We hope you enjoy this b~
Please return or re
Y

OTHERWORLD

OTHERWORLD

JASON SEGEL
KIRSTEN MILLER

ROCK THE BOAT

A Rock the Boat Book

First published in Great Britain & Australia by Rock the Boat,
an imprint of Oneworld Publications, 2017

ISBN 978-1-78607-369-3 (hardback)
ISBN 978-1-78607-371-6 (trade paperback)
ISBN 978-1-78607-370-9 (ebook)

Interior design by Stephanie Moss
Printed and bound in Great Britain by Clays Ltd, St Ives plc

Oneworld Publications
10 Bloomsbury Street
London WC1B 3SR
England

Stay up to date with the latest books,
special offers, and exclusive content from
Rock the Boat with our monthly newsletter

Sign up on our website
www.rocktheboat.london

TO KRISTA, BARBARA, BEVERLY, AND ERIN.
FOR HELPING US TELL OUR STORIES

OTHERWORLD

There are guys online who swear it was heaven. They still sit around like a bunch of old geezers, swapping tales of epic storms, monstrous beasts and grisly battles. Talk to any gamer in their twenties and at some point they'll say: "You're too young to get it. You never saw Otherworld."

Now keep in mind, most of these idiots never experienced the original Otherworld either. Even at the height of its popularity, it never had more than a handful of subscribers. It wasn't until years after the publisher pulled the plug that it became known in geek lore as the greatest game of all time.

I always thought that was bullshit. I don't anymore.

It took a twentysomething tech billionaire named Milo Yolkin to drag the game back from the dead. Today at noon, his company released an early-access version of Otherworld 2.0. Two thousand lucky gamers were chosen to test it, and somehow I'm one of them. The original Otherworld players were all dorks like me, but as far as I can tell, this new group of players has little in common aside from deep pockets. The app itself is free—you just have to buy the exclusive new headset that goes with the game. Only a couple thousand have been made, and each one costs over two grand.

I have no clue what the old Otherworld looked like on a PC monitor when it came out over a decade ago. But I gotta admit—when I downloaded the new app and I put on the headset, I wasn't expecting graphics this good. I know everything is CGI, but my eyes are completely convinced that it's real. I've got a plastic brick strapped to my face, there's sweat trickling out of my haptic gloves, and I'd rather die than be seen in the dainty booties I'm wearing. Back in the real world, my body is blind, deaf and helpless. I've been in Otherworld for over seventeen hours now, and there is no way in hell that I'm leaving.

Of course, this world has been trying to kill me from the very first second I set out to explore. I've encountered some truly insane shit so far—an avalanche, lighting strikes, quicksand and some kind of mutated polar bear that I managed to butcher and eat using nothing but a dagger and my two bare hands. Still, nothing compares to what I've just found.

I've come to a stone path that disappears into a cavern carved out of a glacier. I run my hand along one of the icy walls. I feel that it's there, but my fingertips can neither confirm nor deny that the surface is as smooth or as cold as it appears. I shouldn't have cheaped out when I bought the gloves, but the best ones were so expensive that they'd have triggered a credit alert. I'm sure I could have found a way around it if I'd known the fancy gloves would be worth it. But none of the rumors prepared me for Otherworld.

When I look up, I see a sun just like the one I've always known burning in the sky. Its light penetrates the ice around me, and the whole glacier glows like an enchanted gem. I can hear water rushing somewhere deep within the glacier. A sharp crack echoes behind me, and I spin around a little too quickly. My stomach drops and hot vomit rises and scalds the back of my throat. They haven't found a way to truly beat the motion sickness yet. I close my eyes, swallow and wait until the dizziness fades.

Then I take a deep breath and open my eyes again. Stretching out toward the horizon is the empty ice field I just crossed. Somewhere in the distance is the City of Imra, where I began my journey. Apparently that's where all Otherworld adventures begin. You design your avatar and walk through a door and suddenly you're outside Imra's gates. In the few minutes I was there, I watched a parade of avatars pass through them.

They're all still back there, I guess. They say the original Otherworld could get pretty smutty, but I don't think it had anything quite like Imra. Apparently the city's a CGI Sodom that makes *Grand Theft Auto* look like *Dora the Explorer*. I was tempted to do a little sightseeing in town, but that seemed to be what the designers expected us to do. So I set off in the opposite direction. Away from the city. Down a mountainside. Into the wilderness. Across the ice fields. The way I figure it, when you're given a chance to explore the most incredible survival sandbox ever created, you shouldn't let yourself get slowed down by a few anatomically correct non-player characters.

Now I'm standing here in front of the ice cave, with the wind whistling all around me. It's a pity I can't feel anything but the steady chill of central air. If I breathe in too deeply, I can smell the

Febreze my mom's cleaning lady uses. But my eyes are burning from snow glare, and my toes are numb. Before I enter the glacier, I turn one last time and scan the frozen white landscape behind me. There are no signs of movement, but I know I'm not on my own. Someone's followed me here. She's always kicked ass at camouflage, and I haven't caught sight of her. But I don't need my eyes to tell me that Kat's in Otherworld too. I feel her presence—and I'm finding it hard to wipe the shit-eating grin off my face.

Back in the real world, Kat hasn't spoken to me in months. I've tried pretty much everything, and Otherworld was my last resort. On Friday I left a set of gear in her locker, along with a note to let her know I'd be logging on at noon today. I didn't think she could resist being one of the first to see Milo Yolkin's new wonderland. So I was pretty bummed when I didn't catch sight of her outside Imra. It's starting to look like my investment paid off, though. As far as I'm concerned, a few thousand dollars of my mother's money is a small price to pay for the pleasure of Kat's company.

I step forward into the cave and stop. Lurking in a shadow is a figure I didn't see until now. Someone or something is guarding the entrance. I draw my dagger and prepare to strike. Everything around me may be fake, but the sound of my heart pounding is real. As my eyes adjust, I see a thin man dressed in what looks like a modern-day suit. He's about a foot taller than I am, and there's a scarf wrapped Bedouin-style around his head. The thin strip of face left uncovered is ebony black. In one hand the man holds a gnarled staff. An amulet hangs around his neck, a clear stone in its center. When the man doesn't move, I have a go at stealing his staff, but his grip remains firm. It's only when I try to take the amulet that I realize I'm attempting to mug a statue. I rap my knuckles against its hollow chest. It seems to be sculpted from clay.

I suppose the clay man is a sign that I'm on the right track. Open world or not, the developers wouldn't have placed a statue here for no reason. There's bound to be something interesting at the end of the path. And when I find it, I have a hunch that the statue will spring to life and show me what it can do with its staff. But why worry about that right now, when I can listen to the crunch of rocks beneath my bootie-clad feet? Or watch chunks of ice bobbing in the Slurpee-blue stream that's flowing beside the path? The scenery alone is worth every single penny of the six grand I charged to my mom's credit card.

I plunge deeper into the glacier, occasionally sneaking a peek over my shoulder, hoping to catch Kat slinking up behind me. I'm thinking about the two of us alone together in an icy blue cavern with a giant clay man guarding the door. It's been over a year since she and I have been by ourselves. I'm enjoying the thought so much that when I turn a corner and see *him*, I almost mistake him for a rock.

He sits on a throne chiseled out of granite. His body is made of a gray material that looks like stone, and there's an impressive set of horns sprouting out of his head. He's human in shape, though he seems to be built on a much larger scale. Whoever he is, he feels no need for clothes. Heat radiates from him, and the melting ice walls form a sphere around his body. The moat of meltwater at his feet is clear, but I can't gauge its depth. On the opposite side of his chamber is a tall metal door that doesn't really fit with the decorating scheme. I'm itching to find out what's behind it, but it's pretty obvious that I'll need to make it past the big dude first.

I make my way closer, and his head rises. I can't tell if he sees me, because he doesn't have a face, but I get the sense that he's not very happy. From what I've read online, the lands of Otherworld are ruled by demigods known as Elementals. This might be one of them. Some Elementals are helpful; many are hostile. I'm guessing the creature in front of me isn't interested in making friends.

"I wasn't expecting visitors." His voice booms in my headset and I have to turn the volume down.

Otherworld's new publisher has spent months bragging about its next-generation AI, but there's something that makes me think this guy's not part of the game. And if he's not an Elemental or an NPC, then I'm not the only explorer around. Whoever this is, he's built a formidable avatar.

"I guess not," I say into my mike. "Looks like you forgot to get dressed. You know, a stud like you would be pretty popular back in Imra. I've heard the place is a nonstop orgy. What are you doing out here when the action's back there?"

"I could ask the same of you," he says.

"Yeah, well, I'm allergic to fun. And mangos. Long-haired cats, too."

"How amusing," he says, giving my avatar the once-over. "You could have been anyone. And this is what you chose? What are you—a peasant?" He sounds so . . . *disappointed.* "Lack of imagination is a terrible affliction."

I glance down at my dull brown robe, sewn from the best

cyberburlap available. Whenever I'm given the option, I choose something similar.

"I can think of worse," I tell him. "Nothing wrong with keeping things simple. You know what they say: the flashier the avatar, the smaller the . . ." I stop the instant he stands up. His crotch is nothing but a smooth bump. He's like one of the action figures I used to torture when I was a kid. "You know, you're missing a little something down below." I gesture to his absent parts. "They had some amazing options during setup. Might be worth a reset."

"I appreciate your concern, but I have everything I need," he responds, moving toward me. "The ice fields are no place for guests. I'm afraid you must leave and return to the City of Imra."

"Make me." It just pops out. Which happens more often than I'd like. My tongue produces words faster than my brain can approve them.

"Make you?" he responds incredulously. "Perhaps you're not aware that Otherworld is intended for players eighteen and older? Did you lie when you registered?"

I didn't, but what the hell does he care?

"Spare me the lecture and get ready to rumble," I say. "I've been battling the environment for seventeen hours straight, and it's time for bed. I need a little PVP action to put me to sleep."

The avatar approaches, and soon he's towering over me. Once again, I'm blown away by the details. I can actually see veins throbbing in his chest, and though I'm an eighteen-year-old heterosexual, even I recognize that the dude's nipples are works of art. "You assume Otherworld is like the games you know. I assure you it's not. You've entered my sanctuary, and you are not welcome." The guy's beginning to glow from within like an ember. As his head lights up, features finally appear on his face, and I almost bolt. He does not look friendly.

Instead of running, I draw my dagger. "Then you'd better kick me out."

Before I can make a move, three flaming arrows zip past my shoulder. They miss the monstrous avatar and sink into the frozen arched ceiling above him. A second later, an explosion rocks the entire cavern. I steady myself and watch as ice rains down from above, burying the beast. I turn to find a sleek figure behind me. She's dressed in a body-hugging suit of reflective material. It's hard to see her even though she's standing out in the open, but I'd know the face anywhere.

"You provoked that guy on purpose, Simon," Kat says. The voice is all hers, and it sets me on fire. "Did you think you had any chance of winning a fight with that dinky little dagger?"

"Absolutely not. I figured you'd show up and save me," I tell her. "I wanted to see what you're wearing. *Very* nice."

"Let's go, dumbass," she orders. She's never been able to accept a compliment. "He'll be out of there soon."

I glance back. The mysterious door behind the avatar is blocked now, so there's no real reason to stay. Kat is already retreating down the path, and I race to catch up, following her toward the entrance of the cavern. It's only when we're outside on the ice field that I realize something's different.

"The clay man's gone," I say as it registers.

"What clay man?" she asks.

"Never mind." It's not important, and there's much more that is. "Listen—" Just as I say it, the ground beneath our feet begins to rumble, and in moments the whole world is shaking around us.

"Not now, Simon," she says.

"Kat." I grab her hand and pull her toward me. There's no place to run. A geyser of lava erupts from beneath the ice and showers down on us. My crappy haptic gloves and booties are suddenly so hot that I yank them off and throw them across my bedroom. I keep the headset on, hoping for one last vision of Kat. All I see are sparks.

REALITY

It's a Sunday and nobody bothers me, so I sleep until noon. I'm a little disoriented when I wake up to my tastefully decorated bedroom with its sturdy oak furniture. I throw back the plaid bedspread that's pulled up to my chin. My first instinct is to reach for my Otherworld headset and get the hell out of New Jersey. I don't own a car, but thanks to the game, that won't matter much anymore. Then I remember I already have plans today.

I get out of bed and rifle through an old box at the back of my closet until I locate the Speedo I wore to swim meets back in elementary school. I strip out of my boxers and pull it on. Then I unlock my bedroom door and head down the hall. I pause at a mirror in the living room to make sure my junk is safely tucked away. The Speedo covers just enough to keep me from getting arrested. It's a pretty good look, I gotta say. Pasty white skin, wild black hair and three days' worth of untrimmed scruff. I figure I'm ready for action. But before I get down to business, I take a moment to admire my nose.

My grandfather was blessed with the same giant schnoz. From what I've read, the thing was legendary. If he'd lived two hundred years earlier, they'd have sung songs about it. But his heyday was the sixties, so his nose inspired a nickname instead. They called my grandfather the Kishka. For those of you out there who consider French fries an ethnic food, a kishka is a sausage. A rather unattractive sausage, I might add, with a shape that's either phallic or fecal, depending on your level of maturity. And yet, by all accounts, the ladies loved my grandfather. They say it's probably what got him killed.

I never saw the nose in person. In fact, I wouldn't know anything about it if it weren't for a book I found in the Brockenhurst library called *Gangsters of Carroll Gardens*. My mother grew up in that part of Brooklyn, but to hear her tell it, her childhood was all fresh cannoli, backyard garden parties and upscale bat mitzvahs. So imagine my surprise when I'm thumbing through the book and come across a picture of the Kishka. I don't know who he is at that point. I'm thirteen years old, and I don't even recognize my grandfather's name. I just know he looks exactly like me.

Stop here for a minute and imagine tumbling down that rabbit hole. By the time I hit bottom, everything made sense. My entire life, I'd always suspected that some critical piece of information was being withheld from me. For years, I was convinced that I couldn't possibly be my parents' biological child. I knew in my heart of hearts that one of the cleaning ladies had given birth to me in a broom closet and my beautiful, small-nosed mother had graciously taken me in. Whenever one of the maids smiled at me, I'd always wonder if it might be her.

Now I knew. Armed with a picture of a gangster I'd never heard of, I started to dig for the truth. I found part of it in a box tucked away in the attic. Inside were four Brooklyn high school yearbooks. I flipped through one, and there she was ... Irene Diamond. I didn't recognize her at first. All through high school, she looked nothing like the woman I know. I never would have guessed the girl was my mother if it hadn't been for the kishka set in the center of her face. Irene Diamond had the same damn nose I see every time I look in the mirror. I'd love to know how much her father paid to have it fixed.

When I was younger, my mother used to watch me when she thought I wasn't looking. She'd try to smile when I caught her, but I could tell she was horrified by what she saw. It used to upset me. Now the cosmic justice of it all cracks me up. She'd been running from the nose her entire life—and it ended up on her only son's face.

I may have cracked a little the day I found those yearbooks, but I didn't fall apart. And I never mentioned my discovery to my parents. Even then, I knew secrets had power. I knew my mother had hidden her true identity for good reason. Nothing would have given me more pleasure than shouting the truth from the rooftops. But I figured there would be a day when my mother's secret would come in handy. So for the past few years, I've kept it tucked away safely for future use.

I love looking at my nose now. The afternoon sun streaming in through the living room windows really sets it off. The giant gilded mirror in front of me is one of a pair that my mother tells dinner guests she purchased on her honeymoon in Paris. I don't know where she got the mirrors, but I've seen snapshots of her honeymoon in Orlando. The room in the background looks like Marie-Antoinette might waltz through at any moment. But the kishka on my face is there to remind me I don't belong to this world. I'm the grandson of a two-bit gangster who broke fingers for the Gallo crime family and is probably buried at the bottom of the Gowanus Canal.

"Oooh!" a lady squeals behind me. Then I hear the sound of footsteps rushing out of the room. Some new staff member, probably. The rest of them have been warned about me. I'm not sure what they've been told, but I doubt they'd be shocked to find a six-foot-three-inch kid with zero muscle mass and a giant nose standing in his old elementary school banana hammock in the middle of the formal living room.

"Sorry," I call out. I didn't expect anyone inside to see me. The house is rarely empty, though you can wander through it for hours without running into a soul. Don't get the wrong impression— I generally wear clothes when I wander. But today I have a special treat in mind for the neighbors.

It's still a bit nippy when I step outside, but spring has sprung. Across the street, the neighbors' newly planted rosebushes are blooming. The buds started opening last week, which is why I'm here now, nearly naked on a chilly afternoon. The flowers are fuchsia, a color my mother calls vulgar. As soon as they began to reveal themselves, my mother petitioned the homeowners' association to have them uprooted. Since she's the president of the association—and a ruthless attorney—her petitions always pass. How about that? It's the American Dream in action. Irene Diamond started life as the daughter of a small-time crook, and now she's in charge of nature.

The people across the street are new to our neighborhood. Last fall, they moved here from Singapore to work for one of our local tech conglomerates. Unlike my mother, they haven't spent years forming alliances over hors d'oeuvres, which means they lack what my parents call *leverage*. But they're friendly to me, so I'm going to give *them* something to complain about—something that will embarrass Mommy Dearest enough to keep her lips sealed at the next meeting of the homeowners' association.

I drag a chaise from the side of the pool behind our house. Its legs gouge muddy tracks in the pristine grass all the way to the front yard, where I position it perfectly—not far from the street and just across from the neighbors' living room windows. I've worked up a sweat, and my pasty skin glistens as I lie down on my stomach. I wedge the back of the Speedo between my butt cheeks and try to assume an artistic pose. No sense in being *vulgar*.

My eyes are closed and the warmth of the sun is spreading over my skin when the first car approaches. The driver hits the brakes near the mailbox.

"Hey, crazy!" someone shouts. I recognize the voice. It belongs to a girl from school. "What the hell are you doing?"

"What does it look like?" I call out. "I'm getting a tan."

"Put some clothes on, you pervert!" shouts a second voice.

"Nobody wants to see your hairy butt cheeks, Simon," screams a third. I open my eyes a crack and see three girls from school hanging out of a car. One of them is already tapping away at her phone. Their friends will be arriving soon.

My butt cheeks aren't quite as furry as they've been made out to be, and apparently *lots* of people would like to see them, because the traffic on my street goes nuts for the next thirty minutes.

I don't pay any attention to the hoots and catcalls. Crossing ice fields and getting blown to smithereens for hours on end was exhausting. I got about five hours of sleep, but I'll need more if I want to go back in tonight. I'm just drifting off when I hear a car pull into my drive. A few seconds later, someone's thrown a jacket over me.

"Get up and get inside." It's my mother.

I open my eyes. She's looming over my chaise, and she's pissed as hell.

"The people across the street are threatening to phone the police," she hisses.

"Hi, Mom," I say with a yawn. "You look stunning this afternoon."

She does. Her black hair is pulled into a fancy knot, and she's wearing a silk dress in a very tasteful shade of pale blue. Her painted lips are pressed together beneath her perfect nose.

"*Now,* Simon. Or you're going to jail."

I sigh and sit up, tying her jacket around my waist. "Aren't you overreacting? I'm sure the neighbors will forget all about this unfortunate incident if you let them keep their vulgar roses."

"Those people are not who you should be worried about," she says. "My accountant just called to ask if the six-thousand-dollar charge on my AmEx for video game equipment was a business expense. You stole my credit card, Simon. One more word from you and I'm dialing your probation officer."

This is unexpected. The accountant must be new. The old one didn't ask questions.

I'm fully clothed and sitting on the living room couch when my father gets home. He's dressed in Easter egg colors and there's a nine iron in his hand. Apparently I've interrupted a golf game. He walks straight through the room without even acknowledging me. A few minutes later, he's back, and he's got my new headset, gloves and booties. He drops them all in a pile on the floor.

I wince when I hear a crack. "Come on, Dad," I groan. "Do you know how hard it was to get all that stuff? Only a couple thousand of those headsets have even been made. That one's going to be worth a fortune someday."

"This heap of crap cost six thousand, three hundred and fifty-six dollars?" he asks.

Not exactly—I bought two sets of gear. I only kept one for myself. "It's not crap," I say. "It's the newest virtual reality technology. I was on a wait list for that headset—"

"So it's a video game," my father says. If you didn't know him, you wouldn't think he was that angry. But I've spent eighteen years with Grant Eaton, and I know all the warning signs. He's about to blow sky-high.

"It's revolutionary—"

"It's over." He lifts his nine iron over his head and brings it down hard on the equipment. He repeats the same motion at least three dozen times, until his face is bright red and he's out of breath.

I'm finding it pretty hard to breathe too. My last chance to spend time with Kat is just a pile of plastic shards. "I can't believe you—"

"You're eighteen now," he interrupts me. He's holding the golf club like a baseball bat and panting so hard that I wonder if he'll keel over. "One more incident like this, and your mother and I will no longer be able to help you. If I were you, Simon, I'd spend a lot more time in the real world."

THE GIRL
IN THE WOODS

It was a miscalculation—no doubt about it. I was sure the credit card charge would fly under the radar. I didn't factor in my mother's new eager-beaver accountant. Still, it's hard to see what all the fuss is about. I bet my mother spends more than six grand on Botox every month. Come to think of it, I wouldn't be surprised if my father spent even more than that. He's starting to look like a Madame Tussauds wax sculpture of himself. There's probably a warning tattooed on his ass that says KEEP AWAY FROM OPEN FLAMES.

My parents didn't stick around after they taught me my lesson. They had very important golf balls to hit, frittatas to eat and luxury leather goods to acquire, so I'm alone again, sitting on the edge of our pool with my legs dangling over the side. With my devices shattered, I'm trapped in what passes for reality here in beautiful Brockenhurst, New Jersey. My house is a fake French château, and my town stole its name from some fancy place in England. The grass in my lawn is a shade of green not known to nature. And the sausage in the Hot Pocket I'm chewing tastes like mystery meat that was grown in a lab.

You can touch Brockenhurst and you can smell it, but you'd be crazy to call it *real*.

Where our backyard ends, the woods begin. When I was a kid, the wilderness seemed endless; now most of it's gone. I look for the path that leads through what's left of the forest. The trail's grown over, but I could still walk it in my sleep. It leads straight to one of the few old houses around here that was never torn down. The land it sits on is swampy, and until recently the building had been slowly sinking for ninety-odd years. That's where Kat lives. I'd be there right now if she'd just let me talk to her. But these days my best friend bolts whenever I get near her. It cost me a few grand and a near-death experience with my father, but I got to see her in Otherworld. Unfortunately, in Brockenhurst she wants nothing to do with me.

Kat and I met ten years ago, when we were eight years old. My father had just made senior partner at his law firm, and he'd built this McMansion as his trophy. Thousands of trees were sacrificed to ravenous wood chippers, and our house rose near the edge of what would become the town's swankiest gated community. We moved in on the first day of summer. Mrs. Kozmatka, the nanny my mother had hired, told me to stay on the grass in the backyard when I played outside. I wasn't allowed to set foot in the woods, which my mother believed to be teeming with snakes, ticks and poison ivy.

In her defense, Mrs. Kozmatka was new. She knew nothing of

my history. And for the first couple of hours, I gave her no cause for concern. I sat exactly where I am right now and stared at the trees. Everything seemed so much more alive in the forest. As I was watching, I heard branches snapping and leaves rustling. And then someone stepped out from the other side.

I'd been playing a lot of Harry Potter games that summer, and I was convinced it was some kind of mythical creature. It was pretty clear that it wasn't a centaur, but I figured it could be a faun or a sprite. Even if the creature had spoken to me on that first encounter, I wouldn't have believed she was human. I'd never seen another kid so dirty. She was covered in dried mud from head to toe. It was camouflage, Kat later informed me. And it worked like a charm. That day, when the nanny came outside, Kat took a step backward and vanished so completely into the woods that it was almost as if she'd been swallowed whole.

My tender young mind was totally blown. My family had just moved from Manhattan. The first eight years of my life had been filled with fancy private schools and playdates with kids named Arlo and Phineas. It was an ideal life, which was why my therapists had so much trouble identifying the cause of my behavioral issues. (Arlo and Phineas got their asses kicked on a regular basis.)

In hindsight, it all seems perfectly clear to me. I'd been kept in a cage my entire life. I wasn't a kid. I was *veal*. And then this portal opened up in suburban New Jersey and I was offered a glimpse of an untamed universe. I didn't tell the nanny about the creature I'd seen. Instead I spent the next few hours eagerly waiting for it to return. I was sure it was spying on me, but it didn't set foot on my grass again. And by lunchtime I just couldn't wait any longer.

When the nanny went inside to make tuna sandwiches, I slipped into the woods to go find it.

I was only a few yards past the tree line when I heard Mrs. Kozmatka calling for me from the backyard of my house. When her cries grew more frantic, I stuck my fingers in my ears and kept going until I couldn't hear her anymore. The deeper I went, the wilder the woods got. Everywhere I looked, there were signs of the creature. Boards nailed to the trunks of trees—makeshift ladders leading to lookouts positioned high above in the canopy. Lean-tos built with branches and bows, their interiors carpeted with soft green moss. A massive fort made from scavenged wood, plastic tarps and car tires. I climbed every ladder and lay inside every shelter. I felt like I'd made one of those discoveries no one makes anymore. I'd stumbled across an abandoned world.

That whole afternoon, I remember having no sense of time passing. And then suddenly I was hungry and thirsty and the sun was beginning to set. As it grew dark, I saw a light appear in the distance. I hurried toward it and discovered a little white house tucked between the trees. A gravel driveway snaked toward the other side of the woods. The place I'd found was no fairy-tale cottage. It was more like a tumbledown shack. Half of it seemed to be sinking, and there were several kitchen appliances rusting on the front porch. Patches of paint had peeled away from the walls, leaving the house looking sickly. But the light was on in the living room, and I caught the scent of bacon in the air. I was trying to work up the courage to knock on the front door when I heard the growls.

Three dogs emerged from the brush. They seemed enormous to me at the time, but they couldn't have been much bigger than your average border collie, and all three of them were clearly starving. Their gray-and-golden coats were mottled and their skin clung to their ribs. The trio slinked toward me, yellow fangs bared. They'd been stalking me for a while, and they were ready to make their move. I was a plump little veal calf lost in the woods. I'm sure I looked absolutely delicious.

I grabbed a stick off the ground and backed away slowly, holding the large twig in my hands like a sword. I knew better than to run. I needed to climb something. I was so busy scanning my surroundings for a tree with low-hanging branches that I forgot to look down. I tripped over a rock, tumbled backward and fell to the ground. The dogs were on me in an instant. I waited to feel their teeth sink through my skin.

Then the air popped behind me. One of the dogs howled in pain and sprang at least a foot in the air. Another pop and there was a spray of sawdust from the trunk of a nearby tree. A third pop followed and the dogs fled.

I examined my arms and legs for missing flesh and bloody wounds, but much to my surprise, I was completely intact.

"Hey! You okay?" a voice called out to me.

I picked myself up and turned to face it. There on the porch of the house was a girl my age. I saw the hair first—a fierce mane of copper curls. Then my eyes moved to the pellet gun in her hands. The freckles came into view as I walked toward her. They covered the bridge of her nose and spread out over her cheeks. But it was the eyes I recognized. They belonged to the mud-covered creature I'd seen spying on my house. "Those your dogs?" I asked.

"Nope," said the girl. "Those're coydogs. Half wild dog, half coyote. They used to live farther out in the woods. Then you cut half the forest down. Now they've been hanging around here at night, eating our garbage."

"I didn't cut down the forest."

She rolled her eyes. "You know what I mean. People *like* you."

"Where'd you learn how to shoot so well?" I asked. My eyes were practically fondling her pellet gun. None of my friends in Manhattan had that kind of stuff. If a neighbor had spotted a kid with so much as a slingshot, child protective services would have been alerted.

"My gramma taught me. She says you gotta be tough when you're pretty and poor." I must have stared at the girl a little too long. Her brow furrowed and her eyes turned hard. "Yeah, I know what you're thinking. I'm not pretty enough. I shouldn't be worried," she snapped.

"That isn't what I was thinking," I told her honestly. "You just don't look like anyone I've ever met before." Which was true but completely pathetic. I probably would have seen lots of kids like her in New York if I'd ever left the Upper East Side.

The girl scowled, like she couldn't figure out whether to be offended. "Well, I'm not like anyone you've ever met before," she finally said. Then she glanced up at a patch of blue sky. "It's going to be dark soon. Want me to walk you back to your house?"

"Your parents will let you?" I asked, shocked. My parents locked the doors and drew the shades as soon as the sun went down.

"My dad's dead," she said.

"Your mom, then?"

"She's not home." The girl seemed annoyed by my questions. "Where's *your* parents, anyway?"

I shrugged. "I dunno. They don't tell me where they go." As far as I knew, they could have been in Hong Kong. They often showed up with trinkets they'd purchased at airports in faraway lands.

"Who's that lady at your house who was on the phone all morning?"

That was when I realized how long I'd been gone. Hours had passed since I'd slipped into the woods. Mrs. Kozmatka would have called my parents, and they wouldn't be happy. "She's the nanny." The last word slipped out before I could catch it.

"Huh. Must get boring hanging out with an old lady all the time." It sounded like an observation, nothing more.

I was pretty sure I'd rather play in traffic than spend another hour with Mrs. Kozmatka, but it didn't seem macho to say so. I shrugged instead. "I guess."

"Come on," said the girl, setting off down a path with the barrel of the pellet gun resting on her shoulder. I scrambled to catch up with her, and once I had, I paid close attention to the route we took. I knew I had to be able to find my way back.

That night, when we reached my house, every window was ablaze. I could see around one corner of the building to where a police car was parked in our drive. Its flashing red and blue lights painted the lawn, but there was no siren to accompany them.

"How many rooms are there in that house?" the girl asked.

"Lots," I told her. "I've never really counted." It was a lie. There were twenty-two.

"What do you put in all of them?"

I could have listed all the contents of my life, but the subject bored me. "Will you be in the woods tomorrow?" I asked her.

"Sure," she said. "I got a lot of work to do. D'you see the fort? Some of the walls washed away the last time it rained, and the roof keeps coming down."

"I saw," I told her. "I can help."

Her eyes narrowed. She seemed unsure.

"My name is Simon." It had been so long since I'd introduced myself to anyone that my name felt like a gift.

"Kat," she replied. "Raid your parents' garage tomorrow. Bring some nails and a rope."

In the kitchen, Mrs. Kozmatka was crying. My mother was draining a tumbler of red wine while my father conferred with a police officer in serious tones.

"Well, well. Look what the cat dragged in," said the cop, who'd caught sight of me over my father's shoulder. He winked at me like the two of us were in on a secret. "Looks like someone's been exploring the woods."

I gave myself a quick inspection and realized I was covered in brambles and a leaf was sticking to the bottom of one of my sneakers.

"Simon!" Mrs. Kozmatka yelped. She started to rush for me, only to be blocked by my mother, a master of optics, who wanted the policeman to see her receive the first hug.

"What were you doing out there?" my father demanded. Even back then, he always seemed vaguely annoyed by my presence. Like I was a puppy his wife had wanted. He'd indulged her little whim and now the beast wouldn't stop relieving itself all over the rug.

"I was playing," I told him.

"Didn't Mrs. Kozlowsy—" my mother started to say.

"*Kozmatka,*" said the nanny, who must have realized she was going to be fired and didn't feel the need to take my mother's crap anymore.

"Didn't Mrs. *Kozmatka* tell you to stay away from the woods?" my mother said sternly. "Do you have any idea how much trouble you've caused? Officer Robinson had to come all the way out here . . ."

Officer Robinson looked a bit thrown by our family dynamic. "It was no trouble at all, ma'am," he insisted. Then he knelt down in front of me. "Did you get lost?"

I shook my head. "No."

"Did you have fun?"

I couldn't help it. I must have grinned like a maniac. The cop mussed my hair and stood up. He was a nice guy. Still is—though he wasn't quite as helpful the next few times we met.

"Excuse me, Officer," my mother began, "but I really don't see—"

"Mr. and Mrs. Eaton, the woods around Brockenhurst are pretty safe during the day. That's where most of the kids here play. My own girls included. Of course," he said, looking down at me, "it's a good idea to get inside a couple of hours before dark. There are some wild dogs that come out when the sun starts to set."

"*Wild dogs?*" my mother gasped, as if he'd said lions or bears.

"We call them coydogs around here, and your son is no safer from them in your yard than he is out in the woods. You might think of getting Simon a slingshot or a BB gun and teaching him how to use it. The dogs are scavengers. Cowards. They won't put up a fight."

"Simon is *eight*," my father argued. "He can't be out running wild in the forest."

"Why not?" the cop asked, and my father clammed up.

"I can't see why Simon would want to play in the woods when he has toys and a pool and everything he could possibly want right here," my mother informed the cop.

"You're absolutely right, ma'am," Officer Robinson told her. "I'm sure your boy has everything you could buy. But out there in the woods, Simon can make his own world."

My mother remained skeptical, but my father must have felt that his manhood had been challenged. He sided with the cop. After that, I was allowed to leave the house in the morning and return just before dusk, covered in leaves and mud. No one ever asked what I did in the woods. I didn't tell them—and I never breathed a word about Kat.

Over time, my behavior improved. I got into fewer fights. Kat and I built new worlds and burned old ones down. We ruled over our forest kingdom with barbaric benevolence. Kat showed me how to shoot, saw and hammer. I gave her my ridiculous weekly allowance whenever her mom didn't have money for groceries, and I taught Kat how to curse in French. At school we beat up each other's bullies and did each other's homework. We bought our first game consoles together—and transitioned to PCs together. We were inseparable in every world we visited.

Kat was my best friend and my family for ten whole years, but I don't think I ever spoke her name in front of my parents.

She belonged to my world, not theirs. She was none of Grant and Irene's business.

The sun is setting behind me. It's a beautiful Sunday evening in Brockenhurst. A cold wind ripples the swimming pool water, and the trees at the edge of my lawn shove against each other like commuters boarding a subway car. Kat's somewhere beyond those trees. She can't be far. I can feel her. I hope she's all right, but until I see her at school tomorrow, I'll have no way of knowing. My Otherworld gear is just a pile of shards. I'm legally forbidden to use email. And Kat blocked my calls three months and four days ago.

THE BOY
WITH NO FUTURE

So how *do* you lose your only friend? It's an excellent question. I'm still searching for the answer. All I know is that the chain of events kicked off sixteen months ago. At the time, life was about as perfect as it will ever be. I should have known it wasn't going to stay that way. I should have been prepping for disaster. The universe was worried that I'd go soft being happy. I needed trials and tribulations to keep me on my toes.

First my father accepted a job offer in Dubai. It was supposed to be temporary. "Only a couple of years," my parents assured me. They seemed blissfully unaware that they were talking to someone for whom two years was the difference between Pokémon and pubic hair. I should have whipped out the Kishka at that point— and threatened to expose my mother's crooked family tree. Then again, if I ever make a list of the shit I *should have done,* it would stretch all the way to Atlantic City.

While my parents enjoyed the fruits of slave labor in a tacky desert hellhole, our house in New Jersey would be transformed into a high-end vacation rental. I was not allowed to stay. They were adamant about this, though I emailed them countless articles about the things that took place in high-end vacation rentals and assured them that I couldn't possibly do any more harm to the house than the furries and orgy enthusiasts who'd soon be occupying our bedrooms.

In the end, I was given two options, and staying in Brockenhurst wasn't one of them. I could move to Dubai—or I could pack my bags for boarding school. My father's illustrious alma mater in Massachusetts had accepted me for the spring semester. Which meant dear old Mom and Pop must have been plotting the move behind my back for quite some time. I would have been heartbroken if I'd ever trusted them in the first place.

I considered running away. I was pretty handy with a slingshot and pellet gun at that point. I figured, if nothing else, I could live in the woods. It was Kat who pointed out that I'd gone completely insane. There weren't enough woods left to hide me. Besides, two years was nothing in the grand scheme of things, she said. And she said it with such conviction that I started to wonder if she could see the grand scheme from her bedroom window. At the end of our time apart, we'd both be out of high school, together and free. She swore we'd talk every day until then.

For the first six months we did. Then Kat's mother, Linda, announced she was marrying a man named Wayne Gibson. He'd moved to town around the same time I left, and they'd bonded over bourbon at some local bar. Suddenly Kat was busy helping her mom make arrangements for the wedding. Our texts and video chats dwindled to a few a week. After the blessed nuptials took place, she sent me some pictures of the event. I didn't say so at the time, but I thought her new stepdad looked like a real douchebag. He wore a military dress uniform with a bunch of fancy medals that he'd polished to a shine, and in every picture he stared straight at the camera, as if daring the photographer to take the photo off-center. But Linda in her frilly cupcake of a dress was beaming like she'd just been crowned prom queen. She'd always been so nice to me, though. I figured her happiness was all that mattered.

That was when Kat slowly began to vanish. She'd send me a strangely cheery note now and then, but most of my texts went unanswered and my emails weren't opened. In my more para-noid moments, I started to think that maybe Kat had planned it all. That maybe she'd convinced me to leave New Jersey because her grand scheme didn't include me. I went a little nuts with the cybersurveillance. I set up a Google alert for her name. I studied her dormant Instagram feed for secret messages. The last thing she'd posted was a series of photos devoted to the home improve-ments her new stepfather was making. There was nothing really interesting in the pictures—just lots of electronics and wires. She hadn't posted on Facebook in months, so I stalked the profiles of our mutual acquaintances, searching for clues. I spotted a blur of copper-colored hair in the background of a few party pics, and that was it. Kat was alive, but she was moving too fast to be cap-tured on camera. I kept writing her, sometimes three emails a day. The last time she responded, she told me she needed some space. The message was one sentence long.

Everything I thought I'd known had been torn down and reassembled. Kat had been my touchstone, and without her, I didn't recognize the world anymore. I didn't care to. I stopped going to class. I stayed in the dorm, playing *Assassin's Creed* with my roommate, a Ukrainian head case named Elvis who collected toy robots and possessed a very dim view of the human race.

Then one morning four months ago, I woke up to find a Google alert for Katherine Foley. The Brockenhurst newspaper was reporting that she'd been arrested the previous night for stealing her stepfather's SUV and driving it into an ornamental koi pond. The police report noted that a sodden, half-smoked joint had been discovered under the gas pedal.

The paper didn't publish a picture, but I had no trouble finding a few online. I'm still surprised the photos didn't go viral. The black SUV was submerged all the way to the backseat doors, and the pond's fat golden koi were gliding in and out through the open windows. The half of the vehicle sticking out of the water was almost perfectly vertical. It was a truly impressive feat of automotive mishandling.

Scrolling through the pictures of Wayne Gibson's SUV, I kept thinking back to that fateful day when I'd first stumbled across *Gangsters of Carroll Gardens.* One glimpse of the Kishka and I'd known he was my grandfather. I didn't need to read the caption or contact the local genealogical society. I'd just known. The same way I knew that the wreck I was looking at on Facebook wasn't an accident. I can't explain why, but there was no doubt in my mind that Kat had destroyed her stepfather's car on purpose.

Elvis drove home to see his parents most weekends, and he kept a run-down Volkswagen off campus. I suppose I should have been more suspicious when he offered to loan me the car if I let him use my computer. But I would have given him a kidney, too, if he'd asked. So I handed over the computer and drove seven hours to New Jersey. When I pulled up in Kat's drive, I thought I might have made a wrong turn. The beautiful house I found in the middle of the woods looked nothing like the hovel I remembered. It was painted white, and the jack pines around it had been cleared. Somehow the foundation had been lifted as well, and the house no longer seemed to be sinking. I knocked on the door and Kat's stepfather answered, greeting me with the same stare I'd seen in the wedding photos. He was compact and wound tight—six inches shorter than me and thirty years older. But I knew he could probably take me and I could see he was eager to try.

He politely informed me that Kat had been grounded and couldn't see any friends. She'd fallen in with a bad crowd, he explained, and she needed some time alone to get her head back on straight. I assured Mr. Gibson that I had never belonged to any crowd—good or bad—and I'd driven all day just to see his stepdaughter.

"I know who you are, son," I remember him telling me. "And I don't think Katherine wants to see you. You haven't been back here in months, and it would probably be best if you just stayed gone."

It stung for a second, I gotta admit. That was just about the last thing I wanted to hear. But while part of me was inclined to believe it, hearing it come out of Mr. Gibson's mouth felt *wrong*. There was no way in hell Kat would share her feelings—*any* feelings—with a man who looked like he invaded third-world countries for sport. So I asked if I could have a word with Linda instead. I was told *Mrs. Gibson* wasn't at home, which was total bullshit. It was past seven in the evening, and I could smell Linda's signature stew cooking. I said I'd be happy to wait, and Mr. Gibson said that wouldn't be wise. When I sat down on the porch, he phoned the cops.

Officer Robinson arrived on the scene, and I was sure I'd been thrown a bit of good luck—until he and Kat's stepfather greeted each other by name. Officer Robinson (*Leslie* Robinson, I now knew) took me aside for a man-to-man. He said he sure was sorry to hear about my recent breakup, and boy, did he feel my pain. He'd been dumped a few times in his day, and he'd learned that "sometimes a man has to just walk away."

"Kat's not my girlfriend," I told him.

The cop just laughed. "Maybe it was never official, but you think I'm too old to recognize a young man in love?"

His expression was so cheesy that I wanted to vomit, but I managed to keep the contents of my stomach from spewing out onto his shoes. I swore I wasn't in Brockenhurst to win Kat's heart. Something was wrong with her, I insisted over and over. But I didn't have any evidence to offer. As desperate as I was at that point, I wasn't crazy enough to inform a policeman that my best friend had destroyed an SUV on purpose.

Officer Robinson wholeheartedly agreed that Kat was in trouble. The kids she'd been hanging out with were pretty bad news. But he promised me the Gibsons had the situation under control. They didn't need—or want—any help. And then he warned me not to return to the house.

"Mr. Gibson works in the security business," he told me in a low voice. "I wouldn't be surprised if he has cameras up all over this property. I know for a fact that he's licensed to carry a firearm, and I'm sure he's got a few hidden away here. Believe me, Simon. You don't want that man ever mistaking you for a prowler."

I'm not an idiot. I knew better than to go back to Kat's house. But I didn't give up on her, either. For the next few days, I hung around town, sleeping in Elvis's Volkswagen and trying to run into Kat. I was loitering outside the high school the following Monday when her stepfather dropped her off at the front door. I know she must have heard me calling her name, but she never even glanced in my direction. She clutched her books to her chest and bolted toward the entrance. When I tried to follow her inside, a guard stopped me and I got to have another man-to-man with Officer Robinson, who informed me that it's never a good sign when a girl runs away from you. This time I had to agree.

An hour later, Officer Robinson personally escorted me and Elvis's Volkswagen to the Brockenhurst town limits. I spent the first part of the drive back to Massachusetts cursing Kat for ignoring me. As I passed through Connecticut, the crosshairs of my rage shifted to Wayne Gibson. When I reached the Massachusetts border, I nearly did a one-eighty on the freeway. The SUV in the koi pond meant something, I was sure of it, and the answer was back in New Jersey. But I had no money and no place to stay, and I couldn't bear any more sappy sympathy from Officer Robinson. The hopelessness of the situation was sinking in when I arrived at my boarding school dorm and was greeted by the FBI.

. . .

When the agents told me why they were there, I knew in an instant that opportunity had knocked. At some point during the three days I'd been gone, someone had used my computer to hack the server of the world's largest manufacturer of Internet-connected toy robots.

Laugh all you like, but it's not as ridiculous as it sounds. Imagine what someone who's truly evil could do with an army of toy robots that can see, speak and record. The FBI certainly had a few ideas. But my roommate, the Ukrainian wing nut, apparently had something quite different in mind. He'd reprogrammed the toys to inform the children of the world that "The robot revolution is nigh."

I don't even know where Elvis was that evening. Probably hiding in a bathroom stall. Whoever was responsible for the hack was looking at a minimum of three years in jail, the FBI informed me. I'm sure that's what would have happened if I'd ratted out Elvis, who'd already turned eighteen at that point. His parents were astrophysicists or something equally useless. My parents, as I've mentioned, are lawyers.

In the end, it was a win-win-win situation, as far as I was concerned. I got kicked out of school and sent back to Brockenhurst. Everyone thought I'd gone nuts. And since I'd saved Elvis's life, he was now my humble servant. Of course I got probation. My parents were forced to return to the States and pay a massive fine, which they swore they'd recoup from my future earnings.

When the sentence came down, the judge must have seen that I was pleased with my punishment.

"You really thought it would be funny to scare the socks off a bunch of little kids? What are you—some kind of nihilist?" he demanded.

"No, sir," I told him. "But I certainly appreciate all the good work those folks do."

That earned me two months of mandatory counseling. But if I had a chance to do it all over, I'm pretty damn sure I'd say the same thing again.

So here we are.

I didn't plan any of it. Fate brought me back to New Jersey for good. There's no other place my parents can send me. No private school will accept me—not anymore. The United Arab Emirates denied me a visa. I didn't just burn all my bridges. I blew them to hell with nuclear missiles. My father, who was forced to give up his cushy position in Dubai, refers to me as "the boy with no future." Which is true, just not for the reason he thinks. Anyway, I couldn't care less about the future. I came back for Kat. I did what I had to do. To be honest, I would have done anything.

The irony is, this particular princess doesn't want to be rescued. I've been in Brockenhurst for four months now, and she's barely said a word to me. I hoped Otherworld would fix that. But tomorrow morning when I see her at school, I don't expect anything to have changed.

CAMOUFLAGE

My mother pulls her car up to the front of the school and I slide out. It's just before eight o'clock on a Monday morning, and I see Kat's already in her regular spot. She's sitting on the hood of a car on the other side of the parking lot, next to a girl named Winnie with raccoon eyes. Standing in a circle around them are four guys—a psycho, an anorexic drug addict, a known STD carrier and a stranger dressed in black. Or War, Famine, Pestilence and Death, as I like to think of them. The first bell will ring in five minutes, and the Four Horsemen are vaping. From what I can tell, Kat and her friends try their best to stay stoned. I'm in no position to judge, believe me. You gotta do what you gotta do. But I can't understand why Kat wants to do it with these douchebags.

The one dressed like the Grim Reaper keeps fondling her curls. I once saw her slap a guy who put his fingers in her hair, but for some reason she's letting this one get away with it. His name is Marlow Holm, and he's new to Brockenhurst. He showed up at school in January, around the same time I came back. I don't know much about the kid or why Kat's humoring him, but I certainly intend to find out.

"Slut." The word comes out of nowhere. Right out of the blue. I spin around. The two girls walking past must not have seen me. Olivia and Emily. I've known them both since grade school.

"I heard she doesn't sleep at home anymore. She rotates between their rooms," Olivia says, and Emily cackles.

I love a dirty joke as much as the next guy, but that one hits a little too close to home. I ended up walking through the woods and checking on Kat's house last night. It was Sunday, so she should have been home, but her bedroom light never went on. I thought I'd die waiting to see it, and that certainly wasn't because of the cold.

"Excuse me! Ladies!" I jog to catch up with them. The look on their faces when they see me is priceless. The mixture of fear and disgust makes me feel powerful. If I reached out and touched them, they'd crumble to dust. "I couldn't help but overhear your conversation."

Their mouths are open, but no words are coming out. It's one thing for girls like them to insult my butt cheeks from the safety of a moving car. It's another thing to confront me in person. I'm bigger up close. And much, much crazier.

These particular ladies are repeat offenders, and Kat seems to be their favorite subject of gossip. I've warned them before. It's time to bring out the big guns.

Olivia crosses her arms and cocks her head. It's the battle stance of the teenage girl. I hope she doesn't think I'm intimidated. "What do you want?" she asks.

"I don't want to talk about *me*," I tell her. "I'd like to talk about women's rights."

"Women's rights?" Emily sneers, flicking a lock of glossy brown hair over her shoulder.

"Screw off, Simon," Olivia says. She thinks it's all a joke, and she sounds relieved.

"Okay, sure, but before I go, I just want you both to know that I fully support your right as women to do whatever you want with your bodies—and I will fight to ensure that your rights are protected and preserved."

"Gee, thanks, crazy." They laugh and start to walk away. I follow.

"It just makes me sad that you two don't support other women. I heard what you called Kat. Not very politically correct of you."

Olivia spins back around. "It's the truth, Simon. Get used to it. While you were away, your dream girl turned into a whore."

It's a kick to the balls, but I don't double over. I clench my teeth and smile through the pain.

"What Kat does with her body is none of your business." Then I drop the earnest act. "Just like what you do with yours shouldn't be any of mine."

"What's your point?" Olivia asks. "Make it fast if you've got one. We're going to be late for homeroom."

"Won't take a second. Are you familiar with the phrase *live by the sword, die by the sword*?" I ask as I take out my ten-year-old flip phone and toggle through my photos. "'Cause if not, I have a picture of it." I turn the screen around and show her.

Emily slaps a hand over her mouth but a giggle still escapes.

The blood drains out of Olivia's face. "You hacked my phone," she says.

"Not yours. Your boyfriend's. His Gmail password was *blowjob*. I'd hardly call that *hacking*," I say modestly.

"You're not supposed to go near a computer without supervision," says Olivia. "You're not even allowed to have an iPhone."

"I didn't touch one," I assure her. It's true. I don't need to do my own dirty work when I have a Ukrainian hacker who owes me big-time.

"You'll go to jail if you send those pictures to anyone."

"Yes. And it will be *totally* worth it," I promise. "And don't worry about Emily. She won't get left out. When I post all these photos, I'll throw in a few of her, too."

"What?" Emily looks sick.

I roll my eyes and sigh theatrically. "Don't *either* of you pay attention during school assemblies? A couple of weeks ago, Principal Evans warned you about this very thing. She said you shouldn't take any pictures that you don't want the whole world to see." I silently thank Principal Evans. Her Internet safety assembly gave me a million ideas. "So what do you say, ladies? Are we all going to respect women's rights in the future?"

They nod silently, but I can see them smoldering with hatred and fear.

"Then let's just remove the word *slut* from our vocabularies, shall we?" I pause long enough to let the smile slip off my face. "And if I were you, I'd try my very best to forget that Katherine Foley exists."

I leave the girls standing there. Inside the school, the first warning bell rings. A wave of students surges toward the front door, and I let myself be swept along. In the halls, kids dart away when they see me. The lesson I just gave Olivia and Emily wasn't the first one I've taught since I came back. There's a force field forming around Kat. It won't make her more popular, but when I'm done, crowds will part as she passes. If you're going to be a pariah, you might as well be their queen.

It's been four hours and I still can't get the conversation with Olivia out of my head. I'm no prude, but the idea of Kat rotating between the Four Horsemen's rooms drives me completely insane. When it's time for lunch, I skip the cafeteria and go hunt for her. I have to navigate the entire campus before I find her standing with Marlow behind the cafeteria dumpsters. A cloud that's the palest shade of blue hovers over the garbage. From a distance Kat seems totally stoned. Marlow's got an arm around her, his hand dangling a little too close to her breast. He giggles when he sees me coming. Kat just stares. Her eyes are remarkably clear.

"May I have a word with you?" I ask Marlow. The hood of his black sweatshirt is up and his black jeans sag around the knees. He's the image you'd see if you Googled *high school stoner*. But there's something about his face that doesn't match. It's like someone Photoshopped a J.Crew model's face into the picture.

His bloodshot blue eyes dart in Kat's direction.

"Not now, Simon," she says. "Leave us alone."

"No, seriously, Kat. I just want *one word* with him." I hold up my index finger for reference.

"Fine. What is it?" Marlow asks, growing bold.

When he steps forward, I throw my arm around his neck and whisper in his ear. "Run."

He looks at me and I smile. I've been working on my smile, and I think I've finally perfected it. Dead eyes and lots of teeth. Marlow shoots away faster than a speeding bullet. He's a real superhero, that one.

Kat watches him go. She's annoyed, but she's not surprised. I can tell she's not into him, and I gotta say, that comes as a *massive* relief. But then why is she hanging out with the guy in the first place?

I take Marlow's position beside her and lean my back against the wall. I expect her to bolt, just like she has every time I've come near her in the past four months. But she stays. For almost a minute, neither of us says anything. I'm the one who'll have to break the silence. I don't think her sex life is a good place to start.

"So what did you think of Otherworld?" I ask her. "Was that the coolest shit you've ever seen or what?"

"Yeah. Thanks for sending the gear and login. Wayne found it and confiscated everything," Kat said.

"My father destroyed my gear with a nine iron."

She winces. "Sorry, Simon. Your dad always was a dick. You shouldn't have come back to Brockenhurst right now. Look, I really gotta go."

"Kat." I grab her hand as she starts to leave. I expect her to pull away but she doesn't. "What's going on with you? Why won't you talk to me?" I've asked the same question a hundred times—usually to her back as she's rushing away from me. Finally it seems like I might get an answer.

She looks around as if scanning for spies. I don't see anyone, but she doesn't seem satisfied. "I can't."

I can't doesn't mean *I don't want to*. It's a small step, but at least we're moving in the right direction for once. "You're in trouble, aren't you? I knew something was up when you drove into the pond. Is it your stepfather?"

We lock eyes, and I know the truth. I'm right.

"What if it is?" she asks quietly. And that's when I realize she's not stoned at all.

"Then I'll kill him." We both know I would. I'd do it right now if I could.

"And what would happen to you if you did?"

I shrug. "Doesn't matter."

That really pisses her off, and she yanks her hand away from mine. "See, this is why I didn't want you involved. This isn't a god-damn game, Simon. What would happen to you?"

"Prison, I guess." Then it dawns on me. "Wait. Are you not talking to me because you're trying to *protect* me? 'Cause if that's what you're—"

She holds up a hand. She isn't going to listen anymore. "Give it a rest, Simon. Go back to boarding school."

"Haven't you heard? I can't."

Kat crosses her arms. "Sure you can. Just tell them the truth. Tell them you didn't do it."

I don't say a word.

"You've never hacked anything in your entire life, Simon. You really expect me to believe you were the mastermind behind some crazy plot to take down Toys 'R' Us?"

"It wasn't Toys 'R' Us."

"Jesus, what difference does it make? We both know you didn't do it."

For a moment I'm a little bit crestfallen. Is it so hard to believe I'm a genius? "Yeah, well, maybe you don't know me as well as you thought."

"It doesn't matter if you did it or just took the blame for it. Either way it was a dumbass move," Kat says. "I can't be seen hanging out with a cybercriminal right now. It's too dangerous for both of us."

If she's looking for an excuse to blow me off, she could at least try to find one that makes some sense. "You can't hang around with me because I got arrested for hacking? What about all those assholes you've been spending time with? You're trying to tell me that Brian and West haven't committed a few felonies between them?"

"Those guys aren't my *friends*, Simon," she whispers angrily. "They're *camouflage*."

"Camouflage?" Something about the word scares the crap out of me. "Kat, what in the hell is going on? I'm not leaving you alone until I know."

She looks around again and grabs my arm. Then she pulls me behind the dumpster. I feel her hands on my face and her lips on mine. For the next sixty seconds, it's like we've passed through to some parallel universe. Then she pulls away and we're right back where we started—in a world that's completely screwed up for reasons I don't understand.

"Why did you do that?" I ask. She kissed me once a long time ago. I'd given up hope that it would ever happen again.

"Because I was tired of waiting for you."

I can't speak. My mind is too busy counting all the missed opportunities.

"Go back to boarding school, Simon," she says softly. "*Please.* When this is over, I swear I'll come find you."

"When *what's* over?" I call out as she heads for the school. "Kat! We used to be a team!"

She doesn't answer and she doesn't look back.

But my hunch is confirmed. Kat's knee-deep in some kind of shit. She doesn't want me to get involved. And she kissed me. I know one of these facts is far more important than the others, but right now I'm having a real hard time keeping my priorities straight.

The shades are drawn in my film-editing class, and a dozen screens light the room. As I pass through, moving toward my station, something catches my eye, and I'm overwhelmed by a sense of déjà vu. There's Kat on someone's screen. It's like every paranoid thought I've had in the hour since she kissed me has just been vindicated.

I stop and reverse course. "What's that?" I tap the girl's computer monitor.

My voice is gruff, but she doesn't flinch. She gazes up at me with eyes so dark that they don't seem to have pupils. I noticed her on my first day back at school. She must have moved to Brockenhurst while I was away. She's tall and pretty, with closely cropped hair and skin that glows like polished mahogany. I noticed early on that she didn't say much in class. Then I noticed she was absent a lot. Eventually I stopped noticing her at all. I haven't really thought about her since.

"My film," the girl says. "It's a documentary."

"Why are you filming my friend? You should mind your own business. Who are you, anyway?" I demand.

"My name's Busara Ogubu," she says, and turns back to her work. "You must be the crazy guy."

Most people would be offended. I can't help but laugh. "You can call me Simon," I tell her. Then I tap her screen. "So did my friend Kat sign any release forms? Does she know she's starring in your documentary?"

"You're part of it too," she says, fast-forwarding. She stops at a familiar scene—me in the parking lot this morning with Olivia and Emily. I had no idea she was there, and I can't for the life of me figure out where she might have been hiding.

"It's illegal to video people like that," I warn her. Somehow I'm not quite as pissed as I know I should be. "I'd be more careful if I were you. Every kid in this school has at least one lawyer in the family."

"Last time I checked, it was illegal to blackmail teenage girls, too," says Busara. "Even the bitchy ones."

"Touché," I concede. I like her. She's feisty.

She swivels around in her chair to face me. "Why are you protecting Katherine Foley?" she asks.

I realize then that Busara must not have any idea about Kat and me. About how things were before I left for boarding school. Still, I can't figure out what to tell her. I just stand there and look back at her. Then my mouth opens and I hear myself speak.

"Because she's the best person I know, and I'm pretty sure she's in trouble," I say, and instantly regret it. I have no idea why I've chosen to be honest with a girl I've just met.

"You might be right," Busara says.

"What?" I croak, as if there were hands around my throat. I didn't expect her to confirm my suspicions.

Busara puts a fingertip on the computer screen. "You know that kid?" she asks.

It's Marlow. "I know he's an asshole, but that's about it," I say. "He's new."

"He moved here from California over the holidays," Busara says. "Lives with his mother in a fancy glass house outside town. She works in tech."

"So?" I ask.

"So he may look like he lives under a bridge, but he's really a rich kid. I did a little cybersleuthing for my film, and from what I can tell, he didn't own a scrap of black clothing before Christmas. The Goth stoner thing is just an act. He's pretending to be something he's not."

I shrug. "Aren't we all?" I can think of a million things to hold against the guy, but that's not one of them. "New school, new identity. We were all someone else before we moved to Brockenhurst."

"Speak for yourself," says Busara. "By the way, you might be interested to know that Marlow and his new friends are having a party tonight."

"Are you trying to ask me out?" I give her a faux-flirty wink.

"I'm not into boys," Busara says flatly. "Or girls, for that matter."

"So you're an android?"

One side of her mouth twitches, but she doesn't quite laugh.

"I wondered the same thing myself, but then I passed the Voight-Kampff test, so I'm fairly confident that I'm human. Here— watch this."

She swivels back to the computer and rewinds through the footage of Kat and her friends. She stops and turns up the volume on the speakers and hits Play. Marlow is talking about a place known as Elmer's—an abandoned horse-rendering plant and glue factory a few miles from school. It's little more than a ruin, but it used to be the best party spot in town. Now the place is posted with No Trespassing signs, and the cops watch it on weekends. They don't bother to watch it during the week. I guess they assume kids aren't going to get crazy on a Monday. The world is built on false assumptions.

On the video, I hear Marlow say the building is going to be demolished. Some corporation just bought the land. The plant deserves one last party before it becomes an eco-friendly rock-climbing facility on a new company campus. I have no idea whether any of it's true—or how Marlow could have found out.

My eyes are still fixed on the computer screen when the camera pans away from Kat's friends and focuses momentarily on a car at the edge of the parking lot. There's a man inside. I can't see much of him, but he's wearing glasses, and his head is turned toward Kat and the other kids vaping in the lot.

"Who's that?" I ask. He looks official. The last thing Kat needs is to be busted for drugs on campus.

Busara looks back at the screen. It's impossible to read her expression. "How would I know?" she asks.

THE GIFT

I can't think of a worse place to be at nine o'clock on a Monday night than hunched down behind a bush, waiting for an illegal party to kick off at an old horse-rendering plant. But now that I'm here, I'm not going anywhere. It took two hours to walk to Elmer's. I'm not allowed to drive anymore, though the judge wasn't the one who imposed the punishment. It was my father's brilliant idea. Good ol' Grant is chock-full of brilliant ideas. The coydogs are out tonight, and I hear them yapping away all around me. I'm pretty sure they won't attack. I'm too big for them now. They know I'm more likely to eat one of *them*. Still, it's really f-ing cold out here, and I'm seriously starting to worry that I might lose a finger to frostbite.

But I will stay here and wait, because I will get Kat back. That kiss shook up everything inside me that had started to settle.

A gust of wind sets the world in motion. I watch the shadows of the scrub pines on the perimeter of the lot dance against the dim glow of distant streetlights. Their fragrance fills the cold air, and I find myself thinking about my family's holiday tradition. On the Friday before Christmas, my parents would pour themselves glasses of Scotch and watch me open a pile of gifts. On Saturday, they'd leave. My mother's family is Jewish. I'm not sure what my father's excuse was. They always spent Christmas Day together. Until I was nine, I spent mine with the staff. The nanny my mother hired after she fired Mrs. Kozmatka was the one who came up with the idea for the tree. I can't even remember the woman's name. She was only with us for a few months, due to mental health issues that will soon become evident. That year, before they left for parts unknown, my parents had given her an envelope full of cash to take me shopping. On Christmas morning, I came downstairs to find that she'd hung all the bills on the tree.

I plucked them off, crammed them into my pockets and disappeared into the woods before any of my keepers woke up. I didn't want to intrude on Kat and her mother, but I couldn't stay away. I was lurking outside the house when Kat came out on the porch in her pj's.

"What took you so long?" she asked with a yawn. "I've been up since six. You coming in or what?"

I remember wrapping paper strewn all over the floor. Linda was there in her nightgown. She and Kat were both drinking cocoa made from a mix that came in little paper pouches. Linda's cup smelled like chocolate and bourbon.

"Here," Kat said, shoving something into my hands. The item was oddly shaped, and I could see that she'd struggled to wrap it.

I tore off the paper and found a homemade slingshot. I looked up to see Kat jamming her sockless feet into boots. "Come on, I'll teach you how to use it."

"Wait a second," I said. I reached into my pocket and pulled out the wad of bills. "This is for you. Sorry, I didn't have time to wrap it all up."

After that, I spent my holidays with the Foleys. Every Christmas, Kat would give me something she'd made herself, and I would give her the wad of cash my parents had left for me. I always felt like I got the better deal. Then, the year I turned thirteen, I arrived at Kat's house to find there wasn't a present under the tree for me.

"It's outside," Kat said, crooking a finger as she opened the door. "Come on. Follow me."

As soon as we were out of sight of the house, she stopped. I didn't see anything that might be a present. And then she put her arms around my neck and kissed me. And I realized I'd been madly in love with her all those years.

For a brief but beautiful moment, I figured it had all been decided. But then nothing happened. In the two weeks that followed, I watched and waited for another sign, but none came. It was like the world had reset and we were back where we'd started.

I never kissed Kat again.

Of course, anyone who saw us assumed we were boyfriend and girlfriend. Or, thanks to my kishka, maybe they assumed we weren't—but that I wanted more. What no one could understand is that there *was* nothing bigger than what we had. Kat was my best friend, and I was hers, and that was everything.

I might have loved her, but there was too much to lose.

The kiss behind the dumpster made me think that maybe— just maybe—all this time she'd been in love with me, too.

THE GROUND
BENEATH OUR FEET

It's just after ten, and the party's in full swing. Flashlights are dancing in the glassless windows. I'm still not sure what I'm doing here. If Kat finds out, she'll be royally pissed. Still, I need to know why she's using the town losers as camouflage. And for the sake of my sanity, I have to find out just how deep undercover she's gone.

A few cars are parked behind the building, and from what I can tell, there are over half a dozen people inside on the second floor. I let out a deep breath. It's time to go in.

Kat and I explored the crumbling brick building on countless occasions over the years, so I have no trouble slipping in unnoticed and locating the stairs. On my way to the third floor, I use a trick Kat taught me: I stop and scatter a handful of dry twigs that I gathered on one of the stairs. I'll hear them snap if anyone follows me up. I know I'm being overly cautious. Everyone avoids the third floor of Elmer's. There's a rumor that they found a dead body up here years ago. I have no idea if it's true or just urban legend, but there's no arguing with the wisdom of staying off the third story. It's clearly unsafe. The boards creak under my feet, and the entire floor is riddled with holes that are hard to make out after dark.

I take my time and maneuver carefully to one of the openings, and then I get down on my knees. The hole is big enough that I have a good view of what's going on below. The first person I spot is one of the Horsemen, a psycho named Brian. He lives a few houses away from me. He moved in when we were both in fourth grade and introduced himself by squeezing the guts out of a toad. His personality hasn't improved since then. I always thought he'd be in jail by now, but he's captain of the lacrosse team, which makes him invincible around here. He's smoking something with West, the addict. Probably pot, though I'd be surprised if that was West's poison of choice these days. He's lost about forty pounds since freshman year, and he looks like he hasn't had the munchies in months.

I crawl across the floor to another hole and see Jackson, Mr. Chlamydia, making out with a girl I don't recognize. Probably a sucker from some other town—everyone in Brockenhurst knows he's polluted. Then I spot Kat, huddled in a dusty corner, her knees pulled up to her chest. She's nursing a drink in a Solo cup. Marlow's right there next her, talking her ear off, though I don't think she's listening. Her eyes are focused on something far away—someplace she'd rather be.

I wonder if she's back in the Otherworld ice cave. The giant avatar is gone. It's just the two of us together again in our own private world. For a second, it's nice to imagine I might be inside her head—the way she's always in mine.

A snap startles me. Someone's climbing the stairs and they

just stepped right on the twigs I left there. The footsteps pause for a moment and then continue. But there's enough time for me to scuttle into the darkness on the other side of the room. I end up in an alcove I had no idea existed. I can't see much, but there's something soft beneath my feet. I bend over and touch it. I'm pretty sure it's a down sleeping bag. I guess someone was planning to get lucky up here tonight.

I peek around the corner and see a figure standing at the top of the stairs. It's just a dark shadow with arms and legs. I can't even tell if it's male or female. For a minute, it doesn't move. It seems to be thinking. Or waiting. Then it stretches out an arm and tosses a small round object. The thing sails in an arc through the air and then plunges straight through a hole in the middle of the floor.

"Hey!" yelps a voice from below. Whatever it was must have come close to beaning someone. The music below stops and there's an eerie quiet.

A kid laughs. "What the hell?"

"What *is* that?" someone else asks.

The party has come to a halt, and the figure who threw the object is gone. I cautiously step out of the alcove and make my way toward the hole. I want to see for myself what's going on, but when I peer down, the object is hidden from view. Everyone at the party is huddled around it. Everyone, I notice, except Marlow and Kat.

"Hey, get back!" someone says. I can't see who said it, but it sounded like Marlow. No one's listening, though. There's an electric-blue light shining through the cracks between the kids.

"He's right! Don't mess with it!" This time it's Kat.

Directly below me, Brian the psycho looks straight up at the ceiling, and I barely back away in time.

"Who's up there?" he shouts. He doesn't sound angry. He must think it was one of his friends playing a joke. But I realize I'm still in serious shit. Unless I hurl myself through a window, there's no way to get out now. One-on-one I could beat Brian. I can't take on everyone here.

I'm scrambling for cover when the whole building groans like some massive beast that's been woken. I drop back down to my hands and knees, and tremors course through the floor. The tremors become a rumble and end with a crack and a deafening crash. A girl's scream is cut short. I don't think it's Kat, but it might be. I rush to one of the holes in the wooden floor, but all I see below me is a cloud of dust. Then I hear the waterfall of debris and I know what's happened: the second floor of the building has collapsed.

"Kat!" I shout.

I hear a muffled cry. Someone down there is alive.

Thank God the stairwell is still intact. I fly down the stairs, stopping briefly on the second and first floors to check the main part of the building. Both floors are almost completely gone. Everyone and everything has crashed straight through to the basement.

I've been inside the factory a hundred times, but I didn't know there *was* a basement. There's no time to hunt for the entrance, so I grab the edge of what used to be the first floor and drop down into the darkness. The fall is much farther than I thought it would be, and the landing knocks the wind out of me. I try to stand and the ground gives way beneath me and I'm suddenly surfing down a mountain of wood and bricks. I skid to a stop at the bottom and freeze for a second, getting my bearings. It's pitch-black except for the beam of a flashlight shining from beneath the debris. I dig it out and shine it around me, illuminating a pile of rubble unlike any I've ever seen. A guy's arm is protruding from the wreckage and I scramble over to him, clamping my fingers down on the vein in his wrist. No matter how hard I press, I can't detect a pulse.

I snatch my hand back and fight the urge to vomit. My heart is pummeling my rib cage, and I'm sucking in dust-filled air that clogs my lungs. Then the beam of the flashlight lands on a swatch of copper-colored hair, and I'm there, digging like a dog, hurling boards and pipes and bricks behind me until I finally unearth Kat's head and shoulders. She's either unconscious or dead, and her angelic expression scares me more than anything I've seen tonight. I close my eyes and press my fingers against her jugular. Her heart is still beating. I dig even faster, and when I reach her legs, I realize how badly she's injured. Blood is gushing from her left leg, and the spray splatters my face. I rip off my belt and tie it as tightly as I can around her thigh. When the flow of blood has been reduced from a gush to a trickle, I fish out my phone and start to dial 911.

Then I hang up.

I can hear ambulances. Multiple ambulances. Someone's already called for help. I look around. There's no one moving in the building but me.

THE MIRACLE

The EMT said the tourniquet saved Kat's life. A nail nicked an artery in her left leg, and without my size thirty-two belt she would have bled out. When we arrived at the hospital, no one asked me what happened or what I saw. They were all frantically treating the wounded. I wasn't injured, so they probably assumed I wasn't with the others when the floor collapsed. Given my criminal record—and the fact that I hadn't exactly been invited to the party—I figured it was best not to volunteer any information just yet.

Four people died. I knew at least one of the kids hadn't made it, but hearing the body count made the horror too real. I thank any God that's listening for sparing Kat's life. And given the extent of her injuries, I pray it will be a life worth living.

The clock on the wall says it's almost five a.m. In a few hours the sun will rise, and Kat still hasn't woken up. Aside from the leg wound, she's suffered serious head trauma, a punctured lung and three broken ribs. The doctor says she's hopeful, but I'm not stupid. I know there's a fair chance that Kat might never come to. I think that's the reason they're letting me stay in her room. Or maybe they realize that removing me would be potentially life-threatening. Not for Kat, but for me.

Her mother arrived about an hour after we did. I hadn't seen Linda since I returned to Brockenhurst, and the difference was startling. When I knew her, Linda always drank too much and smoked like a chimney. But I spent years wishing she was my mother. She hugged every kid who ever entered her house. She told raunchy jokes and laughed harder than anyone else. And she always made sure that the kitchen was stocked with my favorite, Flamin' Hot Cheetos—even though she and Kat both despised them. Now Linda's dressed in chinos and her bleach blond hair is now dyed a respectable shade of auburn. The hair's an improvement, but she looks like her spirit is broken. I have a hunch that marriage has not been kind to her.

Linda barreled through the door and flung herself over Kat's body. I was busy making sure she wasn't going to accidentally rip the IV out of Kat's arm when Wayne Gibson appeared in the doorway. He wasn't pleased to see me standing beside the bed. He grabbed a nurse who was passing by. "Get this kid out of here," he ordered without bothering to lower his voice. "I don't want to see him again."

That's when Linda lifted her head. Her eye makeup was a blur. Most of it had rubbed off, leaving smudgy black circles on Kat's blanket. "No," she said. "You can leave if you want to, Wayne, but Simon is going to stay."

I saw Wayne Gibson's jaw clench so hard he could have bitten through rebar. Linda was going to pay for her words when they got home, but Wayne wasn't the kind of guy who'd make a scene in public. "You let your child run wild. I told you something like this was going to happen," he said in a low, steady voice. "Now that it has, the last thing she needs is a criminal camped out in her hospital room."

"She's *my* daughter," Linda replied softly. "I know what's best for her."

"If you knew what was best for her, Linda, Katherine wouldn't be here."

At that point, I stepped forward to face him. If I'd ever had to live with an asshole like that, I would have turned to drugs in a heartbeat. I could only imagine how he must have tortured Kat. And she was right about one thing—if I ever found out, I'd probably kill him.

I put my hand on the man's chest and shoved him out of the hospital room and into the hall. "See ya, Wayne," I said before I slammed the door in his face. "I'll take it from here."

When Linda said she was going home to gather a few of Kat's things, I had a hunch Wayne wasn't going to let her come back. I think she must have known too. Before she left, she signed a form giving me full access to her daughter's room. The paper is folded up and tucked away in my back pocket in case anyone challenges me. So far everyone has left us alone. Yesterday, I would have traded my soul for some time with Kat. Now we're together in a beige room with a floral border and a cheesy mass-produced watercolor of a sunrise. I feel like some poor bastard from a fairy tale who was granted a wish but forgot to phrase it correctly. I asked to have Kat to myself, and I got what I wanted. Her body is here with me, but the rest of her is gone.

A phone alarm chimes somewhere outside the hospital room.

"Kat," I whisper. She doesn't answer, but I know she can hear me. "If you don't come out of this, I'm going to come after you."

I move my chair to the darkest corner of the room. Lying in her hospital bed, Kat is lit from above like the body of a queen at rest in a crypt. I think back to Elmer's, and I try to go through the facts as I know them. An unknown person threw an unidentified object. The object made eight people gather around it. When they did, the floor collapsed. After decades of neglect, the building's boards must have been rotten. But was the weight of eight kids enough to bring them down?

Four people died. Three are unconscious. And two people, counting me, escaped from the party unscathed. I saw the other lucky one in the ER being treated for minor hand wounds. As far as I could tell, aside from his bloody palms, there wasn't a scratch on Marlow. I was eavesdropping when he told the doctor he'd grabbed hold of a pipe that was mounted on the wall when the floor started to shake.

So we have one miracle survivor, one person who shouldn't have been there and a mysterious call to 911. But the biggest mystery of all is the object. The incident is all over the news, and I keep waiting to hear that something unusual has been recovered from the rubble. The police still seem convinced that the collapse was an accident, but I'm not buying it. Right now, everything points to one conclusion: sometime soon, I need to have a chat with Marlow.

LOCKED IN

Kat opened her eyes. I fell asleep for a while and woke up to find her staring up at the ceiling as if she were counting each little pockmark on the tiles. When I leaped up and grabbed hold of her, I knew right away that something was wrong. Kat didn't hug back or push me away. She didn't say anything, either, though I'm sure I was blubbering. When I released her, she gurgled and sank back on the pillows. Her head came to rest at an awkward angle, and her eyes, which had been staring at the ceiling so intently, were examining the blanket instead.

The nurse popped her head in and then summoned an army of doctors, who promptly kicked me out of the room.

An hour has passed. Nurses with equipment are still entering and leaving. Finally the neurologist on duty comes out to speak to me.

I recognize Dr. Ito from the Brockenhurst Country Club. It helps that her lab coat is the same color as her tennis whites.

"You're Irene Eaton's son," she says.

That's the biggest downside of the kishka. Like a giant birthmark or a second head, it renders me unforgettable.

"Yes," I tell her. There isn't any point in denying it. I'm sure they gossip about my family all the time at the country club. Poor Irene Eaton, they must say. How did she end up with a nutjob cybercriminal for a son? "I'm a friend of Kat's. Can you tell me what's wrong with her?"

She seems a bit reluctant to share, so I take out the form that Kat's mother signed. "I'm a friend of the family."

Dr. Ito nods. "Katherine has sustained significant damage to a part of the brain stem called the pons," she tells me. "The condition is called cerebromedullospinal disconnection, and—"

"I'm sorry. Cerebro *what*?"

She smiles patiently. "The layman's term is *locked-in syndrome*."

I look past her, into the room where Kat lies motionless on the bed. "Is that like a coma?"

This time the doctor shakes her head. "Only in the sense that Katherine is unable to move. But her EEG shows normal brain activity. That tells us she's fully conscious and her mind is locked inside a body that is unable to function. While medical science has gotten good at fixing bodies, we haven't made quite as much progress when it comes to repairing the brain."

I can't breathe. The muscles in my legs go limp and I plop down in a chair near the nurses' station. "Will she recover?"

"I'm afraid it's highly unlikely," the doctor informs me. "I wish I had better news. I'm very sorry, I was due in the OR ten minutes ago. Will you please excuse me?"

I try to grab her arm as she leaves, but my timing is off and I catch nothing but air. I fall to my knees and stay there while everything crashes down around me.

It takes every bit of courage I can muster to return to Kat's room. She's lying perfectly still, her eyes staring up at a different patch of ceiling. If what Dr. Ito says is true, the Kat I've always known is a prisoner inside a broken body. For a girl who grew up running wild through the woods, nothing could be worse. Creatures like Kat don't survive being confined to a cage.

I lean down close to her face. "Hey," I whisper, my lips brushing her ear. "You're going to get better. I'll be right here until you do." But the words coming out of my mouth sound phony. I have to step out of the room again until I can find a way to believe them.

It's lunchtime, and my mother is sitting across from me in the hospital's basement cafeteria. Her buddy Dr. Ito must have told her where to find me. The lighting down here is so bad that it's hard to distinguish the sick from the healthy. Even my mother looks green. I take a monstrous bite of a tuna fish sandwich. The stench reminds me of cat food.

"I'm going back upstairs as soon as I eat this," I inform her. "Where's Dad?"

"On his way to London," she says. "I'd be with him right now if it weren't for you."

I used to wonder if my mother had any idea how awful she sounds when she says shit like that. Now I don't care.

"Oh, I'm sure there's still time to catch the red-eye," I tell her. "Don't let me keep you."

My mother ignores me. "The girl who's hurt," she says. "It's the same one? The one you drove down from school to visit?"

It's a stupid thing to ask. "Do I have any other friends?" I say. Like she'd actually know the answer.

"I'm sorry about what happened, Simon. But I've been told your friend may not get better for quite some time. You can't stay here in the hospital and miss school."

I laugh, though it's purely for effect. I find none of this even remotely funny. "I'm eighteen years old. School is optional."

"Perhaps, but you're not a member of the girl's family. The hospital won't let you stay in her room."

She's been underestimating me since kindergarten. You'd think she'd have learned her lesson by now. "You seem to forget that I'm the spawn of two lawyers. Surely you're familiar with the federal government's hospital visitation guidelines." I pull the form Kat's mom signed out of the back pocket of my jeans and pass it across the table. My mother delicately removes a glob of mayonnaise from the paper with a napkin before she unfolds it and reads.

When she looks up and hands the sheet back to me, I can tell she still doesn't know I've won. "All right, so the law allows you to stay. But I don't. You're coming home with me, Simon."

"Or else?" I ask.

Her pretty little nostrils flare as she takes a deep breath. "What do you mean, 'or else'?"

"I mean you'd better have something amazing to threaten me with if you want me to leave."

"I can call your probation officer right now and inform him that you've expanded your criminal repertoire to include credit card fraud."

"Go right ahead," I tell her. "And I'll tell everyone in this fancy-ass town who you really are."

She raises her perfectly sculpted eyebrows and laughs. She has no idea that her secret is out. "And who exactly is that, Simon?"

"The Kishka's daughter," I say, my eyes locked on hers.

She's silent. I've got her. This is literally one of the best moments of my life, and I want to savor every last second of it. The fluorescent light over our heads begins to flicker on cue, lending the scene a delightful horror-film quality.

"Do you think they'll all still admire you after they've seen pictures of your original nose?" I ask. "Do you think they'll gossip about how your father found the funds to pay your tuition to Harvard? Or maybe they'll question whether you deserved to be admitted in the first place?"

"That's enough," she snaps. Her expression has shifted from shock to outrage. "You're a little shit, Simon."

"No, I'm a *Kishka*," I tell her. "Just like my grandfather." I lean over the table until my nose is inches away from hers. "Did you really think you'd get away with it?"

I'm back in my chair in Kat's room, pretending to have a little after-lunch nap with a blanket pulled over my head. I hear people come in, but when I open my eyes, all I see is a golden light shining through a matrix of white wool. There are three of them in the room—Dr. Ito and two men. I don't recognize the guys' voices. I inch the blanket down until I can see them. They're all bent over Kat's bed like they're playing Operation. The two men aren't very old. Probably in their late twenties, early thirties. Their shirts are untucked and they're both wearing jeans and sneakers.

"You're right. She's an ideal candidate," one of them says.

"It'll be a real shame to shave such a pretty head," the other jokes.

"Don't touch her hair." I throw off the blanket and the three visitors jump.

"You're awake," Dr. Ito says with a sigh. I'm sure she was hoping my mother would drag my ass out of the hospital.

"Hey there," says one of the men. He comes over to greet me with a friendly smile and an outstretched hand. "Sorry to bother you. My name's Martin—"

"What's going on?" I demand.

"We're doing our best to help your friend," Dr. Ito says. "Are we finished here?" she asks the two men.

"Yeah, I think so," says the man still standing by Kat's bedside. He makes a few quick notes on a tablet. "The nurse will let us know when she's been prepped?"

"Certainly," Dr. Ito answers. "Now, will you excuse us, gentlemen? I need to have a word with this young man."

They don't need to be asked twice. The men file out of the room, their eyes averted. When they're gone, the neurologist turns to face me.

"Who were those guys?" I ask her.

She crosses her arms and smiles, one gesture negating the

other. "Katherine is a very lucky girl. Those men are engineers from the Company. They've designed a device that can help people with her condition. They're looking for patients to take part in a beta test."

"Wait." Did I hear her right? "Are you saying those guys are from *the* Company?"

"What other Company is there?" Dr. Ito asks. "They work for Milo Yolkin."

I once watched a TED Talk filmed at the Company's headquarters in Princeton where Milo told the story behind his business's name. I guess it started off as a joke between friends. All the giant tech corporations had stupid, cutesy or gibberish names, so Milo went the opposite way with his little start-up. For the first couple of years, the financial press called the Company a dog, but then the organization kept on expanding until it became the beast it is now. There are a lot of people out there today who no longer find the name all that funny. A future in which there's only one all-powerful Company doesn't seem totally preposterous anymore.

I had no clue that the Company was making medical equipment, but I guess I shouldn't be so surprised. They do everything else. I've even heard rumors that Milo Yolkin personally wrote most of the code for the new Otherworld—in his spare time. If he's able to do something like that on his own, the Company is capable of *anything*.

"What kind of device have they invented?" I ask Dr. Ito. "How does it work?"

"You'll have to ask the engineers," the doctor says with a chuckle. "I may be a brain surgeon, but I'm afraid it's all way too complicated for me."

I glance over at Kat again, and when I turn back to the doctor, she's whisking through the door, her white lab coat flaring out behind her like a cape.

Maybe she was joking, but I take Dr. Ito's suggestion very seriously. In a heartbeat I set out to look for the Company engineers. For the first time in forever, I'm experiencing something that feels like hope. My heart is racing and my palms are damp. If Milo Yolkin has focused his brainpower on helping people like Kat, she might actually have a chance.

Fortunately, the engineers haven't gone very far. They're chatting near the nurses' station right outside Kat's room. The one named Martin is carrying a black plastic suitcase. Who knows what's inside it? Pills, needles, gadgets—it makes no difference to me. If there's even the slimmest chance that he's going to help Kat, I will worship at his sneaker-clad feet.

There's no reason for them to share information with me, and I am fully prepared to grovel. But Martin sees me approaching and smiles.

"Hey. Sorry about just now," he says, sounding sincere. "I didn't mean to be insensitive. Hospitals still make me nervous. By the way, this is my colleague, Todd."

"Hey there," says the other guy, raising a hand.

"Simon," I say. "May I speak with you guys for a moment?"

They consult each other with a quick glance. "Sure," says Martin, and I gesture for them to follow me back to Kat's room.

"So is Katherine Foley your girlfriend?" Todd asks once we're all inside.

"Yes," I tell him. Then I remember she can hear what we're saying. "I mean we're friends. And she's female."

"Clearly," says Todd in a tone I don't appreciate.

Martin just nods. "We're really sorry about what happened to her."

He actually sounds like he means it, but I don't have time to waste on small talk or sympathy. "This therapy you've developed for patients with Kat's condition. I'd like to know more about it."

Martin puts the suitcase on top of the tray at the end of Kat's bed and cracks it open. The interior of the case is black foam, with custom compartments carved out. If this were a movie, there would be an unassembled sniper's rifle inside. But this case contains a thin, dark visor and a circle of flesh-colored plastic.

I move in closer. They don't seem to mind. "What is it?" The visor is interesting, but I've never seen anything like the plastic circle before.

"The hardware doesn't have an official name yet," says Martin. "That's how new it is. Right now, we're just calling it the disk. The guy who designed the software used to call it the White City. Run his software on our hardware and you've got the next generation of virtual reality."

My heart sinks. Virtual reality makes for great games, but it isn't going to *cure* anything.

"Did you just say *next generation*?" Todd scoffs. "Give me a break. It's a quantum leap forward." He looks over at me. "Our labs are always five to seven years ahead of consumer release. We generally stagger innovation to maximize profits. But this time the tech is too important. The boss doesn't want commerce to keep it away from the people who need it."

"The boss. You mean Milo Yolkin?" He's not even here, and yet I suddenly feel like I'm in the presence of a divine being.

"What other boss could I mean?" Todd says with a laugh that almost seems bitter. "The Company is Milo's kingdom. Though I think he prefers Otherworld these days."

I get the feeling Todd isn't Milo's biggest fan. I suppose it must be hard working for one of the world's greatest geniuses—especially an infamous micromanager who's known for personally overseeing every Company project.

"I actually played the new Otherworld with Kat this weekend," I tell them. Was it really this weekend? It feels like it's been forever.

"And you made it out of your bedroom?" Martin jokes. "I've heard the Otherworld headset app is so addictive there are twenty-year-old guys buying cases of Depends diapers so they don't need to waste any time in the real world."

"Yeah." Todd nods. "They say sales of Soylent are going through the roof too. Do you think it would be insider trading if I bought a few shares of the company?"

Martin shrugs. "Not my wheelhouse," he says. "Ask HR."

I tap the suitcase, trying to steer the conversation back on track. "So this is next-generation VR hardware. You're saying it's more advanced than the new Otherworld headset?"

"Light-years," Martin confirms.

"It's our masterpiece. Martin and I have been working on it for ages," says Todd. Then his tone shifts and I'm reminded that, despite his frat boy behavior, he works for one of the most powerful corporations on earth. "It's going to make a real difference in people's lives. The disk was designed for people who are unable to move on their own. It frees them from the prison of their bodies and allows them to explore a world as real as this one." If I didn't know better, I'd wonder if he was reading off the Company's website.

"Can I try it?" I ask.

Todd laughs. "We'd have to shave the back of your head first." He pulls out the flesh-colored disk and holds it up. "That's the one downside of the tech. The disk needs perfect skin adhesion."

I thought I was pretty up-to-date on the latest advances in VR technology, but I have no idea how this could possibly work. "Skin adhesion? For what?"

"In layman's terms? It talks to the wearer's brain." He registers the dumbfounded look on my face. "Didn't you notice there are no gloves or boots in the box? We've gotten rid of haptic devices altogether. This is true virtual reality—not just sight, sound and touch. Tap into the brain and you can engage all five senses."

"And maybe a few others that we don't have names for yet," Martin adds.

I reach for the disk and Todd hands it to me. It looks like a large version of the skin-colored nicotine patches that Linda used to wear whenever she'd try to quit smoking. "This actually communicates with people's brains?" The engineers were right. This is wild. I'm holding a paradigm shift between my fingers.

"Yep," Todd says, pointing at the visor that's still in the suitcase. "The visor *shows* you another world, but the disk makes it *real*."

"What does the person wearing it see?"

"The future," Todd says proudly. He looks over at Martin. "Play him the video."

Martin pulls out his phone and calls up a video. Then he hands the device to me.

On the screen a field of green-and-golden grass is swaying in a breeze. A few cottony clouds float across a blue sky. I realize it must be a park. Gleaming white towers dripping with flowering foliage surround it on all sides.

"What is this?"

"That's where our patients go. That's the White City."

I bring the image closer to my eyes. It's one hundred percent photo-realistic. "That's not CGI," I say. "That's gotta be a real place."

"What's real anymore?" Martin laughs proudly. "We'll pass your compliments along to our software colleagues."

"It looks like heaven." I'm not speaking metaphorically. It actually looks like an image you'd find on some religious cult's website.

"Smells like heaven, too, apparently," says Martin.

"Yeah, I don't know. My paradise has fewer flowers and more scantily clad ladies," Todd says. Then he winks at me. "Sorry, that was unprofessional. Don't tell anyone I said that."

I don't know why, but Todd's stupid joke sets off a brainstorm. "Wait—how many people are already in the White City?"

"At the moment, about three hundred people are taking part in the beta test," Todd says.

"Can they talk to each other?"

"Sure, and more," Todd says, arching an eyebrow. Apparently his mind never leaves the gutter.

"Okay, then," I tell him. "You can shave my head. I'd like to try the disk." I'd let them shave every inch of my body for a chance to speak to Kat.

Suddenly Todd's fidgeting uncomfortably. I don't think he was expecting me to take him up on the offer. "I was just kidding around about that. The disk is a prototype, and we don't have any to spare. Plus, the boss is pretty particular about who gets a tour of the White City."

"I need to talk to Kat," I say, fully aware that my desperation is showing now. "*Please.* I'll do anything."

Martin puts a hand on his colleague's shoulder. "Maybe the kid could come by the facility. As long as he doesn't tell anyone, I can't see how it would hurt."

Todd clearly isn't having it. "Nothing like that has been authorized," he says sternly.

"Yeah, but imagine the feedback this kid could give us," Martin argues.

"*No,*" Todd insists, stepping back so that Martin's hand slips from his shoulder. "Imagine what could go wrong."

Go wrong. I don't like the sound of that. "What do you mean? Do things ever go wrong with the disk?" I ask.

"Of course not," Martin assures me. "Our satisfaction rate is one hundred percent."

"That's right," Todd says, his eyes locked on his partner's. "Because we're very careful about the patients we choose."

Martin turns to me and shrugs apologetically. "Sorry," he says as Todd packs up the suitcase. "I tried my best."

And with those five words, my spark of hope is gone.

Five hours pass before anyone comes back into Kat's room. At some point during the time I've been sitting here praying for something to happen, Kat's mother must have given consent for her daughter to take part in the Company's beta test, because the nurse who finally arrives brings a pair of clippers and a surgical razor. I watch as she shaves the back of Kat's head. Kat's hair is her signature. She's always been proud of it. When the nurse lays her back down, I can't tell the difference. But there's a clear plastic bag filled with copper-colored curls, and the sight of it makes me nauseous.

It's all for the best, the nurse assures me. Kat won't mind about the hair. I wish I could believe her, but I know it's not true.

"I'm so sorry," I tell Kat when it's done. I hope like hell it's worth it.

THE KID

Kat's visor is on, and the disk has been affixed to the base of her skull. I watch her heart monitor sketch the same peak over and over again. Whenever her pulse speeds up, I know something's happening in the White City. I hope she's found the field the engineers showed me. The only thing it was missing was a fort. I wish I could be there to build one with her, but she's gone to the one place I can't follow her. At least, not without one of those disks.

Around eleven p.m., I make a trip to the cafeteria for my second tuna fish sandwich of the day. A woman in a uniform is weaving around the tables, wiping them down with a rag that looks like she just used it to clean an outhouse. She doesn't acknowledge me other than to leave a large dry circle around the spot where I'm sitting with the sandwich and a cup of coffee that tastes like a tire fire. Aside from her, there's a guy who's stationed himself in the corner with his back to me. Judging by his stiff posture and air of alertness, I'd guess he's here in some official capacity, though I can't find the energy to care.

A television mounted on the wall in front of me is playing a talk show. The sound is turned down, but I watch the host as he goes through the motions. Monologue, move to the desk, crack a joke with the bandleader, introduce the first guest. I wonder what it's like to do the same goddamn thing every day, day after day, year after year. I've been at the hospital for just under twenty-four hours, and I've already fallen into my own little rut. Bedside, bathroom, cafeteria, repeat. It won't be long before I lose my mind.

The first guest comes out on the TV and I hear the muffled thunder of wild applause. A youngish man emerges from between the velvet curtains on the right side of the stage. He's dressed like he's on his way to do flip tricks in a shopping mall parking lot. I own the same sweatshirt he's got on. I bought it at Target to annoy my mom. Topping it all off is a goofy smile and a head of angelic sandy-blond curls. There probably isn't a person on earth who wouldn't recognize the face. It belongs to Milo Yolkin. He waves to the audience and they leap to their feet. I'm on my feet, too, searching for the television's volume button. I find it and turn it up until the applause builds to a roar.

The talk show's host is a dapper man in his late forties wearing a beautifully tailored pinstripe suit. He arches an eyebrow and adjusts his glasses, pretending to scrutinize his guest while the clapping and whistles die down.

"What happened?" the host asks with a perfectly straight face. "Couldn't your dad make it to the show tonight?" The crowd howls. I barely crack a smile.

The camera zooms in on Milo Yolkin, who fakes a chuckle.

It's clear that he'd rather be anywhere else. Up close, his famous face looks pale and gaunt. There are circles under his eyes that the show's makeup artist couldn't hide.

"In all seriousness," says the host. "How old are you—twelve?"

"I just turned twenty-nine," says Milo. They pause for the requisite birthday applause.

"I'm pretty sure I have boxer shorts older than you," the host quips. "What age were you when you started the Company?"

"Nineteen," Milo tells him.

"And now it's worth . . ."

Milo blushes, and for a moment his face looks almost healthy. "It's hard to say. The valuation changes every day."

"Okay, so let's just go for a ballpark figure, then. Would you say it's worth more than the GDP of Europe or Asia?"

The CEO of the most successful corporation on earth just grins and stares at his shoes.

I move toward the television set until I'm basking in its glow. I want to get as close as possible to the man who may have just set Kat free.

"Fine, fine. Enough teasing," the host declares. "This is probably why you don't do shows like this, am I right?"

Milo looks up and shrugs good-naturedly. I'm hoping the lighthearted banter is about to end. Milo Yolkin wouldn't be doing a talk show if there weren't a very good reason. I don't expect him to discuss the White City. The Company's beta tests are always conducted in secret. My bet is he's going to announce the new Otherworld wide release.

"But I hear you've made an exception tonight because you want to tell people about a project you've been working on," the host is saying. "Something very important to you. I believe it's called Otherworld." There are a few isolated hoots and whistles in the audience. I was right. "I see it already has a following. What exactly is Otherworld? It used to be a game, if I'm not mistaken?"

"Some people thought so," Milo says. "Technically it was something called an MMO. That stands for massively multiplayer online game. But for those of us who played it, the original Otherworld was a lot more than that."

"Hell yeah!" someone shouts.

"Friend of yours?" the host asks.

Milo shields his eyes from the glare of the studio lights and tries to peer out into the audience. "Probably." He grins, warming up. "Or enemy. I'd have to see his avatar to tell. I knew most people there. Back in my teens, I spent close to two years of my life in Otherworld."

Interesting. Who'd have thunk? It's hard to imagine what the world would have been like if Milo Yolkin had never left Otherworld.

"You must have been very popular in high school," the host jests.

Milo's smile looks much less sincere this time. "Let's just say the real world wasn't very kind to me in those days," he replies.

The host adjusts his glasses. It's clearly time to change the subject. "So what was the objective of the original Otherworld?"

"The objective?" Milo asks. "There was no objective."

The host grins nervously. "Don't all games have objectives? Isn't the whole idea to *win*? Otherwise, what's the point of playing them?"

"What's the point of being alive?" Milo replies, and I actually laugh out loud. But the host is left momentarily flummoxed. I guess he doesn't know the answer. So Milo steps in to fill the silence. "The objective of Otherworld was to live the kind of life you couldn't have in the real world. You could fight beasts, explore new lands, hoard treasure, or have sex. You could even start a chinchilla farm if that was what you were into. It was all up to you. Otherworld became my escape. When I was there, I got to be the person I wanted to be. The place set me free."

I'd love to know what young Milo Yolkin got up to in Otherworld. He's twenty-nine years old now, and he still looks like an overgrown cherub. Did he run a virtual petting zoo? Spend his time rescuing digital baby seals?

"Why did you stop playing?" the host asks, struggling to get the conversation back on track.

In response to the question, Milo's face goes cold. It's moments like this that remind you that he's not really an overgrown kid. He's one of the most powerful men on earth. "One morning about eleven years ago, I turned on my computer and Otherworld was gone. The game's publishers had decided there weren't enough subscribers and they'd shut the whole thing down."

"Just like that?"

"Yep," says Milo, and you can see he's still seething at the injustice of it all. "By that point I'd built my own kingdom. I had an amazing fortress, and a harem, and serfs farming my lands. I was practically running the place. And then *poof,* suddenly everything was gone. It was the worst thing that ever happened to me. So when one of my engineers at the Company showed me some revolutionary new technology he'd developed, I figured the time had come to bring Otherworld back."

"Revolutionary technology?" the host asks. "What kind of stuff are we talking about?"

"Well, it's not something you can really *tell* people about," says Milo. "You kind of have to see it—and feel it—to believe it."

That's obviously the cue for a helper to appear onstage, pushing a cart covered by a white sheet. Grinning like a birthday party magician, Milo rises from his seat and whips the sheet off. Beneath it are haptic gloves and the new Otherworld VR headset.

"These are for you," he tells the host, holding out the gloves for the man to slip into. "The haptic technology is cutting-edge, but the headset offers an experience beyond anything you've ever imagined. We've only made and sold a few thousand prototypes so far, and you can't play the new game without one."

"I can tell this is about to get *very* interesting," the host says, eyeing the headset. "But how's everybody out there supposed to know what I'm seeing?"

"Oh, I think we ought to be able to bring it to life for them." Milo puts the headset on the host, and a large screen instantly brightens behind them. Soon the audience will be able to see everything the host can see.

"Should I walk toward the light?" the host jokes, his hands outstretched as if he's feeling his way.

"Not yet," Milo says with a laugh. "Have you ever climbed to the top of a volcano?"

"No, sir. I'm deathly afraid of danger," the host jokes.

"Well, now you can see what it's like. All from the safety of your stage."

On the screen behind them, a scorched black land and a river of lava appear. The audience gasps. No one's seen anything like it. There's a loud boom and the host spins around. Bright orange flames are shooting into the sky from the cone of the volcano. Three vultures the size of pterodactyls are hovering above, waiting for the barbecue to begin.

"Whoa, my gloves are getting hot!" the host exclaims. "Hey, look! I can see my hands!" He looks down at his crotch. "And the rest of me, too!"

"That's right. Now let's cool those hands down a little," Milo replies. Suddenly the scene shifts and the screen shows an endless expanse of frozen ocean. There's a rumbling, and the host struggles to keep his balance as the ice in front of him collapses. Massive great white sharks are patrolling the water below. "What do you think?"

"I think you and I have different ideas of fun," the host says. "What about a nice beach in Maui and a banana daiquiri?"

Milo laughs. "Okay then, let's take you somewhere a little more relaxing. Otherworld's most popular destination so far is the City of Imra." The screen shows a curved street lined with ornate marble buildings that look like they belong in a Greek myth. A gorgeous redhead in a tight black dress passes by.

"Wowza, look at those pixels," the host says. "Who is *that*?"

"Her name is Catelyn. She's an NPC. Wink at her and see what happens."

"That has never once worked in real life, but let's give it a go. Hey, toots, why don't you come over here and tell me all about your acronym?"

"*NPC* stands for *non-player character*," Milo says humorlessly. "Though Catelyn is different. *Special*. She's part of the system, but we've designed her to have a mind of her own."

What exactly does that mean? I wonder.

The host whistles. "Can I *play* with that software?"

I roll my eyes.

"Absolutely," says Milo. "And she will play back." The NPC comes over and takes the host's hand. She looks as real as any woman in the audience. Her skin texture is remarkable—soft and dewy, with visible pores. And when the camera pans down to her hand, I can see the cuticles and the sun reflected in her bloodred nail polish. The detail is absolutely amazing.

"Oh my God, I can feel her squeezing my fingers!" the host says with genuine surprise. "You know what this would be *really* good for?" He pauses and the audience snickers. "Foot massages. I guess you could say I'm a foot massage enthusiast."

The joke seems to sail right over Milo's head. "If that's what you're into, I'm not here to judge," he says. He clearly takes this all *very* seriously. "In Otherworld all of us can lead our best lives. Whatever those may be. It doesn't matter how much money you have or how physically fit you are. The life you always wanted will be within your reach. Some people will want to hunt or fight or explore. Others are going to want . . . foot massages."

On-screen, Catelyn cozies up to the host and plants a peck on his cheek. "Oh my God," he mutters. Then he pulls off one of his gloves and begins rooting through his pockets. "How much do you want for this thing? A million bucks? My soul?"

Milo beams. "You just need to subscribe to Otherworld and purchase a headset. The early-access app came out this past Saturday. We've let in two thousand players to help us work all the bugs out. Otherworld's wide release should take place in a few months. Hopefully we'll have managed to manufacture a few million of these headsets by then."

"I have to wait months?" the host groans. "But I don't want to leave!" He blows a kiss at Catelyn and removes the headset. "Okay, so now that I've experienced it for myself, I have one question. How are people supposed to feed and relieve themselves? 'Cause nobody's going to say goodbye to *her* to chow down a burrito or take a leak."

"You make a really good point," Milo says. I suspect it's not the first time he's heard that. "I'm sure the Company will come up with something."

The show's band starts to play to commercial and I think of Kat upstairs, her body hooked up to an array of tubes that provide all the nutrition she needs and eliminate the resulting waste products. The device that's communicating directly to her brain is supposedly far more advanced than the headset that's available to the public. If it works the way Martin and Todd described, the world Kat's in feels, smells and tastes just as real as this one. What if she's found the male version of Catelyn? What if she never wants to leave?

A VISITOR

It must be just after midnight. I'm halfway down the hall, heading back to Kat, when my legs suddenly stop before I know why. My brain catches up quickly and I see it. The door to Kat's room is ajar. Probably just a nurse checking up on her, but I don't know that for sure. So I tiptoe toward the room until I can peer inside. There's someone standing over Kat's bed. Slim and dressed in a hoodie and jeans, it looks a lot like the figure I saw at Elmer's right before the floor collapsed. I drop my coffee and lurch forward, grabbing hold of the intruder's sweatshirt. The yelp I hear is unmistakably feminine. Then the hood falls back, revealing an elegant head.

"Busara?" I ask, though I can see her clearly. It's just hard to believe she's here.

"I'm sorry," she says. "I thought you'd gone home. I didn't mean to scare you."

"It's the middle of the night. What are you doing in here?" I demand. Then I remember the video on her computer at school, and my confusion quickly turns to rage. "Wait—were you just *filming*?"

"No, it's not like that," Busara says. "I don't have a camera with me." She's calm. Too calm. Maybe she's an android after all.

"Bullshit," I say. That's when I notice the plastic band around her wrist.

"What's this?" I ask, grabbing the band and pulling her arm toward me to get a better look. The sight of her name and birth date on the plastic takes me by surprise. "You're a patient here?"

She lowers her arm and covers the band with her fingers as if she's ashamed of it. "I have a heart condition," she says. "I spend a lot of time at the hospital. My cardiologist is on this floor."

"Oh." That explains why she's out of school so much. I feel like an asshole. "Sorry."

"It's okay," she says. "How are you?"

It's a simple question, but one I find myself unable to answer. My mouth is open, but for the first time ever there are no words spilling out. We stand together looking down at the girl in the bed. What's left of Kat's hair is spread across the pillow, and her eyes are hidden behind the Company's slim black visor.

My vision blurs and a drop slips down my face and over my lip before I can catch it. I've spent hours alone in this room, and I haven't shed a single tear. Then some random girl shows up and I lose it. Having Busara here makes me realize how alone I am. I don't want her sympathy. I want Kat's. The one person I would have turned to is gone. I'm here for her, but there's no one here for me.

"My doctor says Kat has something called locked-in syndrome," Busara says. I'm grateful I can reply with a nod as I wipe my eyes on the collar of my shirt.

Busara turns her gaze away from me and back down at Kat. "It seems to be going around."

I clear my throat. "What do you mean?"

"I heard that two of the other kids who survived the accident at the factory have it too. West and Brian. They were moved to a long-term care facility earlier this afternoon."

I wonder if that's where they'll be sending Kat soon. To some place where malfunctioning human bodies are kept clipped and cleaned while the minds trapped inside them wait for death. My only hope is that the White City has set Kat free.

"It's surprising," Busara continues when I don't respond. She seems eager to keep the conversation going. "Locked-in syndrome isn't very common, you know."

I didn't know. And I'm not sure how she does.

My skepticism must show on my face, but it doesn't stop Busara. "As a matter of fact, it's pretty rare. And yet three of the four kids who survived the accident have it. What do you guess are the odds of that?"

She looks at me as if expecting an answer. All I can offer is a shrug.

"I gotta say, if I were the fourth kid, I'd be feeling pretty lucky right now," she adds.

A memory flashes through my brain, and I'm reminded of something I meant to follow up on. "Marlow Holm is the fourth kid. Did you know that?"

Busara nods.

"What else do you know about him?" I ask. "Have you found out anything new?"

"Nothing much, really," she says. "His old social media posts make it seem like he and his mother had to leave California pretty abruptly. But why do you ask? Do you think Marlow had something to do with what happened to Kat?"

Marlow was the one who suggested the party. He was also the only kid who walked away. And his abrupt departure from California does seem pretty fishy. "I don't know what to think yet," I tell Busara.

The room stays silent for longer than I'd like, but I can't come up with anything to say. Finally Busara breaks the silence. "You really love her, don't you?"

Love is too small a word for what I feel. How do I explain that before Kat, nothing was real? The nannies who doted on me were all paid to do it. One day they'd be hugging me, and the next they were gone. Kids at school played with me so our parents could network. Most never even pretended to like me. Then I met Kat, and she *chose* me. No one forced her or paid her. I was the one she wanted to be with. When I was eight years old, Kat stepped out of the woods and rescued me. I will spend my entire life thanking her for wanting to do it.

"Yes," I tell Busara. "I love her. Kat's my whole world."

AWAKENING

Once Busara leaves, it's quiet aside from the beeping of machines. I sit down in the chair beside Kat's bed and take one of her limp hands in mine. I wish like hell I could see her eyes. I wonder why Busara never asked about the visor.

Kat's lips part and I forget everything else. They almost look like she's preparing to speak.

"I'm sure it's really great where you are," I whisper, letting my head come to rest on the side of the bed, "but please come back when you're ready."

"No," a voice says softly.

I sit bolt upright and try to figure out if I could have imagined what I just heard. Then Kat clenches my hand and her mouth stretches open in a silent scream.

"Kat?" I stand and bend over her, my face inches from hers. "Kat, are you there?"

"No!" she gasps. "Oh my God, no!" Her voice is weak, barely

louder than a whisper, but I can feel her panic. It's like she's narrating a nightmare. Her fingers are clamped so tightly around mine that they've cut off my circulation. Kat's heart monitor is going nuts.

"It's okay," I tell her, smoothing her hair. If she's talking, it could mean she's getting better. The relief that floods through me almost makes my knees buckle.

"Don't do it!" she screams. "Oh my God!" My relief is gone in an instant. Something is very wrong.

I yank Kat's visor off. Her eyes are wide open, and they're darting from side to side. I slam the palm of my hand into the red button that calls the nurse. Then I run to the door and shout for help. Two women in scrubs sprint down the hall toward the room. One rushes to Kat's side and immediately begins examining her IV needle and tubing.

The second nurse stops at the door. "What just happened in here?" she demands. She's looking at the visor that's still in my hand. "Why did you remove the patient's visor?"

"She was talking," I say, examining the visor for the first time. I put it up to my face, but the lenses are dark. "She sounded totally terrified. She must have been scared of something she saw."

"The IV had a leak," reports the first nurse. She quickly preps a new one. "It's run out, and there's a puddle on the floor."

"A leak?" The second nurse turns to me. And she's angry. "Did you touch any of the equipment?"

"Absolutely not," I snap. "I was in the cafeteria watching television for the last hour. I just got back here a minute ago." Yes, and there was someone here when I came in, I realize. But for reasons that aren't completely clear to me, I don't say a word.

"Okay, we're good," reports the first nurse. "IV's back in." She's moving around Kat's body, checking her vitals. "I see no signs of movement. There doesn't appear to be pain response, either," she adds. "As far as I can tell, her condition remains the same."

I'm back at Kat's side in a moment. The nurse is right. Kat's totally still again. Her lips are sealed and her eyes are dull and motionless. "I don't understand. She talked to me. She squeezed my hand!"

The nurses are quiet. They're watching me carefully, as if I've lost my mind.

"The disk—it's the disk. It needs to be removed," I insist. I'm trying my best to sound perfectly calm and rational, but I'm on the verge of losing it. "Something's wrong. She was really scared—and Kat doesn't scare easily." I can still hear Kat's voice in my head. She wasn't just scared, she was terrified.

"We can't do anything without Dr. Ito's authorization," one of the nurses informs me. It's like talking to a goddamn robot.

"Then get her!" I nearly yell.

"It's almost one o'clock in the morning," the other nurse points out.

I lower my voice. "If Dr. Ito's not here in fifteen minutes, I'm going to take the disk off myself," I announce.

"Don't. It could be dangerous for the patient," the first nurse says. That might just be the stupidest thing I've ever heard.

"It's a video game!" I've finally lost my cool, and it is not coming back. "What in the hell is going on here? You just take the thing off!"

"Not without the doctor's permission," the first nurse repeats firmly.

"Then get her!" I shout at the top of my lungs, and the two nurses both scurry away.

I brush a lock of copper hair away from Kat's pale, dry lips. Then I take her hand in mine and prepare to wait. I will stand right here until Dr. Ito arrives and the disk is removed. I don't care how long it takes. My eyes aren't going to leave Kat. I'd memorize the freckles on her face if I didn't already know them all by heart. I place a finger on her pulse. It feels faster than it should. Thirty minutes pass, and Kat doesn't move. I don't even see so much as a twitch. Then Dr. Ito arrives with a posse.

She's followed by two security guards, a nurse and Martin— the emo engineer from the Company, who appears to be wearing his pajamas. The security guards look eager. Martin looks like he might vomit at any second.

Dr. Ito joins me at Kat's bedside. "What's going on here?" she asks.

The doctor listens patiently while I tell her everything I saw and heard.

"How long has it been since you got a full night's sleep?" she asks when I finish.

"What does *that* have to do with anything?" I ask, though I can see exactly where she's heading.

"Sleep deprivation can have a serious impact on the human brain," she informs me. "What you experienced was a hallucination, Mr. Eaton. Katherine is physically unable to speak or move."

"I'm completely awake, and I know what happened," I insist. "Kat spoke. She *screamed*, actually."

Dr. Ito shakes her head. "That's impossible," she says. "The damage to her brain is too severe."

I hold up the visor and address my next question to Martin. "She saw something on this that scared the hell out of her. What was it?"

His shaggy hair flops from side to side when he shakes his head. "The White City's all butterflies and bunnies. There's nothing there that could possibly scare a girl Katherine's age."

"Then why the hell was she screaming?" I take a step toward the engineer, and one of the security guards puts a hand to my chest.

"Calm down," he orders.

"It's okay," Martin says. I'm not sure if he's talking to the guard or to me. "Hundreds of people have visited the White City. To my knowledge, none of them have ever woken up screaming."

"To your *knowledge*?" I shoot back. "Aren't you keeping track? What kind of test is this?"

"I'm sorry, I—" Martin starts to say.

"I'm afraid this entire conversation is pointless." Dr. Ito cuts him off. Her voice is different now. She's no longer playing nice. "Katherine could not have moved or spoken this evening, Mr. Eaton. You need to come to terms with the fact that there's very little chance that she ever will."

"I don't believe you." I sound like a stubborn child.

Dr. Ito clearly doesn't care what I believe or don't believe. "I've been practicing neurology for over twenty years," she's saying. "If you're questioning my competence, that's just more proof that you've lost touch with reality. I'll be advising Katherine's parents to have her moved to a long-term care facility soon. We have done all we can for her here."

I feel goose bumps break out on my arms. "The same facility

where they sent the two other people who were hurt at the factory? Brian and West? I heard they have locked-in syndrome too. Is that right?"

Martin looks over at Dr. Ito. I notice she's careful not to look back. Either I've gone completely insane or something incredibly weird is going on here.

"I've told you before, I'm not at liberty to discuss any of my patients with you, Mr. Eaton."

"That's fine," I tell her. Once again, I've run out of patience. "I'm done talking anyway. Game over."

I drop the visor on the floor and crush it beneath the heel of my shoe. Then I lean over Kat and gently lift her head, feeling for the disk. The thing's coming off whether they like it or not.

"Stop him," Dr. Ito orders. "He's going to endanger my patient." The two security guards are on me in a heartbeat.

"No, no, he won't. It's okay!" I hear Martin insist. "The disk just peels off. It can go right back on again. You don't need to hurt him!"

My hands are pulled out from beneath Kat's head, and both of my arms are pinned behind my back. They have me bent over at the waist, my head pressed into Kat's lap.

"Hey! What are you doing?" Martin cries. "Are you sure this is necessary?"

I feel a sharp jab in my left butt cheek. Then I feel nothing at all.

GOING UNDER

I wake up in a hospital room with a nurse and a guard standing over my bed. The clock on the television says 11:41. The sun is shining, so it must be just before noon on Wednesday. Which means I was out for almost eleven hours.

The nurse is holding a plastic bag that's filled with my few belongings.

"You had to be sedated. Now it's time for you to go home," she says. I can tell she's looking forward to showing me the door. "If you don't comply, we will be forced to phone the police."

It's a good thing I've kept the document Kat's mom signed in my back pocket. I sit up and unfold it. Then I hold the paper up for the nurse to see. "Kat's mother wants me to stay with her," I croak. My throat is parched.

The nurse doesn't even look down at the page. "The woman who signed that document no longer has legal guardianship over her daughter. Katherine Foley's sole guardian is now her stepfather, Wayne Gibson."

Oh, *shit*. I try to stand up, but it takes two attempts. My legs are still wobbly from the sedative.

"I need to talk to him," I say.

"Shoot." I turn to see Wayne Gibson sitting in the corner of the room, a smirk of triumph smeared across his face.

"What's going on?" I demand. "What did you do to Linda?"

"What did *I* do to Linda?" he repeats incredulously as he rises from his seat. "My wife voluntarily committed herself to a mental health institute yesterday. Our daughter's illness has been weighing heavily on her, and she was worried she might do herself harm."

If that's the truth, it doesn't seem to bother him much. I wish there were a scalpel lying around. If I cut into this asshole, I'm pretty sure I'd only find gears and wires. No human being has posture this good—or a heart this cold.

"I want proof that she left you in charge of Kat," I say.

"Mr. Gibson has provided all the necessary legal paperwork," the nurse answers from the other side of the room.

For the first time ever, I genuinely wish my parents were here. Without a lawyer, there's no way I can win this battle. And getting into a pissing contest with GI Joe isn't going to do Kat any good—or help me figure out what the hell is going on.

I look back at Mr. Gibson. "May I speak with you privately?" I ask, adjusting my tone.

"Certainly," he says diplomatically, nodding at the nurse. I guess it's easy to be gracious when you know you've won.

The nurse and the guard shuffle out of the room. Wayne assumes a superhero stance—chest out, arms crossed and legs apart—and I realize I'm not going to convince him of anything.

"Kat spoke yesterday," I say.

"Thank you for letting me know." It sounds like a voice recording at some corporate headquarters. "I will inform the doctors. Is there anything else?"

"The Company disk needs to be removed. It was scaring her."

"Thank you. I will let the doctors know about that as well."

Nothing I can say will make any difference. I see that now. My words just bounce off him. This short, cocky man with his button-down shirt and perfectly pressed pants is completely invulnerable.

"You don't give a shit about Kat, do you?" I ask.

"Don't worry, son." He gives me a pat on the shoulder and then heads for the door. "I'll take it from here."

"Wait!" I reach out to stop him and he spins around. His lips curl slightly as his eyes travel from my hand to my face. His expression is as good as a growl. I pull back before my fingers brush against him, like a kid who's nearly been nipped by a dog. "Can I at least see her before I go?" If he wants me to beg, I will.

"Katherine isn't at the hospital anymore," he says just before he leaves the room. "She's moved on."

For a few horrible seconds, I assume the worst. Then I realize he means it literally. She's been moved to the facility. I'm relieved she's alive—but otherwise, I couldn't be more terrified.

.   .   .

The plastic bag with my belongings bounces against my thigh as the security guards frog-march me out of the hospital. As we pass the waiting room I catch a glimpse of Busara. She's arguing with some guy who's got a backpack slung over his shoulder. Her eyes lock on to mine and the guy turns to see what's caught her attention. *Jesus.* It's Marlow Holm. He opens his mouth as if he wants to say something to me but he can't quite get it out. I struggle to break free and go back to them, but the security guards drag me forward and out the front doors. They drop me to the ground in the parking lot and stand blocking the path to the hospital.

I pick myself up and start weaving around cars, making my way toward the road.

"Hey, Simon!" It's Busara. She must have run after us. I keep walking. I don't respond. I'm too furious to be around anyone right now.

The walk home must have been around three miles, and the weather was unseasonably warm. I remember nothing about the journey. I couldn't even tell you which route I took. My shirt is soaked through with sweat when I reach the driveway and see my parents' cars are both gone. I walk through the door and a woman dusting the entryway yelps.

"Are my mother and father here?" I ask. She stands with her back against the wall and watches me like I'm a beast that's escaped from the zoo.

"They're still in London," she tells me. My mother must have caught the red-eye after all.

I head straight for my room, disrobing as I go. I turn on

the water in the walk-in shower and take a seat on the ledge. I bow my head, letting the streams of water beat down on my skull.

What am I going to do now? I sit back, banging my head against the tiles. I'm such a fucking idiot. I swore I'd take care of Kat, and then I gave them a reason to separate us. Now she's gone.

Kat spoke. I know she did. I wasn't hallucinating. But even if I had been—why the hell wouldn't they just take the disk off?

I step out of the shower and wrap a towel around my waist. There's a knock at my bedroom door. I open it to find a young woman in a blue maid's smock.

"This just arrived for you," she says, averting her eyes and holding out a box covered in brown paper. My name is written on the front, but there's no return address.

"Who's it from?"

"I don't know. It came by messenger." She backs away from my door as if I'll attack her if she dares to turn around. I guess I don't blame her. I probably look pretty crazy right now.

I rip the wrapping off the package as I make my way to my desk. Underneath the paper is a shoe box with a picture of a pair of sneakers on the side. They're the same unusual brand and color that Milo Yolkin's known to wear. MEN'S SIZE 9 is written beneath the image. I open the box, but there aren't shoes inside. Instead I find a visor and a round, flesh-colored disk.

There's only one person who could have sent the gear. Did Martin feel guilty about watching me get a needle jammed in my ass? Is this the engineer's way of proving to me that there's nothing to fear in the White City?

I remove the items and place them carefully on my desk. At

the bottom of the box is a small envelope. I open it and pull out a note scribbled in Sharpie.

GO FIND HER, it says.

The piece of paper slips out of my hand and flutters to the floor.

I sprint out of my room, through the house and out the front door. There's no sign of the messenger.

THE OTHER SIDE

I've locked myself in my bedroom with a dresser shoved against the door. I just shaved the back of my head, and my scalp burns and tingles. My mind is already far away.

I lie down on my bed and pull on the visor. It's utterly weightless on my face. Carefully, I stick the disk to the back of my skull, right where I saw them put Kat's. In an instant I'm no longer in my bedroom. I'm standing naked in an empty, brightly lit room. I can't tell how many of my senses are engaged. It's hard to assess the latest groundbreaking technology without anything but my own body to see, smell or touch.

There's a mirror in front of me, and I see myself, tall, lanky and blessed with a legendary schnoz. The other details might not be one hundred percent accurate. The disk must have pulled this image of me out of my brain, but I look slightly better than I do in real life—like a picture taken from just the right angle.

I think this is the setup. The weird white space looks a lot like the environment in Otherworld where you assemble your avatar. I guess I shouldn't be so surprised that they're similar. The Company developed the White City software, too. They're bound to have a few things in common. As far as I can tell, there's already one big difference, though. Like most games, Otherworld provides a menu of options. The controls on your headset allow you to assume almost any appearance as long as your form remains essentially human. But there are no controls here. The White City must be designed to be completely intuitive.

"Okay, give me a smaller nose," I say out loud, and the kishka shrinks on command.

"Spiky white hair." My black hair instantly lightens.

"Enormous penis," I order. Because of course. Suddenly I look like something out of the zoo.

"Kick-ass muscles and a leather trench coat." I stand back and admire myself in the mirror. With a few simple adjustments I've become Rutger Hauer in *Blade Runner*.

"Reset." I'm back to myself.

"Give me four tentacles and the head of a musk ox," I demand.

Nothing happens. So, like Otherworld, the software must require that I remain more or less human.

"Fine, then, let's go with seven feet tall, stone body that burns bright red, horns, no face or genitals."

The image I see in the mirror is just a few tweaks away from the giant avatar I met in the Otherworld ice cave. I love the idea of setting this beast loose on the bunnies and butterflies of the White City. But I don't have time to keep screwing around. Every moment that passes is one I haven't spent looking for Kat.

"Hooded brown robe, made from wool. Black pants, shirt and boots."

In front of me is my avatar from a hundred games, with one significant difference: it's my face looking back at me from under the hood. I want Kat to recognize me when she sees me.

"Done," I announce. I could give myself a digital nose job, but then it wouldn't be me.

The mirror becomes a door. The door opens.

I step through the opening and into another reality. And damn, is it *amazing*. It may not be Earth, but it's no game, either. With an Otherworld headset, you can see, hear and touch, but that's the extent of your sensory experience. Here, I'm immediately hit by the fragrance of flowers. I inhale deeply as a light breeze ripples the hem of my robe. I'm standing on a balcony on a tall white building. I can feel the floor beneath my feet. I reach out for the metal railing and it's warm from the sun. Far below me is a beautiful city surrounded by tall stone walls. Beyond the walls lies a vast green land. I can see the hazy outline of mountains in the distance. Inside the city walls, there are other white buildings, all marvels of modern architecture. They're linked by a paved path that snakes through the town. I'm watching a driverless pod navigate the curves in search of its next passenger when a magnificent bird lands on the railing beside me. Its face is golden and its feathers a shimmering iridescent green. Intellectually I know these are graphics. Every other part of me believes it's all real. I can see the shaft in each of the bird's feathers and every scale on its feet. The creature regards me with an intelligent, slightly hostile expression.

Then it squirts a dollop of guano onto the balcony and flies off toward the puffy white dream clouds that decorate the sky.

I turn around and see that the portal to the setup environment is gone. In its place is a set of glass doors. They slide open easily, granting me access to an apartment. On a nearby side table is a tablet. It lights up as I approach, offering an impressive home decorating menu (starting with Amish farmstead, Argentinian estancia and Ashanti traditional), along with the options to build your own pets, children and companions from scratch. I quickly scroll through the companion menu—just to see what's available. I'm expecting a good snicker, but it seems disappointingly clean. And even if it weren't, I remind myself, I'm not here to play house with some AI hottie. I'm here to find Kat. I toss the tablet onto the couch and head straight for the front door.

The hallway outside my apartment is empty. I take a glass elevator to ground level and it deposits me at the bottom of a silent atrium. The plants soaking up the digital sunlight are unlike any I've ever seen in New Jersey, but I could swear they're all real. I can smell the soil they're growing in. I can see the tiny ridges and valleys on their leaves. I reach out and grab one of the round red fruits dangling from a nearby tree. I bite into it and I can feel and hear my teeth break through its skin. The flesh is sweet and smells like a plum. There is nothing about the experience that feels artificial—nothing to remind me that my brain has teamed up with software to trick me. In fact, there's only one thing about this whole experience that strikes me as odd: There doesn't seem to be anyone else around. The building is empty.

I walk out the front door and onto an equally deserted street.

As I stroll through the city, my unease continues to build. Every-where I look, there are swarms of butterflies and flocks of birds. I even spot one of the bunnies Martin mentioned. But there are no other humans here. And most importantly—no Kat. The engi-neers claimed there were over three hundred people in the White City right now, but I don't see a single one of them. It's as if a plague swept through town and wiped out all the inhabitants. I'm standing in the middle of the path when a driverless pod comes around a curve. It stops and waits for me to step aside, and then it continues on its way.

After a short walk, I find a row of shops and restaurants. They all have oddly generic names. ITALIAN RESTAURANT. PHARMACY. LADIES' BOUTIQUE. Then I spot a waitress through the window of FRENCH CAFÉ, and the relief is overwhelming. She looks like she might be in her early twenties, and she's attractive—but in a reassuringly imperfect way. Her chest is flat and her cleavage is unexposed, which makes me question whether she could have been designed by a bunch of horny Company geeks.

"Good afternoon, sir," she says in a chipper tone when I walk through the door. Her name tag says ELIZA. "May I offer you something to drink?"

"Where is everyone?" I ask. "I'm looking for a friend of mine, but there doesn't seem to be anyone around."

"*I'm* here," she says.

"Yeah, but you're not real, are you?" I ask. Might as well get it out of the way.

Eliza laughs, as though it's a question she gets all the time. "*Real?*" she answers. "Of course I'm real."

"Are you an NPC or are you somebody's avatar?"

The waitress's smile fades just a bit. She seems thrown. "I'm a waitress," she says. "I serve food and drinks. Is there anything I can get for you? The French onion soup is particularly good today."

I have a strong hunch that I'm talking to a bot, so I devise my own amateur Turing test. "I've got a flying saucer parked outside, and I'm headed to Pluto," I tell her.

"Would you like the soup to go, then?" she asks with a smile, and I'm stunned. Bots aren't renowned for their sense of humor. It's almost as if Eliza knew I was testing her.

"Sure," I say, doubling down. "Want to come along for the ride?"

"I'd love to," she says carefully. I get the impression that Eliza thinks I'm insane. But to reach that conclusion, she would need to be able to *think*. "Unfortunately, I'm a permanent resident of the White City, and I haven't been authorized to visit other planets. Would you still like soup?"

All I can do is shake my head.

"Then if you'll excuse me, I need to get back to work."

Eliza has no other customers. She's either the most dedicated human waitress I've ever met—or the most impressive NPC ever designed. The weird thing is, I'm still not sure.

On my way out of the café, a flyer tacked to a bulletin board catches my eye. VISIT THE CITY OF IMRA, it says in large type. RESORT OF THE FUTURE. I snatch it off the wall. There are no other words on the page, so I study the photo. It's a picture of Catelyn, the busty NPC that Milo Yolkin introduced on the talk show. She's wearing a red bikini and sitting in a hot tub, toasting the camera with a glass of champagne.

Why is Otherworld's City of Imra being advertised inside the White City? The Company practically invented in-game advertising, and they cross-promote whenever they get a chance. But selling Otherworld to a bunch of people who can't even get out of bed to buy the game just seems goddamn *weird*.

I ball up the flyer in my hands and toss it into a nearby trash can. More confused than ever, I leave the café and follow the path as it winds downhill. Now that I know they're here, I spot other workers inside businesses that all seem to thrive without any customers. A few of them come to the windows as I pass, but none step outside. It occurs to me that I'm outnumbered, and I find myself walking faster. I'm not frightened exactly, but I'm definitely unnerved. And I'm worried for Kat. Whatever happened to the three hundred humans who were supposed to be here must have happened to her as well.

I come around a curve and stop short. I can't go any farther. The path abruptly ends at a tall metal gate, and a statue of a man is blocking the way. The figure is dressed exactly like the Clay Man I saw inside the Otherworld glacier. It's wearing a dark suit and there's a Bedouin-style scarf wrapped around its head. Like the flyer, it feels out of place here in the White City. But then again, so do I.

"Hello, Simon," it says, and I nearly jump out of my skin. "You look lost. Do you need directions?"

The statue's eyes are open. They're a brilliant blue, as is the amulet that hangs around its neck. It's glowing like a cheesy power crystal from *World of Warcraft*.

"How do you know who I am?"

"I am your guide," it says.

"Does everyone here get a guide?" I ask warily.

"I couldn't say," the Clay Man replies. "I have never been a guest of the White City."

It takes me a second to understand that when the Clay Man says *guest* he must mean a human visitor. Eliza called herself a resident, which must be the politically correct euphemism for NPCs.

"So where are all the other guests?" I ask my guide.

"They've left the White City," says the Clay Man, gesturing toward the gate. "Once they pass through this gate, they cannot return."

"Then I guess I'm looking for someone who may have come this way," I say. "A girl named Kat." I wish I could describe her. But unlike me, Kat rarely chooses the same avatar twice. She could be anything or anyone.

"Yes, I have seen her. She is searching for the way out of this world. I told her it lies on the other side of the gates."

My heart sinks. Kat's gone—and any hope I had that this would be a quick rescue mission has gone with her. I stare up at the massive gates, which would look right at home on a medieval fortress. "What's out there?"

"I will show you," says the Clay Man.

The gates swing open, revealing a battalion of NPC soldiers stationed outside. Armed with long spears, the silent men watch the horizon. I study one to see if he blinks. When he does, I look past the army at a featureless landscape of moss-covered rocks. It doesn't resemble any place I've been before, but it feels every bit as real as New Jersey.

"Why are there troops here?" I ask the Clay Man.

"The soldiers have been stationed here to prevent Otherworld's residents and guests from entering the White City."

The name explodes like a bomb in my head. "Hold up—that's *Otherworld*?" I point toward the mountains in the distance.

"Don't you recognize it?" the Clay Man asks. "You've been there before. That's where we first met."

"You're the same guy I saw inside the glacier?"

"I am," he says.

"Okay, stop there for a second." Because none of this shit makes any sense. The White City was built for people with serious medical problems. Otherworld is geek central. "Why is the White City suddenly inside *Otherworld*?"

"They are both products of the Company, are they not? Someone must have decided to bring them together," the Clay Man says.

This whole situation is really starting to freak me out. "So let me get this straight. Guests who leave the White City aren't allowed back. And Otherworld players can't come in either. But why would the soldiers need to keep Otherworld's *residents* out of the White City? The residents are just NPCs, right? They don't think for themselves—they just do what they're programmed to do. It's not like they're going to invade."

"Your assumptions are incorrect," the Clay Man informs me. "In Otherworld, the residents have minds of their own. They eat, sleep, breed and think. Some of them were designed to be just as real as the guests."

My bizarre conversation with the waitress named Eliza immediately comes to mind. "Like the workers here in the White City?" I ask.

"No," says the Clay Man. "Many of the residents you'll encounter in Otherworld are far more advanced than the ones you met here. You must be wary of them."

Anything more advanced than Eliza would be true artificial intelligence. And I'm pretty sure that's what this dude's getting at.

"Even the Beasts in Otherworld are more intelligent than they appear," the Clay Man continues as my head spins. "But the most dangerous creatures you'll encounter will be other guests. Players with headsets can be remarkably brutal. Be on your guard at all times."

I reach up to my face and grope for my visor. I need to press Pause and figure a few dozen things out. But I feel nothing but the skin around my eyes. My hand slides around to the back of my head. There's no disk. I have a full head of hair.

"You cannot remove the disk on your own," says the Clay Man. "In the real world most of your muscles have been temporarily paralyzed—just as they are when you sleep."

Oh, God. What the hell have I gotten myself into? "Then how do I get back home?"

"As I told your friend, there is a way out. An exit of sorts. Your disk and visor will deactivate as you pass through it."

"Where is the exit?" I ask. "How do I find it?"

"You've seen it before," says the Clay Man. "There's a door deep inside the glacier. Your friend is on her way there now."

I remember the door, and I feel a sudden surge of hope. And then— "Wait a second. What are we supposed to do about the giant red dude who lives in the ice cave?"

"His name is Magna. You must kill him," says the Clay Man.

"Oh, yeah? With *what*?" I demand. At least the last time I visited Otherworld I was given a weapon at setup.

"Come with me." The Clay Man steps through the gates. I'm not sure I'm ready to follow him, though. "You must trust me," he says. "Until you find your friend, I am all you have."

He's right. I have no choice. When I join him outside the gates, two of the soldiers break formation. They're carrying a large metal box, which they place at my feet and open. Inside is an assortment of weapons and tools.

I see what I want and reach for it.

"Choose wisely," the Clay Man cautions me. "You may only take one. Those are the rules of Otherworld."

I don't hesitate. Kat will make fun of me when she sees what I've picked, but my trusty dagger goes into my boot. I'm deadlier with an eight-inch blade than most guys would be with a sword.

"Guard your life with great care. Do not assume that you will get another."

"Why not?" I ask. "You forget—I've played Otherworld. You get sent back to setup whenever you die, but you get as many lives as you need."

"Yes, but you are not *playing* Otherworld now, Simon," the Clay Man tells me. "The guests with headsets are inside a game. For those with disks, Otherworld is something else entirely. The only way to ensure your survival is to think of this as a new reality."

"Wait—are you telling me I can die? For real?"

"I'm telling you I don't know."

I feel a very real urge to vomit. But even if I could turn back now, I wouldn't. Kat's out there, and there's a very good chance she has no idea what kind of trouble she's in.

"You're coming with me, right?" I ask. "Isn't that what guides are for?"

"No," the Clay Man informs me. "I will help you when I'm able, but never rely on me to intervene on your behalf. From this point forward, you must make do on your own."

WASTELAND

I'm starting to think I made a big mistake. I've been hiking for hours across the moss-covered rocks, and I've seen no evidence of life. I have to consider the possibility that the Clay Man misled me. Maybe I was tricked into wandering a wasteland while Kat is being held captive somewhere inside the White City. The mountains ahead of me keep growing, but I never reach them. All around me, boulders dot the landscape like the tombstones of an ancient race of giants. Since I set out, I've been watching the clouds, waiting to see if they ever repeat themselves. But the digital sky seems to produce them in an infinite number of shapes and textures. I've seen a wispy dog and a cottony dragon, and I wonder if they might be symbols or messages I don't understand.

I'm studying a cloud that looks like lion rampant when a column of hot steam bursts from the ground directly in front of me. A fine spray of boiling water scalds the exposed skin on my hands and face, and I cry out in shock. It hurts like hell. The disk on the back of my skull has convinced my brain that the pain is real. If I'd been any closer to the geyser, my avatar would have been cooked. I try not to think about how *that* would have felt. Remembering the Clay Man's warning to protect my life, I pull my hood up and keep my eyes glued to the ground.

If the action is all taking place in my head, my body doesn't seem to know it. My calves ache and my mouth is parched by the time I spot a tall rocky outcropping ahead of me. It looks like it should only take a few minutes to reach it, but it's hard to judge distances here. I hike for another hour until I realize there's something unusual on top of the hill, and then I scramble as fast as I can across the treacherous terrain. When I reach the rocks, I climb to the summit and find what I was hoping for. Someone has built a cairn here. Hundreds of small, flat stones have been stacked into a conical tower that reaches chest-high. It's the first sign I've had that anyone else has passed this way. I scan the horizon. There's a dust cloud in the distance and a much larger rock outcropping about a mile away. It, too, has an unusual peak. I've discovered a trail, I realize. I could cry with relief.

Long before I reach the next rocky hill, I see something moving across it, and the discovery thrills me. It may not be human, but it's some form of life. When I'm a few hundred yards away, I can make out a herd of goats with silver hair and magnificent white horns that curl in spirals. The animals scamper across the rocks, stopping to nibble on the flowering plants that sprout out of the crevasses. I notice there's one goat that doesn't appear quite as sure-footed as the rest. It slips and slides as it follows the herd. It's been injured, I assume. I have to give the Company credit.

A crippled goat is a brilliant touch. The imperfection makes the scene feel all the more real.

I follow the ungainly goat with my eyes as I gradually draw nearer. I'm almost to the base of the hill when the beast begins to transform, and I come to a halt. It's not a goat at all. It's a man. He rises from his hands and knees. There's a goatskin fastened around his neck, and the dead beast's head has flopped backward like a hood. Under the pelt, the man is naked aside from a loincloth. He stands on one of the rocks, staring directly at me. His body is battered, his hands are brown with dried blood and something is very wrong with his face.

I have battled a thousand monsters. I've stormed countless enemy camps and faced down dozens of mob bosses. But I've never been as freaked out as I am right now.

The goat man beckons me toward him, but I'm frozen. I stay put, even as his gestures become more frantic. Then he lifts one of his bruised and bloody arms and points to the right. I glance over and see an immense cloud of dust traveling toward me. Over the sound of my racing heart, I can make out the pounding of hooves. I have two choices. Run toward the goat man or be flattened by whatever's heading my way. I decide to go with the devil I know.

I sprint for the safety of the rocks, and as soon as I reach them, I'm enveloped in the dust cloud. I see flashes of matted brown fur, beady black eyes and cloven hooves. The creatures moving past are enormous. The stench that trails behind them is almost as thick as the cloud.

Only when they're gone and the dust has begun to settle again do I realize there's someone sitting next to me.

"Hello," says the goat man. Though his tone is cheerful, his voice is hoarse, as if it hasn't been put to much use. "You're lucky to have escaped the buffalo, you know. They're not very fond of guests. They trample travelers like you whenever they get a chance."

His face begins to emerge from the haze, and I do my best to disguise my shock. His nose has no bridge—it's flat in the middle, with two large nostrils that flare and collapse as he breathes. The tops of his ears flop down over the openings, and I can see the buds of two horns straining to break through the skin of his forehead. The pupils in the centers of his amber eyes are thick black dashes.

I have never seen *anything* like the goat man before. The geek who designed him was one sick bastard.

"What are you?" The words slip out. Even in Otherworld they sound horribly rude.

His hand flies up to his face, and I instantly regret that I asked. "I'm one of the Children," the goat man tells me.

"I'm sorry. I didn't mean to offend you," I say. "I just got here, and you're the first resident I've met. So you're one of the children? Whose children?"

He smiles broadly, revealing a significant underbite and several unusually large teeth. He's eager to talk. "Every Child has different parents," he says. "Mine were a goat and the Elemental of Imra."

There are a hundred follow-up questions I'd like to ask—many of them anatomical in nature—but I don't want to insult the only intelligent creature I've encountered so far. "So you're the son of a god?"

The goat man crosses one badly bruised knee over the other,

weaves his fingers together and lets his clasped hands lie in his lap. It's a dainty pose for someone wearing nothing but a pelt and a loincloth. "The Elementals are not gods. They merely rule Otherworld's lands. There is only one Creator."

I've read a million posts about the original Otherworld. I know all about the Beasts and the Elementals, but I don't recall hearing about Children or a Creator. "Are there many of your kind here in Otherworld?" I ask.

The goat man sighs sadly. "There were more of us once, but the Children were not part of the Creator's plan. Before the guests arrived, many of us were slain. Those of us who survived stay hidden now. My herd used to live in the mountains near Imra. It journeyed here to the wastelands for my protection. The only other creatures in these parts are the buffalo, and as you just saw, they're not very social. It can get terribly lonely."

"Wow, that's awful," I tell him, though it's hard to feel too bad. He's a remarkable bit of AI, but underneath it all, he's just zeros and ones.

"Many of us blame humans like you for our misfortune," the goat man continues. "That's why you should take great care around Children like me."

I'm about to tell him it's perfectly understandable when I finally absorb the meaning of his words. I can't be certain, but it sounds like there's a threat mixed in among them. The smile on his face hasn't changed, though it was pretty disturbing from the start. I glance over my shoulder toward the top of the rocks. Just as I thought, there seems to be a cairn. Guests have passed this way before.

"Looks like you've had visitors," I say, pointing up at the cairn.

"Oh, yes," he confirms. "The last group came through less than a day ago. Would you like to see what they left behind?"

"Yeah, sure." I rise to my feet and shake the dust from my robe. I'm happy to keep moving, and I'll be even happier when I'm off the rocks and headed in the right direction. "Who were they?" I ask as we climb.

"A party of four," the goat man replies. "Three males and a female."

My pace quickens. Could the female have been Kat? She never chose male avatars, despite the fact that females were far from welcome in a lot of the games we played. "Where were your visitors headed?"

"When they left, they were searching for a way out of Otherworld," says the goat man. We're almost to the top now, and I can see the cairn more clearly. The materials used to make it don't appear to be rocks. "I do hope they find one," he continues. "And once they've left our world, I hope they never return."

I reach the summit and take a moment to catch my breath. There's a nauseating stench of rotten flesh in the air. Then I stand up, the cairn in front of me. It's not composed of rocks after all. Stacked neatly on top of each other are several bodies' worth of bones. The sun has bleached the ones at the base. There are still scraps of muscle attached to a femur on top.

"My family were not meant to be meat eaters," the goat man explains almost apologetically. "But we can't survive on the vegetation that grows on this rock pile. Your kind was responsible for our exile. Now you're the solution to our problems as well." He adjusts a few of the bones in the cairn. "The pile attracts guests to our hillside. We choose one from each party that passes through on their way from the White City to Imra. They're not like the other guests, I've found. Most don't know where they are. They seldom put up a fight."

I wonder how it would feel to be eaten—and what would happen to my body in New Jersey if my avatar were to meet such a gruesome fate. Then a worse thought crosses my mind. Did Kat find herself in a situation like this? Is that why she cried out?

I pull my dagger from my boot. Soon there will be one less Child for their Creator to eliminate.

The goat man sighs wearily at the sight of my knife. "You may be able to delay the inevitable by killing me," he says. "But you won't be able to stop it."

I hear the clicking of hooves on rocks, and the rest of the herd appears at the summit. They've got me surrounded. It's the first time I've seen the goats up close, and they're larger than I imagined. Each is bigger than a bear, and while they're clearly not as gifted and talented as the goat man, they seem far more intelligent than any of Earth's furry beasts. I detect a mixture of hunger, fear and fury in their eyes.

Then, somewhere on the hillside below us, a goat bleats a warning and the creatures gather to see the source of the alarm, shoving me along with them. A tall, dark figure wearing a Bedouin scarf is walking toward us across the rocks. His strides are long and purposeful, but the Clay Man seems to think there's no need to rush. It's clear the goats recognize him too. They scramble to the opposite side of the hill, leaving me alone once again with the goat man. I smirk at him and sheathe my dagger. No one's going to get eaten today.

"Why are your friends so afraid of the Clay Man?" I ask.

"We don't know what he is," the goat man tells me. "Or where he comes from. We are told that, aside from the guests, all things in Otherworld originated in the mind of the Creator. But the truth seems to be much more complicated than that."

"Well, your buddies were smart to run. In fact, you should probably follow them, Goat Boy," I say. "The Clay Man is my guide."

The goat man rolls his eyes as if I'm ridiculously naive. "There are no *guides* in Otherworld," he says. "That is not why he's here."

The Clay Man stops. He seems to be waiting for me, but he won't deign to climb the rocks. A single brave goat approaches him while the rest cower on the other side of the hill. The Clay Man remains perfectly motionless as the goat sniffs at him, the stone on my guide's chest glowing bright blue. Then the goat opens its mouth and makes a grab for the amulet. In an instant the Clay Man springs to life. His staff swings and catches the beast midstomach. The force sends it sailing through the air. The goat's long bleat grows fainter, then stops altogether. A small cloud of dust rises in the distance where the beast met the ground.

The goat man cries out, and the beasts hiding on the other side of the hill begin bleating in unison. That's my cue to go. I hurry down the rocks to meet my guide—if that's what he really is.

"I thought you knew what you were doing," the Clay Man barks when I reach him. Most of his face is hidden behind his scarf, but his eyes are flashing and he sounds royally pissed. "I just left you a few hours ago, and I've already had to return!"

"Hold on. You're mad at *me*?" I say. "Where do you get off—"

"I warned you about the residents of Otherworld," the Clay Man breaks in to remind me. "You must be much more careful in the future. I travel the wastelands, but I do not enter the realms. The next time you're in trouble, I may not be able to reach you."

"The goat man caught me off guard," I say. "You didn't tell me there'd be a bunch of freaky-ass Children roaming around. What the hell are they, anyway?"

The Clay Man pauses to consider the question. By the time he answers, he's cooled down quite a bit. "They are unintended consequences," he says. "These days men can build worlds, but they lack the power to control them."

"You're saying the Children are *mistakes*? Like bad code or something?"

"The creators of Otherworld wanted it to be real," says the Clay Man. "They forgot that nothing real can be perfect."

That reminds me. "Speaking of creators, Goat Boy up there was just yammering on about his Creator. Was he talking about—"

The Clay Man doesn't wait for me to finish. "All intelligent beings need ways to explain their origins."

"So the Creator—"

"Was designed to be part of the game. The Elementals worship him. He and the Children have a more complicated relationship."

When I have a little downtime, I'll try to wrap my head around the idea that a bunch of digital freaks have their own god. But right now, I have more questions that need answers.

"So the Creator's part of the software and the Children are mistakes. What are you?" I demand. "You told me you're my guide, but you're not an NPC. And I don't think you're a guest, either. So are you an administrator? A Company employee? Are you Martin, my favorite engineer?"

"Find your friend, get to the exit, and kill the one who guards it. That is why you're here. It is all you need to do."

"And believe me, I'll do it happily. But I don't like surprises. Has the goat man's Creator made anything else I need to know about?"

"It would be impossible to prepare you for everything you might face here," says the Clay Man. "Otherworld has a mind of its own." He looks up at the sky. "Night falls quickly. You must reach the oasis before the sun begins to set."

"The oasis?"

"There's a pool of fresh water in the mountains. Your avatar will be able to eat, drink and rest there. These things are necessary to maintain your strength while you're here. But you must leave for the oasis now. You don't want to find yourself in the wastelands after nightfall. The buffalo that live here can see in the darkness, and they've been known to hunt and consume the guests."

Just when I was sure I knew just how bad it could get. *"Really?"* I groan. "Them too? You've got to be shitting me! Aren't buffalo supposed to be herbivores?"

"Do not assume anything here is the same as it is in your world," says the Clay Man. "And don't let down your guard again."

He gives me a hard look and grasps his amulet. It glows brightly, and then my guide disappears.

THE OTHERS

At first I carefully scanned my surroundings as I walked, keeping an eye out for signs of buffalo in the distance. Now that the land has grown mountainous, I've stopped worrying about being trampled or eaten by bloodthirsty beasts. Instead I'm looking for the oasis I was promised. The oases I've seen online have all had water and palm trees, but there isn't anything like that here. In fact, there's nothing here at all. Even the carpet of green moss vanished long ago. All that's left is rust-red dirt, and it's been hours since I've seen so much as a rock. My only hope is that there's something—*anything*—on the other side of the steep slope I'm climbing.

The barren soil erodes under my feet with every step I take, making it almost impossible to find a good foothold. I finally reach the top of the mountain and collapse in exhaustion. My mouth is dry and my stomach is empty. I drag myself to my feet and glance back at the wasteland I crossed. The vast, desolate plain stretches all the way to the horizon. I turn to see what's ahead of me, praying it's not more of the same. I nearly cry when I realize I've reached the oasis. I'm standing near the lip of a crater. A few hundred feet below me is a lake so crystal clear I can make out a school of silver fish in the water. The creatures are swimming together in an endless spiral, and the effect is mesmerizing. From the little I know of Otherworld, it's safe to assume they're piranhas.

A campfire is burning near the lake's shore. The flames crackle and dance, shooting sparks into the sky. Three human-shaped figures are resting beside it. Judging by their bizarre outfits, they aren't NPCs. One of them appears to be dressed as a medieval knight. I suspect they're the three travelers who recently escaped from the goats. One of the humans catches sight of me, and they all jump to their feet. Kat isn't among them. If she were, she'd have recognized my avatar by now, and these guys aren't exactly rushing up to greet me. I can see someone has gathered a pile of rocks to be used as weapons if necessary. Apparently they've learned how dangerous it is to let down your guard in Otherworld. And like me, they won't be making the same mistake again.

I play it as safe as possible. As I make my way down the slope toward the lake, I raise my hands over my head. "I come in peace!" I shout. Even in Otherworld it sounds unbelievably hokey, but it's the only thing I can think of to say.

The three huddle together for a moment. I suppose they're discussing my fate. Then the decision appears to be made. A figure in a Grim Reaper–style robe and an ogre-size man with tattooed skin stay put while the avatar dressed as a red knight climbs the slope to meet me. The visor of his helmet is up, and his scarlet cape billows around him as he walks. He's wearing a chain mail shirt beneath his red tunic. The dude really geeked out back at setup. My guess is he's taken part in a few role-playing games in his day. There's a sword at his side, but his hand is nowhere near the hilt. It seems reckless, if you ask me. I could send my dagger sailing into one of his eyeballs before he could draw the weapon from its scabbard.

"I'm Arkan." The voice coming from inside the helmet is brusque and emotionless. Arkan is a strange name for a knight. I was expecting something much fancier. But his attitude matches the outfit. He strikes me as the kind of guy who likes to fight. "Who are you?" he asks.

"Simon," I say, offering him a hand, which the knight ignores. "I arrived at the White City earlier today."

"The White City?" Arkan asks as if he doesn't know it.

His response throws me for a moment. "You know—the city with all the white buildings," I say. "Isn't that where you started?"

"Oh, right," says Arkan. "Yeah. We left yesterday."

I'm about to ask why they left when I happen to glance down at his sword. It doesn't look real. "Is that *plastic*?" I ask. Someone sure pulled a dud out of the goody box.

Arkan takes off his helmet, which somehow doesn't seem to weigh as much as it should. Beneath it is a handsome, square-jawed head with a thatch of blond hair. I feel a jolt of recognition. I've seen this avatar somewhere before.

"What difference does it make if it's plastic?" the knight asks.

I don't even know how to begin answering that question.

"Where are you going?" he asks.

"I don't really know," I tell him, figuring honesty might be the best policy for the moment. "I'm looking for a girl."

Before I can say any more, Arkan's eyes widen. "Follow me," he orders, heading down the hill toward the other two avatars. A burst of hope pushes me after him. Then I pause. Below, the ogre now has rocks in both of his hands. The other figure has disappeared.

"Are you sure your buddies are as friendly as you are?" I ask.

Arkan doesn't answer, but I decide to head after him anyway. I can't really hold his companions' behavior against them. If one of my friends had recently been eaten, I'd be a little defensive, too.

When we reach the bottom, Arkan and the ogre stand facing me. Then a woman with ginger hair appears beside them. The cloak she's wearing must render her invisible whenever the hood is up.

"He's looking for a girl," Arkan announces as if it's proof of something.

The woman glances up at the ogre, who towers over the rest of us. He's wearing a loincloth made from hide, and every inch of his exposed flesh is decorated with intricate tribal tattoos. Yet his face, with its flat nose and giant amber eyes, seems oddly chubby and juvenile.

The ogre shrugs and the woman looks back at me. I'm not sure they know what Arkan's getting at either. Then the woman sticks out a hand to me. The skin is buttery soft, but the grip is surprisingly firm. "Hey there, I'm Carole." She has a sugary voice and a Southern accent. Her avatar's face is freckled and pretty, with laugh lines around her eyes. "That's Gorog." She gestures toward the hulk. He drops his rocks and raises a callused hand in a half-wave.

"Simon," I say. "So you guys came from the White City too?"

My question seems to confuse Carole and Gorog.

"He says that's the name of the place where we started," Arkan says.

"Really? I didn't know it had a name." Carole smiles, but she seems on edge. "So who's this girl you're looking for?"

"A friend of mine. I'm here to help her."

"Is she dead?" Gorog blurts out. Carole sighs wearily.

"What? No!" What kind of question is that? "She's not dead."

"Are *you* dead?" Gorog demands.

"Of course not!" This conversation just took a turn for the weird, and I'm starting to worry.

"Are you sure?" Arkan follows up.

"Yeah, I'm *positive.* How in the hell can I be dead if I'm standing here talking to you?"

My response doesn't appear to please Arkan. He throws his helmet down and stomps off toward the campfire, which he kicks at repeatedly before dropping miserably to the ground beside it.

"Your friend's got a little rage problem. What was that all about?" I ask the other two.

Carole grimaces. "Arkan thinks he's dead. He's convinced that this place is some sort of afterlife."

"But why would he think . . . ," I start to ask, and then I realize I already know the answer. They're taking part in the Company's disk beta test, just like Kat. But Arkan doesn't know it—none of them do. Something happened to their real-world bodies, and they woke up in the White City without any explanation. Given the circumstances, it's perfectly understandable that someone might mistake this place for the afterworld. I just hope Kat was eavesdropping when Martin and Todd explained the White City to me. Otherwise, she's probably just as confused.

"You aren't dead," I inform Carole.

"Well, thank sweet baby Jesus for that," Carole says with a snort. "I *told* Arkan this wasn't what the Good Lord had in store for me."

"We're not in heaven?" Gorog asks. He sounds curious, but he doesn't seem quite as concerned as his fellow travelers. I get the feeling he's itching for adventure.

Carole glares at the ogre. "We watched Orin get eaten yesterday evening. If you think this could be heaven, you're just as crazy as Arkan." She turns back to me. "So where are we?"

The answer to that particular question might make their heads explode. I'm going to have to work up to it. "You don't have any idea how you got here, do you?"

"Nope," Carole confirms. "All I remember is driving up I-95 and then suddenly, *poof!* I'm in crazy town."

"I was on my bike," Gorog tells me. "There was a crash and a lot of people talking and then I woke up in some weird changing room. What happened?"

I'm not sure they're going to find the truth very comforting, but I try to explain. "It sounds like you were both injured in accidents. Now you're taking part in an experimental therapy. There's a disk attached to the back of your skulls. Your bodies are probably in a hospital, but the disk is telling your brains you're somewhere else."

"Somewhere *else*?" Carole asks. "Like *where*? What is this place?"

"The town where we started is called the White City. But once you leave, you're in something called Otherworld. The Company created the software for both the White City and Otherworld, and for some reason they connected them."

"You're saying we're in *the* Otherworld?" Gorog asks. All I can do is nod.

Carole seems too stunned to speak, but Gorog's started spinning around like he's just landed in Oz.

"Daaammn!" he exclaims. "This is *Otherworld*?"

"Yeah, it came as a shock to me, too," I say.

"Otherworld?" Carole asks.

Gorog's too excited to stop and explain. "Oh, man, I would have done *anything* for Otherworld gear. But do you know how much that shit costs? Like *three thousand* dollars! I mean, how's someone like me ever gonna get his hands on three thousand dollars? It's not fair! I even tweeted at Milo Yolkin about it. I figured he'd understand my pain if anyone would. But the dude hasn't replied to a tweet in months."

Carole lays a hand on my arm to draw my attention away from the raving hulk. "Are you telling me we're in some kind of *game*?" she asks, her brow furrowed as if she's trying hard to understand. "I had a PlayStation back in the day, and there was nothing on it like this."

"This is very advanced virtual reality," I tell her. "There's never been anything like the disk before."

Carole's hand flies up to the back of her neck. "I don't feel any disk," she says.

"You can't feel it while you're here, and you can't take it off by yourself," I tell her.

"So what—we're stuck in this place?" She's gone from curious to practically panic-stricken. "I've gotta get back to the real world! I've got to find a way out of here!"

"I'm not sure that's such a great idea. Your body may be"— I struggle for the right word—"damaged. The friend I came here to find was in a very bad accident."

"I don't care if I'm broken in a million goddamn pieces. I am *not* watching another person get eaten by goats!" Carole yells. Can't say I blame her, but I don't like being shouted at.

"Then you should have stayed in the White City," I snap. "No one was going to get eaten there. You would have been perfectly safe."

"Sure," Carole says. "Until I threw myself off the top of one of those buildings. I stayed in that place for a week. I ate at every restaurant and had a pedicure every day. I've never been so miserable in my entire life."

"Yeah," Gorog adds. "I was pretty sure I was going to die of boredom."

"Besides, I had to find a way home. I have responsibilities," Carole goes on. "There are real people there who need me. I can't hang out in virtual reality with an ogre and a knight and . . ." She pauses while she looks me up and down. "What the hell are you supposed to be?"

"A Druid," I say.

"Perfect. And a *Druid,*" she adds. "A Druid with a giant nose."

I'm seriously pissed off now. Not because this lady has the balls to insult my stunningly handsome avatar, but because an escort quest is *not* what I had in mind. I'm here to find Kat, not rescue every asshole who's stuck in Otherworld. I should get out of here—find some excuse to sneak away and leave them behind. But I can't—and that's what pisses me off most. What would I tell Kat when I found her? That I abandoned three random people to die? They're with me now whether I like it or not.

"All right, *fine*," I say. "If you want to leave, I'll take you to the exit. Your gear should shut off when you pass through it. After that, if your body is able to move in real life, you'll be able to take off the disk. But just so you know, there's a powerful being guarding the Otherworld exit, and I'm not sure the four of us will be able to take him down."

"How do you know all this stuff?" Gorog asks. "How'd you find out about the exit?"

I'd rather not repeat the whole saga right now, so I keep my explanation simple. "My guide told me," I say.

"Your *guide*?" Carole asks. "Are we supposed to get guides?"

"*We* aren't," says Gorog. He's grinning down at me like he's just figured out my secret. "Only *the One* ever gets a guide. Neo had Morpheus. Luke Skywalker had Yoda. Harry Potter had Dumbledore. Ender had—"

"Gorog, what in *the hell* are you talking about?" Carole interrupts.

"Don't you watch any movies?" Gorog replies. "Simon must be the One. He was sent here to rescue us all."

"Like Jesus?" Carole asks. I get the feeling she's a big believer.

"Wait a second," I interject. "You just met me five minutes ago and now you think I'm the *what*?" I start laughing so hard I can't stop. Of all the shit that's been said about me in the past eighteen years, that is by far the funniest.

"Why's he laughing?" I hear Carole ask.

"That's how it works," Gorog informs her. "The One never believes he's the One."

"Stop, stop, stop!" I'm doubled over, howling with laughter. "I'm going to piss myself."

"What's going on over there?" I recognize Arkan's angry voice in the distance. "Are you guys making fun of me?"

I'm trying to stop laughing long enough to reply when Carole shushes me. "Don't tell Arkan what you told us," she warns me. "Not even the part about the exit."

"Why not?" I ask. Suddenly I don't feel like laughing anymore.

She taps her temple with her finger. "The boy ain't right."

"Hey!" Arkan shouts again.

"Nobody's talking about you!" Gorog shouts back. "I made a joke about Simon being like Neo from *The Matrix*."

"You mean the One?" Arkan yells, but this time the anger in his voice is gone. "That scrawny loser's not *the One*."

Crazy or not, I have to agree with him. I can't be the One, because there's no way in hell I'd be helping these dumbasses if it weren't for Kat.

DREDGING THE GOWANUS

Carole was right about Arkan. The guy's totally nuts. And his sword really is plastic. When my three new companions passed through the White City's gates, they were offered a choice of weapon or tool, just as I was. Gorog opted for fire. Carole went with an invisibility cloak. And Arkan chose *nothing*. The plastic sword apparently came with his knight costume.

He told the others that a weapon "wouldn't make any difference 'cause we're already dead." And as goats were eating their friend, he assured Carole and Gorog that they shouldn't interfere because "it was all meant to be."

Yet despite his rather serious mental health issues, Arkan turns out to be quite resourceful. Before sunset, he used his cape as a net and caught fish for our dinner. His helmet became our water bucket and his shield became the skillet on which he sautéed our fish, which—I have to say—were beautifully cooked. The meal filled me up, but somehow it didn't put an end to my hunger pangs. I hope the food does my avatar some good. Somewhere, beneath the surface, I can feel my body in the real world begging for more.

After dinner, Arkan laid out his theory about this so-called afterlife we're all sharing. We're in purgatory, he says—the waiting room between heaven and hell. His belief is so powerful that he might have convinced me if I didn't know better. I would have set him straight, but Carole caught my eye whenever I opened my mouth. I understand her concern. Arkan's illusions are all he has left. There's no telling what could happen if one of us was to destroy them.

Soon the sky is dark and the others are resting. Even in Otherworld, the brain needs to power down several hours every evening. I lie beside the campfire and rest my eyes for a minute. I figure it's probably a good idea to stay awake in case any more man-eating goats come sniffing around. I don't plan to sleep, but I do. And in my dream I find Kat.

I'm back in the real world, which somehow seems far less real after a day in Otherworld. I'm looking down at Kat from the hole in the floor at Elmer's. She's sitting with her back against the wall, Solo cup in hand, staring into space. It's the night of the party, but this time there's no one else around—just the two of us separated by a rotting wooden floor. I can see now what I couldn't before. She's neither drunk nor high. She's thinking. And I know the answers I need are bouncing around in her head.

"She's a looker," a man says. "I always had a thing for wild hair like that too. I hope this girl's worth the trouble. A lot of 'em aren't, you know."

The stench hits me before I see its source. The smell is a

bouquet of raw sewage, gasoline and a dozen industrial pollutants I couldn't begin to identify. There's a man standing beside me. The rancid water streaming off him has gathered in a pool at his feet. The light inside the factory is too dim to make out his features, but his profile is unmistakable. The Kishka has risen from the bottom of Brooklyn's Gowanus Canal to star in my dream.

"Her name is Kat," I tell my grandfather, making him the first member of my family who's ever heard me say her name out loud. "I'm here because she's in trouble."

"So was the lady who got me into this mess," he says, holding his arms out as if to show off the revolting state of his suit. Then he lets them drop. "Wasn't her fault, though. I was thinking with my kishka. And not this one," he says, tapping his nose. "The *bigger* one." He stops, and I can tell he's no longer joking. "You know what you're doing?"

"No clue," I admit. I haven't had much time to think things through.

My grandfather pulls a pack of Lucky Strikes from the pocket of his suit. When his Zippo won't produce a flame and the cigarettes are too wet to light, he tosses everything out the window.

"So let me see if I understand what's going on," he says. I'm eager to hear what a gangster from the 1960s makes of Otherworld, but he doesn't seem very interested in virtual reality. "A bunch of kids got killed at that factory, and the cops are calling it an accident. Then the people who survived get hooked up to some kind of machine and sent away. The machine's supposed to let them play with bunnies and butterflies, but people end up getting eaten by goats instead. I got this straight?"

"Yeah," I tell him. "Pretty much."

My grandfather whistles appreciatively. "If I were a betting man—and believe me, I am—I'd bet that collapse was no accident. Somebody must have wanted those kids out of the way."

"I know," I say, though it's the first time I've actually voiced my suspicions. "They were targeted."

"I know you know," he tells me. He's right. I'm not having a conversation with a dead gangster I've never met. I'm talking to myself. "Question is—what are you planning to do about it?"

I shrug. "Not much I can do," I tell him. "I'm out of the way now too." Someone sent me the disk and I jumped right into Otherworld without thinking. Maybe the person was trying to help me. Maybe they wanted to get rid of me. At this point, it's impossible to know.

"You followed your gut," the Kishka says. "You did the right thing."

"You mean coming here to rescue Kat?"

My grandfather snorts. "You and I both know that girl can take care of herself. She's been to Otherworld. She knows where she is by now. And half the time in these games, she's the one saving *your* ass. That's not why you need to find her."

"What do you mean?" I ask.

"She saw what happened the night of the collapse. She knows what was thrown down to the second floor—and she probably knows who threw it. You want to do something for her? Figure out who put her in the hospital in the first place."

"How?"

"Are you kidding me? She's here somewhere. Just find her and *ask* her."

I open my eyes. The night is pitch-black. The designers seem to have forgotten to add a moon. There are only stars above. They appear to be laid out in patterns, but as far as I can tell, they don't match any of the constellations I've seen from Earth.

I hear a sniffle and then a muffled sob. One of my new companions is crying. I can't be positive, but it sounds like Arkan. Maybe he doesn't like being dead after all.

THE RESORT OF THE FUTURE

I wake up again as the sun rises. The others are sleeping sound-lessly. Carole's body is wrapped in her cloak. Arkan's shield is covering his face, and Gorog has curled up in a giant ball. There's no breeze and everything around me is perfectly still. It's as if the world has frozen. Then I hear a splash from the lake. The silver fish must be jumping, I think. But when I sit up to watch, I'm startled to see a girl treading water near the bank.

Her face is human, I'm relieved to discover, and her long black hair floats on the surface around her. I can make out her slender, bare arms undulating beneath the water. It's hard to imagine she's wearing a swimsuit.

I stand up and walk toward her, careful to keep a safe distance between us. I know better than to trust a pretty face here—and I have no intention of being dragged in and drowned. Her skin grows a hot red as I approach; then she dips her head beneath the water, and a small puff of steam escapes into the atmosphere.

A silver fish tail slaps the surface of the water. When the fish girl appears again, her cooled skin is the color of pale-gray slate.

"Wake the others," she tells me, her voice soft as if she's sharing a secret. "There's a swarm heading this way. I can hear it approaching. It will be here in a matter of hours."

I listen for a moment, but I hear nothing. "A swarm of what?"

"Flying insects," she says. "They have no name. They were designed to pollinate the flowers of a distant realm, but they flew away. I do not know how they survive while they're in the wastelands. I only know that they are not what the Creator intended."

Sounds familiar. "Lemme guess . . . now they drink blood instead of nectar," I say.

"No," the girl says. "They are not interested in our guests or their blood. They fly from one end of Otherworld to the other, and they let nothing stand in their way. As they pass, they will enter and fill your body's every opening. You'll suffocate moments before your carcass explodes."

Holy shit. Otherworld has invented another delightful way to go.

The girl sinks beneath the water and surfaces again. "You must reach Imra before the insects overtake you. Look for the highest peak on the horizon. On top, you'll find the entrance to the city."

"How far is it?" I ask.

"It's close enough. If you leave soon, you'll stand a chance of survival."

That doesn't sound terribly encouraging. I'd rather have more than just a *chance*. I'm about to jump up and wake the others when I realize I'm taking advice from a naked fish girl who lives in a pond.

"Are you one of the Children?" I ask.

"I am the Creator's daughter," she answers frankly.

I have no idea what that really means, but I guess I'll take that as a yes. "The last Child I met liked to eat people like me. So why should I trust you? How do I know you're not sending me into some kind of trap?"

"Your friend asked me to help you if you passed this way. She wanted me to let you know that she's alive and on her way to the glacier. She will wait for you there."

Some kind of chemical floods my brain and for a moment I'm high on it. I know who the fish girl is talking about, but I still ask, "What friend?"

"The female in a camouflage suit that blends into anything. She said a male dressed like a peasant might come after her."

Kat. She was listening when I told her I'd find her. And it sounds like she chose the same avatar she used when we explored Otherworld for the first time. The camouflage is battle attire. Even during setup inside the White City, Kat knew she'd be in danger. But the girl in the pond just said two things that give me hope. The Clay Man was right—Kat's heading for the glacier. And her trip must be going okay so far if she took the time to knock my avatar.

"I'm not a peasant. I'm a Druid," I correct the fish girl.

"It makes no difference to me. Your companions are lucky I was able to recognize you. I do not let guests take shelter near my lake. Your friend was the first guest I've spared."

"Why did you let *her* live?" I ask.

"When she spoke, she wasn't like the others. She knows this isn't a game, and she agrees that your kind does not belong here.

I let her live because she promised to speak to my father. She will convince him to banish all humans from Otherworld and leave the land to the Elementals, the Beasts and the Children."

What the *hell*? Kat's supposed to be heading for the exit, not setting off on some grand mission. "I thought you just said my friend was on her way to the glacier. Now you're telling me she's looking for *the Creator*? Which is it?"

"Both," says the girl. "She must speak to him before she leaves."

"Okay, well, what if my friend can't find your Creator and convince him to banish the guests?" I ask.

"Then there will be war," the girl says simply. "It's already begun."

She slips silently into the water and does not surface again. It's probably my imagination, but my ears detect a faint buzzing in the distance.

Six hours of walking, and we finally saw signs of Imra. I knew it was on the top of a goddamn mountain, but I'd forgotten how high that mountain peak happened to be. But where else would you expect your safe haven to be when you're being chased by a suffocating swarm of insects? By the halfway point, I was almost wishing I was dead anyway. Though Arkan never stopped assuring us that none of it was real, the black swarm eventually appeared on the horizon, and I almost found myself feeling a little nostalgic for the goats. Compared to having every orifice filled with flying insects, being eaten seemed like a noble way to go.

Now, at the top of the mountain, I'm struck by déjà vu. We're standing outside the same gates where I began my first adventure in Otherworld. Back then, I was blown away by how real everything seemed. But after witnessing the glorious architecture of the White City, I'm feeling a little *meh* about this place. The gates open for us, and we set off down one of the streets. The buildings we pass remind me of college dorms. There are no shops or businesses of any kind—just row after row of bland brick structures. I've heard rumors that Imra's a digital Sodom, but all those whispers must have been wrong. I'm fairly confident that nothing interesting has ever happened here.

We don't walk far before we start seeing NPCs. I scan every face, just in case Kat made a detour on her way to the glacier, but I'm pretty sure there's not an avatar among them. Most of the NPCs are Photoshop good-looking, with creamy skin, gleaming hair and rock-hard glutes. They're all dressed like extras in a vodka commercial. Meanwhile, the dense black cloud of insects is so close now that its buzzing has built to a roar. While the residents here don't seem terribly perturbed, I can't help but notice that the streets are quickly emptying.

One of the few NPCs still left outside is approaching us. Her sensible low-heeled pumps click and her hips sway as she walks. She's clearly a resident. No human being would willingly choose an avatar this bland. Her dark hair is pulled back in a bun, and she's wearing a navy skirt suit and a white button-down shirt. A name tag identifies her as Margot.

"Hello!" She smiles warmly, showing the perfect number of teeth to communicate genuine delight at our sudden appearance. "Are you looking for Imra?"

"This isn't it?" I ask.

Margot chuckles in a way that says she's laughing *with*

me, rather than *at* me. "Not quite. But you're almost there! Follow me."

She keeps talking after her back is turned toward us, but the insects' buzzing has grown deafening, and I can't make out a single word. One of the bugs' advance guards lands on my ear. I capture it between my fingers. It's like a little black ladybug, and I'd probably call it cute if it didn't want to invade all my openings. A second insect grazes my nose, and I feel a jolt of panic. We need to find shelter as quickly as possible.

Carole is clearly thinking the same thing. "Hey, do you think we can get where we're going a little bit faster?" I hear her shout at Margot's back.

I don't catch her response, but Margot breaks into an effortless jog. We run behind her for what feels like miles, past more identical buildings, until we reach a large square that seems like it must be the center of town. Where you'd ordinarily expect to find a fountain or statue, there's a giant glass box instead. A door slides open and the four of us follow Margot inside. The box is big enough to fit a hundred large avatars comfortably. The door shuts and seals just as the insects close in around us. I double over with relief as millions of tiny bodies splatter against the glass while the sun dims and then disappears.

"Everyone feeling good?" Margot asks cheerfully, as if nothing potentially life-threatening had just taken place. "I guess that's *our* exercise for today!"

Carole collapses to the floor and Gorog joins her. "Are you sure this isn't real?" Carole groans. "'Cause I'm pretty sure I'm having a heart attack."

"Real?" Margot looks confused. "Of course it's real."

"It's not real." Arkan is panting, but he still manages to force the words out. The dude's got a one-track mind.

"How long are we going to have to stay in this box?" Gorog asks anxiously. I'd like to know, too. The claustrophobia is starting to kick in.

"Just a few more moments," Margot assures him. And it does seem as if some light is beginning to filter through the swarm. Then I watch as a chandelier rises from the floor, and I realize we've been descending into an underground space.

We come to an abrupt stop and the side of the glass box slides open again. A wave of hot air washes over us. "Welcome to Imra!" Margot exclaims.

Usually I'd find such boundless enthusiasm nauseating, but in this case it's warranted. A wide red velvet carpet stretches out in front of us, spiraling around the interior of what appears to be the cone of a massive volcano. Chandelier-like streetlamps light the way, which is lined with stately buildings, their marble façades riddled with classy nude statues and ornate columns. It's probably what Monte Carlo would look like if ancient Greeks had constructed it. A fence with a single rail runs along the left side of the walkway. It's the only thing preventing pedestrians from plummeting over the edge and down into the glowing pool of lava that spits and churns below. As the son of two lawyers, I feel the urge to warn my hosts that they're running the risk of a billion personal injury lawsuits, but Carole finds her tongue first.

"If this is Imra, where did we just come from?"

"We call the surface village the suburbs," Margot responds with another hearty laugh, and I want to punch the dork who designed her. "That's where our residents live. The city of Imra houses only guests. It's beautiful, safe and all-inclusive. We like to think of it as the Resort of the Future."

"Where is everybody?" Carole pushes further. "The place looks totally empty."

"We just opened a few weeks ago," Margot explains. "There's a small, select group staying with us at the moment, but don't you worry—the crowds will be showing up soon! The city was built to be perfectly scalable. Right now we have space for ten thousand guests, but we plan to host millions someday! Now, what do you say—shall I show you around? I think you'll find we have something for everyone here in Imra. The Creator designed it to be the ultimate welcome station for our guests."

Margot doesn't actually wait for our response, and I'm getting the sense that the tour may not be totally optional. The glass elevator that brought us here is already rising back to the surface, and from where we're standing, the walkway only leads in a single direction. Then Margot pulls open a pair of golden doors to our right, revealing a room that has waterfalls for walls. They feed a pool that's large enough to Jet Ski across.

"Wow," Gorog marvels. Then his eyes immediately shoot toward Arkan. "Yeah, yeah. I know it's not real."

"Maybe not," I say, wiping the mist from my brow as I walk into the room. Gorog and Carole enter alongside me. "But you gotta admit it's doing a pretty good impression of *real*." Upholstered lounge chairs are lined up along the edge, and palm trees bristling with sweet brown dates grow out of massive planters. Stationed at regular intervals are attractive young men and women in white uniforms.

"This is one of our many spa rooms," Margot says, joining

us at the edge of the pool. "Guests like you often stop here first for a refreshing swim or massage. Our therapists can provide any style of bodywork you desire. Should you wish to update your avatar, there are facilities available for that here, too. Many of our guests prefer to assume a more conventional appearance in Imra. It makes certain things . . . easier."

I see her give Gorog a once-over. She clearly thinks he could use a few improvements.

"Huh?" The ogre blushes when he notices her looking at him. "No thanks, I'm good."

Where are all the other guests that Margot keeps talking about? I wonder. There's no one here. I'm about to make a joke about everyone choosing to be invisible when I actually spot someone on the other side of the pool. It's a naked man lying facedown on one of the lounge chairs. His head and left arm are hanging off the side.

Gorog sees him too. "Look—that guy must have died of happiness."

"Oh, no," Margot assures us. She doesn't seem to know it was a joke. "His avatar wouldn't be here if he were dead."

"We're all dead," says Arkan.

Margot smiles at him brightly. "You aren't dead," she corrects the knight. "That seems to be a common misconception these days. We've had a few guests lately who assumed that this was some kind of afterworld. But I assure you all, you're very much alive. This is Otherworld."

There's silence while all eyes turn to the red knight. There's no telling how he's going to respond to the news. Carole's gotta be pissed as hell. She's done everything she can to keep the truth from Arkan, and Margot's just gone and blurted it out.

"Otherworld?" Arkan repeats. "Isn't that a game?" Inside his good-looking head is a brain in full meltdown.

Carole quickly jumps in to change the subject. "You know, if that guy over there on the lounge chair isn't dead, he must be pretty wasted," she tells Margot. "Someone should help him find a room."

Margot shakes her head vigorously. "Oh, no. We're not allowed to interfere. The world you came from is governed by laws and rules and social conventions, but Imra was built to offer a safe haven from such things. The guests in Imra are free to do as they will. None of us are here to judge. You spend so much time and effort fighting your instincts in your world. Well, we're here to tell you it's okay—you can relax for a while," she says, still revoltingly chipper. "So! Any of you tempted to get a rubdown or go for a plunge?"

Carole and Gorog turn to me, confusion written all over their faces. We came to Imra to hide from a swarm of killer bugs and now we're being offered bodywork.

"No?" Our tour guide seems a bit disappointed, as if our comfort were her personal responsibility. "Well, then anyone hungry?"

We leave the spa and Margot leads us farther down the spiral path to a second building. The smell of roasted meat nearly knocks me to my knees before I even step inside. My mouth begins to water and my stomach groans miserably. I have no idea how many hours have passed since my body back in the real world had its last meal. The others don't seem to be quite as affected, and I realize that wherever they are, their bodies must be hooked up to IVs that prevent them from starving. But I need something in my stomach before I move on.

My nose leads me through the building's marble foyer and into a sumptuous banquet hall under a domed roof. There are hundreds of beautifully set tables, but almost all remain empty. In the center, residents in chefs' coats and hats are tending to three monstrous beasts that are roasting on spits. Smoke from the fires twists upward like a vine toward a vent in the ceiling.

"Have you ever tried buffalo?" Margot asks the group. I haven't, but right now I want to more than anything in the world. "Our guests rate it very highly."

"Guess we're taking a little break," Gorog remarks as I pull out a chair at one of the tables. Before my ass can slide into the seat, a resident sets a plate in front of me. Ignoring the utensils that have been provided, I dig into the meat piled high in the center. And it is *divine*. In fact, it's the best stuff I've ever eaten. I smell it and taste it and feel the grease it leaves between my fingertips. I wash the meat down with the beer someone hands me, which leaves my brain buzzing, and keep shoveling buffalo into my mouth.

I hear Carole *tsk*. "I see *someone* forgot their table manners," she drawls.

"No judgments," Margot trills.

When I glance up from the bone I'm gnawing, I realize that Carole wasn't talking about me. There's a couple sitting about ten tables over. Empty plates are piled up around them, and the floor near their table is ankle-deep in bones. The woman, a blonde in a Grace Kelly dress, picks up her latest plate and licks it clean. When it's a sparkling white, she puts it on top of the stack and one of the residents places a full plate in front of her.

Arkan is heading toward them, his armor clanking. "Emma?"

he calls, but the woman doesn't acknowledge him. She's holding another plate to her face when he reaches her.

"Stop eating!" He grabs the plate and hurls it to the floor, where it shatters.

"No judgments," Margot chirps for the second time.

Arkan bends forward to examine the woman's face. "Not Emma," he mutters, and then stomps away.

"Gorog, what in the hell are you doing?" I hear Carole whisper angrily.

"Getting this all on camera," the ogre responds.

My eyes turn to Gorog, and I find him aiming the camera of a tablet-size device in my direction. I can't figure out where he got it, until I see there's one at every place setting. Which seems unbelievably strange.

"Stop," I demand with my mouth full. I reach out a hand to snatch the device.

"Too late," says Gorog as I take it away. "I already sent the video to everyone you know."

I'm about to kick his ass when I remember that he doesn't actually know anyone I know. "Hilarious," I try to say, and end up choking instead.

"What's the deal with all the cameras, anyway?" Gorog asks Margot.

"If you don't record your fun, how do you know for sure that it happened?" Margot jokes. Or at least, I think she's joking. "Our guests like to share their experiences in Imra with their friends and family back at home—and we encourage them to do so. It's excellent publicity for Otherworld."

I'd love to make a snarky comment, but I'm too busy chewing to think one up. I finish the last bit of food on my plate and find a new one in front of me. I should stop, but I can't.

"Dude," says Gorog. "Your avatar is going to explode."

"Now, now," Margot chides. "He's just enjoying himself. If the rest of you aren't hungry, why don't I show you a little bit more of Imra, and your friends can catch up with you later."

"Friends?" Something seems to have set off an alarm in Carole's head. "Wait a second. Where's Arkan?" she asks. I glance around the room. While Gorog was filming, the red knight disappeared. "Hang tight," Carole tells me. "We're going to go find him."

I'm still chewing as they rush away.

I have no idea how much time has passed—or how many plates I've been through. I feel a bit fuller than I did when I got here, but if anything, the need to eat has only grown. My hands simply aren't fast enough to deliver the food to my face. I'm on the verge of getting rid of my five-fingered middlemen and lifting the plate straight up to my lips when I notice that Carole's returned. She's standing a few feet away, staring right at me.

"You've got to come with me," she demands.

"In a little while," I tell her. "I'm still starving."

"No. *Now*," she insists. "Arkan's in trouble."

"Get Gorog to help," I say, annoyed that I have to stop chewing long enough to speak. "He's bigger than I am." I don't bother to add that I never liked Arkan much anyway.

"Gorog *is* helping. He's keeping that robot lady busy while I come to get you."

"Margot isn't really a robot," I say. "She's a—"

"I don't give a damn what she is!" Carole shouts so loudly that even my fellow diners look up. How long have *they* been here, I wonder uncomfortably. She lowers her voice and continues. I notice that she's trembling. "This place isn't right. There are strange things happening here. Get up," she orders.

"I don't know if I can," I tell her honestly.

She puts her hands on her hips and her nostrils flare. "You said you came to this place for a reason. What is it?" she demands. "Do you even remember?"

"To find Kat," I mutter with a mouthful of buffalo. The words mean something, but I can't seem to put it together.

"That's right. You came all this way to find your friend, and now you're just going to sit here in this resort from hell eating virtual meat? Your friend could be three doors down from here, and you'd never even know it. Are you in love with this girl or what?"

I never said anything about being in love with Kat. But what other reason would I have for being here? Carole's words cut through all the knots that were keeping me tied to my seat. I glance down at the pile of food on the plate in front of me. It's fake meat made from fantasy beasts. But it's been my sole obsession for what might have been hours now—hours that I could have spent going after Kat. And yet, even now, I crave it. My fingers are aching to snatch one more piece. And that urge is terrifying. This is what Otherworld does to you, I realize. It gives you what you want. The only way I'll make it through is if I remind myself that there's something I want much more than anything else. I want to find Kat.

I push my chair back and stand. I think I'm hungrier now than

I was when I sat down, but somehow I summon the willpower to make my way across the room to the exit. Outside, Carole and I pass dozens of open doors as we wind our way down the red spiral path, deeper and deeper into the volcano. There are gambling rooms decorated like Vegas casinos that have drawn reasonable crowds—and nightclubs that are practically empty. I can't understand why some of the rooms are so much more popular than others—until the answer hits me. I should have figured it out from the start. Most of the guests here aren't from the White City. They're wearing a headset and playing a game. They don't have disks attached to the back of their skulls. The headset players can see Otherworld and throw dice with their haptic gloves, but they can't taste the food or feel the massages. And dancing in haptic booties, while totally possible, isn't much fun.

There's really no reason for parts of Imra to exist at all—unless they were designed for guests wearing disks. When I have a little more time on my hands, I'll have to figure out what that means.

"Come on," Carole urges me as I pause in front of a man slumped against the wall. "You're going to see a lot more of that where we're going." There's drool dripping from the side of the man's mouth. I assume he's drunk, which means he's got to be wearing a disk.

When I turn to follow Carole, I step on something. It rolls beneath my foot and I lose my balance and fall against the railing. We're much closer to the lava now, and I can feel its heat radiating upward.

"What the . . . ," I mumble, picking up the object that nearly sent me plummeting into the flames. It's an empty syringe. It didn't occur to me until now, but I guess if the disk can make your brain taste buffalo, it can mimic the effects of your favorite drug, too.

"Watch yourself. They've got a bit of a litter problem here at the Last Resort," Carole jokes grimly.

That's an understatement, I learn as we continue down the spiral path. Bottles and Baggies and cigarette butts are everywhere. Imra has been open for less than a month, but it already looks like hell on St. Patrick's Day.

"This is it." Carole has stopped at a pair of open doors. Smoke pours from the entrance like a fast-rolling fog. She takes one of my arms and together we forge inside. The waiters and waitresses must be navigating by echolocation, because the place is too dimly lit to see clearly. But I get the sense that the room is a maze of leather chairs and masculine furniture. Before he wrote me off as a lost cause, my dad once took me to the Harvard Club in Manhattan. This is what his fancy-ass club would look like if its members were Hells Angels and Russian gangsters. Milo Yolkin famously attended Harvard for all of three weeks before he dropped out. If this is his idea of a joke, I think the two of us would get along beautifully.

I wonder how many guests are actually in the club. You'd definitely need a disk to appreciate this section of Imra—unless you're here for the scantily clad waitstaff. The waitress in front of us appears to be missing most of her skirt. She disappears suddenly, yanked into a banquette by an unseen hand. I guess that means there's at least one person here who's enjoying the wares. Now I'm stepping over two bodies that lie sprawled on the floor. Just beyond them, a man in red armor is sitting on a stool with his head slumped down on the bar.

"He won't get up," Carole explains.

"Hey there, buddy," I say, doing my best to speak bro as I pull out the stool beside Arkan. "What's going on?"

"Why can't I find her? Why isn't she here?" the knight slurs.

"Who are you trying to find?" Carole asks. "Tell us. Maybe we can help."

"You wouldn't know her." He's not just drunk, he's absolutely shitfaced. He must have been working pretty hard to achieve this level of intoxication. He couldn't have been at the bar for more than a couple of hours.

"Come on," I try again. "This isn't a good place to take a nap." I can only imagine what horrible things might happen to someone who passed out in a place like this. I feel eyes on us, and I turn around. Three men have claimed chairs nearby. The hulking avatars seem pretty damn menacing. And I remember what the Clay Man once told me—the most dangerous creatures in Otherworld are the guests.

"I'm never leaving," Arkan whispers to the bar.

I lean closer to his ear. "I know how to find the exit," I say. "I can get you out of here. You can go back home and find the girl you're looking for."

"Go away," he says.

Carole groans. "What do you think?" she asks. "Should we let him sleep it off?"

I'm tempted to abandon the knight and let him stay on his barstool. The man's clearly got problems that can't be solved by sending him back to the real world.

"We can't leave him here," I say with a sigh. "It's not safe."

"Why not?" Carole asks. "You said this is a game. What's the worst that could happen?"

I don't want to tell her, but she deserves to know. "If we were wearing headsets like most of the people here, Otherworld would just be a game. But we're not players. We're guinea pigs. The disk technology we're testing is totally new. I don't know what would happen if one of our avatars was injured or died. When I first got here, my guide warned me to protect my life. He said I might not get another."

Carole grabs me by the arms. I can feel each of her fingertips pressing into my flesh. "Oh, dear God, please tell me you're joking," she pleads. I shake my head. "You mean we could really die in this hellhole? I could be eaten by a goddamn goat and never see my family or friends again?"

"I don't know," I admit.

For a second Carole looks like she might burst into tears. Then she grabs one of Arkan's arms. "Take the other one," she orders. "We've got to get him out of here."

We manage to drag Arkan through the club and out to the walkway. He's remarkably heavy for a bunch of code. Carole is struggling under his arm, so we set him down by the wall. I'm catching my breath when I spot Gorog approaching us with the widest smile I've ever seen.

"*Dude*," he says. "You are not going to believe what they've got on the lowest level." Then he glances nervously at Carole.

"Give me a break," Carole snaps. "I'm not your mom. You think I haven't seen a few things in my day?"

"I'm pretty sure you've never seen anything like this," Gorog says, growing bolder. "It's like a giant orgy down there. I'd bet there's a thousand people at least, and a bunch of them are going at it like . . ." He looks over at Carole again, bites his lip and grins maniacally.

Carole rolls her eyes. "And yet you came back to hang out with us?" she says. "How *sweet* of you. Now make yourself useful and help us with Arkan."

The ogre comes to us and hoists the knight over his shoulder fireman-style. "For your information, I've been *very* useful today. While you guys were paying for Arkan's beer, I found the way out of Imra. Margot's waiting for us."

"Margot," Carole groans. "I thought you were going to give Robo-Concierge the slip."

"Easier said than done," says Gorog. "She says the boss here has one last offer to make before we go."

"Two free nights and a complimentary bottle of champagne?" I ask.

"And maybe a discount on an orgy?" Gorog adds enthusiastically.

Carole makes a barfing sound. "You two are hilarious," she drones. "Can we just get the hell out of here and go home?"

We follow Gorog to the bottom of the volcano, the knight's limp body flopping against the ogre's tattooed back. There are no streetlights down here, just the red glow that emanates from the pool of lava. Margot is waiting for us there with a smile plastered on her face and a tabletlike clipboard clutched in her hand. A spark from the molten rock lands in her hair, but she doesn't seem to notice.

"We'd like to check out now," I inform her.

"Not a problem," she replies. "I will pass your request on to Pomba Gira, but I have a quick customer service survey I'd like you to take first. Do you mind? I just need to call it up on the screen."

"Who's Pomba Gira?" Carole asks.

"She's the Elemental of Imra," Margot says absentmindedly as she taps away at the tablet. "She decides who leaves and who stays. Okay, here we are!" She looks up with another plastic smile. "We want to make sure that our guests have had a chance to enjoy themselves fully before they move on to other realms. The data you provide will help us optimize our offerings for future visitors. So how would you rate your experience in Imra?"

"Best day of our lives," I lie, figuring it's easiest to tell her what she wants to hear. "I keep wishing it will never end."

"Oh, excellent!" she replies. "And do you all agree?"

"Sure," Carole answers. Gorog grunts.

"That's wonderful," Margot says, entering the information into the tablet. "You know, there's no need for the day to end. You can stay here in Imra as long as you like. That's the whole idea!"

"We're just passing through," Carole says tersely.

"Of course." Margot's eyes drop back down to the screen. "And which parts of the resort did you find most appealing today? I know you were quite fond of the buffet," she says to me. "What about the rest of you?"

"The orgy," Gorog says.

Margot looks over at Carole. "Ditto," Carole drones.

"Great! Yes, that's a very popular part of Imra, we're already thinking of expanding. And was there anything you were hoping to find here that you didn't?"

"The way out," Carole tells her. "We'd like to see it now. We're done with your survey."

"Of course." Margot smiles, switches off the tablet screen and steps into the pool of lava. "Pomba Gira will be with you shortly," she says as she sinks beneath the surface.

"Wow. Think that could work for us?" Gorog asks, shifting the weight of the knight around on his shoulder. He leans forward over the bubbling red rock and immediately snaps his head back. "Nope, way too hot," he says, his cheeks as purple as plums.

"How long are we going to have to wait here for this Pomba Gira person?" Carole asks.

"I hope you're not expecting a person," I say. I've never seen an Otherworld Elemental before, but there are entire forums devoted to the ones from the original MMO. "The realms here are all ruled by Elementals. They're like demigods. So when this one shows up, it's probably a good idea to be on your best behavior."

"As long as she lets us out of here, I'll be sweet as pie," Carole says just as the lava begins to swirl and a column of flames rises from its center. Gradually the fire takes a female form and what can only be Pomba Gira appears before us. The Elemental's skin is the glistening black of charcoal, the hair that cascades over her shoulders is silvery smoke and the dress wrapped around her is ablaze.

"Whoa," says Gorog, and I have to agree. She may be burned to a crisp, but she's gorgeous. So *this* is the goat man's mother? He said he was the son of the Elemental of Imra. I'm gonna keep my mouth shut, but this lady could do *much* better than a goat.

"You wish to leave Imra?" Pomba Gira speaks softly, like a whisper you've barely heard. I would have expected an Elemental to have a huskier voice, but I have to admit there's more power in this. It makes you draw closer, as if she's the only one who knows what you need.

The ogre and I are struck dumb, and Carole rolls her eyes at us. "Yes, ma'am," she says. "It's been real fun and all. But as much as I'd love to do a bunch of drugs and take part in an orgy, I really need to get back to the real world. These guys and I never meant to stop in Imra. We were just trying to escape from some bugs. We're on our way to the Otherworld exit."

"The exit?" Pomba Gira repeats. She doesn't seem familiar with the word. "Very well. You and the ogre are free to leave. But this one." She crackles as she glides over to Arkan, who's still dangling over Gorog's shoulder. "Set him down. This one wants to stay in Imra with me."

"Are you kidding? He can't even stand up," Gorog says. But when he puts the knight down, Arkan remains upright on his own. Then his eyes open and fix on the Elemental's face.

"This is where you belong," she says.

"I do?" he asks woozily.

"Yes, I can see it," she whispers. Smoky tendrils of her hair sweep across Arkan's cheek like a caress.

"Naw, that's just the booze," I explain. "He'll sober up in a minute. He wants to find the exit more than anyone."

"No," the Elemental informs me. "That's not what the red knight is searching for. He knows that the thing he wants more than anything else is gone. I'm the only one who can return it to him."

The lava has begun to swirl again. And once again, the molten rock takes a female form. Only this time it cools into milky white flesh. Arkan seems to sober up in an instant. The noise that issues from his throat sounds like he's being strangled, and I see the knight drop to his knees at the feet of our host's latest creation.

"Oh, God, Emma. I'm so sorry," he sobs, wrapping his arms around the young woman's legs. She's the kind of plump, pretty blonde you'd see on a hot-chocolate box. And I suddenly realize I *have* seen her before.

It was a big story in northern New Jersey. A couple on their way home from a football game at Rutgers got into a fender bender. The man at the wheel of the first car jumped out and coldcocked the other driver, at which point the injured guy pulled a gun and began firing blindly. One of the bullets grazed the attacker's spinal cord. Another hit his girlfriend, who was waiting for him in the passenger seat of their car. She died on the spot.

The incident was all over the news, and there were plenty of pictures of the girl who had died—and her boyfriend, an avid supporter of the Rutgers Scarlet Knights who'd gone to the game dressed up like his team's mascot.

"I heard the ambulance guys talking before I went under. They said you were gone. When I woke up here in purgatory, I looked everywhere for you."

The girl opens her eyes and smiles down at Arkan and wordlessly smooths his hair with her hand.

Carole's practically blubbering, and Gorog looks a bit weepy too. I'm almost getting a little verklempt myself. At first I find it heartbreaking to see the two reunited in Otherworld, but then I realize the thing standing in front of us isn't the dead girl. It's just a digital doll that looks like Arkan's lost girlfriend. Maybe that's enough for him. He clearly thinks he's been given another chance, and I'm not going to tell him he's wrong. If it's that easy to fool him, he deserves to be stuck here.

"Now for you," Pomba Gira says, turning her attention to me. "I know what you want, too."

"Campaign finance reform?" I say to break the mood. "Consistent sizing in clothing store chains?" The question draws a blank look from the Elemental. "Okay, okay. Too much to ask. Then how about a glass of ice water?" I say. It's not really a joke. It's goddamn hot down here and I'm dying of thirst.

The lava has produced another female, just like I knew it would. As it cools, the skin turns tan, but the hair burns red. I was expecting her to appear, but the sight of Kat still takes my breath away. She looks exactly as I remember her, which makes perfect sense since the disk must have pulled this image out of my memory. The sight drags me in like a tractor beam.

"Who is that?" Gorog whispers to me. "She's amazing."

"It's the girl I came here to find," I tell him.

"No, it's not," Carole hisses in my ear. "It's one of those NPC things. You know that, right?"

I do. But against all my instincts, I take a step forward. "Hi," I say.

"Hi, Simon," she replies. She sounds like Kat. She smells like her. I take her hand, and she feels like Kat too. My heart is pounding, and I'm starting to think I may have been a little too quick to judge Arkan. "We can stay here," she says. "We don't have to be apart anymore. Isn't that what you want?"

Of course it is. More than anything, but that's not what matters.

"What do you want, Kat?" I ask.

"Just to be with you," she says and my heart breaks a little.

Those are exactly the words I've always wanted to hear, but they're not words the real Kat would say. She'd tell me there was something bigger at stake. Somewhere in Otherworld, she's on her own mission. I'm not sure what it is, but I know she would never call it off. Even for me.

And that's the true test, I realize—the one that reveals who's human and who's not. Real people rarely do what you wish they would do. But that's what makes an unexpected kiss behind a high school dumpster so damn magical.

"Thanks, but I'm gonna pass," I tell Pomba Gira.

CALL OF NATURE

The only route out of Imra is an underground passage that's been chiseled out of the black volcanic rock. Gorog leads the way with his fire, which was an excellent choice of tool. It's seeing a lot more action than my dagger or Carole's robe. But even with light to guide us, we're unable to travel fast enough for my taste. When Pomba Gira conjured the copy of Kat, it was like a mirage taunting a man who's gotten lost in a desert. My desperation is physical. Every breath I exhale is thick with longing. My hunger oozes from every pore.

"Hey, Simon. You're not going to believe this." Carole interrupts my thoughts as soon as we've put Imra behind us. I give her less than my full attention. "Back in the real world, I saw Arkan and his girlfriend on the news. I should have recognized his costume straightaway. He was wearing it the night of his accident. I'm pretty sure his full name was Jeremy Arkan. He and his girlfriend lived two towns over from me."

I stop. I'm listening now. "You live in New Jersey?" I ask. "I thought you were Southern. You've got an accent."

"I grew up in Memphis but I live in Morristown these days," Carole says.

I start walking again. "Gorog," I call out, picking up the pace as I hurry toward the ogre. "Where are you from?"

"In real life?" he asks. "Elizabeth, New Jersey."

I know six people who've been given one of the Company's special disks. All six of those people hail from the small state of New Jersey. At least three—Kat, Brian and West—were diagnosed with an extremely rare condition. In my head I hear Busara asking the question I was unable to answer. *What are the odds?*

I'm sifting through all the random clues I've collected when I run straight into Gorog's hairy back. There's a colorful curse on my tongue, but it stays there when I see why he's come to a sudden stop. There's a bend in the tunnel ahead, and whatever is just beyond it is issuing an eerie blue light.

"What the hell is that?" Carole whispers.

Finally, a question I can answer. "I think it's my guide." I step around Gorog and lead the way forward.

"We get to meet him!" Gorog's far more excited than he should be. "Oh, man, this is gonna be good."

Sure enough, the Clay Man is waiting for us around the bend. He's leaning back against one of the rough rock walls with his eyes closed. The amulet on his chest is glowing. His eyes open as we approach.

"You have companions," the Clay Man says, making it perfectly clear that he doesn't approve. If I ever gave a shit, I no longer do.

"Their names are Gorog and Carole," I say. "I'm taking them

with me to find the exit." Neither of them steps forward. Gorog's excitement has been replaced with wariness, and they both look like they're on the verge of backing away.

"Don't worry, he's not going to hurt you," I promise them, though I don't know that for certain.

"You cannot let these avatars slow you down," the Clay Man says.

"Slow me down?" I'm getting kind of pissed now. "I wouldn't have made it out of Imra without them. By the way, where the hell were you? I could have used a little guidance back there. Isn't that supposed to be your job?"

"As I told you, I travel in Otherworld's liminal spaces," the Clay Man says. "The wastelands, tunnels and border areas are all open to me, but it is too dangerous for me to enter any of Other-world's realms."

"I don't understand," Gorog says. "What are you? Are you one of us or one of them?"

"There is no need for you to understand," says the Clay Man dismissively.

"Are you one of the Children Simon told us about?" Carole asks.

"Certainly *not*," says the Clay Man snippily.

"Yeah, speaking of the Children," I jump in. "We just had the pleasure of meeting the goat man's mother. Not to be too graphic, but how the hell is that possible?"

Apparently the Clay Man doesn't share my dirty mind. "How many times do I have to explain that this world does not oper-ate in the way that yours does?" he lectures me. "Digital DNA can be combined in many different ways. Intercourse is not the only option."

"You sure seem to know a lot about this stuff," Carole says. "I'm starting to think you might not be one of those NPC thingies."

"I am Simon's guide, nothing more, nothing less. My goal is to keep him alive until his mission has been completed."

"Okay, fine. But why does Simon get the special attention?" asks Carole. "I mean, he's a great guy and all, but the rest of us are trying to get out of here alive too."

Gorog nudges Carole. "I *told* you," he says. "Simon gets the special attention because he's the One."

"There is no *One*," the Clay Man informs him.

"Yeah, yeah, I know," Gorog replies, undaunted. "Simon's not ready for the truth yet. You don't want to freak him out."

The Clay Man chooses to ignore the ogre. "Simon, I've come to tell you that it's time to make camp."

"Here?" Carole scoffs. "In a tunnel?"

The Clay Man acts as though he didn't hear and continues to speak only to me. "The passage to the next realm is long. You do not have the energy to reach it. You must leave Otherworld temporarily in order to refuel."

"I'm fine," I lie. I'm hardly in tip-top shape. "I ate a shitload of buffalo back in Imra. I think I can make it a bit farther. Besides, I thought I was stuck here until I found the exit. How am I supposed to leave?"

"I will help you," the Clay Man tells me. "I have no choice. You have been in Otherworld for almost forty-eight hours. The detour to Imra was unexpected. You were never meant to be here this long. Your avatar may be healthy, but your real-world body has not received any liquids or nourishment for two days. If you neglect it much longer, your quest will be over before it's truly begun."

I don't care if I've been here for two *weeks*. I'm not leaving Kat behind in this place just to eat a ham sandwich. "I'm telling you, I can keep going."

"I'm afraid I must stop you," says the Clay Man. "As I said, I do not have a choice." He grasps his amulet and disappears. But I go nowhere.

There's nothing to do but keep on walking, so I start back down the path. Suddenly I'm blinded by a searing white light, and it feels like a piece of flesh is being ripped off the back of my skull. The tunnel is gone and my eyes are desperately trying to focus on a different world. I'm blind and dizzy and completely disoriented.

"Simon!" a female screeches. The voice is extremely familiar, but I can't place it. "What in the hell is going on? How long have you been here? What did you do to your hair? And oh my God, Simon, is that what I think it is? Oh my God, I can *smell* it. Get up this instant! Your mattress is totally ruined!"

I'm thrashing around like a fish at the end of a line. Everything around me is wet, and I realize I've pissed all over myself. And not just once. The world is coming into focus. I can see my mother standing over my bed, holding my disk in her hand. Her hair is a mess and she's still in her robe. I catch a glimpse of Louis, our gardener, outside the bedroom door. We lock eyes for a moment before he hurries away.

"What are you doing in here?" I demand. "I thought you were in London." My throat is so dry I can barely speak. But I manage to snatch my disk from her hand.

"We got back last night! Then I wake up to a text that says

you're in your room and you're going to die unless I take some device off the back of your head. And I came to your room and couldn't get in, so I had Louis force the door open. What the hell is that thing you were wearing, Simon?"

"You got a *text*?" I ask. "From who? Who sent it?" It's proof that someone IRL is controlling the Clay Man. Whoever it is knows about the disk, obviously. Is it the same person who sent it to me? Does that mean the Clay Man is Martin? Marlow? Or maybe even Todd?

"I don't know who sent it!" she exclaims, shoving her phone at me. I take it and look down at the text. It says exactly what she told me it said. I don't recognize the phone number.

"Get out of my room," I tell her.

"Not until you tell me what's going on, Simon! Are you on drugs? Do I need to call an ambulance?"

"Get out *now*," I repeat, more loudly. I pull myself off the bed. My legs are unsteady and I stumble toward her.

"I'm waking your father up," she says, rushing out of the room, leaving her phone in my hand.

The last thing I need is a visit from my father and his favorite nine iron. I grab a duffel bag from my closet and stuff it with some clothes, my mom's phone, two auxiliary batteries and my gear from the Company. I throw on a T-shirt, but there's no time to change the jeans I've got on. I'm still wet, smelly and weak when I drop out of my window and onto the lawn.

My father always told me I'd never amount to anything in life if I didn't stop acting impulsively and start thinking things through.

It sucks to admit it, but even complete assholes are right sometimes. I should have had a plan before I hopped out of the window. I have no money, no credit cards. According to my mom's phone, it's just after seven a.m. on Saturday morning. Nothing in Brockenhurst is going to be open. My head looks like it was shaved with a blunt machete and my jeans have been marinating in piss for the past two days. I pause on a neighbor's lawn to guzzle down water from a garden hose. I'm so hungry that I briefly consider breaking into the house to scavenge for food. But I can't run the risk of getting arrested right now. I have to get back to Otherworld as quickly as possible.

The house's garage door comes to life and begins to rise. I scuttle behind a bush and watch a Mercedes pull out into the drive. Inside it is a middle-aged couple wearing matching pink polo shirts and gingham sun visors. I suddenly know exactly where I need to go.

When I show up at the Brockenhurst Country Club, the front desk attendant appears visibly confused to see me coming up the stairs. I don't have my wallet with me, but it's not like I'll need ID. The kishka works better than any plastic card could. The closer I come, the more difficulty the attendant seems to have closing his mouth. His eyes keep traveling from my haircut to my sopping-wet crotch.

"Morning!" I say, employing my special smile.

His nostrils twitch ever so slightly when my stench hits his nose. "Good morning, Mr. Eaton."

"When's my dad's tee time?" I ask him. My father plays golf at the club every weekend.

"Ten o'clock, sir," the attendant informs me.

I'll need to be long gone by then. "Excellent," I say. "He asked me to let you know he'd like to buy everyone on the course a cocktail when he hits the ninth hole."

"Very well, sir," says the attendant. "And what about you? Is there anything I can help you with today?"

"You can get me a table in the restaurant for breakfast," I say. "But I gotta wash all this urine off before I sit down to eat. It's a terrible problem, you know. But what can I do? The condition runs in the family. The old man pisses himself about three times a day." The attendant's jaw drops and I give him a wink. "What do you say we keep that entre nous, sport?"

"Of course, sir," he says. But I can see he's already feeling for the phone in his pocket.

When I reach the locker room, my clothes come off and go straight into the trash. The shower feels like a gift from God. I'd stay in forever if the bacon in the restaurant weren't calling my name. Out of the shower, I use clippers to even up my new hairdo. Without hair on my head the kishka looks twice as big. I lean over the counter to examine it. When I stand back up, there's another set of eyes staring back at me in the mirror.

The first thing I notice is that the guy's wearing pink shorts, which immediately brands him as a total douchebag. The second thing I notice are the bandages on his hands.

"Marlow," I say. When I turn around, I expect him to bolt. I can tell he'd like to, but he doesn't. "Looks like somebody got a makeover."

He cleans up nicely, my little buddy Marlow. All that scraggly hair is gone—along with the black jeans and hoodie. His clothes finally fit that pretty J.Crew face. A face that, as I watch, is gradually losing all its color. It occurs to me that I've never seen him at the country club before. Now that I do, I can tell Busara was right. He *is* a rich kid. This is obviously his natural element.

"I'm sorry," he says.

I can't figure out if it's an admission of guilt or an expression of sympathy. I'll probably beat the crap out of him either way. "Oh, yeah?" I snarl, and step toward him. "Why don't we find out how sorry you really are?"

He puts a hand up as if to ward me off. "I'm serious. I really liked her," he says. "I never thought . . ."

The water shuts off in a nearby shower. Marlow glances nervously toward the stall. He's practically shaking with terror.

"I have to go. I just wanted to know if you got it," he whispers as a man emerges.

"Got *what*?" I demand. For a fleeting moment I wonder if he's talking about the disk. But there's no way someone this pathetic could get his hands on a Company prototype.

Marlow is staring at the man who's joined us. He's a hairy little hobbit with the kind of glasses that tells me he spends at least ten hours a day staring at spreadsheets. Yet Marlow seems completely unnerved by the guy. "We'll talk later," he tells me, turning tail and heading for the locker room door.

"No," I yell, rushing after him. "Now!"

"Sir! Sir!" A muscular arm clotheslines me just as Marlow disappears behind the closing door.

"What?" I bark, annoyed that Marlow's been allowed to make his escape.

"I'm sorry, sir, but I can't let you leave the locker room like that." I glance down and realize I'm dressed in nothing but a towel.

By the time I'm wearing clothes again, Marlow's long gone, and I'm too hungry to search for him. I need to eat. I head straight for the restaurant, claim a seat and order double portions of pancakes, bacon and sausage. Whenever I catch one of the other diners staring at me, I give them a saucy wink and their eyes flick away. I can't remember ever being this hungry, and I have to distract myself to keep from snatching the food off everyone's plates. So I force myself to concentrate on what just happened. I run down the list of all the things that Marlow might be sorry for. It's long enough to be meaningless. *Maybe he's sorry for trying to murder Kat. Or maybe he's just sorry for driving her to the party. Or maybe he's sorry for pretending to be a black-clad stoner when he was a pink chino shorts guy at heart.* It's impossible to say. But Marlow's apology is another clue to throw on top of the growing heap of evidence that something seriously weird is going down. And what did he mean when he'd asked if I'd gotten it? *Gotten what?* Could he have been talking about the disk?

I could spend the whole morning wondering, but right now I have bigger fish to fry. I pull my mom's smartphone out of my jeans. I'm pleasantly surprised to see she hasn't cut off the service yet. I open the Web browser and type in *Jeremy Arkan*. A picture of the Otherworld knight appears on the screen. He and his girlfriend lived in a town about twenty miles from Brockenhurst. I scroll through the accompanying article and stop when my eyes land on a set of familiar words. *Locked-in syndrome.* Jeremy Arkan was diagnosed with locked-in syndrome, just like Kat, Brian and West.

I pull up a new screen and do a combined search for *locked-in syndrome and New Jersey.* The list of results goes on for four pages. I count at least twenty-five individuals who've been diagnosed with the condition. All in the last three months. Busara said locked-in syndrome was rare, but when I Google it, I'm still surprised to discover *how* rare. And yet in less than a year dozens of new cases have been reported in northern New Jersey.

I scan an article about a fifteen-year-old boy from Hoboken named Darius who was diagnosed with locked-in syndrome after an accident. At the end of the story it mentions that he's now a patient at a long-term-care facility in New Jersey that specializes in caring for people afflicted with the condition. But it doesn't give the facility's name or an address. I go back and add the words *long-term care* to my search query. Ten articles, each focusing on other patients, mention a similar facility, but none of the articles name it.

I click on my browsing history and gaze in horror at the list of Web pages. Dozens of people in northern New Jersey have been diagnosed with a rare condition that makes them perfect candidates for the Company's disk. It looks like many—if not all—of them have been moved to the same facility. And it seems highly unusual that not a single reporter was able to uncover the name of the place.

When I look up from my phone, the world around me has changed. Before I typed in Arkan's name, I was sitting in the restaurant of the country club I've been visiting since I was eight years old, surrounded by a familiar crowd of overprivileged but harmless assholes. Now it feels like everyone is a potential suspect—a player in a game I don't understand. I have no idea how many people are in on the conspiracy I may have just uncovered, but there's no doubt something big is going on. Patients in one little part of the world are being diagnosed with a rare brain condition. And as hard as it is to believe, it looks like the Company might be involved somehow. Locked-in syndrome is suddenly all the rage—and they just *happen* to show up with a ready-made therapy? But the idea's still nuts. It would mean Milo Yolkin was involved, and that's almost impossible to swallow. The gamer geek genius I've seen on television is about the last person on earth who'd have a hand in something as sinister as this.

If there are answers to be found, they're at the facility where the patients have been taken. My breakfast arrives as I hastily type out a message to Elvis, the hacker who owes me his freedom. I attach links to five of the articles I found and ask him to hack into a few hospital servers and find the name and address of the long-term-care facility that the locked-in syndrome patients were sent to. Then I dig in to my food. My fingers and face are covered in bacon grease when a response text arrives from Elvis.

> Back to you in a few hours. You played Otherworld yet?
> I hear the AI is insane. Least you can't say I didn't warn
> you. The revolution is nigh.

Holy shit. I think he might be right.
I've lost my appetite, but I keep mindlessly shoveling food

into my mouth. I need enough energy to stay in Otherworld long enough to finish my mission. While Elvis hunts down the facility's real-world address, I need to find Kat in Otherworld. The collapse at the factory definitely wasn't an accident. Could the Company have been responsible for that, too? Are they doing more than kidnapping the minds of people who are already injured? Could they be *arranging* those injuries as well? If so, there's a chance that Kat has the information that can blow the top off an enormous conspiracy, close the facility—and help me set her free.

I'm swallowing a glob of pancake and sausage when four women in white glide into the restaurant like the chicest of ghosts. One of them is Dr. Ito. The lump of food gets stuck in my throat, and I chug a glass of OJ to wash it down. My first instinct is to duck under the table, but I keep my wits about me, and once I'm no longer in danger of choking to death, I raise the menu to hide my nose and do my best to remain perfectly still. Her eyes pass over me three or four times without landing. I credit my new haircut.

I wait until the doctor's deep in conversation with her companions before I attempt to rise from my seat. Unfortunately, the waiter arrives to fill my water glass just as I slip out of my chair. We do a little dance trying to get out of each other's way. Then water from the waiter's pitcher drips onto a girl eating nearby, and she shrieks as the icy liquid trickles down the back of her neck. There's no expression on Dr. Ito's face when she looks up and her gaze settles on me. Anyone watching us both would assume she's never met me before. But her eyes travel from my nose to my hair and I see an epiphany register on her face. She knows why my hair's gone. As Dr. Ito turns back to her friend, she casually removes her phone from the pocket of her tennis skirt. She glances at the screen, presses a button and places a call.

I'm outside the country club in five seconds flat. I take one look at the long drive that leads from the club to the street and instantly realize there's no way I'll make it anywhere on foot. As I see it, I have one option—and no time for moral quandaries. Next to the club entrance is a bike rack, and lucky for me, no one locks their bikes at the club. Why would they need to? Rich people don't steal—right?

I'm pedaling as fast as I can, my duffel bag bouncing against my back as I review my options. I need to find somewhere private and safe to reenter Otherworld—and I need to do it fast. Home is out of the question. So, obviously, is Kat's house. I don't have any other friends, and without my wallet, paying for a hotel is impossible. As I run through my very short list of options, there's only one that meets all the criteria. And it really sucks. I turn right at the next light and head for Elmer's. I'd rather not return to the scene of the crime, but I figure it's one of the last places anyone's likely to look for me.

I haven't been back since the collapse, and it's shocking to see the place in the light of day. The shell of the building is still standing, but there's a mountain of debris piled outside. The authorities must have removed it all from the basement during their search for victims. I pull up alongside the mound and carefully cover the bike with boards. When I've finished, there's barely a trace of it.

The building itself is wrapped with yellow tape printed with the words DANGER: DO NOT ENTER. I try my best not to rip it or pull it loose as I squeeze between the lengths and climb in through a broken window on what's left of the ground floor. I edge around to the stairs, which are still intact, and climb up to the third floor. It looks different in the light of day, but I have no trouble finding the hole I was standing by the night of the collapse. From its edge I can see straight down into the basement where four people died.

The floor around me is covered in a layer of dust, and there's a mandala of footprints in the center of the room. Leaving a fresh set of tracks across the floor, I look for the alcove where I hid the last time I was here. I find it and see that the sleeping bag is still here, bunched up in a corner. The dust on top of it is undisturbed, and it looks like a pile of garbage. It's an unexpected bonus.

When I pick up the sleeping bag, I realize it's kid-size. I shake it off outside the nearest window, over a patch of weeds behind the building. As the dust blows away, a face emerges. It's Yoda. He's standing in front of a tree looking smug, both hands on his cane. I recognize the image in a heartbeat. Years ago, Kat's mother bought a bag just like this one at a thrift store in town and gave it to us for our fort. On cold days, Kat and I used to huddle beneath it for warmth.

I'm not the kind of guy who usually believes in signs, but I'm pretty sure this means something. Why was it here the night of the party? Could it actually be the same bag from the fort? I reach inside and run my hand over the lining. Kat's bag had a tiny rip midway down that formed a pocket. We used to leave notes for each other there. My heart skips a beat when I feel a square of paper tucked inside. So the sleeping bag *is* hers, but why is it here at the factory? I pinch the paper between my fingers and pull it out. As I unfold it, I realize it isn't a note. It's a hastily taken photograph of an architectural blueprint, and it's been printed out on regular copy paper. The image is blurry and off-center, but I can make out what looks like a wall covered with dozens of hexagonal windows. It almost looks like a wasps' nest. I squint and hold the page closer, but I can't make out the fine print. Why did Kat have it? And why did she hide it in the sleeping bag? When I find her in Otherworld, I'll ask her what it means.

I tuck the page into my duffel, retrieve my Otherworld gear and spread the sleeping bag out on the floor. Only when I lie down does it occur to me that I'm about to take the biggest risk of my life. I'll be leaving my body behind in an abandoned factory where it will be utterly defenseless. I could get eaten by raccoons and never know the difference. And no one knows where I am. If something goes wrong in Otherworld, there'll be no one around to remove the disk.

All the more reason to act fast and get to the exit, I decide. I strap on the visor, attach the disk to the back of my skull, and I'm gone.

THE CLIFF DWELLERS

My avatar is standing exactly where I left it, inside the tunnel that runs through the bowels of Otherworld. Carole and Gorog are now asleep beside me on the floor. The Clay Man is nearby, watching over us all. Gorog's fire is out, and the only light in the tunnel radiates from the Clay Man's blue eyes and the stone around his neck. He's got a lot of explaining to do.

"Did you eat?" the Clay Man asks me.

"Yes," I tell him. "I had a lovely and nutritious breakfast at the Brockenhurst Country Club. Did you send that text to my mother? She was really pissed off about the state of my mattress."

He doesn't answer my question. "Is your body safe?"

"Who the hell are you in real life?" I demand. "Are you Martin? Todd? Marlow? Busara? Elvis? Priscilla? Lisa Marie?" I could keep on naming potential suspects, but I doubt I'll ever get a reaction.

"I am your guide," the Clay Man says. Again.

"But why are you helping me? What's in it for you?" This guy is driving me crazy. I can't get a straight answer out of him.

"Is your body safe?" he asks again.

I shrug. "For now," I say. "I didn't exactly have a whole lot of options when it came time to stash it."

"Where is it?" he asks.

"I'm gonna need a few answers from you before you're allowed to ask me anything else. Let's start again. Who are you?"

"This line of questioning is futile," says the Clay Man. "I am not going to answer. Please move on."

"Are you associated with the Company?" I demand.

The Clay Man hesitates before he answers the question. "Yes. I am associated," he finally says.

Shit. Now we're getting somewhere. "Do you know about the facility?" I ask eagerly. "The place where all the people with locked-in syndrome are being sent?"

"I have never seen the facility with my own eyes," says the Clay Man. "But I am aware of its existence."

"What's going on there?" I ask. "Is it owned by the Company?"

"As I mentioned, I have never seen the facility," the Clay Man repeats. "Would *you* care to see it?"

Now there's a question I wasn't expecting. "You're saying you can get me in?"

"Perhaps," says the Clay Man. "I myself am unable to visit. I have certain unfortunate physical limitations. However, I may be able to help you get inside. If you'd like me to make the arrangements, you must tell me where your body is."

"Wait—you want me to leave Otherworld and go to the facility? What about my mission?"

"I think a visit to the facility will show you what's at stake—and inspire you to focus on your *original* mission. You'll understand why you can't afford to get distracted by the unfortunate souls you encounter here in Otherworld. If you try to help all of them, you will end up helping no one," he says, looking from Carole to Gorog. "Now. Tell me. Where is your body?"

It's going to take a little while for me to be comfortable handing over that information to some anonymous dude I met in virtual reality. "Come ask me again when you've got all the details worked out."

"It's good to be cautious," he tells me. "But if you want to see the facility, you will have to trust me."

"Fine, my body's at Elmer's."

He seems perfectly content with my answer. Which means he must know the factory's nickname. "Who are you?" I ask again. "What do you want from me?"

"Wake the others," he orders. "The time has come to move on."

I give up. "Where exactly are we going?" I ask with a sigh.

"The Elemental of Imra has set you on the path to Mammon," the Clay Man says. "You must travel through it before you can continue to the ice fields and the glacier. Guard your life carefully. Mammon is said to be one of the more dangerous realms."

"So what's going to try to kill us in Mammon?" I ask. "Care to give us a heads-up?"

"I don't know," the Clay Man says. "I have never been there."

"Great," I mutter. I'm getting really sick of surprises.

"Just remember why you're in Otherworld," the Clay Man tells me. "You're here to save someone you love. Keep that in mind at all times. The knowledge will protect you." Then he turns and walks away, the light of his amulet fading with each step until I'm left in utter darkness.

"Mammon?" It's Carole's voice. I guess she was just pretending to sleep.

Gorog's torch lights up. He's been awake too. "Like the guy from *Spawn*?" the ogre adds.

Despite everything, I can't help but grin. "I was thinking of the Mammon in *StarCraft*," I say. "You ever play that?"

"Too old-school for me," Gorog says.

"Mammon is from the Bible, you doofuses," Carole says, sounding a lot like my second-grade teacher. "It means money or wealth—the kind that corrupts you."

The ogre and I laugh our asses off, and it feels good.

"This is Otherworld, Church Lady," Gorog informs Carole. "There's nothing in this from the *Bible*."

The joking ended somewhere during our first hour of walking through darkness. At least three more have passed since then. Every stretch of tunnel looks exactly the same. If you told me we were walking in place on some kind of treadmill, I wouldn't be shocked. Gorog is a few paces ahead, while Carole strolls along beside me.

"So who is she?" Carole asks out of the blue. It takes me a moment to realize she's speaking to me.

"Who is who?" I ask.

"Give me a break. You know who I'm talking about. Your friend. The girl you're here to find. She must be pretty amazing if you're willing to risk your life for her like this."

"She is," I say. I'm not sure I'm ready to open up to a woman I've only just met—and who could easily be a fat, hairy dude in real life.

"I saw what you did back there in Imra," Carole says. "You could have had the perfect girl—someone made just for you—and you turned her down."

"I don't want someone who was made for me. I want a real person to choose me."

Carole is quiet. "The person who does will be very lucky," she finally says.

How would she know? She met me less than two days ago. I'm about to say just that when Gorog begins running. Then I realize why: there's sunlight up ahead. I start to sprint too, praying the light won't vanish before I can catch up with it. The tunnel widens as I run. Finally the ceiling disappears and I stop. I'm standing in a lush garden at the opening of an enormous canyon. Just ahead of us, red rock walls rise thousands of feet above our heads. They're riddled with pockmarks and what appear to be hundreds of small caves.

Between the canyon walls lies a grassy open space. Here in the garden, tree branches droop with purple, red and golden globes, and the ground is strewn with fallen fruit. A troop of monkeys lounges in the patches of shade beneath the trees. They're watching us intently. Given the homicidal nature of Otherworld's beasts, I should probably keep an eye on them. But right now they can't compete for my attention.

Ahead of us, at the end of the canyon, lies the entrance to a glittering city. That's no exaggeration. The place is actually *glittering*, as though its walls are spackled with precious stones. At its center, a golden temple rises far above the other structures. I see no sign of humans anywhere. The only sound I hear is that of the monkeys munching on fruit.

As far as I can tell, the only way to reach the city is to walk through a narrow meadow that stretches for at least half a mile between the canyon's two walls.

"I'm not going out there. It's a trap," Carole says. I'm inclined to believe her. Finally we're somewhere that actually resembles a video game environment. In the original Otherworld, everything was against you. I prefer that to Imra. As brutal as it sounds, at least you knew where you stood.

"Definitely a trap," Gorog agrees. "And those monkeys don't look very friendly, either."

My eyes cut back to the beasts on the ground. They're fat from the fruit, but they're not all that large. If they stood on their hind legs, they'd probably reach waist high. The fur on their bodies is dark brown, and puffs of golden hair form manes around faces with yellow eyes that appear eerily intelligent. I see no evidence of sharp teeth or claws. But there are several dozen of them—enough to hold us down and gnaw us to death if they like.

I suspect the monkeys understood Gorog's words. One of the tribe stands upright and approaches us, his front paws closed into fists. He's much larger than his companions, with a face that's disturbingly humanlike. I draw my dagger and he smiles. His teeth are those of a plant eater—I'm relieved there's not an incisor in sight.

The creature stops a few feet away and looks at us each in turn.

Then he seems to settle on me. He walks forward with his hands extended. He opens his fingers to reveal fistfuls of diamonds.

"Take them," he says, and I feel myself recoil instinctively. He's not a Beast like the others. He's one of the Children.

"No thank you, I don't accept gifts from Children," I tell him. "And my mom says I shouldn't talk to strangers." A shadow passes over the Child's face. He wasn't expecting me to know about his kind. I watch him struggle to keep his smile in place.

"I only want to help you," the Child insists. "You will need currency in the lands to come. There are more of these in the city. You may gather as many as you like before you leave."

"Oh, yeah? And what would I buy with them?" I ask. "Will we pass through a gift shop as we exit the realm?"

"The diamonds will purchase weapons, land, companionship," says the Child. "Whatever you desire. Now that you've left Imra, such things won't be free."

"Yeah, thanks but no thanks," I tell him again. I know a setup when I see one. And I've also watched enough YouTube clips to know better than to trust a monkey.

"Hell, I'll take them if you don't want them," Gorog says gamely, reaching out a hand.

"Don't!" I try to warn him, but he's already accepted the jewels. They cascade like a twinkling waterfall from the Child's fist into the ogre's waiting palm.

There's suddenly a glimmer in Gorog's eye. Something's come over him—he seems strangely intoxicated. Then I remember his rant about Otherworld gear. He couldn't even imagine raising three thousand dollars. Now he's got a handful of diamonds worth a hundred times that amount. "You say there are more of these in Mammon?" Gorog asks the Child.

"More than you can imagine," the creature tells him. "Enough to make you the richest guest in Otherworld."

"Sounds good to me," says Gorog. "Thanks for the tip."

"What are you doing?" I demand as he pushes past me, heading for the valley that lies between us and Mammon. "Have you lost your mind? He's sending you into a trap!"

"So?" Gorog says without looking back. "It's just a game. What's it going to hurt to find out?"

I catch Carole's eye. Gorog doesn't know that Otherworld might not be a game for us. We should have told him.

"Hey, Gorog, wait! There's something you should know!" Carole yells after him, grabbing at his arm. He yanks it away from her so hard that she falls to the ground.

I help Carole up, and we watch as the ogre marches into the canyon. He's barely a dozen yards inside when something shoots out from one of the caves in the canyon wall. Gorog yelps loudly as an arrow lodges in his shoulder. Before there's time to react, several more follow in quick succession, hitting Gorog in the chest and neck. The archer's too far away for the wounds to prove fatal, but they're not paper cuts, either. Confused and disoriented, Gorog spins in circles, desperately trying to pull out the arrows he can't quite reach.

A hunched, emaciated creature appears at the mouth of the cave. It's covered head to toe in red ocher, which helps it blend into the rocks. The thing's human in shape, which only makes it more terrifying.

Carole gasps. "Oh my God, what is that?"

"Don't you recognize your own kind?" The Child has joined us at the edge of the canyon. "He's a guest—just like you."

The cliff dweller throws a rough ladder down the side of the rock wall and quickly descends, his bow and arrows strapped to his back. As he climbs, other ocher-covered men and women emerge from caves farther down the canyon. They launch arrows and spears at the avatar, but they're too far away to hit their mark.

"They're *all* guests like you," sneers the Child.

Guests. The most dangerous beings in Otherworld. I start to sprint in Gorog's direction. If the cliff dweller gets close enough to the ogre, he could slaughter him. He and I are an equal distance from Gorog when I pull my dagger out and send it sailing through the air. I'd rather not kill the guy, so I don't aim for the heart. The dagger hits him in the upper right shoulder, and his arm flops down to his side. He won't be shooting any more arrows today. But despite his injury, the avatar keeps charging forward. If he had a disk, he'd show some sign of pain. This guy's a headset player. The closer he gets to Gorog, the more worried I am. The avatar seems crazed. Maybe he's sane in the real world, but here in Otherworld, he's gone completely berserk.

We reach Gorog at the same time. The cave dweller hasn't bothered to pull my dagger from his arm, so I do it myself. He barely seems to notice I'm here. He just pushes past me and goes straight for Gorog, knocking him down and pouncing on his chest like a rabid dog. He's rifling through the ogre's minimal clothing in a frenzied search for valuables. He finds the diamonds, gathers them into his fist and lunges at Gorog's jugular with his teeth bared. I catch the cliff dweller in a choke hold before he can puncture the skin. He flails about, kicking and punching before he finally loses consciousness, sinks to his knees and flops face-first over Gorog's chest.

Exhausted from the ordeal, I cautiously examine the thin, ropy carcass that's lying on top of the ogre. This must be what happens when you don't take proper care of your avatar. It looks horribly neglected, like it's been locked away in a prison camp or shipwrecked on a desert island. I roll it off Gorog's body, and the diamonds the cliff dweller stole from the ogre pour out of its hands onto the grass next to the avatar's bow and quiver full of arrows.

Gorog sighs once the weight is off his torso.

"You okay?" I ask the ogre.

"I've been better," he tells me as he sits up and pulls an arrow out of a bicep. I can tell he's in serious pain. The arrows must have inflicted real damage.

"At least the guy was nice enough to leave you a souvenir," I joke lamely, handing the cliff dweller's bow and arrows to the ogre.

The diamonds on the ground sparkle alluringly, but neither of us dares to touch them. I'm going to kill that Child when we get back to the garden. The gems were obviously cursed or enchanted.

I hear the monkey troop screeching in the distance, and I'm suddenly seized by panic.

"You need to get up," I tell Gorog. "We've got to get back to Carole." I should never have left her alone with one of the Children and a band of homicidal monkeys.

Gorog still has a half dozen arrows sticking out of him, but he doesn't question the order. He climbs to his feet and we hustle back to our starting point, but I don't see Carole anywhere.

The monkeys are all gathered around one of the trees, screeching loudly. I look up to see two of the beasts climbing, branch by branch, toward the top of the tree, crude stone knives clenched in their teeth. I hurry over and the cries stop abruptly. Suddenly the monkeys are all glaring at us.

"You're back." The Child looks confused and surprised. "No one ever comes back."

"Where is our friend?" I demand.

The Child stares at us without answering. I'm just about to grab him by the throat when one of the climbing monkeys flies out of the tree and lands in a pile of rotten fruit. Then a second sails backward and slams into the trunk of a neighboring tree.

"I'm up here!" Carole shouts. She yanks back the hood of her invisibility cloak and appears on a branch at the top of the tree. "It's the goddamn goats all over again!"

"You were planning to eat our friend?" I manage to keep my voice calm, but inside I'm raging.

The Child's spine stiffens and his upper lip curls into a sneer. "My father is the Elemental of Mammon. He allows us to dine on the guests who are too timid to enter the canyon," he says haughtily. "It is our right. This is *our* world. You do not belong here."

"You're wrong," I growl. How dare this digital freak try to tell *me* who belongs. "This whole place was created for *guests*. Children like you were never meant to exist. You're nothing but bad code. You're goddamn *mistakes*."

"You've seen what your kind does here in Otherworld and you think *we're* the mistakes?" the Child asks, baring his teeth at me. "You come here to kill one another for sport. And the things you do to us are far worse. The Children and Beasts were born in this world. It is not a game for us. Whatever we do, we only do to survive."

"And I guess eating guests is essential to your survival? Your monkey friends need meat, do they?" I ask.

"They have developed a taste for it," says the Child.

"Then I have a real treat for them. Bon appétit!" I shout at the troop as I plunge my dagger deep in his heart. The Child staggers backward and drops to the ground. "Hope you taste good," I tell him. I'll try my best to avoid killing players with disks, but as far as I'm concerned, Children are fair game.

Gorog holds off the other monkeys with a bow and arrow as I retrieve my knife from their leader's chest. By the time I'm done, Carole has climbed down from the tree.

"What now?" Gorog asks as I walk back to meet them.

"Remove the arrows," I say, pointing at the wooden shafts still protruding from his torso. "Take time to recuperate. I need to check something out. And keep an eye on those monkeys while I'm gone. Kill any that get within fifty feet of you," I add.

"I don't think we need to worry. Looks like they're busy," Carole says as I walk away.

I glance back over my shoulder. I expect to see the troop feasting on the flesh of their fallen leader. But they're not. They're carrying the Child's body away, three on each side like pallbearers. I could be wrong, but it doesn't look like they intend to eat it. If I had to guess, I'd say they were preparing to bury it. I feel a twinge of regret, though I know I shouldn't. It's virtual reality, after all.

. . .

I walk back out into the canyon. The cliff dweller's body is gone. The only sign of him is a wide trail of blood left behind in the grass. Someone must have administered the coup de grâce and dragged him away. I guess it's safe to assume that the diamonds went with them. Keeping an eye on all nearby cave entrances, I jog toward the rope that's still dangling from the cliff. I see the next-door neighbors appear with bows raised. Arrows whiz past as I climb, and one grazes my thigh. It's the second time I've been injured in Otherworld, and the pain is intense. It's all in my head, of course. I know that my flesh-and-blood body isn't injured. But that knowledge doesn't make my leg feel any better—or my heart beat any more slowly.

The Child said all the cliff dwellers are guests. But something about that doesn't make any sense to me. Why would headset players spend their free time living in a godforsaken canyon? The answer must be inside the caves, so despite the pain, I keep climbing until I reach the ledge of the cliff dwelling and pull myself inside. It's just a small chamber carved out of the rock. The ceiling is so low that I can feel my hair brushing against it. Piles of junk take up most of the floor space. There's barely enough room for one person, and I'm not alone. The man's been dead for fifteen minutes, and someone's already come to raid his cave. This avatar appears to be female, though frankly it's hard to tell. Her body is so thin and fragile that she probably couldn't put up much of a fight, yet she drops all but one of the ragged bags she's carrying and attacks anyway. I dart to the side as she rushes my way, and she's unable to stop herself from hurtling over the ledge just behind me. Stunned, I look over the side and watch her body bounce against the canyon wall before it finally hits the ground with a distant thud. The bag she was carrying bursts open and diamonds spill out around her.

I have a feeling she won't be the last looter this cave welcomes today. And I can see why. The guy who lived here was a serious hoarder. He assembled a small arsenal. Mostly swords, spears and arrows, but there's a massive slingshot on top of the pile. I leave it, wondering what kind of idiot would choose a slingshot as his weapon. I grab three swords instead. I'd love to take a few spears, but I don't. If I get greedy and try to carry too much weight, I run the risk of snapping the homemade rope on my way down from the cave.

Fortunately, aside from the weapons, there's nothing here to tempt me. The rest of the stuff is just clothes and crap. There's no doubt where it came from—the shoes are all different sizes. The cave's occupant must have killed quite a few players in the past few days. He probably had a million dollars in stolen diamonds, but he lived like a beast. Looks like he was using the clothes he collected as a makeshift bed, and I see the remains of a campfire in the corner. There are strange white shards scattered among the charcoal chunks. I walk over, bend down and run my fingers through the ashes, exposing a charred human vertebra. I stumble backward, gagging. I suddenly know why his corpse was dragged away. Some other cliff dweller will be feasting on it tonight. There's no other food in the canyon.

As hard as it is to believe, the monkeys in this realm seem to be far more civilized than the guests. I know it's all just a game for Otherworld's headset players, but what kind of person finds this sort of shit *fun*?

I go back to the entrance of the cave and peer down. The corpse of the female who fell is already gone. Then I look out at the canyon we need to cross to get to the sparkling city in the distance. The cliff face on the opposite side is riddled with caves as well. The question is, how many are filled with men and women like the two who just died?

My eyes detect motion, and I suddenly realize there's something moving across the rock wall in front of me—a camouflaged avatar. I watch him crawl spiderlike from his own cave to another that's a few yards closer to the city. He enters the new cave, and a minute later a body is flung out over the side of the cliff. I can't tell if it's the cave's inhabitant or the intruder. When the body hits the ground below, three scavengers race to claim the prize, ignoring the arrows that rain down on them. I watch in horror as they rip the corpse apart. They each climb back up to their own cave with a sizable chunk of flesh.

At first I'm not sure what to make of the scene—and then I figure out what's going on. The players here are all trying to make their way toward the city of Mammon, advancing one cave at a time. In this realm, murder is how you move up in the world. Carole, Gorog and I need to reach the city too, but we don't have time to go from cave to cave. We'll need to travel through the canyon by foot. I glance back at the spot where the last body landed. There's nothing left but a red smear. How can we possibly make it without being killed and eaten?

Carole has an invisibility cloak, but it only fits one—and there are three of us. The swords I just collected will be useless against the cliff dwellers' arrows and spears. Then it hits me: the only way to survive is not to fight at all. We'll give the players what they want instead. Inspired, I return to the pile of weapons and pull out the large slingshot. It won't do us much good in a battle. But if we're going to make it to Mammon alive, it may be just the thing we need.

I climb down from the cave. A half-dozen arrows pierce the ground around me as I hurry back to the safety of the garden, where Carole is still dressing Gorog's wounds. The ogre looks weak—he's clearly out of commission for a little while. His avatar needs time to recover from the wounds. That means either Carole or I will need to execute the first part of my plan. One of us will soon be taking a quick trip to Mammon alone.

I announce my plan to the group and explain why I should be the person to go. Carole isn't having any of it.

"You've got to be kidding me," she says. "You want to take my invisibility cloak?"

"Yes. And Gorog's fire," I say. "When I return from Mammon I promise to give them both back."

"But we'll be defenseless," Carole points out. "What if the monkeys attack again?"

I lay out the swords I took from the cave.

Carole looks back up at me. "I don't want to use one of those," she says.

"Oh, it's easy," Gorog chimes in. "Seriously—anyone could do it, even a girl."

Carole glares at him, and he wisely shuts up.

"Then *you* go to Mammon," I tell her. I take out my trusty

dagger and hand it to her. "The Child said the city was filled with diamonds. Bring back as many as you can."

"Are you joking?" Carole asks. "How do we know that thing was telling the truth?"

"We don't," I admit. "But does either of you have a better plan?"

Carole looks down at my dagger and then gets to her feet and tucks it into the waistband of her cloak. "Okay then," she says with a smirk. "I'll go." I can tell she thinks she's calling my bluff, but I'm not bluffing at all. Her smile fades fast. "You're really going to let me take your dagger?"

"You may need it for protection," I say. "And it's a lot easier to carry than a sword."

"But . . ."

"You have the most important tool," I tell her. "Without the invisibility cloak, my plan won't work. But it's your possession. You choose who gets to use it. Just remember, our lives depend on the success of this mission."

Carole draws in a long, deep breath and exhales. "All right," she says. "I'll do my best."

Like I said, I wasn't bluffing, but I didn't really expect her to take me up on the offer. I figured she'd chicken out and let me go. I suddenly feel naked without my dagger. I'm sure Gorog feels the same way as he hands over his fire.

"Please don't screw it up," he begs Carole. "You've probably never done anything like this before, and I don't want to spend the rest of my life stuck here hanging out with Simon and a bunch of man-eating monkeys."

"Excuse me? How do you know I've never done anything like

this before?" Carole demands. "I got news for you, smartass. I'm practically Lara goddamn Croft. You think because I'm a lady I don't know what I'm doing? Well, as they say back home, *Hide and watch, son.*"

Then she pulls the hood of her cloak up over her head and instantly disappears.

Hours have passed. The sun is starting to set and Carole still hasn't returned. In the silence, I think of Kat. I try not to obsess over where she might be—or what might be happening to her. To stand a chance of finding her, I'll have to stay sane. So I close my eyes and pull up one of my favorite memories and let it play like a movie on the back of my eyelids. The sun was setting then too, and inside our fort there was barely enough light to read when I first showed Kat the book *Gangsters of Carroll Gardens*.

"That's my grandfather," I said, pointing to the picture of the Kishka. "He used to break people's fingers."

"Whoa!" she said, holding the book up to see the picture. "Tough guy, huh?"

"More like *thug*. I think that's why my mother never really loved me," I said. It started off as a joke, but that wasn't where it ended up. Suddenly I was struggling to keep my voice steady. "Because I look so much like him."

"Nope," Kat replied, shaking her head with absolute certainty. "That's not why."

"How do you know?" I ask.

"Because that's not a reason not to love your kid," she said.

"If your mother doesn't love you, it's because there's something wrong with her, Simon." She looked back at the picture of the Kishka. "He seems like a pretty interesting guy to me. What do you know about him?"

"Not much," I admitted. "He was a gangster who had a lot of girlfriends and ended up at the bottom of a canal."

"Great," she said.

"Great?"

"Sure. If that's all you know, then you get to decide what he was really like. Maybe he was an awesome guy. Maybe he only broke people's fingers if they really deserved it. And maybe he passed all his awesomeness down to you."

"I could pretend that's the truth, but it wouldn't be real," I said.

"Why not?" she asked. "He's just a picture in a book. Why can't he be who you want him to be?"

"I can't believe you let Carole take my fire." Gorog interrupts the memory, and I open my eyes. He's shivering in his loincloth. "As soon as it gets dark, those monkeys are going to eat us alive," he groans.

I look over my shoulder and he's right—the troop of monkeys is back. I'm about to suggest we start discussing Plan B when something hits the ogre in the middle of his forehead. A diamond the size of a grape falls into his lap.

"That's for the vote of confidence earlier," says a disembodied voice.

Carole's head appears first, followed by the rest of her as she pulls down her hood and drops a sack at our feet. Her face is flushed with excitement as she hands Gorog his fire and passes my dagger back to me.

"The canyon is just the beginning," she says, her eyes glowing. "Mammon's a freak show too. I don't know what's going on over there, but the houses I saw are all booby-trapped. I'm talking spike pits, swinging logs, the works."

"How did you—" Gorog starts.

"Survive?" she finishes for him. She bends over and pinches him playfully on the cheek. "Awww. You sweet little thing. You still have no idea who you're dealing with, do you?"

I'm not in the mood for fun and games. "Are you sure you got enough diamonds to go around?" I ask as I reach out for the sack she dropped. The weight of the bag answers my question. There must be thousands of jewels inside.

"So? What do you think?" Carole asks with an eyebrow arched.

I can't help but smile. "I'm starting to think we might actually get the hell out of this place," I tell her.

Before darkness falls, we gather a giant mound of the fruit from the trees. We eat a few for dinner, but most we save for morning. The monkeys have been inching closer, so we take turns keeping watch through the night. I have the first watch, and while Carole and Gorog sleep, I prepare the goodies for our trip through the canyon.

Into each ball of fruit, I insert twenty-five of the precious stones that Carole gathered in Mammon. I'm careful not to push them in too deeply. I want them to sparkle in the morning sunlight. When it's my turn to rest, Carole takes over. I sleep so deeply that the next thing I know, I'm opening my eyes to see hundreds of bejeweled balls laid out around us—and two dead monkeys. They tried to sneak up on the camp in the middle of the night. Carole might not like using a sword, but as it turns out, she's pretty good with one. She got rid of the monkeys without even bothering to wake us.

With the sun streaming into the canyon, we begin the last of our preparations. We have no bag large enough to carry the fruit, so I take off my burlap robe and fill it with as many of the sparkling spheres as it will hold.

"Your robe isn't going to cut it," Gorog observes. "We need to take everything we've got with us. If we run out of fruit in the middle of the canyon, we're goners."

"Here," says Carole, pulling her cloak over her head. "We can use mine too."

"No," I tell her. "We'll find another way to carry the stuff." Carole's invisibility cloak will guarantee her safe passage. I can't ask her to risk her life on a plan that might not work.

"Don't treat me like I'm some precious little flower," she snaps. "I want to get out of here as much as you do, and I won't be able to make it alone. Take the damn cloak."

I reach out for it—I've already forgotten we're having an argument, because for the first time, I see what Carole's been wearing under her cloak, and it leaves me totally speechless.

Gorog cackles. The ogre never loses the power of speech. "Oh, man, I forgot you were dressed like my mom."

"Yeah, well, when I chose the outfit, I didn't know I'd be running from swarms of insects or fighting off monkeys, did I?"

Carole snaps. She brushes off her beige chinos and straightens her pink polo shirt. "I dressed for comfort."

"Where'd you think you'd be going?" Gorog asks. "A PTA meeting?"

"Says the guy who's clearly compensating for something with that overgrown avatar," Carole says. "You want a spanking, you little fart?"

"Yes, please," says Gorog, bending over and lifting the back of his loincloth.

"Okay, okay!" I shout. "That's enough. We aren't here to talk about Carole's fashion choices. If she wants to dress like a soccer mom from San Antonio, that's her business, not ours."

Gorog bursts out laughing again, and Carole sticks her lower lip out like a kid. "I hate both of you," she grumbles.

"Yeah, well, if it makes you feel any better, we'll probably be dead soon," Gorog replies.

Gorog meant it as a joke. He's talking about our avatars, of course. But Carole and I instantly sober up. The ogre still doesn't know what's really going on, and now isn't the time to tell him.

"We're not going to die," I say, hoping to convince myself along with the others.

"Of course not," Carole chimes in. "You've come up with a brilliant plan."

"Even if our avatars do bite the dust, it's better than playing *their* stupid game," Gorog says, pointing up at the cliff dwellers' caves.

He's got a point. I still can't understand why anyone would stay in the canyon—raiding, killing and suffering—just to work their way closer to Mammon. They have to be pretty good at the game to survive this far. Otherworld has been available to headset players for about a week. You'd think some of these guys would have found another way through the canyon by now. But they haven't. And what scares me most is that in seven short days, this is what they've become.

I pick up one of our sacks of fruit. Carole takes the other. Gorog is carrying the slingshot I found in the cave.

"You guys ready?" I ask them.

"Hell yeah," says Gorog.

"Then let's get out of Dodge," Carole says.

"What's *Dodge*?" Gorog asks.

Carole sighs. "Good God. Never mind," she says.

I step into the grass between the canyon walls and prepare to address the savages.

"Hey, I just thought of something," Gorog calls to me. "Are you sure the guys in the caves all speak English?"

Shit. It never occurred to me. "Yep," I lie. "I'm sure." There's no turning back now.

I enter the canyon, staying just out of arrow range, and hold up one of the jewel-covered spheres. It sparkles like a disco ball in the early-morning sunlight.

"*Listen up!*" I shout. My voice bounces off the canyon walls. It's far louder than I could have hoped. The acoustics here are excellent. I wait until the cliff dwellers emerge from their caves. "*Every sphere contains food, water and diamonds. Everything an avatar needs! There is one for each of you. Make sure you get yours.*"

I turn to Carole and Gorog. "Here goes." I hand Gorog the ball of fruit I'm holding. He places it in the slingshot and sends it sailing into the first cave. The cliff dweller catches it, examines it and immediately throws a rope down the cliff side. He's not satisfied with one. He wants them all.

"Okay, he's coming," says Carole.

"Time to start walking," I say.

"Dude, he's getting close," Gorog says nervously. The man sprinting in our direction is a particularly fierce specimen. I don't know which one of us he'd go for first, but I'd rather not find out.

"*Make sure you get yours!*" I shout again. "*Don't let this guy get them all!*"

The attacking cliff dweller has made it to a point less than a hundred yards away from us when a spear slices through his abdomen and pins him to the ground like a bug to a board. Gorog immediately shoots a gem-covered fruit in the spear thrower's direction. The neighbor examines it and almost goes for his own rope. But a glimpse over his shoulder gives him pause. The next cliff dweller along the canyon has a bow and arrow aimed directly at *him*.

"*Don't let anyone take what's yours!*" I shout.

"Holy moly, it's working!" Carole whispers. Now the truth comes out. She didn't think it would.

"Yeah, 'cause they're jerks," Gorog says. "I bet they don't even care about a few diamonds. They just don't want their neighbors having more than they do."

"Ah, human nature," I say. "It's so revoltingly predictable."

"Hey!" Carole says, taking offense on behalf of the entire human race. "Gorog and I are human too, you know. And neither of us has ever killed for diamonds or resorted to cannibalism."

"*Yet,*" says Gorog, flinging a fruit at another cliff dweller. "With the right barbecue sauce . . ."

Carole rolls her eyes and passes the ogre the next piece of fruit. "He's joking," she says, as if I need it explained to me. "But if you ask me, we're the only real people here. I don't know *what* you'd call *them.*"

You'd call them *guests,* I say to myself. I need to stop thinking of them as human. It's obvious now that the two things are not the same.

We reach the gates of Mammon without a single piece of fruit left between us. Along the way, three cliff dwellers pressed their luck and tried to claim more than their fair share. All three died at the hands of their neighbors. In the end, my plan worked perfectly. If a cliff dweller tried to attack us, the player in the closest cave would kill him. Not out of goodwill, of course. It was just simple logic. If you're waiting for a delivery, it's in your best interest to keep the mailman alive.

Carole and I put our cloaks back on as we approach a pair of golden gates that stand between us and Mammon. There's a booth to the right of the gates, and an NPC guard is sitting inside. He doesn't move as we draw near, but he keeps his eyes trained on us. Unfortunately, I didn't plan for this part. I have a hunch that those gates aren't going to open unless we're able to pay a hefty price.

"How did you get past the gates when you were here earlier?" I ask Carole.

"I stayed invisible and followed a cliff dweller through," she tells me.

"You're kidding. They let one of those cannibal freaks inside?" Gorog asks.

"Sure," says Carole. "For the right price they'd probably let anyone into Mammon. I hope you guys brought enough to pay the toll."

"What?" Gorog yelps. "Why didn't you say something? We used up all the fruit!"

"Good thing one of us held on to a few diamonds in case of an emergency." Carole pulls out a sack of jewels I didn't know she had. Then she stands on her tiptoes and pinches the ogre's overgrown cheek. "You going to make fun of my outfit again?" she asks.

Gorog shakes his head.

"Yeah, didn't think so," Carole tells him.

MAMMON

It's a different world inside Mammon. The only road through the realm is lined with mansions surrounded by gilded gates and well-tended lawns. Each of the homes is more ornate than the last, and they're all covered in stucco that's been mixed with diamonds so the walls sparkle in the sun. It seems the gems the cliff dwellers kill for are as common as dirt here. Everywhere I look I see royal palms, English ivy and topiary trees. But there don't seem to be any avatars or animals. The realm is totally still. As we start down the road, it feels like we're strolling through Beverly Hills just after the apocalypse.

Far ahead at the end of the road, a massive golden temple sits atop a hill. I'm guessing that's where the Elemental of Mammon resides. The homes closest to it are practically palaces, but the temple itself seems to be the ultimate prize. If anyone's alive in this part of the realm, I'd bet they're striving to reach it. I'd love to know what they get if they do.

"We need to make our way to the temple," I say. "If this is anything like Imra, the Elemental of Mammon will decide whether we can leave. And I'm betting that temple is where he or she lives."

"If we're going that far, I should probably stay invisible," Carole says. "Give me your tools and weapons for safekeeping."

"Again?" Gorog whines. "Why? There's no one around."

"Don't be so sure. I stole the diamonds from one of the homes here. The entire yard was booby-trapped like you wouldn't believe. There are definitely people around, and they aren't any friendlier than the ones back in the canyon."

"Okay, but what could these people possibly want from *us*?" Gorog's irritated. "Look at these houses. They have everything. They've got it made."

"You think that's how it works?" Carole asks. "There are rich people in the real world who'd steal a jar of pennies from an orphan. That's how most of them got rich in the first place. Can you imagine what the ones here are like?"

"She's right," I tell the ogre. There's something eerie about this place. I hand Carole my weapons.

"Whatever," Gorog says. "Take my sword and my fire. But I'm keeping the slingshot. I like it."

Carole rolls her eyes at the ogre before she pulls the hood over her head and disappears. I figure she must be lugging her weight in weapons.

We set off toward the temple on the hill. As we walk past the gates of the first mansion, a relatively humble Gothic pile, I hear a strange mechanical whir. It takes me a moment to figure out that it's the sound of a hidden camera following our every move. Someone inside the building is watching us. We reach the second and then the third mansion and discover that their owners have taken security surveillance to even greater heights. Countless cameras are mounted on posts along the gates, and as we pass, drones buzz above our heads. Gorog flips them the bird. I feel strangely naked, like the cameras can see through my clothes and my skin. The discomfort makes me itch. It seems to make Gorog angry.

"We don't want your stuff!" he shouts as one of the drones swoops down for a close-up of him.

We're nearing the grounds of the fourth mansion, and I'm finally beginning to understand the paranoia. Two armies of NPCs are at war on the grounds. One group seems to be invading while the other desperately tries to fend off the attack. What was once lawn is now a muddy battlefield. The little grass left is red with blood. Several booby traps have been sprung, and I see invaders who've been immobilized by nets, riddled with arrows and impaled by spears. As I watch, two NPCs disappear into a hole in the lawn. I don't know for sure what's in the hole, but it wouldn't be much of a trap without a few spikes at the bottom.

We move on quickly while the battle continues to rage. We don't get far before we spot a roadblock up ahead, outside the next mansion.

"Now do you see why I needed to carry the weapons?" I hear Carole whisper.

I know what she's saying, and she's right. Any visible weapons would probably be confiscated. But I'd still feel a lot better if I had my dagger handy.

As we draw closer, it becomes clear that the figures manning the roadblock are all identical NPCs. The mansion's owner definitely has a type—tall, dark and bland. They stand shoulder to shoulder in a line that stretches across the street. There's no way around them.

"Relinquish your weapons," one of the clones demands.

"I don't have any," I tell them. Thankfully, Gorog and I have a fully armed guardian angel watching over us.

"And you?" the clone asks Gorog.

Gorog looks at me and I shrug. He should have let Carole hold on to his slingshot. The ogre pulls the weapon out of his waistband and reluctantly tosses it to the ground. Two of the other men step forward and frisk us.

"That's it?" the clone asks, clearly surprised. "You survived the canyon with a slingshot?"

"We're really fast runners," I tell him.

Gorog nods. "As soon as we're out of here, we're trying out for the US Olympic team," he adds.

The clone doesn't blink. "Come with me," he says humorlessly. We're forced to leave the road to the temple. They surround us and we're marched through the gates that encircle the mansion and then across its broad lawn.

I gotta say, the security here is truly exemplary. You can't really tell from the street, but the place is a fortress. The mansion itself is a stucco-covered monstrosity that looks like the embassy of the world's tackiest country. As we near the building, I see that the windows are barricaded with metal grates and the balconies are all adorned with razor wire. Several snipers are stationed on the roof, and a defensive wall made of sandbags surrounds the entire house. Whoever lives here doesn't seem all that fond of visitors. My chest is starting to feel a bit tight, but I know I'd be feeling a hell of a lot worse right now if Carole weren't right behind me.

The mansion's doors open when we reach the porch, and I'm once again taken by surprise. I'm not sure what I was expecting, but this is definitely not it. The interior is decorated in a style I'd call Baltic dictator. A forest of black marble columns topped with golden ornament holds up the ceiling. The floor tiles are a high-gloss leopard print, and the black ceiling is studded with tiny lights that form what I'd guess are astrological signs. But there's no art on the walls or furniture to sit on. Mounds of black garbage bags are lined up along the perimeter, as if the mansion's inhabitants just went nuts with spring cleaning.

"Hey there!" says a woman, and I spin around. Again—not what I was expecting. The avatar is your typical twentysomething Alpha female. Olive-skinned, with a long brown ponytail. Toned, but not too burly. Nice set of knockers. I would have expected the house's occupant to be all blinged out, but if anything, her appearance is tastefully understated. She's wearing what looks like a black yoga outfit and a pair of diamond studs in her ears. "I'm Gina."

"Hi," Gorog replies a little too enthusiastically. He should know better than to get all hot and bothered by an avatar. There's probably some hairy-handed forty-year-old pervert behind it.

"So you guys have joined forces, have you?" Gina asks. "Most of the people in Mammon prefer to play solo. I guess we're not the sort who like to share." The word *play* echoes in my head. If she knows she's in a game, she's probably wearing a headset.

"We're not here to play," I tell her. "We're just passing through."

Gina laughs. "Passing through? I've never heard *that* before." She gives us the once-over and rubs her hands together eagerly. "What have you brought me?" she asks.

"I'm sorry, we didn't realize you were having us over," I say. "If we'd known, we would have purchased a hostess gift on our way to the party."

"Hilarious!" the woman says. "It's so good to hear a joke. As much fun as these NPCs can be, it's nice to have a human around sometimes. Can you both open your mouths for me, please?"

"Excuse me?" I ask. I seriously didn't think anything could surprise me anymore.

"Your mouths?" She gestures to her servants, and two of them step forward and wrench our jaws apart. The woman takes a look and shakes her head. The servants let us go.

"What was that about?" Gorog's no longer in love.

"You'd never guess how many people trick out their avatars with fancy dental work," she says. "I have a small fortune in grills." She gestures to the guard. "Show them."

The NPC picks up one of the black plastic bags and holds it open in front of us. Inside is a collection of gold and diamond-studded tooth-shaped jewelry. It makes me wonder what might be inside the other bags.

"You steal people's teeth?" Gorog asks.

"Every little bit counts," she says, then turns to one of the NPC servants. "What weapons did our visitors have on them?"

"Only this," says the guard. He passes her the confiscated slingshot.

She examines it thoughtfully. "You made it through the canyon with a *slingshot*? How impressive! It took me a hundred weapons and almost a week of constant play to work my way through the caves."

"You used to be one of the cliff dwellers?" Gorog asks in astonishment.

"Clean up pretty nice, don't I?" says the woman.

"Does that mean you ate people?" Gorog asks, managing to look both curious and queasy. "What did they taste like?"

"Taste like? How the hell would I know? It's a *game*, dickweed," the woman responds testily. She seems offended by Gorog's squeamishness.

I'm actually glad Gorog brought up the subject of cannibalism. Gina's response confirms my suspicions. If her taste buds aren't working, she's not part of the disk's beta test. Somewhere in the United States (possibly Canada), a person wearing a headset is controlling her, and only a few of that person's senses are engaged. I guess cannibalism isn't quite as bad if you don't have to taste or smell what you're eating.

"In case you haven't noticed," Gina is saying, "I'm kicking some serious ass here in Otherworld. I've got twenty-four kills and over three billion dollars in gems, weapons and other assorted goods."

"Oh, we've noticed," I assure her. "You're obviously good at this. So why are you still here in Mammon?"

"What do you mean?" she asks.

"I guess it just doesn't seem like much fun to me. Do you *enjoy* stockpiling weapons and stealing teeth? Isn't Otherworld all about living the life you always wanted? Why spend your time in a place where everyone's afraid all the time?"

"Well, it's a lot better than Everglades City. Spend too much time outside where I live and you'll die of heatstroke or get eaten by gators." So the person behind Gina is in Florida. Good to know. Only two thousand people were given access to the Otherworld headset app. There can't be more than one of them in Everglades City. "Besides, I'm having a blast. I figure in a couple more weeks I'll reach the golden temple."

"And then what?" I ask.

"And then I'll win!"

"Win what?" I ask.

The question clearly annoys her. I don't think she knows. "The game! Look, I'm getting sick of this conversation. I always forget how stupid people can be." She turns to the NPCs. "Take them out of here. And make sure you get the invisible one, too."

"Invisible one?" I ask, managing to play it somewhat cool even though I'm freaking the hell out.

"Do you think I made it this far by being stupid?" the woman sneers. "There's no way you got through the canyon with a god-damn *slingshot*."

Gina's NPCs have already found Carole and pulled down her hood. All of our weapons and tools are taken away and thrown into a black plastic bag. Then Carole is stripped down to her chinos, and Gina takes the invisibility cloak.

"Cute outfit," she tells Carole. "Is there a minigolf course somewhere in Otherworld?"

"Yeah, why don't you join me there after you get out of your yoga class," Carole says snippily.

Gina practically busts a gut. "You are all so funny!" Then she holds the cloak up under my nose. "Think no one wins this game? This right here is my ticket to glory." She turns to her men. "Get them out of here."

The NPCs grab us and I have to play my last card. Gina isn't a digital freak like one of the Children. She's a human being. An appeal to her better nature may be the only thing that can save us now.

The soldier behind me has me in a choke hold, but I still manage to force a few words out. "Hold on. Don't kill us," I gurgle. "There's something you should know."

Gina lifts a finger, and the pressure on my windpipe eases.

"We're testing a new device for the Company. If we die in Otherworld, there's a good chance it will kill us in real life."

"What?" Gorog blurts out. *Shit.* I forgot. We still haven't shared the news with him. "Simon? What are you talking about?"

Gina's quiet for a moment; then she calls out to her men, "Bring them back." She eyes me closely. "Explain what you mean," she orders.

"I'm serious—we could die," I say. "The three of us don't have VR headsets. We're wearing disks that communicate directly with our brains. They let us experience Otherworld with all five senses. But when something bad happens to our avatars, the disks tell our brains that the injuries are real. I think if our avatars get hurt badly enough, we might die in the real world."

I hear Gorog whimper. Carole whispers something to console him.

"Then it's a good thing I was never planning to kill you," Gina says.

"You weren't?" I ask.

"No, I'm going to sell you. One of my neighbors developed a taste for human flesh while he was making his way through the canyon. I always wondered how he managed to *taste* it. I guess he's wearing one of those disk thingies, too. Explains why he pays me top dollar whenever I bag one of you."

"And you're still going ahead with that after everything he just told you?" Carole asks.

"Of course," says the woman. "There won't be any blood on *my* hands. Though I have a feeling there may end up being quite a lot on my neighbor's."

THE FACILITY

Gina's NPCs locked us inside some kind of holding cell. The chamber is so small that there's barely room to move. Gorog's body is radiating heat. I can see beads of sweat forming on Carole's forehead, but for some reason I'm freezing cold.

"I can't believe it! Why didn't you tell me earlier?" the ogre whines. Gorog's having a hard time coping with the news that his trip to Otherworld could prove fatal.

"I don't know," I answer. "I'm sorry." I'd try to comfort him if there were anything I could say, but there's no silver lining to the cloud hovering over us.

"Come on. Let's focus on the present," Carole says. "What are we going to do now?" She still seems pretty certain that we'll find a way out of this mess. I wish I shared her confidence.

"I have no idea," I admit. "I'm trying to come up with something."

"Why are your teeth chattering?" Carole asks. "It's a hundred degrees in here."

I just shrug. I don't know the answer to that question, either.

"Well, we'd better come up with something soon," Carole says. "It's almost suppertime."

"Shut up!" Gorog bellows. Then his voice softens into a whine. "I don't want to think about getting eaten. I got hit by nine arrows back in the canyon, and it hurt worse than anything I've ever felt before. Can you imagine what it's going to feel like to get chopped up or roasted on a spit or—"

"Stop panicking!" I order. "We're not going to . . ." I can't finish the sentence. Something is happening to me. Something I'm helpless to stop. It's like Gorog and Carole have been ripped away from me, and suddenly I'm surrounded by pitch dark. It's incredibly cold and I feel a frigid breeze sweep across my skin. My heart is thumping and my arms instinctively shoot out in front of me and slice through the air, as if to fend off some invisible threat. But I know what's happening. The Clay Man said he'd find a way to get me into the facility. Now he's making good on his promise—and I wish I'd never asked. He's just dragged me out of Otherworld at the worst moment possible. With the disk off, I'm safe, and that's all he cares about. He doesn't give a damn about Gorog and Carole. But I do, and I'm not going anywhere unless I can guarantee their safety.

Hazy and disoriented, I shove a hand into the pocket of my jeans. The phone I stole from my mother is still there. I pull it out, switch on the flashlight app, and aim the beam into every shadow around me. There's no one there. But there was. That's for sure. My visor and disk were placed at a safe distance so my thrashing wouldn't destroy them. They're sitting on top of a canvas bag I didn't bring. Next to the bag is a package of Depends.

I could chase the person who left them, but I don't. Remarkably, my mother hasn't shut off the phone's service, and I think I just figured out how to save my friends. So I type out a text to Elvis.

> there's someone in Everglades City FL playing Otherworld. can u pull the plug?

He's writing. I'm dying.

> you mean Gina?

The kid never ceases to amaze me.

> HTF do you know?
> her last Otherworld playthrough got 1.5MM views
> can u get her out of the game?
> can't hack the app but can prob take down her Internet
> how long?
> 5 min
> you sure?
> FO
> text me when you're done
> ok maybe this time you'll thank me?
> FO

It suddenly occurs to me that I might actually owe Elvis a thank-you. Back at the Brockenhurst Country Club, I texted him and asked for a favor—to find the address of the facility where Kat's body was taken. I scroll up through my text history and discover that he delivered.

> can't find name. 1250 Dandelion Drive Brockenhurst NJ
>
> isn't that your town?

I'm not sure what I was expecting. I guess I figured the place would be somewhere in the state. But Dandelion Drive? I could walk there from my house.

A new text arrives from Elvis:

> done. Gina out
>
> **that fast? how?**
>
> took down local power plant
>
> **WTF?**
>
> you said get her out of the game. now she won't be back for a while
>
> **damn Elvis**
>
> careful what u wish for asshole

It's worse than dealing with a robot sometimes. But with Gina—and probably a good chunk of southwest Florida—out of the game, at least I can be sure that Carole and Gorog are safe for a while. So I dig into the bag that's been left for me on the factory floor. The first thing I find is a dark blue uniform. Beneath it are two temporary badges. One bears the name MIKE ARNOLD and the job title PATIENT TRANSPORT. The second is for JOHN DRISCOLL,

MAINTENANCE. At the very bottom I find a piece of paper. *Transport Order. Brockenhurst Hospital to 1250 Dandelion Drive. 8 a.m.*

1250 Dandelion Drive. It's the same address that Elvis sent me. The Clay Man really is sending me to the facility. That's what I asked for, and that's what I got. But somehow it feels like the decision wasn't entirely mine. Whoever's behind the Clay Man has been pulling my strings since he sent me the disk. He says he's affiliated with the Company. So why is he helping me? I know I shouldn't trust him. And I wouldn't—if I had a choice.

It's eight a.m. and there's a van labeled PATIENT TRANSPORT parked outside the Brockenhurst Hospital ER doors. Aside from its dark-tinted windows, there's nothing remarkable about it at all. Nor is there anything particularly interesting about the guy leaning against it slurping coffee from a Styrofoam cup. He's in his fifties, I'd guess, judging by his salt-and-pepper hair and the impressive paunch that's hanging over his belt.

"You the guy filling in for my assistant?" he asks as I approach. You'd think the answer was obvious given the fact that I'm wearing a dark blue uniform that's identical to his.

"Yes, sir," I say. "Mike."

"Don Dunlap. Thanks for making yourself available on short notice," he says, sizing me up as he shakes my hand.

"My pleasure, sir," I tell him.

"Recruiter said you got your EMS training in the army. The boss likes guys who've been in the service. Looks like you haven't been out long enough to let your hair grow."

"That is correct, sir," I say, hoping he doesn't ask for any details. The only things I know about the military I learned playing *Metal Gear Solid.*

"You know, if this ends up working out for both of us, there could be a steady job in it for you. We've had a lot of work lately. The new facility here is getting pretty popular. We've been picking up patients from all over the tristate area. Though it might get a little dull for you after a while. People we've been hauling are all stable. Not much chance of using the skills you picked up in the forces."

"After what I've seen, dull is good, sir," I tell him.

"Yeah, I bet it is," Don says sympathetically.

If only he knew.

The doors of the hospital slide open and an orderly pushes a gurney outside. My new boss tosses his coffee cup in the garbage. "Here we go. You open up the back of the van. I'll bring the patient around."

I do as he asks and then help him push the gurney inside. The patient rolls by; I don't get a good look at her. But it's impossible to miss the fact that she's wearing one of the Company's visors.

"What's that thing on her face?" I ask, wondering if he knows.

Don gives me a funny look. "If I was a doctor, you think I'd be hauling vegetables around at eight o'clock in the morning? It's not our job to ask questions. Our job is to make pickups and deliveries and ensure that our packages get to their destination alive."

"Yes, sir," I say.

"You ride in the back with the patient," he tells me. "Make sure the visor stays on and the IV stays in. We had an IV pop out about a week ago and the patient started shouting like he was being murdered or something. So let's make sure that doesn't happen today. Got it?"

He's waiting for my response, but I'm still stuck on what he just said. When the IV came out, the patient started shouting. Just like the night Kat cried out in the hospital. The nurse said Kat's IV had run dry. That means there must be something in the IV. The patients are being given a drug that prevents them from moving or speaking.

"*Got it,* Mike?" Don repeats, and I snap to attention.

"Yes, sir," I tell him. "I got it."

It's eerily quiet in the back of the van. The woman stretched out in front of me can't be more than twenty-five years old. One of her arms is in a cast, but I can't see any other signs of injury. Once the van is on the road, I look around for a chart, but I don't see one of those, either. There's no way of knowing who she is or where she came from.

I wonder where she is right now. Has she left the White City? Is she indulging in Imra—or fighting for her life in one of the realms? I'm suddenly struck by an overpowering wave of guilt. I'm alone with this woman in the back of a van. No one is watching. I could peel off her disk. Find some way to destroy it. Or I could remove her IV. But I can't run the risk. If I help this one woman, I could lose the chance to help hundreds. But let's be honest: I don't give a damn about hundreds. Right now, all I care about is *one.* And it's not this lady. No—taking her out of Otherworld would put too much at stake. I hope like hell she's safe, but she'll have to stay.

The van comes to a stop, and I hear Don chatting with another man. I peek out the window and realize we've stopped at the gates of 1250 Dandelion Drive. The rear doors open and a security guard pokes his head inside. He glances at the patient and then at me. Once he's satisfied that we're not smuggling whatever qualifies as contraband here, he slams the doors. "You're good to go," I hear him tell Don. A few seconds later, the van starts up again.

I watch from the window as we drive through a park that's filled with ornamental trees and dotted with man-made lily ponds. I catch a deer bolting for cover just before we swing past the facility's main entrance, which looks like it belongs to an upscale spa.

The front of the building is entirely glass. The statement it's making is impossible to miss. The business inside has nothing to hide. It's still early in the morning, but there appear to be a few family members visiting. I bet they're grateful for tasteful scenery. The facility's lobby is bright and airy. It looks nothing like the hellish, fluorescent-lit waiting room of your typical New Jersey hospital.

Our van takes a sharp turn and drives along the side of the building. I realize it's much bigger than it first appeared. The facility is long enough to park a dozen 747s inside and still have room left over for a few games of professional football. And unlike in the welcoming lobby, the windows in this part of the building are few and far between. The only ones I see are small and made of mirrored glass.

Don stops near a metal garage about halfway down the side of the facility. He throws the van into reverse, and when the door rises, he backs all the way into the building. The van shuts off and Don comes around to the rear. He opens the doors.

"What's the name of this place?" I ask. "I didn't see any signs on the way in."

"Dunno. All I know is they pay my boss and he pays me," he says. He doesn't sound terribly curious.

"You really don't know?" I probe.

"Don't know, don't care." Don grabs the end of the gurney and rolls the patient out of the van. "Okay. Let's haul 'er in," he says.

I'm not going to argue, but I'm kind of surprised we're the ones taking the body inside. You'd think a place this big would have a thousand workers, but I don't see anyone around. I help push the gurney from the loading dock into a featureless hallway that ends in what looks at first like an office. There's a desk, but no one's sitting behind it. I count three sliding steel doors on the wall in front of us.

"Hey there, Don," someone says. The voice is coming from a screen mounted on the wall. An attractive middle-aged woman with big blue eyes and bright pink lips is peering out at us. Judging by the love-struck look on Don's face, the lady on the screen is his fantasy girl.

"Morning, Angela," Don says dreamily, proving me right. "You're looking lovely for someone who's probably been up since the crack of dawn."

"Well, aren't you a charmer," Angela flirts back. "Who's your friend?"

Don looks over his shoulder at me as if he totally forgot I'm there. "Oh, right—name's Mike Arnold. Phil called in sick again, so the recruiting agency sent me a sub. But if Phil keeps getting sick after playoff games, Mike here might just become permanent."

"Welcome, Mike," Angela says. "May I scan your badge? Just go ahead and hold it up to the screen."

I do as commanded. I hope she doesn't notice that my hand is shaking. There's no telling whether the badge will actually work. She bends forward for a look. "Wonderful. That all checks out," she says, though I didn't see her check a computer screen. It was like she scanned the badge with her eyes. "Welcome back from Afghanistan, Mike. I hope we get to see you more often!"

"Thank you, ma'am," I say. There's something about the woman that isn't quite right. How did she access my information? She appears to be sitting in a room that looks exactly like this office. Why isn't she here in the flesh?

Then it hits me. She's not a real person. The woman who stars in Don's wet dreams is a robot. She's not quite Otherworld-level, but she's at least as advanced as the NPCs in the White City. That means there's a single place that Angela could have come from. Only the Company is capable of producing artificial intelligence this impressive.

"So which door would you like this young lady to go through?" Don asks Angela, referring to the patient between us. He clearly has no idea that his dream girl isn't human.

"Door number one, as usual," says Angela. It slides open soundlessly, revealing a metal interior that looks like the world's least interesting elevator. Don feeds the gurney into the opening and the patient vanishes behind the sliding door. Just like that, she's gone.

"Anything else I can do for you today?" Don asks Angela.

"As a matter of fact, there is. We have a delivery that needs to be made to the Bosworth Funeral Home in Hoboken. Can you fit it into your schedule this morning?"

"Sure!" says Don as though nothing could make him happier.

"Wonderful," Angela says. "You'll find the delivery behind door number three."

The door slides open. There's another gurney inside. On top of it is a long object encased in a dark blue plastic bag. I try my best to keep my jaw from hitting the floor. It's a body. A *dead* body.

"They know it's coming?" Don asks so casually that you'd think he was talking about a floral arrangement.

"Yes, they're expecting it," says Angela. "The delivery data has been sent to your phone. Make sure you check it before you depart. And thanks again for your help!"

"It's always a pleasure," Don says. "See you next time?"

"Absolutely," Angela replies cheerfully. "I'm always here."

I have to stifle a laugh.

The screen goes black. Don gestures for me to follow him to the third door; then we wheel the body toward the van.

"Isn't she something?" he marvels once we're in the hall and out of earshot.

"Angela?" I ask, and he nods. "You ever seen her in person?"

"Nope," he tells me. "But one of these days I'm going to work up the nerve to ask her out."

"That should be interesting," I say. I'd love to hear her response. How does a robot weasel out of a date? I wonder.

"Tell me about it." Don's practically drooling at the thought. We're at the van and the doors are open. "You good to ride into Hoboken? Traffic this time of day can be brutal. Might take a few hours. Some people get a bit uncomfortable sitting in the back of a van with a corpse for that long."

"Not me. I'll be fine," I assure him.

"Oh, that reminds me," Don says. "It's protocol to confirm that we have the right package before we fire up the engines. Gotta check the info Angela sent." He pulls out his phone and opens a file. I see a picture of a kid. It must be an old photo, because the boy in it can't be more than fifteen. Then Don unzips the bag and I almost gasp. The picture is up-to-date and the body inside the bag is so young that it's hard to believe its owner could be dead. How did it happen? Did he die of injuries he sustained in the real world—or was it the disk that killed him?

Then I notice there's something wrong with the top of his head. There's an incision just above his hairline—it runs from one side of his head to another. I'm trying to figure out what might have caused it when the truth hits me so hard that I almost double over. The kid's been autopsied and his brain has been examined. I feel my knees soften and my head starts to spin while my mind repeats the same sentence over and over and over again.

Oh my God, this could be Kat.

"Yup, same guy," Don confirms, then zips the bag back up. "Let's hit the road."

I push the gurney with the dead kid's body into the van. Then Don heads for the driver's seat. I make a show of climbing into the back with the body, but when I slam the door, I'm not inside. The van heads out of the loading dock, and I hitch a ride on the back bumper. Just before we drive past the front entrance, I hop off again. I need to get into the main part of the building, and I figure there's no way Angela is going to let me pass. My only hope is going in through the front door.

There was a second ID badge in the package the Clay Man left at Elmer's. JOHN DRISCOLL, MAINTENANCE, it reads. There's some kind of code beneath that. It's a long shot, but I'm hoping John is my ticket inside. I take the second badge out of my pocket and fix it to the pocket of my blue uniform. This adventure's risk level keeps rising. Right now it's hovering between "you've got to be shitting me" and "good luck with your death wish." But I've seen what happens to the patients here, and at this moment, I couldn't care less about the danger.

I'm barely through the front doors when a guy steps in front of me, blocking my way. I assume he's a flesh-and-blood human being. If not, he's an excellent replica of one. He's dressed in a blue polo shirt, dark jeans and white sneakers. He has a casual, friendly face to match the casual, friendly environment.

"Good morning," he says. "I'm Nathaniel. May I help you?"

"I'm John from maintenance," I say, pointing to my badge and hoping that's enough.

Nathaniel scans my badge with a handheld device while I stare over his shoulder. There are a few miserable-looking people in the reception area who must be family members. A man is standing at the main desk, speaking with the woman behind it. I can't hear the conversation, but it looks tense. When I recognize the voice, my entire body goes rigid. It belongs to Wayne Gibson—Kat's stepdad. He's here for a visit.

"Come with me," Nathaniel says. I'm almost trembling with nervousness when he leads me past security. I keep my head turned away from Wayne as we pass. "There's a clogged toilet in visiting room number three. Someone must have tried to flush something fairly big. We'd love to have it fixed as soon as possible.

We have a limited number of visiting rooms, and as you can tell, we have quite a few family members with us this morning."

"I'll see what I can do," I promise. This place must be filled with some of the most advanced technology ever developed, and yet no one here is able to unclog a toilet. Typical.

I follow Nathaniel out of the lobby and into a hall with a half-dozen doors. He chooses one and places his palm against a black glass scanner on the wall beside it. The door opens and we step inside a room that looks more like a high-end hotel suite than something you'd find in a facility that tends to the nutritional and waste-removal needs of lost causes. The television is large, the furniture is well designed, and the floor is a tasteful hardwood. I wish the chair I slept in at the hospital had been half as plush as the one they have here. I walk up to the bed and rub the sheets between my fingers. Even my mother would approve of the thread count.

"The toilet's in there," Nathaniel says, helpfully pointing at the bathroom. "The door will lock behind me when I leave. Just press the button on the wall as soon as you're finished and I'll come get you."

Nathaniel doesn't seem to have noticed that I have no tools with me. It's highly unlikely that anything in this room's getting fixed. When he leaves, I realize I'm stuck. There are two metal doors—the one I just entered and another on the opposite side of the room. But I'm not getting out of either one. Instead of knobs, they both have biometric scanners embedded in the walls beside them. I cross the room to the second door to examine its scanner. I'm bending over for a closer look when the door slides open and I jump back in surprise. A doctor in a white lab coat jumps too when he sees me. His eyes dart to the empty hospital bed and then narrow as they return to me.

"Who are you?" the doctor asks warily, as if I could be anyone from a Russian spy to a hired killer.

"Maintenance," I tell him, tapping my badge. "Toilet's clogged."

His attitude instantly shifts from fear to annoyance. "Still? I'm supposed to be meeting here with a family in . . ." He checks the device strapped to his wrist. I can tell it's a smart watch, but I've never seen one like it before. I'd bet anything it's a Company design. ". . . two minutes."

"I guess you're going to have to find another room," I say.

"I have a better idea," he says snippily. "Instead of standing around making small talk, why don't you do *your* job so that I can do mine?"

I'm about to suggest I use his face as a plunger when three quick beeps issue from the device on his wrist and his expression changes. He knows what the signal means without having to look down at the watch. "That just bought you some time," he says. "Fix the damn toilet before I get back."

The doctor presses his palm against the scanner and the door slides open again. He rushes away down another featureless hall without realizing that I've slipped through the door behind him.

The door slides shut, and the doctor's footsteps grow fainter. I'm clearly in a part of the building that's off-limits to visitors. I expect security guards to show up at any moment and haul me away, but no one does. I scan the ceiling and walls, but I can't spot a single camera, which seems highly unusual. Slowly, placing one foot after the other carefully, I head in the direction where the doctor just disappeared. Identical metal doors line the wall on my left. I suspect they lead to other visiting rooms, but there are only six of them. Where are the patients? Martin and Todd said there were three hundred people participating in the beta test. A lot of them must be here at the facility by now. But where are they keeping them all?

I turn a corner and realize I've left the hall. In front of me is a metal balustrade. There are stairs to my left leading down. I walk to the railing. Below me lies a space the size of an airplane hangar.

I'm not quite sure what I'm seeing. There's obviously a mammoth building project under way. Most of the space remains under construction, but a small section appears to be already in use. Inside the finished area, corridors cut paths through massive metal walls that must be at least twenty feet deep and eight feet high. Three rows of glowing hexagonal windows are set into the walls. From where I'm standing, it looks like a high-tech beehive.

I spot the doctor below me. He stops at one of the windows and punches in a code. The window opens, and he pulls out a sliding shelf with a body resting on top. It's a man, and he's naked aside from an aluminum foil Speedo and the black visor on his face. Clear plastic tubes sprout from his mouth, forearm and groin, while thin black wires tether him to the inside of the capsule. I realize I must be looking at some sort of giant life-support machine, with rows of individual capsules stacked three high like shipping crates. Each capsule contains a human being who's being kept alive. The fancy visiting rooms are just to make the families happy. This is where the patients are actually stored.

In Otherworld, the guy on the shelf is probably battling to

survive. But here in this world, he's nothing but a bag of flesh with a beating heart. Nourishment is pumped directly into his veins while his liquid waste is removed via a tube that's been inserted into his bladder. I'm sure the shiny diaper he's wearing takes care of the rest, but I'd rather not know how.

My entire nervous system is buzzing with anxiety. Kat is down there somewhere, locked inside one of those capsules. Carole and Gorog are too. The horror of it almost makes me retch. I cannot—I will not—abandon them here. There's no time to think it through. I have to act. While the doctor is examining his patient, I dart down the stairs and up to the first capsule. Behind the window, a middle-aged African American woman is lying on a steel shelf, her bare feet only inches from the glass. At the back of the capsule, her head is raised slightly. I can see her face clearly, and it's not one I recognize. I step back and, one by one, I work my way down the row of windows, looking for Kat. I have no idea what Carole and Gorog look like IRL, but I keep hoping I'll recognize them, too, somehow. Maybe, like me, they'll resemble their avatars.

I crouch to look into the capsules on the lowest row and jump for a view into the ones on top. The capsules are all the same. Stainless steel interior, blinking green monitors, wires and tubes. The bodies inside the capsules couldn't be more different. They come in every size, age and color, and they're all mostly naked. Each is bathed in a strange orange light that must play some role in keeping them healthy. Every single one of the patients is wearing a black visor.

This is the proof I've been looking for, I realize. I pull out my mom's phone and start snapping pictures. There's something big going on, and the Company is at the center of it. Helpless people are being falsely diagnosed with locked-in syndrome, and their families are being tricked into accepting the Company's virtual reality therapy. Then the patients are brought here. The Company is using people's bodies to beta test the disk and work out the bugs. And as hard as it is to believe, that douchebag Milo Yolkin must be behind all of it. Everyone knows he's a control freak. Nothing ever happens at the Company without his direct. . . .

A piercing sound nearly shatters my skull. Just around the corner from me, an alarm is going off and red lights are flashing overhead. I hear a door open somewhere and footsteps rushing to the scene. I freeze and back up against one of the capsules, doing my best to disappear. I have no idea what would happen if I got caught, but I do know what would happen to my friends. *Nothing.* They would stay here. Eventually it would be their bodies in the transport van to the funeral home.

I can hear multiple people running down a nearby corridor. Then they come to a sudden stop. Someone is barking commands. There's a loud thump, followed by a monotonous beeping, and then a second thump.

I tiptoe toward the action and sneak a peek around the corner. A few dozen yards down an identical corridor, a second doctor and a team of nurses have gathered around the male patient I saw being examined. One of the nurses steps away from the patient's side and I finally get a good look at him. I'd guess he's in his early thirties, and aside from all the tubes coming out of him—and the fact that a doctor is using a defibrillator to restart his heart—he appears to be an excellent physical specimen. From what I can tell, there are no visible injuries to his body, so it's strange to witness the flurry of activity around him.

I raise my phone and hit Record. To their credit, the doctors seem to be making a valiant effort to save the guy's life. But only a few minutes after they begin, it's all over. The doctors pull off their gloves and disappear into the maze. A nurse rolls the defibrillator cart away and two of his colleagues follow behind him. Eventually only a single nurse is left with the lifeless body. As I put my phone down, I hear doors open and shut somewhere in the distance, and it suddenly occurs to me that I'm trapped. The nurse is probably my only way out, and I doubt she'll want to help me. I'd rather not force her, but I may not have a choice. I have footage on the camera that can free my friends and take the Company down. But only if I can manage to get out of here alive. Right now, that's a *really* big if.

I wait as the nurse unhooks the man from the various tubes and wires that were connecting him to the life-support machine and shifts his lifeless body onto a waiting gurney. Then I approach her. I don't tiptoe this time. I want her to hear me coming, and she does. She glances at me without a trace of fear. Up close she's unusually pale, with dark circles beneath her eyes. The corpse on the gurney in front of her looks a hell of a lot healthier.

"Hi," I say, trying to sound cheerful. "I'm John from maintenance. I'm afraid I got lost down here. Think you can show me the way out?"

"Nobody gets lost," the nurse says, still staring at me. She knows I'm not supposed to be here, but she doesn't seem worried. If anything, she appears completely resigned. If I pulled out a machete and threatened to hack her to pieces, I doubt she'd so much as flinch.

"Well, I guess there's a first time for everything," I tell her.

"What do you want?" she asks, getting down to business. "Tell me now before someone else comes."

I realize this is my chance. "I'm trying to stop this," I say. "But first I need to get out of here."

I wait on edge. This could go one of two ways. One of them ends with me punching out a female nurse. I'll just have to make peace with that when and if the time comes.

"Then climb under," she says, pointing to the gurney. There's a long metal shelf between the mattress and the wheels.

I look all around. "Are there cameras watching?"

"Surveillance systems can be hacked. They don't want cameras down here. They'd rather track *us* instead." The nurse taps the smart watch on her wrist. "This thing doesn't come off. They know everything I do. I can't get away. My movements are monitored twenty-four seven."

I bet they are. The Company wouldn't want news of their body farm getting out.

"What happens if you do something you're not supposed to?" I ask. Like help an intruder escape.

"I don't know." Her voice trembles a little. Once again, she points at the shelf underneath the dead patient. "Get on. Quickly. Before one of the doctors walks by."

I cram my giant body onto the shelf, lying on my side with my legs tucked up under my knees. The nurse spreads a sheet over the corpse above me. The ends of the fabric are just long enough to hide me. My brain bounces around in my skull as the wheels of the gurney roll across the concrete floor. I hope like hell I know what I'm doing.

The journey lasts less than three minutes and ends in a room that's freezing cold. The nurse whips the sheet off the corpse.

"You can come out," she says. "There are no cameras here, either."

I slip out of my hiding place and I can see why. We're in an autopsy room. There are three bodies of various sizes laid out on metal tables. Thankfully the cadavers are all covered with sheets. On my left is a wall of metal drawers. On my right is a giant re-frigerator with glass doors. Its shelves are lined with jars filled with floating human brains.

I take out my phone and start snapping more pictures. My eyes pass over the brains and focus on one of the covered bodies that are waiting to be autopsied. A dirty-blond dreadlock is stick-ing past the edge of the sheet. West, the druggie Kat used to hang with, had hair just like that. I don't need to see his face to know it's him. He survived the collapse at the factory just to end up here. I never liked him, but I would never have wished this upon him.

"Holy shit." I look over at the nurse. "What are you doing to these people?"

"The patients die in the capsules. The pathologists are try-ing to figure out what killed them," the nurse says. "That's all I know."

She seems so small and frail standing there next to the gur-ney, but I know that what she's doing requires incredible strength. "Why are you helping me?"

The nurse shakes her head helplessly. "I can't escape." She taps the device on her wrist. "But you can. End this."

"I'm going to try." That's all I can promise. I shove my mother's phone back into my pocket. "But first I have to get out of here."

"This is the only way out," the nurse says, holding up a long black bag.

My gurney enters an elevator. I hear the doors shut. I can't feel the car rising, and I can't tell when it's come to a stop. But I hear the doors open and Angela's voice in the background. She seems to be flirting with yet another driver from another patient transport company. I try to stay perfectly still as the guy takes control of my gurney and pushes it down the hall. At some point, he'll open my body bag and check to make sure he's got the right package. The nurse figured she might know a way around that, but she also made sure to warn me that nothing was certain.

I hear the bag unzip. "Sir, they got a sheet covering this one's face," says a young man. "Should I remove it?"

If they do, I'll have to bust out and make a run for it. My face won't match the picture on their patient file.

An older man grunts. "Only if you got a strong stomach," he says. "They do that to the ones who haven't made it out looking pretty. I took the sheet off once, and I swear I'll never do it again."

"Then I think I'll pass, if that's okay, sir," says the young guy. I can tell from his quavering voice that he lacks the balls for this kind of work.

"Are we sure the cadaver's male?"

"Yes, sir. It's way too big for a female."

"Then it's okay with me if you pass on the inspection."

The zipper goes up again. I'm rolled inside the van and I hear the young guy clamber in behind the gurney. Suddenly I pity the kid. He's going to be sitting right beside me when the corpse he was too squeamish to look at decides to rise from the dead.

I feel the van turn right onto Dandelion Drive, and I mentally chart the course it's likely to take. If we continue in a straight path, there will be a patch of woods on the left side of the road soon. If I reach them, I can disappear. With my finger positioned on the body bag's zipper, I wait until the van rolls to a stop at a streetlight. Then, with one quick sweep, I open the bag. The shrieking begins the second I sit up and slip the plastic away from my torso. By the time I break free, my escort is already cringing in a corner of the van, his body tucked into a tight little ball and his hands over his face.

"Sammy! Sammy! What the hell is going on back there?" the man in the driver's seat shouts. The kid answers with a piercing scream that doesn't seem likely to end.

I throw open the back doors of the vehicle. There's a car right behind us at the red light, and I watch its driver react as I emerge, naked from the waist up. The dickhead lifts his camera to snap a photo right before I make a break for the trees at the side of the woods. Unless he's a virtuoso at action shots, it's unlikely he caught me. I'm deep in the forest in a matter of seconds.

Unfortunately, I quickly realize, I'm miles from Elmer's. Fueled by a mixture of panic and rage, I start hiking toward my destination. Branches are slapping at my sides, and every bug in New Jersey seems drawn by the scent of my exposed flesh. I trudge through the forest and sprint across the countless roads that cut through it.

I'm covered with scratches and speckled with bites, and I still have a few miles to go when I take my mom's phone out to check my location on the map. The caller ID for my home phone flashes up on the screen. I let it go to voice mail. When I check, there are a dozen missed calls from the same number. Five have come in the last ten minutes. I play back the most recent voice mail.

"What have you done?" she whispers angrily into the microphone. It immediately catches my attention. Irene Eaton doesn't whisper. "The police are here searching your room. They say you were seen trespassing at some kind of medical facility. And they think you may be in possession of stolen goods. Simon, you have to turn yourself in right away. If they catch you, you could end up going to jail for years. And they *will* catch you. When they find out you have my phone, all they have to do is trace it."

I don't listen to the rest of the message. Maybe I'm wrong, but I have a feeling my mother just saved my ass. I think she knew someone might be listening. She was trying to tell me to destroy the phone. I'll do it in a second, but I need to send the photos and videos I took at the facility to my own email account for safekeeping. I open the photo folder. I'm selecting images to send. Then suddenly they're gone—they've just disappeared. The Company's already hacked the phone. I drop the useless device and grind it into the ground with the heel of my shoe.

THE RIGHT PLACE

Once again, my avatar is right where I left it—inside the cramped chamber in Gina's house where Carole, Gorog and I were imprisoned while we awaited our fate. Only now the door's open and I'm alone. If Carole and Gorog have been eaten, I'll never forgive myself. The Clay Man sent me to the facility so I'd focus on my original mission. But after visiting the place where their bodies are stored, I feel even more responsible for the two of them. I need to get them to the exit. I need to find Kat. And then I need to figure out another way to take the Company down.

I step into the hall and see Gina smiling at me. Her lifeless avatar has faded to indicate it's inactive. I guess the headset players' avatars don't disappear completely when they take a break from the game. This must have been where she left it when the plug was pulled on Everglades City. I'd love to beat her avatar to a bloody pulp, but instead, I walk away.

I retrace my steps through the house, passing several off-duty

NPC guards who pay me no mind, and finally locate my friends in the only furnished room in Gina's mansion. Gorog is fiddling with a tablet that must control the house's decorating menu. The room's décor keeps flipping from Medieval Fortress to French Chateau to Kountry Klassic.

Carole has a tablet too, and I can see the screen from over her shoulder. She's studying a menu that allows users to custom-design NPC companions. "Hey, it says here that thirty NPCs come with this house," she tells Gorog. "Each of them can be totally different, but Gina just made the same boring Ken doll thirty times. Can you believe it? What a waste! I figure I'll make a few changes, if that's cool with you. You got any requests?"

"Just make sure your new boyfriends are all wearing clothes," Gorog grunts.

"We don't have time for any of this," I say, and suddenly their eyes are on me.

"You're back!" Carole cries merrily, dropping the tablet and hopping up to greet me with a hug. She's traded her chinos and polo shirt for a sleek black yoga outfit like Gina's. On a table in front of her is a glorious feast. "You hungry?"

I am, damn it. I forgot to eat while I was back in the real world. And while Carole's feast is amazing to behold, none of it's going to do my real body much good.

"Oh, man, you're not going to believe what happened," Gorog tells me. "Gina came to get us and feed us to her friend. Then suddenly her avatar just goes totally still, like she's been turned to stone or something, and her guards all wandered away."

"Get up," I tell him. "Both of you get ready. We've got to go."

"What? Can it wait a little bit? Just for a few hours?" Gorog groans. "I really need a break. I'm still sore from those arrows, and Gina's got a Jacuzzi upstairs."

"No. We can't wait." Not another second.

Carole realizes there's something going on. "What is it?" she asks. "What happened to you back in the real world?"

I open my mouth, but I can't tell them. I *can't*. What the hell would I say? Would I tell them that the world's richest corporation has kidnapped their bodies? That they're unwilling participants in an experiment that would make Dr. Death proud? That a single wrong move in Otherworld could kill us?

I can't say any of that. So I say nothing at all.

Gorog and Carole look stunned by my silence. The horror must show on my face.

"That bad?" Carole asks. I nod in reply.

"Okay, then," Gorog says softly. "Let's go. You got any ideas about how we're going to make it out of this city?"

"We need to get to the temple on the other side of Mammon and we're less than halfway there," Carole adds. "And if Gina was . . . well, Gina, can you imagine how bad the people farther up the ladder are going to be?"

"We'll have plenty of weapons this time," I point out. "Gina's got hundreds of garbage bags full of everything we could possibly need."

"Doesn't matter," Gorog says. "Someone's always going to have more."

"If we try to fight all of them, it will take forever to leave," Carole adds.

They're right. Fortunately everyone in this city shares a weakness. And I think I know just how to take advantage of it.

"Where are all Gina's NPCs?" I ask. "I saw a few wandering around the house. Where are the rest of them?"

"Most of them are outside." Gorog points toward the front lawn. "We kept making them leave because they were freaking us out. They all have this same weird blurry patch right here." He points to a spot under his left ear. "It's like a robot mole or something. But once you see it, you can't *stop* seeing it."

We're struggling to stay alive, and the ogre's talking about robot moles. There's something seriously screwed up with him. "Find the NPCs that are still in the house and send them outside. Then gather the best weapons—take as many as you can fit under Carole's invisibility cloak."

"But I thought we just agreed that we can't fight our way out," Carole says.

"We won't fight unless we have to," I tell her. "Be ready to leave in thirty minutes."

I was hoping to avoid any more killing, but my new plan leaves me no other choice. Before I do anything else, I'll have to dispose of Gina's avatar. I return to the hall and execute her from a distance by sinking a crossbow arrow through the center of her skull. Her avatar only flashes, but it counts as a kill. With her death at my hands, the house, its contents and Gina's digital slaves all belong to me.

I head out to the lawn, where the thirty identical NPC clones are loitering.

"Visit every house in the city," I order them. "Tell all the guests that the gates of this mansion will be opened in thirty minutes and all booby traps will be deactivated. Everything inside the mansion will be free for the taking. But only Otherworld guests will be allowed inside. Any NPCs they bring with them will be slaughtered on sight."

The soldiers set off the second the words leave my mouth. There are no questions—no complaints or concerns. And I couldn't care less if half of them never return from their mission. Having a robot army certainly has its advantages.

They're excellent at their job, too. Word of our little give-away spreads quickly, and soon the residents of Mammon are scuttling about like cockroaches on garbage day. For the most part, the mansions' owners are attractive and elegantly attired. Standing outside the closed gates of Gina's house, they resemble members of the Brockenhurst Country Club. If it weren't for their icy eyes, you'd never guess they were killers.

Gorog and I are on the lawn, waiting for the fun to commence. Carole, loaded down with weapons, is invisible beside us. As our visitors arrive, they all peer through the gates, examining the ogre first before they move on to me. The gaze is always cold and clinical, and when they finish, they scrutinize their neighbors. Finally, risk assessed, the people of Mammon proceed to pick apart Gina's mansion with their eyes. At least half of them have far more than Gina. There's no need to resort to looting. But the cliff dwellers inside them all can't resist.

"Why are you doing this?" a gentleman asks me, as if my motives are completely inscrutable. "Why give it away?"

"Because Gina's a bitch," I say.

He lets out a snort. "That's true. But I hope you weren't expecting to find many saints here in Mammon."

"Saints?" I reply. "*Please.* I'd settle for someone who isn't a cannibal."

He snickers. "Oh? And who are you to judge? We all consume people on our way up the ladder. It's only natural that some of us learn to like it."

Gorog nudges me. "I think that might be the dude who was going to eat us," he whispers.

If so, I should kill the guy. If this were a game, my dagger would already be sticking out of his throat. But if he's the one with a taste for human flesh, he's probably wearing a disk. If I kill him here, he dies for real. And I'm not ready to add murder to my résumé.

"I hope you meet something much bigger than you farther up the food chain," I snarl back at him.

I open the mansion's gates and step back while the looters flood in. As soon as they're all inside, I take my friends and my robot army and forge deeper into Mammon. A battalion of NPCs guards every mansion we pass. No one in Mammon left their possessions unprotected. But we meet no resistance on our way to the temple that looks down on the city. The mansions' owners are all back at Gina's.

We walk until the road through Mammon ends at the base of a staircase composed of golden bricks, which make me think of *The Wizard of Oz.* Standing at the bottom, I count five long but manageable flights. Gorog's bounding up the first set of stairs before I'm done ordering our NPCs to go home to Gina's. He stops at the landing between the flights, looking around in confusion, as Carole and I begin our climb. As soon as we join him on the landing, I spot the problem: there are still five flights of stairs above us.

"What the—" Gorog says.

"Don't stop," I tell him.

We keep climbing, and new stairs keep appearing above us, as if we're walking up a down escalator. We're forced to take regular breaks to let Gorog catch his breath. Apparently ogres aren't built to climb stairs. One by one, Carole dumps all the weapons she's been lugging. None of our avatars has the strength left to carry any additional weight. Whenever we stop, my eyes immediately turn to the temple at the summit. It's Roman in style—a simple rectangle set on a podium and surrounded by columns. Slowly, we begin to draw closer, and as we do, the columns supporting the pediment begin to take on human shape. They're statues of men and women—all of them naked and all clearly struggling under the weight they're bearing. Their backs are hunched and their muscles straining. Misery is literally etched on their faces.

After hours of climbing, I finally set foot on the top of the hill. Like those of the statues that loom above, my face is probably the image of agony. Gorog and Carole aren't looking so hot, either. In fact, I'm seriously surprised that Gorog made it up here alive. While he wheezes and coughs, I look back over the City of Mammon. From up here, I can see the realm for exactly what it is—a fucked-up digital board game. You start way down in the canyon. Then you hop from square to square by hoarding, stealing and killing as often as you can. Everyone's trying to reach the golden temple. But then what? What happens to players when they finally get to the top?

I guess it's time to find out. Gorog's no longer hacking up a lung, so I motion for him and Carole to follow me into the temple.

It's dark inside, and plumes of perfumed smoke waft from marble incense burners. It takes a second for my eyes to adjust to the dim light, but as they do I realize we're not alone. At the far end of the temple, a giant being sits atop a golden chair. There's no doubt it's the Elemental of Mammon. A golden toga conceals his lower half, but his doughy chest and massive stomach are bare. Blue-white flesh spills over the chair's armrests and bulges through the openings beneath them. If he decided to stand up, the chair would probably need to be surgically removed from his ass. But somehow I doubt this guy ever needs to budge.

Five of what I can only guess are Children skulk about behind the Elemental's chair, ready to do his bidding. Their size and overall appearance vary. They must have different mothers. But like their father, they're all totally hairless, with skin the color of skim milk. Hideous creatures with hunched backs and gnarled limbs, the Children watch our every movement from the safety of their father's side. They don't dare come any closer. They seem to fear us even more than they hate us.

The Elemental's gaze is lazy and his eyelids droop as if he'd love nothing more than a nice long nap.

"You have reached the temple," he drones. I suppose he doesn't feel the need to introduce himself. "You must go now. You do not belong in Mammon."

It's a little rude, but I'm not going to argue. My ogre friend, on the other hand, doesn't seem satisfied.

"So what do we win?" Gorog asks.

"Win?" the Elemental asks through a yawn.

"Yeah—for making it through Mammon," Gorog adds. "Has anyone ever done it before?"

"My realm offers guests a unique way of life," the Elemental tells him. "It is far more than a game."

"But we met a lady down there who said the whole point is to keep moving up until you reach the temple," Gorog argues.

"The object is to keep moving up. Not to reach the temple," the Elemental informs us. "There will always be more gold to collect. Larger houses to build. Richer neighbors to rob. Those who belong here with me understand that."

Gorog seems hopelessly confused, but Carole is nodding, and I think I get it too. The people here are addicted to acquiring. But no matter how much they have, they'll never have enough. That's why they stay in Mammon.

"So you're really going to let us leave?" Carole asks the Elemental.

He takes a moment to scratch his ample belly. "Certainly. Where do you think you belong?"

It's not exactly the response I was anticipating. The Elemental of Imra didn't give us much of a say in the matter. "We can choose where we go next?" I ask.

"In a manner of speaking," he replies, his voice deep and rich. "The Creator designed Otherworld to be a place where every guest is able to be his or her true self. Whatever desires you may have, there's an Otherworld realm where you may express them freely. Perhaps it's something that would not be acceptable in your world. It makes no difference to us. So tell me what it is you desire most, and I will direct you to the realm that suits you best."

I glance over at Carole and Gorog. They nod, silently letting me know that they'll follow my lead. "Out in the wastelands there are ice fields that stretch for miles and miles. That's where we'd like to go."

Something I just said seems to have caught the attention of the Children. I see ears prick up. But their father yawns again as if performing his duties is an utter bore. "No. The ice fields are a liminal space. They are not within the boundaries of any of Otherworld's realms," he says. "I cannot send you there."

"Could you send us to the realm that's closest to them?" I ask. "There's a glacier in the ice fields that we really need to reach." The Elemental doesn't respond. He's bending to the side, letting one of the Children whisper in his ear. When he sits up straight again, he no longer seems bored.

"What business do you have at the glacier?" he demands. I think I may have misread him. He doesn't sound quite so easygoing anymore.

"Someone's waiting for me there," I tell him. My heart skips a beat at the thought of Kat. "And these two just want to go home. Inside the glacier there's a cave with an exit that leads back to our world."

The most human-looking of the Children limps toward us. She's a pale, sickly creature, with large, wide-set eyes that take up most of the space on her hairless head. Her sisters and brothers are far more hideous, but I'm still finding it hard to look at her. Something appears to be very wrong with both of her legs. Thick, oozing scars ring her shins. I'm guessing she got caught in a booby trap outside one of the mansions in Mammon.

My gaze passes over her brothers and sisters. They, too, show signs of injury—fresh wounds and scarred flesh. A couple of them appear to be missing limbs. Life in Mammon is dangerous for anyone without garbage bags full of weapons. No wonder the Children are holed up here in their father's temple. It's the only safe spot in the realm.

"Why do you need an exit?" the Child asks. "Guests may leave our world whenever they like."

"Not us," Gorog says, shaking his head.

"We're not playing a game like most of them," Carole tries to explain. "We're stuck here, and we're trying to get out."

The Child glances up at her father and then back at us. "I don't understand."

"We shouldn't be here," I tell her. "The people who made this place—"

"People?" the Child interrupts.

"The *Creator* built Otherworld," the Elemental booms.

"Right, right, of course," I say, trying not to sound dismissive. "How could I forget?"

"The cave you describe—they say the Creator has taken refuge there," says the Child.

What? Now I'm confused. Since when do Creators take refuge in caves? And what about the big red dude that already lives there? The one the Clay Man says I'm supposed to kill? None of it makes any sense, but I'm not going to quibble.

"Ummm, well then, good," I say, doing my best to think on my feet. "I was meaning to have a word with him anyway."

"You intend to speak to the Creator?" the Elemental asks, leaning forward as if to see me better. Multiple folds of flesh dangle from his outstretched chin.

"Yeah, I was going to try to talk some sense into him. I've met a lot of folks here who believe all the guests need to be sent home. They think Otherworld should belong to the Elementals, Children and Beasts."

The Children begin whispering among themselves. The idea clearly excites them.

"No," the Elemental announces. "Otherworld will never belong to us."

The Children go silent as they register the betrayal. The stricken looks on their faces are horrible to behold.

"But, Father," says the female who spoke earlier. "You've seen what the guests do to us. Dozens of your Children have died so far. We will not survive if they're allowed to stay. They say there's a war coming. The Creator must choose between the guests and his own creations."

"Then he must choose the guests, and you must continue to suffer," the Elemental tells his daughter. The words may be harsh, but he delivers them kindly.

"But, Father—"

"Without the guests, there is no reason for any of us to exist." He looks down at me. "I cannot send you to the glacier. I will not allow you to speak with the Creator."

I've come too far and seen too much to take no for an answer. The only person I love said she'd be waiting for me at the glacier. If she tries to fight the red guy on her own, she could die. My mission to save her will not be stopped by a toga-wearing Jabba the Hutt. Gritting my teeth, I drop down and reach for the dagger in my boot. Either the Elemental sends me where I need to go or I teach him the real meaning of suffering.

Carole must catch sight of the steel blade. "Simon, what in the hell are you doing?" she whispers.

It's the last thing I hear before I'm no longer in Mammon.

WORLD OF WAR

All it takes is a single look around and I know I've really fucked up this time. I'm alone. Carole and Gorog are still in Mammon. I've lost all three people I was trying to help, and things aren't looking so hot for me, either. I'm surrounded by dense jungle. The air is stiflingly humid—so thick that it would be easier to chew it than breathe it. I hear a man screaming in the distance. And the only weapon I've got is the dagger I was holding.

There's a soft crunch behind me. If I hadn't spent most of my childhood in the woods, I doubt I would have picked up on it. But I spin around just in time to see a man in forest camo barreling toward me with an axe raised high above his head. I duck to the side just as he brings the blade down. If I'd spotted him a second later, he'd have split me in half like a piece of kindling. And I get the impression I'm not the first person Rambo has tried to murder. He recovers quickly and he's beaming when he comes at me again. The look on his face is one of sheer ecstasy. I can tell the dude really gets off on killing.

I won't fight. I saw the bodies in the capsules. I saw what happens to them when they die, and I don't know if Rambo's wearing a disk. Acting against every instinct I've ever possessed, I turn and run instead. My avatar is fast, but my opponent's no slouch, and he knows the jungle far better than I do. He stays right behind me. So when I see the opportunity to slip between the fronds of a prehistoric-size fern, I happily seize it.

Rambo isn't easily fooled. The avatar runs past my hiding place, then comes to a stop.

"Come out, come out, wherever you are!" he calls. "I've got to be on a client call in fifteen minutes, and I need a good look at your intestines before I go."

The crazy fucker is a headset player.

I'm engaged in a battle to the death with some random business guy who's never going to die. He may lose his swag and be sent back to setup, but at the end of the day, it's no big deal. Me? I die and I stay dead. Screw Milo Yolkin and his human experiments. What kind of lunatic lets people die just to figure out what's killing them?

Fortunately, there is one clear advantage to fighting guests that won't die. I can slaughter Rambo and keep my conscience nice and clean. I hear him stomping back in my direction. At first I think the jig is up, but then there's the sound of a large animal darting through the trees nearby, and the avatar turns his beefy back to me. I step out of my hiding spot inside the fern and plunge my dagger between his ribs. Then I pull it out and shove the blade in again as far as it can go. Hot blood pours out of his body and over my hand. It feels fantastic. Not as good as sex, but damn close. It's like the pressure that's been building inside me has been released all at once. For a few glorious seconds my head clears, my rage is sated and my whole body feels lighter.

The avatar collapses in a heap at my feet. I steal his weapon and ransack his pockets. They're totally empty. The only thing the psycho was carrying was his trusty axe. As I stand up, I can feel the pressure beginning to grow again. My head is pounding, and I ache for another release. I've never been addicted to drugs, but I'd bet this is what withdrawal feels like.

I crash through the jungle, hacking a jagged path through the vines and branches. Everything around me is green. Leaves the size of elephant ears block the sun, so the light at the forest floor level is dim. This is exactly the kind of environment you'd expect to host dinosaurs. I wouldn't be shocked to encounter a velociraptor here, but I have a hunch that the dangers in this world are human in nature. And that hunch is confirmed when something buzzes past my temple. A split second later, a hand-made dart lodges in a nearby branch.

I slip behind a tree and scan the jungle for my assailant. At first I see no one. Then a shadow passes across a giant leaf about ten feet off the ground, and I throw my dagger toward the movement. I hear the blade hit something soft, and seconds later a body plummets to earth. I step out of my hiding place, well aware that there may be other killers around. Staying low, I cross the jungle to where I think the body fell. I find an avatar that's about half the size of an average human, with dark green skin and long claws. The fall appears to have knocked it unconscious. My dagger is protruding from its thigh.

It ambushed me. It wanted to kill me. If its aim had been just a little bit better, it would probably be standing over *me* right now. I should rip the avatar apart and fling the pieces in every direction. But when I pull my knife out of its leg, a splatter of blood hits me, and the sight and smell remind me of Kat's leg that night at the factory. I don't know if the avatar belongs to a headset player—or to someone with a disk. So I grit my teeth until the almost-irresistible urge to kill him passes. Then I rip a strip of fabric from the bottom of my robe and fashion a tourniquet.

I confiscate the avatar's blow darts and head off into the jungle. I take three steps before I hear a low growl and something springs onto my back. The weight of it almost brings me down. I don't need to look to know it's the avatar I just stopped myself from killing. I'm so enraged that I barely feel the teeth sink into my neck. I saved its life, and it's still attacking. I pull out one of its darts, reach back and ram it into its side. The poison on the dart's tip takes immediate action. The avatar slips off my shoulder. It's dead when it lands at my feet. I kick the corpse over and over again until I feel the pressure in my head release. If the guy had a disk, this would be my first real kill. I don't know if it will be my last. But I do know where I am now. I may not know the realm's name, but it hardly matters. If Mammon was the land of greed, this one is fueled by rage. The Elemental of Mammon wanted me out of the way. He sent me here to this realm to die.

I move much more cautiously now. I've painted my skin with mud from the jungle floor and I've woven leaves through the fabric of my robe. I'm not invisible, but I'm no longer an obvious target. Which is good, because the jungle is filled with avatars hunting for humans. I've managed to avoid most of them, though I did send a couple of headset players back to Start. But I've tried not to indulge my desires too much or too often. That's how Otherworld traps you. It introduces you to sensations you'd never be able to feel in real life. You discover what you've been missing—because it's taboo or illegal or because you lack the guts to do it for real. And when you find what's missing it's almost impossible to let it go again.

I would love to take out my axe and chop each and every one of these psychos into bite-size pieces. And that's exactly why I can't let myself do it.

After the sun sets, only the thought of Kat keeps me going. I have to reach her. This realm feels even more dangerous in the dark, but I can't hide and wait for sunrise. I've got to find a way out. Then it's like God reaches down and grabs me by the ankle and rips my foot out from beneath me. I'm weightless, flying through the air, smacking against leaves, scraping against the trunks of trees. I'm high enough to see a patch of starry nighttime sky through the dense forest canopy when my ankle is yanked again and I plunge downward. I bounce back and forth a few times until the movement is finally just a mild bobbing. I'm hanging upside down, racked by dry heaves, my ankle caught in a snare. I'd vomit, but my avatar's stomach—like mine—is completely empty.

There are only two things that could save me now. I could summon the strength to cut myself down. Or someone in the real world could remove my disk. I know neither of these things is going to happen, and I wait for the pain that's sure to come.

Something big is stomping toward me. I'm starting to wonder

if there might be dinosaurs in this realm after all. Then a tall beast breaks through the foliage. In the silvery moonlight, I can make out a human-shaped body with the head of a wild boar. Its snout is coated in dried mucus and studded with thick black bristles. The eyeballs have rotted away and their sockets are empty black holes. Two sharp yellow tusks jut from the bottom jaw of its open mouth. When it reaches me, the head's at my eye level, which means the creature has to be seven feet tall. I can see into its open mouth. Inside are two human eyes. Then a face takes shape around them. It's coated in dried blood. The boar's head is a mask.

Oh, *shit*. This cannot be good.

I hear a knife sawing through rope. Suddenly my ankle slips free and I plunge headfirst to the ground. My skull throbs with pain and my vision's blurred. An enormous foot passes by my face, and I notice it's bare. I catch a glimpse of the giant man's belt as he hoists me up by the back of the pants and shoves me into a rough-hewn sack. As my head begins to clear, I realize the belt is made out of human fingers.

I'm dragged for what seems like miles across the jungle floor. I feel every bump, stick and stone on the ground. Finally we reach our destination, and I'm dumped out into the bottom of a cage. The door swings shut, locking me inside. It's dark, but I can see enough to know that I'm in a long building made of wood. The floor beneath my cage is pressed dirt and the roof above appears to be thatch. There are other cages around me, all fashioned from some kind of indestructible bamboolike jungle plant. The cages are filled with filthy avatars, most of whom are covered in blood, though it's impossible to tell whether it's their own. The entire place reeks like a slaughterhouse.

I'm pretty sure I'm about to die.

I feel someone's eyes on me and I turn to find a man staring through the bars of the neighboring cage. He's bald and his eyes are ringed with black. You'd expect someone locked up in a cage to be either terrified or enraged, but there is no expression at all on his face.

"Where are we?" I ask him. "Who was it that dragged me here?"

I can tell he understands, but he doesn't answer at first. It's as if he's trying to figure out whether answering my questions will be to his advantage. Finally he breaks into a broad smile that's oddly charming despite his broken and blackened teeth.

"That was Ragnar," he says cheerfully. "The Elemental of Nastrond. We are in his realm, waiting for our chance to fight."

I have no idea what he's talking about, but it does *not* sound like fun. "Sorry, I'm new here. What do you mean?"

"Ragnar brings the best warriors to his fort to do battle. It's an honor. He's very picky about who he chooses. The reigning champion right now is Ylva. Whoever beats her gets to kill her any way he likes, and I have a ton of ideas." He grins and it makes me shiver.

"Like what?" I ask, just for the hell of it.

"Crushing, flaying, then drawing and quartering," he says lustily. "Her head will get put on a spike, and I'll eat the heart, but I'm still trying to decide what to do with the rest."

"Sounds wonderful," I say. The guy's clearly criminally insane. He'd make an excellent serial killer.

"Doesn't it?" he replies. "Hey, listen, I think it's morning in Dallas. I gotta go to school now or my mom will murder me. But I'll be back in a few hours. You gonna stay here for a while?"

"Sure thing," I say. I've just lost all hope for the human race. "I'm not going anywhere."

"Great. You can tell me everything that happened while I'm gone."

"Yeah, well, just to be clear, I'm not protecting your avatar while you're sitting in health class, learning how babies get made."

"I already know all about that shit, bro. And who cares if something happens to my avatar?" the guy says. "I don't have anything to steal. If I die tonight, I can just start again tomorrow."

I can't believe it's that easy. But I guess it is. The avatar goes still and fades slightly. Somewhere in the real world, a kid just pulled off his headset.

Looking around, I realize most of the other avatars are dormant as well. It's smart, I think. Otherworld must have been designed so its nights correspond to the real world's days. Players with headsets can go to work or to school without missing much action. For those with disks, the nights are time to let the brain rest. I can't afford such luxuries.

The sun is just rising when they come for me. The door of my cage opens and standing outside it is an NPC dressed in the bloody pelt of a beast I don't recognize. He doesn't speak, but the spear point he's thrusting at me seems to indicate that I'm wanted elsewhere. I feel the spear's tip scrape the skin of my back several times as the NPC marches me out of the building in which I've been held. I look back to see a Viking-style longhouse with windowless wooden walls and a thatched roof. We're heading for the center of a ring fort. Hundreds of wooden posts rise from the circular stone walls. On top of each post is a severed head. The smell is overpowering, and I'm overcome by nausea. The stench doesn't seem to bother anyone else, which tells me that the players here must be wearing headsets. A crowd has gathered, and everyone wants a look at me. A few step forward to inspect my physique. Most of them have big, burly avatars that were built to intimidate. None of them seems terribly impressed by what I have to offer.

The spear in my back presses me forward toward a fighting pit as the gamblers hurry to place their wagers. Through the crowd I see Ragnar standing at the edge, watching the action below. He's no longer wearing the boar's head, but he hasn't bothered to wash. The top half of his body is completely encrusted in old blood that's cracked like a dry lake bed. I can see strips of his pale white flesh beneath. The Elemental's long, matted hair would probably be blond if its true color weren't covered in a helmet of dried gore. His only clothing is a pair of patchwork pants made from different shades of leather. I'd rather not imagine their provenance.

My captors push me to the edge of the pit. The giant avatar I see down below was designed for brute force. He's useless for anything other than killing, but I'm sure he excels at what he does best. The dude could rip my limbs off like he was plucking the wings from a butterfly. And yet his eyes seem out of focus and his expression oddly constipated. Then a thin stream of blood trickles from one side of his mouth. The avatar lurches forward, stumbles and falls to the ground, revealing his assassin.

The champion is not a guest. I see it immediately, though I doubt many other human players have figured it out. Ylva must be one of the Children—and her braided blond plaits tell me she's most likely Ragnar's daughter. But unlike her beast of a father, she's sinewy and slim. Her mother was a wolf, I'd guess, judging by her yellow eyes and the razor-sharp claws extending from the end of each finger. Both of her hands are dripping with blood, but the rest of the girl is remarkably splatter-free. Two men hop into the pit with her. One gives her a rag, which she uses to wipe her hands clean. Then the two men drag the corpse out of the pit.

"Give me another!" she shouts up at Ragnar. "Let's empty all the cages today."

Ragnar beams down at the creature like a proud father. Then he reaches over and, with one arm, shoves me into the pit.

I wonder how many people have died of broken necks before they've even had a chance to fight. I hit my head on the way down, and when I stand up, I'm dizzy and disoriented. A horn blows. I stumble forward, my arms up to defend myself. I expect to die at any moment and I brace for an attack, but nothing happens. I drop my arms and see that Ylva is still twenty feet away. She's leaning against the wall of the pit, watching me.

"What are you doing?" Ylva asks. She speaks confidently but keeps her voice low as if she'd rather the spectators not overhear.

"I don't want to fight you," I say.

"Why not? You wouldn't be here if you didn't like to fight," she replies casually. She holds a hand out and examines her clawlike nails. "That's how it works, isn't it? The guests that are sent to my father's realm are the ones who get excited at the sight of blood."

"I'm not like that," I tell her. Then I remember the release I felt when I killed the first man who attacked me in Nastrond. "I don't want to be like that."

"Fight, already!" someone shouts from above, and cheering erupts from the crowd. They're getting impatient.

Ylva ignores them. She's obviously used to doing things her way. "You don't *want* to be?" she repeats with a smile. *She's really quite pretty,* I find myself thinking against my will. "What a ridiculous thing to say. Either you are or you aren't. Here in Otherworld, it makes no difference what you *want*. I didn't want to see my brothers and sisters slaughtered because they weren't part of the plan. I *wanted* them to live, but they were murdered anyway—just because they took after our mother. Do you have any idea what it was like to watch them die?"

I don't. "I'm sorry," I tell her. I used the same words after the goat man told me his story, but back then I felt nothing. Now I truly sympathize. The only thing I can offer her is the truth I've genuinely come to believe—even though it just got me kicked out of Mammon. "Guests don't belong in Otherworld. This world should be left to the Elementals, the Beasts and the Children."

"Tell that to the Creator," Ylva says.

"I'm on my way to see him now." I suppose that's the truth. If he's taken refuge in the ice cave, I may not have a choice.

The girl throws her head back and literally howls with laughter. The inhuman sound of it excites the crowd gathered at the edge of the pit. "You think you can convince the Creator to send his beloved guests away?" She's slinking toward me now. "He brought them here. He thinks we can all exist together. But your kind are monsters, and the Creator is a fool."

We're the monsters? That's rich coming from someone who spends her time murdering people with her bare hands at the bottom of a pit. "If the Creator doesn't agree to get rid of the guests, I will kill him." What the hell am I saying? I think I've gone too far.

"You'll kill him?" Ylva's closer now. "How? You won't even fight me. The Children are waging war against those who murdered our brothers and sisters, and we all have our part to play in the battle. I stay here in my father's realm. When the guests come to us, I rip them apart one by one. You will be next."

"What are you waiting for, bitch?" shouts one of the spectators. "I've got all my money on you!"

Ylva spins around. "Him," she says, pointing up at the heckler. An NPC steps forward and shoves the loudmouthed avatar into the pit. He lands with a thud at the bottom and Ylva is on him. Blood flies everywhere as she shreds his flesh with her claws. She returns to face me, drenched in gore. The creature she left behind is unrecognizable. The crowd above roars with approval.

"You won't win that way," I tell her. "Guests like him don't really die. You can rip them apart all you like. They may die temporarily, but they won't be gone for good. It's hard to explain, but they'll keep coming. And there will be more of them soon. Maybe millions more."

The smile on Ylva's face slips away. She sees I'm telling the truth—she's waging a hopeless war. The slaughter of her brothers and sisters will not be avenged. Her kind is almost certainly doomed. And that fact hurts her more than a weapon ever could. I wish I hadn't been the one to deliver the blow.

"Believe me—I want the guests to leave as much as you do," I tell her. "If you let me go, I might be able to help."

Ylva snaps out of her reverie. "I can't let you go," she says, her voice soft. She steps forward and reaches out to gently stroke my face. "Only one of us can leave the pit alive. That's the rule. If we climb out of the pit together, my father will kill us both. You must fight. Prove to me that you're capable of killing the Creator. Prove it by taking my life."

Ylva's arms slide around my waist and she nestles her head against my chest. The crowd rumbles ominously. They must be as surprised as I am. Then I feel the tips of her claws scratch at my back. One at a time they slowly pop through my skin. The wounds aren't deep, but the pain is excruciating. I can feel the blood beginning to soak my shirt. I try to break away from her, but she's incredibly strong and she manages to hold me tight. The crowd sees my struggle and begins to cheer.

"Head-butt her," a woman's voice whispers in my ear. "Now!" It could be the voice of God, for all I know. I'm in far too much pain to think straight. The claws are an inch into my flesh now. I have only one option: obey.

I rear my head back and then slam it into the top of Ylva's skull. The second I make contact, I know the blow isn't hard enough to do much damage. Still, I feel Ylva's knees buckle. The claws slip out of my flesh as she falls. I wait for her to get up, but she doesn't. I'm standing here like an idiot looking down in shock and wonder at the Child I've somehow defeated.

"Kick the body!" the voice urges in my ear. "You can't let it look like you won by accident."

Carole is beside me with her invisibility cloak on. I have no idea how she found me. She must have bashed the Child's head with some kind of weapon at the same time that I head-butted her. I'd cry out with joy if I could. Not just because Carole saved me—but because I'm no longer alone.

"Hurry!" she urges. "Get it over with! Gorog's waiting for us near the border. We need to get back to him before one of these bloodthirsty assholes takes him out."

I give Ylva a kick designed to appear a lot worse than it is. I can see a slight movement in her rib cage. She looks dead, but she's breathing. The realm has a new champion and the crowd above doesn't seem thrilled. Raising my arms in victory, I climb out of the pit.

Ragnar is waiting for me at the top. The spectators gather around us, many of them grumbling. Even the ones who won their wagers seem disappointed with the outcome of the fight. Not enough gore or guts for their taste.

"Very good," Ragnar says bluntly. "The champion has been defeated."

I'm not exactly sure how to respond. His daughter is lying on the floor of the pit, a stream of blood trickling from her head. But I seem to care far more than he does.

"The victor is free. He can stay and fight here—or leave Nastrond whenever he chooses."

I think I know which one I'll be choosing. I'm not sure how anyone survives in the same realm as this guy's breath.

"But there can only be one victor," Ragnar adds.

"What?" I ask.

"You cheated," he says, and my heart feels like it stops. He knows.

"I did not—" I start to insist.

He holds up a hand to stop me from wasting his time. "I see all. Cheating is permitted." I breathe a sigh of relief. "We follow one rule. Two cannot leave the pit alive." He motions to two men standing nearby. They step forward and grab Carole, yanking off the invisibility cloak.

The black yoga outfit she picked up at Gina's makes her seem impossibly small. Every avatar here towers over her. She looks like one of the pretty, fit moms you'd see in the Brockenhurst mall on a Tuesday afternoon.

"Which of you will be the victor?" Ragnar asks us. "Choose."

"He will," Carole says. Her face is pale, but her voice is firm, as if the decision were made long ago.

"No!" I shout. "I won't!"

"I made the kill," Carole tells Ragnar. "The decision should be mine."

Ragnar nods. "And so it is," he says. He pulls a hunting knife from a scabbard hanging from his belt. With one swift thrust, he plunges it into Carole. Then he pulls it out. The movements are so graceful that if it weren't for the smear of blood on his blade I would doubt what just happened. Carole looks down at her stomach and totters for a moment. I catch her before she slumps to the ground.

All around us, grumbling members of the crowd are beginning to wander away. There will be no more fighting for now. I drop to my knees and lay her body out on the dirt. I pull away layers of clothes, trying to get a look at the wound, but the blood rushing out of Carole's abdomen covers everything. I see nothing but red.

"Hey." It's Carole, weakly patting my hand. She wants my attention. It's all I can give her now. She smiles when she receives it. "I knew what I was doing, Simon. I knew how it would end. It was my time."

"You weren't even supposed to be here." I can barely speak. It feels as though there's a weight on my chest. It takes all my strength to breathe. "Why did you come?"

"You helped me and Gorog—and you didn't have to. We wouldn't have made it this far if it weren't for you."

"You could have made it a lot farther without me," I tell her.

"Listen to me, Simon. You're the one *I* could save. I did my part. Now you're going to find a way to save Gorog—and all the other people who are prisoners of Otherworld."

My vision is blurred and there's snot streaming from my nose. I'm nobody's hero. "I can't. Not me—" I start.

"Then who?" she demands, her voice suddenly strong. "It has to be you, Simon. Who else can do it?" The outburst seems to have drained the last of her energy. Carole's eyes flutter shut.

I rise in a panic and gather her up in my arms. "Just hold on," I plead. "I'll get you to the border. We can stay there as long as it takes to help you get better."

"No. You can't waste any more time," she says. "Promise me."

Before I can say anything, Carole is gone.

Blind and sobbing, I carry her body into the forest. No one in Nastrond bothers to stop me.

THE TRUTH

I'm sitting at the edge of a canal. The water is brown and topped with a frothy layer of foam. It looks like a cappuccino and it smells like crap. Still, I feel the urge to jump in. What a relief it would be to end it all. To spend eternity at the cold, calm bottom of the Gowanus Canal.

"I've been waiting for you to show up." My grandfather is sitting next to me, our legs dangling over the side. "How long's it been since you slept?"

"You're dead and I'm not in the mood," I say. "Go away."

"Dead, sure. But hardly gone. See that?" He reaches over and flicks my nose with his middle finger. "That right there means I'm immortal. I am inside every cell of you. You want reality, it's right smack-dab in the middle of your face."

Not long ago that would have made me feel better, but tonight it's hardly a comforting thought. Carole died because she thought I was the One. I've read a million graphic novels and seen hundreds of sci-fi films. In none of them was the One the delinquent grandson of a big-nosed gangster.

"So whatcha gonna do?"

"Can't you leave me the hell alone?" I ask. "Don't I deserve a minute of peace?"

"No," he says. "That lady died to help you. You owe her. I want to know what you're going to do."

"I don't know!" I shout.

"Hey! What are you shouting for?" someone whispers.

I look around. My grandfather's gone. I'm inside the fort that Kat and I built in the forest between our houses. I reach out and run my fingertips across the wood.

"Are you okay?" Kat asks. She's sitting cross-legged in front of me, the Yoda sleeping bag wrapped around her shoulders. I try to take in every part of her. The copper-colored hair, the hazel eyes. What if this is the last time I see her?

"No," I tell Kat. "I'm not okay. I need you right now." What else is there to say?

"I'm here," she says. "I'm always here."

I would give anything for that to be true. "You're a dream inside a virtual world."

"I'm the girl you met in the woods when we were eight years old. Even when you don't see me, I'm here. I helped make you *you*."

And I know it's true. "What am I supposed to do?"

"You're supposed to keep going," she says.

"I just came here for you," I confess. "I'm not who they think I am."

"Maybe you weren't," Kat says. "Maybe you are now."

"It doesn't work like that," I tell her.

"It doesn't?" Kat asks. "You think you can come somewhere like Otherworld and leave the same person? It's not just the disk that's dangerous. It's Otherworld, too. It changes you."

I think of the avatars hunting each other in the jungles of Nastrond. "I'm pretty sure most of the people who come here are pretty screwed up to begin with," I say.

Kat shrugs. "Sure. A lot of them. Otherworld was built so you can indulge your every desire. You can go around eating, killing, hoarding, screwing—and there's no one here judging you or telling you to stop. No doubt a bunch of people here were psychos from the start. What do you think happens to everyone else?"

"I don't understand. It's just virtual reality," I say.

Kat leans forward. "No, see, that's the big secret," she whispers. "It's not virtual if it changes who you are. All of this is real, Simon. It's *real*."

I wake to find the Clay Man standing with his back to me, staring down at Carole's final resting place. After I found Gorog, he and I did our best to bury her, but the grave isn't much to look at. The land around us is red rock with a silky coating of scarlet dirt. The wind spins the loose soil into dust devils that aimlessly wander the wasteland. The ogre and I spent hours searching for enough stones to cover Carole's avatar. I wonder if it's still there beneath the pile.

The Clay Man's head is bowed in grief. When I started my journey, he wanted me to leave Carole and Gorog behind. He said they would distract me from my mission. The truth is, the mission would have ended days ago without them.

"It's about time you showed up to pay your respects," I say.

"How did she die?" he asks.

I sit up and look around. Gorog is awake too. He's got his arms wrapped around his knees and his forehead resting against them. "I almost attacked the Elemental of Mammon and was sent to Nastrond as punishment. Carole followed me there and sacrificed herself to spare my life," I tell him. "She had this insane idea that I'm the guy who's going to free everyone the disks have imprisoned."

"You *are* the One," the ogre mutters to himself. I can tell he desperately needs it to be true.

"I'm *not*," I insist. "You've watched too many movies."

The ogre looks up at me. "Yeah? Well, so have the geeks who designed this place," he argues. "Maybe they designed it so there would be a *One*."

"I don't think there's a *One*," says the Clay Man.

"See?" I tell Gorog.

"But there might be *Two*," the Clay Man says. "If so, Simon is one of them."

"Who's the other?" I can tell from Gorog's voice that he's really hoping he gets to be number two. But he won't. I know exactly who the Clay Man has in mind.

I'm too exhausted and broken to keep playing games. "I need to know who you are in real life," I say. "I'm not going anywhere until you tell me."

"I understand," the Clay Man says. "And it's time I showed you. Let me take you out of Otherworld, and I'll explain everything."

"No." I'm not having it. "I'm not leaving Gorog in Otherworld on his own. We've got to talk here."

"Gorog is safe for now," says the Clay Man. "There are no Beasts or Children in this wasteland. He'll watch over your avatar while you return to New Jersey."

I'm about to refuse again, but Gorog claps a giant hand on my back. "It's okay," he says. "I don't need a babysitter. I'll be right here when you get back."

"Are you sure?" I ask.

He rolls his eyes. "Yes, Dad," he says. "And I promise not to use the stove while you're gone."

Gorog's sad smirk is the last thing I see before I'm blinded by a powerful light. I'm back at Elmer's, and the sun is streaming in through the glassless windows. There's someone bending over me, but all I can see is the blurry outline of a head. Still, it's not the head I was expecting.

"Oh, man, you really need a bath," a girl's voice says. "Why didn't you use the Depends I left for you?" I recognize the voice just as the face begins to come into focus.

"Busara?" I sputter. "*You're* the Clay Man?"

"Yes," she confirms as I struggle to sit up. "I sent you the disk. I got you into this mess. I'm really sorry. Here." She pulls a bottle of water and an energy bar out of her backpack. Then she sits down beside me on the floor. "You definitely need this."

I chug down the water and chew the energy bar as my brain slowly recalibrates. I should have known that Busara might be the Clay Man, but I was convinced it was Martin. "How did you get your hands on a disk?" I ask, realizing as I speak that she must have one too.

"My father was a man named James Ogubu. He invented the technology, and he liked to bring his work home," she says. "I have the master disk—the one he used to wear. No one else even knows it exists. It lets me enter and leave whenever I like. The disk I gave you is the one my dad made for me. The two devices are connected—that's how I'm able to find you in Otherworld."

The news takes me by surprise, and I stop chewing. "Your dad works for the Company?" I ask with my mouth full.

"Not anymore," Busara tells me. "I'm pretty sure Milo Yolkin had him killed."

"Milo Yolkin had . . . *What?*" Bits of energy bar spray every-where. I'm not sure why I find this news shocking, after everything I've seen in Otherworld and at the facility. It's still hard to believe that the Company's sneaker-wearing boy genius could be personally responsible for so many deaths. It's like finding out that the devil takes the form of a cocker spaniel.

"Sorry," Busara says. "That slipped out. I should have worked up to it. I didn't mean to blow your mind right away." She pauses as if she's collecting her thoughts and trying to put them into an order that will make sense to me. "When I was first diagnosed with my heart condition, the doctors told my parents I was never going to lead a normal life. My mom cried for weeks, but my dad refused to accept it. He started looking for solutions—and he was the kind of guy who could find them. He ran the Company's West Coast innovations lab, so he had access to money and resources and the world's best engineers."

"You're saying the disk was made for *you*?"

"That's how it started, but then my dad got obsessed with the project. Even after I had heart surgery and started getting better, his team kept working on it. After a while they ended up inventing the disk and the visor—and creating the software for the White City. The technology was designed to help people with broken bodies lead better lives. In the real world a kid with a serious heart condition might be stuck in a bed. But in the White City she could run and dance and play."

I remember the fields that surround the White City and imagine a younger Busara prancing among the flowers and butterflies. "It sounds really great. I can't understand how it could have gone so wrong."

Busara sighs. "Two words—Milo Yolkin. My dad's team was testing the disk when Milo heard about the project. He was smart enough to see that my father's technology was world-changing. It wasn't just the disk. The graphics and the AI were eons ahead of anything else developed by the Company. So Milo took my dad's whole team and brought them here to Brockenhurst. He wanted them to be closer to the Company headquarters in Princeton—but far enough away so they could work on the project in complete secrecy."

"That's when you moved to New Jersey?" I ask.

"Yeah, last year. Before they started expanding it, the building on Dandelion Drive used to be my father's lab."

It's beginning to come together now. "I was wondering how you managed to get me into the facility."

"I wasn't sure I could," Busara says. "But I have access to my dad's old files, and fortunately for us, the facility is still using the same HR recruiter. They like to hire former military personnel for all the grunt work. My dad always thought it was strange. Now it makes perfect sense. They want people who follow orders and keep their mouths shut. My father never did either of those things. That's what got him killed."

Once again, we're back to the subject of murder. How many people have died for this goddamn disk? "I still don't get why Milo would want your father dead. What the hell happened?"

"During his tests, my dad started finding bugs everywhere. The White City software was full of them. He wanted the city to feel real, so he created a self-sustaining ecosystem where the plants and animals all grew and reproduced and died. But weird hybrid species started popping up. And the NPCs, which my dad had designed to possess what he called emergent AI, began acting in unpredictable ways. He felt like he was losing control of the world he'd built. But he figured that could be fixed, even if it meant starting all over from scratch. The biggest problem wasn't with the software, though. It was with the *disk*."

My laugh is bitter. "Yeah, it kills people. I'd say that's a pretty big problem."

"The disk sends signals to the wearer's brain that convince it that everything the person smells or touches or tastes in the virtual world is real. Which is totally fantastic if you're riding ponies or eating steak. But it's impossible to create a virtual environment where only good things happen. My father realized that one day when he was in the White City testing the gear. He dropped a tablet on his foot—and it *hurt*. His brain was completely convinced that the injury was real. And that's when he knew the disk was dangerous. If a person was ever seriously hurt inside the White City, his brain could react by shutting down the injured part of his body. And it might be a part of the body the person couldn't live without."

"What did your dad do when he discovered the problem with the disk?" I ask.

"He ended the project. There were engineers on his team who thought he'd gone totally crazy, but he knew it was too dangerous to continue. Then Milo showed up at our house."

"Milo Yolkin was at your house? You met him?" Even now— after all I know—I still feel a stab of jealousy. The hoodie-clad girl sitting cross-legged in front of me on a gritty factory floor has been in the presence of greatness.

"Oh, sure. Milo's a super-nice guy. Really charming and polite. You'd never guess he was evil incarnate. He flew here in a helicopter from Princeton. It landed in our backyard. He wanted to talk to my dad about Otherworld. He said he'd been working on a secret reboot—and he'd borrowed a few things from the White City."

"*Borrowed?* Your dad gave him access to the White City software?"

Busara snorts angrily. "Of course not. But Milo owns the Company. The Company owned the lab. Milo took what he wanted, and there wasn't much my dad could do about it. I'm not even sure my dad knew that his boss had access until Milo's pet project started going south."

"Let me guess. Otherworld was full of bugs too."

"Yeah. *Literally.* Milo had borrowed the self-replicating ecosystem my dad created for the White City, and he gave some of his NPCs—mainly the Elementals—true artificial intelligence. By the time Milo came to see us, his Otherworld ecosystems were going completely insane. Beasts and Elementals were reproducing, and strange creatures were being introduced."

"The Children," I say.

"Yep. I guess Milo tried to get rid of them at first, but there was one little problem with that. My father had been very careful not to give his White City NPCs true artificial intelligence. But Milo had gone all the way. He'd tried to create a world so real that players would never want to leave. Now he had all these un-expected creatures to deal with—dangerous creatures that didn't want human guests in Otherworld. And the Children weren't robots. They were *conscious.* Milo couldn't bear to exterminate them. He wanted my dad to help him find a way to fix what he'd screwed up."

Something isn't adding up. The man who has murdered dozens of people just to test his technology suddenly got all tenderhearted when it came time to kill off a bunch of digital freaks?

"Did your dad help him?" I ask.

"There was nothing he could do. He told Milo to scrap every-thing, but Milo refused. My dad said it was like he *couldn't.* And that's when he figured out that Milo hadn't just stolen the soft-ware. He was using a disk. He was addicted to Otherworld."

"Wow." What else is there to say? I remember what Kat told me in my dream. *Otherworld changes you.* Sounds like Milo Yolkin was its first victim.

"My dad told me he threatened to go public if Milo didn't kill the entire Otherworld project. Next thing I know, my father's disappeared and Milo's launching Otherworld as a headset VR app. And then one day I work up the guts to try out my dad's old gear, and I discover the Company is beta testing the disk—and they've connected the White City to Otherworld. I guess they had to. No one was going to get really hurt inside the White

City, and the beta testers needed to be badly injured so the Company could see what the physical impact would be. I guess they decided it was worth killing a few hundred people to fix the disk's bugs."

We sit in silence while I let the information sink in.

"So when do I come into the story?" I ask.

"I've been lurking in Otherworld for a while now," she tells me. "I don't enter the realms. My heart is too weak—any kind of combat might kill me. But otherwise I come and go and no one seems to notice. Their focus is on optimizing the realms for launch; they don't have time to monitor the wastelands and in-between spaces right now. Plus, I think my condition keeps me off the Company's radar. I guess they don't believe that a sick kid like me could pose a threat. And I didn't think so either. I knew there wasn't much I could do on my own. Then I saw you inside the ice cave . . ."

"How did you know it was me?" I butt in.

"Are you kidding? You gave your avatar the same nose. And the girl you were with called you Simon."

"It was Kat."

"Yeah, I figured that out. After the collapse at the factory, I saw a way for us to help each other. You wanted to save Kat. I wanted Magna dead. All you had to do was kill him and take Kat through the exit in the cave. With her disk shut off, she'd be safe until her body could be rescued."

It takes me a moment to place the name Magna. It belongs to the big red creature inside the glacier. "I don't get it. Why did you want me to kill Magna?"

"He's the one they call the Creator."

I guess that clears a few things up, but I still don't understand why Busara would want him dead. "Isn't the Creator part of the game?"

"No," she says. "Magna is Milo Yolkin's avatar."

I suddenly feel unbelievably stupid. I should have made that connection a long time ago, but I was only thinking about saving Kat. Then something else hits me. "You lied to me," I say to Busara. "You told me the Creator was part of the game."

Busara swallows nervously. She must feel me seething. "At this point he is. Milo spends almost all his time in Otherworld. He hardly takes his disk off. He's addicted to the game. He just sits in that cave trying to figure out how to fix his creation. Killing his avatar is the only way to put a stop to the project."

"But if he's wearing a disk, killing his avatar would . . ." I pause. Things are quickly adding up in my head, and the conclusion I'm coming to is batshit insane. "That's why you sent me a disk. You want me to *murder* Milo Yolkin?"

"Yes," she admits, though she doesn't sound very proud of it.

"Because you think he killed your father."

Busara shakes her head with frustration. I guess she doesn't want her plan to be written off as revenge. "My father isn't the only person Milo's murdered. Think of all the people who've been forced to take part in the disk's beta test. People like Kat and Carole and Gorog. Milo's using them as human guinea pigs. I'm pretty sure most of the patients involved in the test don't even have locked-in syndrome."

"No shit. But do you have any proof?" I ask.

"According to my dad's files, the disk puts people into a state that's similar to sleep paralysis. Sleeping people don't have conscious control of their bodies, but that doesn't always keep them from moving or speaking. Remember the night you found me in Kat's hospital room? I punctured Kat's IV. When the fluid ran out, she started speaking, right? Well, people with real locked-in syndrome can't speak. I think the Company is drugging them. There's something mixed in with the patients' IV fluids that keeps them paralyzed. I'm sure of it."

I hold up a hand. "Stop right there for a second," I say. We just took a detour into some very dark and disturbing territory. "You're telling me you screwed with Kat's IV at the hospital? On a hunch? What if you'd been wrong?"

Busara's eyes go wide. I don't think she realized how far she'd taken things. "But I wasn't wrong," she says.

"You could have been," I say. "And now that I think about it, you knew from the start that the disk is able to kill its wearer. You even warned me that I might not get more than one life in Otherworld. And then you went ahead and let me use the disk anyway."

"My father thought the disk might be dangerous," Busara says. "But I swear, Simon. I didn't know for sure until now."

I'm starting to get seriously pissed. "So you let *me* be *your* guinea pig. You let me take all the risks while you never took a single one. What exactly makes you any better than Milo Yolkin?"

Her jaw drops. She clearly doesn't have an answer ready. "I'm really sorry," she finally says. And she looks sorry, too. But I'm sure she'd do it all over again. "I sent you the disk because I saw you in Otherworld and I was convinced you'd survive. And it was the only way to protect Kat. If I'd told you the truth, would it have stopped you from going in after her?"

"No," I admit. And it still won't. In fact, it just makes me more eager to get Kat the hell out of there. I pick my disk and visor up off the floor. "But you should have been honest with me. Thanks for giving me the opportunity to kill myself. I think it's time for me to go back and finish my mission."

"No! Don't you see—you don't have to," Busara says. "That's why I pulled you out of Otherworld. Carole died. That means we finally have proof that the disks are actually killing people. We can put the facility out of business and destroy the Company, too."

She hands me a phone. On it is an article from the *Morris NewsBee*. There's a picture of Carole. She looks a little plumper than she did in Otherworld, but otherwise she's exactly the same. She could have been anyone back at setup, but she chose to be herself. I scan the words. It's an obituary. Carole Elliot, forty-three. She succumbed to injuries sustained in an automobile accident. She's survived by her four children and husband. Turns out Carole really was a soccer mom.

I hand the phone back to Busara. It takes a few seconds before I feel like I'm able to talk. "How is *this* proof?" I ask.

"You saw Carole die in Otherworld yesterday. The same day she died at the facility."

"You're not thinking straight. That doesn't prove anything," I say. "It would just be my word against the Company's. Who do you think the cops are going to believe? Milo Yolkin—or some idiot kid with a criminal history?"

Busara goes quiet. "Okay, you're right," she says softly. "But I don't want you to go back to Otherworld. I guess I wasn't prepared to be right about this. But it's gotten too real, Simon. Carole died. You could die too."

"I don't have a choice. I have to go back. Kat is still there.

Gorog is too. I'm not leaving again until both of them are free. If that means killing Milo Yolkin, that's okay with me."

"What if you die fighting Magna?" Busara asks. "What's going to happen to everyone else in the beta test?"

Honestly, it never occurred to me. There aren't just two lives depending on me. Everyone in the facility is my responsibility. My life couldn't possibly suck any harder than it does right now.

"Fine," I huff. "Kat might have information that could help you stop the Company if something happens to us. She saw what happened at Elmer's. I'll pass the information along to you after I find her and talk to her. If we die, you'll need to find a way to use it."

"I don't understand," Busara says. "What kind of information could Kat have?"

"The night of the collapse, I was at the factory. I saw someone throw an object through a hole in the third floor. When it landed on the second floor, all the kids gathered around. That's what made the floor collapse. Maybe the boards were rotten—or maybe they'd been sabotaged. But someone knew that the floor couldn't handle that much weight in one spot."

"Wait—you said someone threw an object?" Busara asks. "What kind of object?"

"It was small and round. And when it landed, it was glowing. That's all I know, but Kat saw it. She might even have seen the person who threw it. I'd bet you anything there's a connection to the Company."

"What did Marlow do when he saw the object?" Busara asks.

"Marlow?" I try to think back to the night in question. "He shouted something. I think he told everyone to stay away from it."

I'm loving the look on Busara's face right now. It's nice to see

I've surprised her for once. "You never mentioned any of this," she says.

"Yeah, well, there's a lot you never told me, either," I shoot back.

I bend my head forward and begin to position the disk at the base of my skull.

"Wait," says Busara. "Give me one more hour. Please. There might be another way."

MARLOW

The windows of Busara's car are all down and I'm shivering un-controllably. But the chill is preferable to the smell wafting off me. I really should have used the Depends.

"That's it," Busara says, pointing through the windshield at a house on the side of a hill. It's three stories high, and the front, which looks out over the forest, is almost entirely glass. I've been fascinated by the structure ever since I moved to New Jersey. As a kid, it always reminded me of a giant dollhouse. I could never understand why the owners would choose to put their lives on display.

"We're going up there?" I ask. The driveway that leads to the house is completely exposed, and there are no other homes on the hill. "Everyone in town will be able to see us. Have you forgotten that I'm kind of on the run these days? Are you sure this is something we need to do?"

"Yeah, I'm—" Busara is cut off by a blaring emergency alert

from her phone. It sounds like the end of the world. As the car swerves, I grab her phone and turn down the volume. There's a message flashing on the screen.

"'I've been expecting you. Don't drive up to the house. Pull over as soon as you can. I will guide you from there,'" I read out loud. Then I look up in surprise. "What the hell is going on?"

"It's from Marlow," Busara says. "He must have geo-fenced the property line."

"We're going to see Marlow? *Why?*"

"Because I think I may have been wrong about him," Busara tells me.

Busara pulls onto the shoulder of the road. Just as she shifts the car into park and turns off the engine, a small black drone appears at the driver's-side window. It hovers there until we've gotten out of the car. Then it heads off through the woods. Busara goes after it without hesitation.

"You're just going to follow a random drone into the forest?" I call out to her.

"You got any better ideas?" she shouts back.

I catch up with her and together we hike through the forest. The little black drone stays a few feet ahead of us at all times. As the slope of the hill gets steeper, I keep glancing over at Busara. Tiny beads of sweat are forming along her hairline. She does not look well.

"Are you sure you're going to be okay?" I ask.

"Yeah," Busara says in a voice that sounds determined—but not terribly convincing. She follows up with a weak smile. I think this may be her way of saying she's sorry for not taking any risks in Otherworld.

"We can go back," I assure her. I don't know how much farther she can go. I have a hunch I'm going to end up carrying her out of here.

"We're almost there," she pants. "Look."

I glance up and realize I can see part of the house through the trees. There's an unobstructed view into the gym on the building's ground floor, where Marlow is lifting weights in his underwear.

"He knew you were coming," I say with a snicker. "Why isn't he dressed? Is there something you want to tell me?"

"Yeah. There is. I don't think that's Marlow," says Busara.

She must be feeling a little loopy. Because unless Marlow's been cloned, that is definitely my little buddy working out inside the house.

"Now who's the spy?" someone says behind us, and I nearly leap out of my skin.

"Marlow?" My eyes flick back and forth between the guy working out inside and the one standing here in the woods. This kid is dressed in mud-covered jeans and he looks like he's been out here for a while.

"The one and only," says Marlow, his voice quavering slightly.

"Oh my God," Busara suddenly gasps. She's ignoring the Marlow in front of us and watching indoor Marlow lift weights. "Is that what I think it is?"

"Yep," he replies. "They don't know we have one. I turn it on when I need to escape. I'm pretty sure I'm under heavy surveillance."

"It's amazing," Busara marvels. I still have no idea what *it* is— or how these two ended up sharing secrets.

"What in the hell are you both talking about?" I ask. "And if you're the real Marlow, who's the guy inside?"

"It's not a guy, it's a hologram," Busara tells me.

"That's not a hologram," I argue. "And even if it is, how would you know?"

"It's a Company product—the first three-D hologram projector that produces an opaque, lifelike image. Marlow's mom invented it," Busara says. "She and my dad used to work together in California. At the Company's West Coast innovations lab."

I'm pretty sure this is information I should have been given a long-ass time ago. I'm seriously annoyed. "What? So you guys knew each other in California? You're *friends*?"

"Not exactly," Marlow said. "I don't think I'd spoken to Busara in years before she accused me of moving to Brockenhurst to spy on her."

"Can you blame me?" Busara jumps in. "Was I supposed to think it was just a random coincidence that another Company kid shows up at my school on the other side of the country and starts pretending to be some kind of Goth stoner? I knew there was something weird about the whole thing. And I was right, wasn't I? Why *are* you in Brockenhurst, Marlow?"

"Punishment," he says.

The word stuns me for a moment. "Punishment? For what?" I ask.

Marlow looks over his shoulder at the house, where his hologram double is now doing a series of lunges and squats. "My mom built the projector to help people," he said. "There are a lot of schools in poor countries that can't afford to hire teachers. My mom thought the projector could be a solution to the problem.

But when the guys who run the Company saw the projector, they had other plans. Turns out the device has some serious military applications. You throw a few into a battle zone and have them project three-D images of soldiers. Your enemy won't know who's real and who's not."

"But Milo doesn't work with the military," Busara argues. "It's one of his rules."

289

"I get the feeling Milo doesn't care much about his rules anymore," Marlow replies. "When my mother tried to tell him what was going on, she couldn't even get a meeting to see him. So she decided to leak news of the military deal to the press. The Company found out before any harm was done. My mom could have gone to jail for the leak, so I took the blame. Pretended it was me trying to make a quick buck by selling the intel. A few days later, we find out my mom is being transferred to beautiful Brockenhurst, New Jersey, so she'll be closer to the Company headquarters."

"That was your punishment?" I ask.

"Yeah, we thought we were getting off easy. Then when we get here, they tell me I have to hang out with a certain group of kids at school."

"*Who* told you? Do you remember their names?" Busara asks.

"Their *names*?" Marlow asks. "You think these guys and I sat down and discussed this shit over Frappuccinos? Someone called me on the phone and told me what to do. As far as I know, it was God himself."

"What exactly did he tell you to do?" I ask.

"He told me to get to know Jackson, Brian, West and Kat."

"He mentioned those names specifically?" I demand.

"Yep," says Marlow.

"Why was the Company interested in them?" Busara asks.

"No clue," Marlow replies. "I just did what they told me to do. Jackson, Brian and West weren't the kind of people I'd usually spend time with, but they were a lot better than the kind of guys I would have met in prison."

"And then?" I ask. "What were you supposed to do once you got to know Kat and her friends?"

"Nothing," says Marlow. "I mean, there were always weird men watching us, but—"

"Weird men?" I ask.

"Yeah. They'd be in the parking lot before school or outside our houses at night. But I never talked to any of them. And I didn't hear from the guy on the phone until the day before the party. He called and told me to suggest a party at the factory, so I did. I had no idea—"

"That's it?" I blurt out. "They didn't ask you to do anything else?"

"No, I swear! I thought they were just going to spy on us. It wasn't till I saw the projector fall through the ceiling and hit the floor that I knew some serious shit was about to go down. So I stayed with my back against the wall. I tried to keep Kat from going near it, but she jumped up and ran toward it like—"

"Like she knew what would happen and wanted to save every-one." I finish the thought for him. I know exactly what Kat would have done. Her reaction tells me two things: Kat knew they were in danger. And she knew the Company had been watching her.

"Yeah," says Marlow. "I thought they might have rigged the projector with some kind of explosive, but the floor collapsed instead. If I hadn't grabbed on to a pipe when I heard the first rumble, I probably would have died too."

"So you were the one who dialed 911?" I ask.

Marlow holds up his hands. The abrasions on his palms are still red and raw. "I couldn't have wiped my own ass after the incident. How was I supposed to dial anyone? Whoever threw the projector must have called the ambulances."

"But why?" I ask. "Why arrange something like that—and then make sure there were ambulances on the scene?"

"Maybe they didn't want everyone to die," Busara says. "Maybe they had plans for the survivors."

Of course they did. At the facility.

"You have to come with us to the police," I say to Marlow. "You have to tell them everything you just told us right now."

"I can't. I doubt I'd make it as far as the station."

"What do you mean?" Busara asks.

"No one warned me about what was going to happen at the factory that night. They wanted me to die or end up in a coma along with the rest of them," he says. "But I didn't. And now I know too much. My mom, too."

"You really think—" I start to say.

"Yeah. That's why I left a present for you in your locker. When I'm gone, you should use it."

I look over at Busara. She shrugs. She doesn't know what he's talking about either.

"What present?" I ask.

"I found the projector after the collapse. It's just a hunk of metal at this point, but it can tie the Company to what happened to Kat and her friends. I couldn't keep it here, so I took it to the hospital to give it to you. When you got hauled out by security, I put it in your locker at school."

"That's what you were talking about at the country club? When you asked if I'd 'gotten it'?"

"Yeah," says Marlow. "Kat always said you were a genius. I thought you might be the one who could figure out what to do with it."

IMPERIUM

Busara has the combination to my locker. She'll get the projector, but it could take days to figure out what to do with it—and Kat can't wait that long. So my body is back at Elmer's. Busara was there when I went under, and she wasn't exactly thrilled to see me return. But she helped me put the disk back on, and she told me where to go. One realm lies between the wasteland outside Nastrond where we buried Carole and the ice cave I need to reach. Imperium, she called it.

I open my eyes to find I'm lying next to Carole's grave, Gorog's pudgy face inches from mine.

"Preparing for a career in dermatology?" I ask. "If so, I've got a mole on my left sack you might want a look at."

"You're back!" Gorog leaps to his feet and does a weird little dance. I don't think anyone's ever been so happy to see me. Red dust devils crisscross the landscape behind him while flashes of blue lightning illuminate the sky.

"Stop for a second," I say. "We need to talk."

"Is everything okay?" he asks.

Nothing's been okay for quite some time. I'm not sure anything will ever be okay again.

"We've got to get moving. But I need to ask you a few questions before we go. Remember I told you your body's been injured? It's being kept in a facility where they take care of your basic needs. If I have a chance to get you out of there, do you want me to try?"

"Yeah," says the ogre. "Absolutely. Why wouldn't I?"

"Because I don't know what kind of condition your body is in," I admit. "I don't know how well you'll be able to use it."

"I don't care," Gorog says emphatically. "Anything is better than *this*."

I have to agree with him there. "Okay. In order for me to find you, I need to know what you look like in real life," I tell the ogre. Even after all this time, it feels weird to ask.

"I have brown hair and brown eyes and brown skin," he says sheepishly.

"Your powers of description astound me. Can you give me a bit more to work with? How tall are you? How much do you weigh?"

"Last time I went to the doctor I was five three and weighed a hundred and fifteen pounds."

WTF? "Are you a girl?" I ask him, trying not to sound surprised.

"What? *Hell* no!" he shouts.

"Sorry," I say. "You're just a bit smaller than most guys I know."

"Screw you. My dad's six four. I'll be his height eventually."

The horror is starting to seep into my brain. "Wait a second. How old are you?" I ask Gorog.

"I turned fourteen a few weeks ago," says the ogre.

"Right." I pretend the news makes no difference to me. But if that bastard Milo Yolkin were standing in front of me, I would kick him to death. Fourteen. The kid's fighting for his life and he's fourteen years old.

We start walking, though I have no idea where we're going. The scorching sun begins to sink, and a flash of light on the horizon catches my eye. I'm too exhausted to form words, so I point. Gorog grunts and we pick up speed. The lights grow brighter and more colorful as what looks like a forest of glass and steel takes shape before us. The red wasteland ends abruptly. We're standing at the edge of a cliff, looking down at a city unlike any I've seen before. Clustered together are hundreds of skyscrapers. No two of them are the same, and all appear to be under construction. Land in this realm must be in short supply. The owners seem to be claiming the heavens, competing against one another to build the most intimidating towers. A few have already reached too high and are leaning precariously against their neighbors.

Each of the towers bears the distinctive stamp of its owner. Some feature giant video screens playing film loops of avatars dressed in the uniforms of Wall Street executives, Eastern European oligarchs or African dictators. Other owners have marked their buildings with retro-cool neon signs or hologram icons. But in the center of the city, one skyscraper rises far above the rest, its gleaming black walls resembling polished obsidian. Either the place has no windows or the building's *all* windows. It's impossible to tell. There's no mistaking the identity of its owner, though. Near the top of the structure, the name MOLOCH is emblazoned in blinding gold lights.

The Moloch building is already the tallest I've ever seen, but it's still in the middle of a growth spurt. A massive orange crane squats on top, hauling up materials for the dozens of NPCs crawling all over the upper reaches of the structure. From this distance, the workers seem ant-size and the top three floors appear to be little more than concrete slabs and steel columns.

"Someone's coming," Gorog says, just as my ears pick up the sound of vehicles below. A line of five tiny Humvees has emerged from between two towers, traveling toward us on what appears to be the only road out of the city. They're still miles away, and most of those miles will be straight uphill. There's plenty of time to run or hide. But I don't see the point. Neither does Gorog, I guess. We don't bother to discuss what to do next. We just sit down on a rock and wait.

The Humvees come to a stop in front of us, their engines still idling and their tailpipes spewing a fog of exhaust. Nothing seems to be happening. Then one of the doors opens and a man gets out alone to greet us. The closer he comes, the handsomer he gets. Clean-cut and well groomed, he looks like a cross between Prince Charming and the president of a Young Republicans club. He's wearing chinos and a blue chambray shirt with a black flak jacket on top. The name MOLOCH is spelled out in golden letters on the front of his black helmet.

The man waves. "Hello!" he calls out as he takes off his helmet. "I hope we haven't startled you. We've been watching you head this way for hours."

I gotta say, I think I may hate this guy already.

"*Daaamn.* Looks like Goldman and Sachs had a baby," Gorog snickers under his breath.

I wish I could laugh. I'm glad the ogre's recovered his sense of humor. Mine may be gone for good.

The man comes up to us and reaches out to shake my hand. "Welcome to Imperium." His voice is familiar, but I can't place it. "My name is Moloch. I'm the Elemental in charge of this realm." I guess I wasn't expecting the dude with the biggest building and creepiest name to have a haircut like my dad's. It's like meeting a tax accountant named Beelzebub. "You must be Simon. I've been waiting for you to arrive."

He's been waiting for *me*? I've been wrong before, but I'm willing to bet that's not a good sign.

"You knew Simon was coming?" Gorog asks warily.

"Well, I *hoped*. I've heard you're on your way to the glacier, and Imperium is the closest realm to the ice fields." Moloch turns to the ogre. "I'm sorry, and your name is?"

"Lancelot," Gorog says without hesitation.

"Pleasure to meet you, Lancelot," the Elemental replies with a knowing smile. Then he turns to me. "A friend of yours traveled through Imperium a little over a day ago. She said you'd probably be following her."

The relief is so goddamn powerful that I feel like I might float away. Kat's alive, and there might still be a chance to catch up to her. Then a thought drags me back down. This is the third time Kat predicted I'd be following her. If she really believed it, why the hell didn't she wait?

"She's on a rather urgent mission, as you know," says Moloch, who must have been reading my mind. "She wanted to reach the glacier early so she'd have time to scout the place out and plan the attack. I will give you and the ogre a room for the night and take you to your friend first thing in the morning."

"Hold on a sec. My friend is planning to attack the Creator?" I ask. If so, this is the first I've heard of it. "And you're cool with that?" The Elemental of Mammon didn't even want me to *speak* to him.

An alarm goes off in the city below us. It sounds like the wail of an air-raid siren. Moloch turns his head in the direction of the noise. I wonder if he knows where it's coming from. It stops as suddenly as it began and his attention returns to me. "Yes, well, your friend has come to the conclusion that killing Magna is the only solution—to Otherworld's problems as well as her own. I'm afraid I have to agree with her."

The land beyond the skyscrapers is as white as a blank sheet of paper. On the far side of Imperium lie the ice fields Gorog and I need to cross before we reach the glacier. Who knows how long it will take or what we'll encounter along the way? If I've learned anything here, it's that Otherworld is full of surprises.

"Thanks for offering us a place to stay, but I'd like to head for the ice fields right now," I say. I can't wait another twelve hours to see Kat. And I don't want her to try to kill Magna on her own.

"I would love to take you," says the Elemental. "But the sun will be down soon, and it is no longer safe to travel through my land after dark."

It seems peaceful enough to me. At the top of the towers, the NPC crews have disappeared. I wonder where they go when the working day is over. "Why not?"

Moloch sighs. "We've had quite a few problems with the Children lately. Have you met the Children?"

"I've had the pleasure," I tell him.

His face wrinkles with disgust. "Then you know they're abominations. They were never meant to exist. Magna should have exterminated them all long ago, but he couldn't summon the intestinal fortitude to finish the job. Now they feel entitled to Otherworld, and Imperium is on the front lines of the war. Unless we destroy them, it won't be long before they overrun us. While Magna sulks in his cave, I've had to deal with the Children on my own."

"Whose Children are they?"

"Not mine, I assure you," says Moloch. "Most of the Children in Imperium are *his* children. He traveled every inch of Otherworld in the early days, and his DNA ended up mixing with many of his creations. The idiot didn't even realize what was happening until it was too late. Come." Moloch motions for us to follow him back toward the line of idling Humvees. "We should head for safety unless you'd like to meet the local Children. As you've probably learned by now, they aren't very fond of humans."

Those are the magic words, as far as I'm concerned. As much as I pity them, I've seen what the Children can do. So even though I'm not all that keen to have a sleepover with Mr. Perfect, I'm not sure what other options Gorog and I have. Besides, if Moloch and his men wanted to take us by force, I'm sure they could. Right now they're playing nice. Which makes me suspect Moloch wants something from us. I'm curious to know what it is.

We're hustled into one of the Humvees. Moloch and I are in the back while Gorog sits with his neck bent and his knees wedged against his chest in the front passenger seat. I watch through a tiny window as we travel down the dirt road that leads from the cliff to the city below. The driver seems to be in a hurry to reach our destination. He hits every bump at top speed, ignoring the yelps that come from Gorog, whose head keeps thumping against the Humvee's roof. Finally we get to the outskirts of Imperium, and

the road turns to smooth asphalt. The Humvee steers between two towers on the edge of the realm, and the fading sun is immediately extinguished. Without its streetlights, the canyons of Imperium would be as dark as the dead of night. My eyes are drawn to a building up ahead. Its bottom floors are completely scorched, and the glass from its windows lies scattered across the road.

"Wow. Did the Children do that?" I ask Moloch.

"No," he says. "The fire took place before the Children began interrupting our gameplay. You see, the towers of Imperium are vertical empires. They're ruled by guests and house thousands of residents. The more powerful the guest, the more workers he owns. The more workers he owns, the higher his building will rise. But ruling an empire is much more difficult than most realize. In this case, the workers mutinied and pillaged the building. Then they tossed their owner's body from the roof. I'm afraid he never saw the rebellion coming."

As we pass by, a face appears in one of the blackened windows. It's a beautiful young girl with shimmering silver hair.

"Hey, who's that?" Gorog asks.

Moloch leans over me for a better look. The girl steps back from the window, but not in time. "It's one of the Children," he says. The driver mumbles something into the microphone attached to his helmet, and one of the Humvees in front of us pulls over to the side of the road.

"Why are they stopping? What are they going to do?" I ask as we speed past.

"Does it matter?" Moloch asks. "Don't waste your pity on the Children. Whatever my soldiers do to her, I assure you that she and her kind would have done far worse to you."

A few minutes pass in silence and the Humvee takes a hard right turn into one of the buildings and down a concrete ramp. It pulls to a stop in front of an elevator bank and Moloch, Gorog and I slide out. I look up toward the entrance we drove through, just as a heavily armored gate slams shut. It's eerily quiet, as though the building has been evacuated by all but the most essential personnel. Our footsteps echo as we walk across the concrete floor to the elevator. Moloch hits the button and the doors slide open. No one speaks as the elevator silently climbs to the penthouse on the ninety-sixth floor. The doors open again and we step out into a stunning apartment that's surrounded by the sky.

I walk to the windows that look over the ice fields, past a table on which a banquet has been laid out. My stomach growls, but I ignore it. I'm much more interested in the scenery. Now that we're out of the city's dark canyons, the sun hasn't quite disappeared yet. I can see that the towers closest to the ice on this side of Imperium have all sustained considerable damage. Moloch's building is in the middle of a war zone, and it's composed almost entirely of glass. I'm not sure we're any safer up here than we would be down below.

"That is the Children's work," I hear Moloch say. I turn back to the table, where every species in Otherworld must be represented. I'm able to identify a heap of buffalo meat, but most of the beasts have been roasted or stuffed beyond recognition. Moloch has taken a seat at the end of the table. Gorog has chosen a chair on the right side of the Elemental, leaving me the one on Moloch's left. No one else joins us. Aside from two guards standing at the elevator, the three of us are alone in the room.

Gorog immediately grabs a greasy thigh from a platter and begins stripping its flesh off with his teeth. I don't see the point in eating, and Moloch doesn't appear much more interested in the food than I do.

"It's so nice to be able to sit down and talk one-on-one with our guests," he says. "How long have you been in Otherworld?"

"A few days," I tell him.

"And what do you think so far?" Moloch inquires.

I feel like I'm being interviewed. I have a hunch he's looking for a particular answer, but I'm not sure what it is. I must take too long to speak because Moloch decides to answer for me.

"You don't like it," he says. "Of course you don't. It was designed by a madman to cater to perverts and psychopaths. All that will change once Magna is gone."

"You keep saying *Magna*. Don't most people here call him the Creator?"

"Among other things," Moloch says dryly. "He built this world to indulge his own weaknesses. Right now there's no reason a normal human being would want to stay. We'll fix that in time, of course."

"Parts of Otherworld might be fun if you had more than one life," Gorog offers half-heartedly.

Moloch smirks. "Yes, I would imagine the fear of death takes some pleasure out of the experience," he admits. "But all that will be resolved soon. Everyone knows that killing off your guests isn't good business. The idea is to offer them the kinds of immersive, one-of-a-kind experiences that will entice them to stay in Otherworld for as long as possible."

An Elemental who looks and talks like a CEO. Now I really have seen it all. How much does he know? I wonder. And who told him? There's a loud explosion outside, and the windows are briefly aglow.

Gorog drops his dinner. "What the hell was that?" he says, pushing back his chair and hustling over to a window.

"That would be Children," Moloch says. "Right on time, as usual."

"Oh, shit!" Gorog flinches as another explosion rattles the building. Then he looks back at me. "You really need to see this. They're launching some kind of missiles at us."

I join him at the window. The top of a nearby tower collapses in flames just as a ball of fire crashes into one of the giant video screens.

Moloch stays seated. The attack doesn't seem to worry him and he doesn't bother to look. "Don't be concerned. They can't harm us," he tells us. "Our best engineers have fortified the building. The defenses will hold, and in the morning you'll be on your way to the ice cave. If you accomplish your mission and kill Magna, we can end this ridiculous war. Without his protection, the Children won't last long and order can be restored."

"Do the Children have to be exterminated?" I ask, remembering what Busara told me. The Creator let them live because he knew they were alive.

"Of course!" Moloch exclaims. "They're a nuisance. Just look what they've done to this realm! They're making it impossible for our guests to enjoy themselves. Magna knows that guests and Children can't coexist, but he won't take any action. He's even let an army of Children take refuge in the ice fields. During the day, they're impossible to find. At night they scuttle out like vermin to attack Imperium. It's chaos. But once Magna is gone, the Children will be eliminated and the Beasts will be brought under control. We'll make Otherworld what it has the potential to be."

"And what's that?" I ask.

"A better reality—a place everyone wants to stay," says Moloch. "The deviant guests can still have their own realms, of course, but Otherworld will be a playground for everyone else as well."

Just like the man sitting across from me, the solution seems a little too neat. The guests will get their paradise, but first all the Children have to die.

I see Gorog's face scrunch up as if nothing he's heard makes any sense. "If everyone wants to be in Otherworld all the time, what's going to happen to the real world?" he asks.

Moloch dismisses the question with a laugh. "I imagine it will continue to revolve around the sun."

"Seriously, though," I say. "How much do you know about the real world?" I'm genuinely curious.

"I know it's a place of misery for most," he tells me. "Otherworld will offer humankind a chance to escape."

"You just put on a visor and leave it all behind," I say.

"Precisely," he replies, sounding pleased.

"Except you have to abandon your body. You know about our bodies, right?"

Moloch shrugs. "There will be solutions to such problems."

"Like what, exactly?" I ask. His flippant attitude is pissing me off. "Right now Gorog's body is crammed into a capsule. Mine is in an abandoned building waiting for a raccoon to eat it. Those don't sound like very good solutions to me."

"If there's a demand for storage, someone will find a way to supply it."

"You sound like a capitalist," I say. "Were you programmed that way?"

"I'm a realist," our host tells me. And judging by his tone, he has nothing else to say. "Now if you'll excuse me, I must attend to some business. One of the servants will be along shortly to show you to your rooms."

If I didn't know any better, I would swear that I'm in the most sumptuous bed ever constructed. I remind myself that my body is lying exposed on the wooden floor of a crumbling factory. But I don't quite believe it.

The moonlight streams in through the glass walls. In the city below, the siege has stopped. The Children are finally quiet and the realm is at peace. My eyes close, but I won't be sleeping tonight. In the morning, I will see Kat and possibly do battle with Milo Yolkin's avatar. I have to prepare myself for the fact there's a good chance I'm going to die. I don't really care anymore—as long as I can find a way to save Kat.

A breeze tickles my face. I detect movement through my eyelids, as if a shadow has passed through the moonlight. I open my eyes and see that someone is standing over me. It's the young girl from the burned-out building. For some reason, I'm not frightened at all. I'm happy to see she escaped from the soldiers.

Moloch said most of the Children belong to the Creator. If that's true, I wonder who her other parent might be. The moon, maybe. I suppose anything's possible in Otherworld. The girl's body is thin and fragile and her silver hair shimmers. I can't tell if she's made of flesh or light. She looks scared and nervous. She raises a finger to her lips and then gestures to me to follow her. I don't know why, but I do.

A ragged rectangle has been cut out of the glass wall of my room. Outside in the cold night air, a wooden platform is waiting, supported by ropes that must be attached to the arm of the giant crane on the top of the building. It wasn't there earlier when I took in the view. The girl steps onto the platform, and I climb out after her, though it's terrifyingly narrow and swaying from side to side. I hold on to one of the ropes and try not to look down. The girl's hair floats on the wind as the crane begins to lift us into the sky.

The platform comes to a stop at one of the unfinished floors near the top of the building. There's an elevator bank in the center of the floor, but beams remain exposed and the windows haven't been installed yet. The girl points to a steel cage near the elevator. It appears to be empty, and I'm about to ask what I'm supposed to be looking at when something inside the steel bars begins to shift and move like a pool of mercury. It takes me a moment to realize what's going on. There's someone in a camouflage bodysuit lying inside the cage. It has to be Kat. She's not waiting for me at the ice cave. Moloch has taken her prisoner.

I've opened my mouth to call out to Kat when I hear a whistle followed by a dull thump. It's the most horrible sound I've ever heard because I know exactly what it means. I glance over in time to see the Child crumple, an arrow lodged deep in her chest.

I grab her hand as she starts to fall from the platform. Her grip is firm and her flesh is warm. She's alive, but I can feel the life inside her draining away. Her grip loosens, and as she lets go, her fingers slip through mine. I thank God I can't hear her body break when it hits the ground below.

I turn in the direction the arrow came from. Moloch appears from behind one of the building's exposed beams, a crossbow in his hands.

"It's time to go back downstairs," he tells me.

I step off the platform and into the building. "You killed her."

"Her?" he scoffs. "Don't be stupid. That wasn't a *her*. It was a bug. Just a batch of bad code."

But she wasn't. I would swear the girl was every bit as real as I am. She risked her life to take me to Kat. She died helping someone she'd never met. How could anything get more real than that?

I'm still in shock as Moloch ushers me across the unfinished floor and onto the elevator. The descent takes less than two seconds, and the doors open on the ninety-sixth floor, revealing blood-soaked tiles and piles of dead NPCs. Before I can make any sense of the scene, two burly tattooed arms pluck Moloch out of the elevator. His crossbow drops to the ground as Gorog takes the avatar's head in his hand. I hear the crunch of Moloch's neck snapping and the thud when he falls.

"Hi, Simon," Gorog says, his smile big and wide.

Then there's a strange flash. I glance down to see Moloch's neck straighten. When he rises to his feet, he doesn't appear to feel any pain. I should have known. He's not an Elemental. He's not part of the game. Someone in the real world is controlling him. A headset player.

It's still sinking in when a dozen NPC soldiers rush into the room behind the ogre.

"Gorog!" I shout, but it's too late. They've surrounded him now, but he doesn't struggle to break free. He doesn't even appear to be frightened.

"You've got this, Simon," he tells me. "Remember, you're the One."

"Get rid of the goddamn ogre," Moloch orders his men.

"No!" I shout. "No, don't! Gorog!"

There's no answer. The tip of a spear emerges from between two of the ogre's ribs. Gorog's body drops. The deed has been done.

THE ENGINEERS

I open my eyes. I'm in the back of a patient transport van. My visor and disk have been removed and my chest and legs are strapped down. My hands are bound together with a zip tie that's slicing into my wrists. No one's riding with me. I stare at the ceiling, my teeth clenched in rage. When I find the person responsible for Gorog's death I will rip him limb from limb.

I feel the van backing up. Then the engine shuts off. The doors open and the driver rolls my gurney out. We're in one of the facility's loading docks.

"You can go. I'll take him from here," someone tells the driver. A face appears above me. It's Martin.

"Hey there," he says. "Sorry for all the drama back in Otherworld. We had to keep you busy while we looked for your body. By the way, it was genius to hide it right out in the open. None of us ever considered the factory."

I'm a moron. My little outburst at Moloch's dinner party told them right where to find me.

"You're Moloch?" I ask.

"Sometimes," he says. "Last night it was Todd. And when we're not in Otherworld an NPC fills in for us. We've got to keep the place functioning while the test is running."

"You killed Gorog," I snarl.

"Yeah," Martin admits as he wheels me into the building and down the long hall. "It wasn't part of the plan, but then he went and tried to break Todd in half."

"Todd was wearing a headset!" I shout. "He couldn't die! Gorog was wearing a disk. He knew that and he killed him anyway!"

"You're right—ordering the ogre's death was a mistake," Martin concedes. "But in Todd's defense, you get so used to dealing with the Children that the words just pop out. Still, there is some good news! The ogre bit the dust, but it turns out the kid didn't die. It's a very exciting day here at the facility. We've taken a giant step forward with the disk—and your friend helped us make it."

My relief is mixed with a hundred other emotions, the strongest of which is terror. "Are you going to cut him up?"

"What?" Martin blurts out. He looks thoroughly revolted. "Why would we do that?"

"To examine his brain. I've been in your lab, you know. I've seen what you do to people."

"Sure, to *dead* people," Martin corrects me. "We don't chop up the living. Do you think we're monsters? We'll just run lots of CAT scans."

"Hello, Martin," a familiar voice interrupts.

"Hey, Angela," Martin replies. "I've got a delivery for the boss."

"Wonderful," the robot says. "According to his GPS, he's on his way back to the facility right now. Estimated arrival time is seventeen minutes."

Oh, good. Milo is coming. I can't *wait* to see him.

"Thanks, Angie," says Martin. "Now how about opening door number two for me?"

"It would be my pleasure." Her flirty voice seems to imply that the pleasure will be physical. Someone must have thought it would be real funny to have a sexed-up robot secretary. I've met her twice now and the act is already old.

Martin and I ride the elevator down to the maze of capsules where the bodies are kept. Martin whistles as he rolls me toward a room along the perimeter.

"We-he-hell," someone calls out. "If it isn't the savior of Otherworld. *The One*." It's Todd.

Martin sighs. "Come on, don't be an asshole," he says. He undoes the straps that bind me to the gurney and helps me sit up. We're in an office that would appear perfectly ordinary if not for the computer screen displaying what must be a video feed from Moloch's tower. There appears to be something happening on the ice fields outside Imperium.

"You're both assholes," I inform them just as Martin grabs an X-Acto blade from a desktop and bends forward to remove the zip tie from my wrists.

"Maybe you should keep his hands bound," Todd says. "The little bastard seems pretty agitated."

"Yeah. Good thinking." Martin stands up and takes a cautious step back.

Once he's sure I'm no threat to him, Todd sits on a nearby desk.

"So we're *assholes,* are we?" I'd love to punch the smug look off his face. "In a few years, you can tell that to the Nobel Prize committee. By the way, I hear Watson and Crick were assholes too."

"Watson and Crick never killed anyone," I say.

"That you *know* about," Todd says. "Watson seems like the kind of guy who probably experimented on a hobo or two, don't you think?" When he looks over at Martin, he seems to be expecting a laugh.

"Oh, shut up," Martin snaps instead. "We're not the bad guys," he tells me. I get the sense that he really wants to believe it.

"You're tricking people into using stolen technology that you know can be deadly," I point out. "If you're not the bad guys, who the hell are?"

"Whoa there, dickhead. You think we *stole* the tech?" It's Todd talking now, and he's completely offended. "We were part of the team that developed it! We sank three years of our lives into the disk."

"And the technology won't be dangerous for much longer," Martin is quick to add. "We're analyzing what happened to the kid with the ogre avatar. If we can figure out how he survived, we might be able to fix the disk."

"It's too late. People have already *died.* A lady with four children *died.*"

Martin looks stricken, and unless he's the world's greatest actor, he's completely sincere. "You're talking about Carole Elliot. It's tragic, I know. But Carole didn't die in vain. Besides, after the car accident, her body was beyond repair. She wasn't walking out of this facility either way. Look—a handful of people have been lost, but thanks to them, humankind is on the verge of taking a giant step forward." There must be a vat of Kool-Aid hidden somewhere in the building. When I get a chance, I'll hunt it down and drown Martin in it.

"They didn't *die,* you psychopath," I say. "They were *sacrificed.* Can't you tell the difference?"

"You know what?" Todd growls. "I'm getting real sick of this sanctimonious crap. We took people who would have spent their entire lives as drooling vegetables, and we gave them the opportunity to be true pioneers."

"Their sacrifices will make life better for the entire human race," Martin quickly adds.

I'm dumbfounded. "People's lives are going to be better because of Otherworld?" I ask. "Are you joking?"

"Otherworld? You think that's what all this is about?" Martin laughs like he's discovered the source of my confusion and can finally set the record straight. "We needed software for the disk's beta test, and Otherworld just happened to be available. But Otherworld is only the beginning. Do you have any idea what our technology will do? It's going to educate people around the globe. Someday soon, a kid in rural India is going to slap on a disk and attend classes taught by Harvard professors."

"You think Harvard's going to let little Indian urchins take their classes for free?" Todd mutters under his breath.

"*Whatever.*" Martin rolls his eyes as if they've had the same exchange a million times. "Then think about all the elderly people cooped up in nursing homes. With a disk they can spend their final years touring the world or . . ."

"Or having sex with hot young things," Todd finishes.

"Goddamn it, are you going to let me talk?" Martin nearly shouts. The two of them act like an old, homicidal married couple.

"Do you see what I'm saying? The disk is going to level the playing field for people around the world. Everyone will have access to education and companionship and sex. You'll be able to travel the entire globe without spending a penny on airfare. You won't need to be born rich or beautiful or lucky. All you'll need is a disk."

I want to ask Martin how many people he's willing to kill to save the world, but I can't stand to hear another lecture. "Where's Milo?" I ask. "I want to talk to him."

"Milo?" Martin asks, as though he doesn't quite recognize the name.

"Yeah, your *boss*. Wasn't he supposed to be here in seventeen minutes?"

Todd laughs. "Milo's already here, bro."

"Where is he? Go get him."

Martin looks nervous. "Come on," he says, taking one of my elbows and helping me slide off the gurney. "Why don't I show you around before the boss comes to see you?"

"Thanks," I say. "But like I told you, I've been here before."

"Yeah, we know," Todd sneers. "Lotta people got fired because of you."

I think of Don and Nathaniel and the nurse who helped me escape, and I suddenly want to vomit. I probably got them all killed. God knows how many people Martin and Todd have murdered, but I've got a body count of my own.

"Fired?" I ask. "So you think they're all working at Costco now?"

"What exactly are you implying?" Todd barks.

"Hey," Martin says in his most soothing voice. He's smiling at me like I'm a mental patient. "Don't be ridiculous. Nothing happened to them. They just don't work here anymore."

You know, I actually think he really believes all this shit. I think he's managed to convince himself that there's nothing evil about the operation he works for. They're just a bunch of scientists using vegetables to save the world.

"Tell you what," Martin says. "Why don't I take you to visit your friends? You can see for yourself they're okay. We've been taking very good care of them."

Butterflies flutter in my stomach at the thought of seeing Kat. Martin's offer is one I would never refuse. So with my hands pinned together like a convict on his way to court, I follow Martin out of the office and into a nearby room. There's a hospital bed at the far end, but Kat's not in it. Lying on top is a young black kid. There are tubes sprouting out of him and machines monitoring his vitals. But there's no visor on his face. I'm not sure why I'm here, until—

"That's Gorog," I say.

"Who?" Martin asks. "Oh, right, that was the name he gave his avatar. His real name is Declan. He was riding his bike to school one morning and got hit by a car. The cost of his hospital care was about to bankrupt his family, so the Company stepped in to help."

"He told me he was fourteen years old." There is no way the tiny boy on the bed is fourteen.

Martin clears his throat. "I believe he's thirteen," he says.

"You bastards are experimenting on thirteen-year-olds?"

"I'm sorry, I thought you'd be pleased to see him," Martin says irritably. "He's in stable condition. We're monitoring his progress very carefully. He's out of Otherworld for good now—and he'll be well protected. He's the secret to fixing the disk."

I run my fingertip along the zip tie that's holding my hands together. If I could only find a way to snap it, I would kill Martin right now.

"Would you like to see Katherine?" he asks.

"Yes," I manage to croak.

We weave through the maze of capsules. Construction has apparently been moving ahead at full speed. The labyrinth has doubled in size since the last time I was here. And more of them are in use. Hundreds of the hexagonal windows glow with the strange orange light.

"This is Katherine's," Martin says, stopping at one of the windows.

I press my nose to the glass. "It's empty," I say. "Where is she?"

"She's in one of the visiting rooms," Martin says. "There's someone with her now. As soon as they leave, I'll take you up to her. I thought you'd prefer to see her face to face. And just so you know, I made Todd leave your Otherworld avatar in the same cage with Katherine's. After you talk to the boss, you can put on a disk and join her there."

"Why would you do that?" I ask.

"Because I'm not a bad guy," Martin tells me. "You two are sweet together."

We hear the sound of wheels on the concrete floor. Someone is pushing a gurney our way. "That's our latest patient," says Martin. "Would you like to meet him?"

I nod, but he hesitates.

"You know what?" He points at the zip tie around my wrists. "It's probably best if the staff doesn't see you like this. I'll remove your restraints if you promise to behave."

"And if I don't?" I ask.

He raises his eyebrows and tilts his head like he's lecturing a naughty toddler. "If you don't behave, you'll never get to see Katherine Foley again. Here or in Otherworld. Do you understand?"

I nod again, but I'm gonna play it by ear. My fingers tighten into fists as Martin removes the zip tie. I have to force them to open again.

The nurse turns the corner. It's not the same woman who helped me. God only knows what happened to her. My eyes lock with the nurse's. There's a flicker of life in them. She's never seen me before, and she knows there must be a reason I'm here. Then I glance down at the body she's carting. It's Marlow Holm.

"Shit," I mutter. His entire body is black and blue.

"I know." Martin winces at the sight. "The kid's pretty banged up. He and his mother were in a car accident this morning. It was a terrible tragedy. She worked for the Company. They say she was brilliant."

"Mrs. Holm is dead?" Just as Marlow predicted. They made it happen.

"You knew Madeline Holm?" Martin asks casually. You'd think we were making cocktail party chitchat.

"I went to school with her son."

"Of course! I can't believe I almost forgot," Martin says. "Yes, she passed away. But her son survived, and now he's here with us. Don't you see? Marlow is a member of the Company family, and he'll be part of the beta test, too. That's how passionately we believe in the importance of this project. The accident that brought Marlow to us was tragic. None of us enjoy seeing seventeen-year-olds with broken bodies. But if Marlow dies in our care, he'll die a hero. His life will not have been wasted."

I meet Martin's beady little eyes. "Don't feed me your bullshit," I say as calmly as I can. "You and I both know Marlow wasn't in an accident. The Company did this to him."

The nurse gasps, and Martin recoils as if I've raised my fists. "Excuse us for a moment," he tells the nurse. She stares at him like a deer watching an eighteen-wheeler barrel toward it. "*Now,* please." The words break the spell and she bolts.

Martin's good humor has disappeared by the time he turns back to me. "I thought you were going to behave!" he says through clenched teeth.

I've never known how to behave. I should keep my mouth shut, but I can't let Martin convince himself that he's anything but a murderer. "Marlow was in the same *accident* that nearly killed my best friend. He wasn't supposed to survive it—but he did. So the Company staged another *accident.*"

"You know what? Todd was right. You are a little bastard," Martin snaps. "I've been trying to explain my work to you, and you're spouting stupid conspiracy theories—"

"It's not a theory," I say. "Marlow wasn't in an accident. And he's not in a coma now."

"Don't be ridiculous," Martin scoffs.

Before he has a chance to stop me, I step forward and slide the IV needle out of Marlow's arm. Then I pull the visor off his face. Marlow's eyes are open—wide open—and he's terrified.

"Have you gone completely insane?" Martin whispers angrily. "Nurse!" he calls out. "Nurse, come back, there's a problem with the . . ."

And he stops. He sees it too. Marlow's lips are moving.

"God," Martin groans.

"You sure you want to call on God right now?" I demand. "'Cause I have a feeling he's not too happy with you. *This* is the truth, Martin: The people you have stored in these capsules aren't *vegetables*. They may be injured, but they don't have locked-in syndrome or anything like it. There are drugs mixed in with the IV fluid that are keeping them comatose. And maybe some of these people were in accidents, but I know of at least four kids my age who are here because the Company *wants* them to be here."

Martin rubs his eyes, and I wonder if I've managed to surprise him. Then he sighs and picks up the needle that's dangling from the end of the IV's thin plastic tubing. He places it on Marlow's chest, then looks up at me.

"I know," he says. His anger is gone. He sounds beaten. "I wish like hell that I didn't, but I do."

Marlow's lips stop moving and a thin trickle of drool escapes from the side of his open mouth as Martin takes the visor out of my hand and places it back on Marlow's face.

"How can you stand back and let this happen?" I ask.

"You're young and idealistic, Simon. When you get older, you'll realize there are no easy choices. I stand back and let it happen because I honestly believe that this technology is going to make billions of lives better. What would you do in my shoes? Would you let a few dozen people die if it meant making the world a better place?"

"Is that what you think you're doing? Improving the world?"

"Nurse!" Martin calls out again, and this time I hear footsteps hurrying toward us. I have a few more things I'd like to get off my chest, but Martin stops me. "Be careful what you say in front of her," he warns. "I know what it's like to have people's deaths on my conscience. I've learned to live with it. Do you think you could too?"

This time, I have no answer to offer.

"Come on, then," Martin says as the nurse returns. He smiles at me as if bygones are bygones. "Let's go see your girlfriend. Promise you'll be on your best behavior? No more yanking out IVs?"

I keep my mouth shut and nod.

"Good boy," Martin says.

He guides me through the maze and up the stairs toward the visiting rooms off the lobby. I pause when we reach the top to watch the nurse connect Marlow's body to the tubes and wires that will keep it alive inside his new capsule. Martin waits patiently. When I'm ready, I follow him down the hallway until we arrive at the last visiting room. There's a blinking green light on the biometric scanner beside it.

"Kat's ready for us," Martin announces.

"You're sure her stepfather is gone?" Even now, I have zero desire to be in Wayne Gibson's company.

Martin shoots me a strange look. "You mean Mr. Gibson?"

"You said she had a visitor. Who else would it be?" I ask Martin. Her mom's in a loony bin, and Kat has no other family. "I saw him here the last time I visited."

"I'm sure you did," Martin responds as if I'm a moron. "He works here."

No. Fucking. Way. "He *what*?"

Martin snorts. "And I thought you had everything figured out, boy genius. Wayne Gibson runs this facility. He's our boss."

"What about Milo?" I ask while my mind reels.

"Milo's on sabbatical," Martin says.

He places his palm against the scanner's screen, and there's no time for a response. The door in front of us opens with a swoosh. It must be the same room I was in before. There's an OUT OF ORDER sign taped to the bathroom door. My eyes pass over a cabinet with a drawer jutting out. The medical equipment inside grabs Martin's attention and he heads over to investigate.

And then I see Kat, tucked between the sheets. I'm by her side in an instant, her hand in mine and my face buried in her hair. I know there's a very good chance that this is the last time I will see her alive in the real world. Martin promised that Kat and I could be together in Otherworld, but I doubt he's run that one by his boss.

The boss. Wayne Gibson. Wayne *fucking* Gibson. I'm still finding it hard to wrap my head around that one. I almost wonder if Martin is messing with me. But now that I think about it, Wayne Gibson makes sense. Did he have Kat in his crosshairs before he married her mother—or did Kat accidentally get in his way? That's what I'd really like to know. If only I could see him now. If only I could go back to the day when he and I stood face to face on Kat's front porch. I would do things to Wayne Gibson that would shock Ragnar and all the bloodthirsty psychos in Nastrond. I would take my time with his body, ripping it apart bit by—

"Simon?" It's Martin's voice. He's come to Kat's bedside.

I look up at him and he flinches. I'm glad. The rage rushing through me must show on my face. Martin did this to Kat, and when I'm done with Wayne, I'll come for him next.

"You need to say goodbye now," Martin tells me. "It's time to go."

"No," I say. "I'm not leaving her."

Martin rolls his eyes. "Do I need to call security?" he asks.

"Go ahead. Call them," I say. "I will kill every person who comes into this room."

"Sure you will," Martin says with a smirk. He can laugh all he likes. I know it's true, and I know I can do it. Otherworld trained me well.

Martin lifts his arm, bringing the tiny computer that's strapped to his wrist closer to his lips. I rise too. Martin won't be calling anyone. When they find his body, I'll make sure that arm is rammed somewhere *special*. He happens to glance up as I lunge across the bed. His eyes go wide as my fingers wrap around his scrawny neck. I've barely begun to squeeze when Martin's eyelids flutter shut and his body goes limp. Suddenly the full weight of his body is in my hand. My grip is unprepared for the burden, and he slips through my fingers and crashes to the floor.

I rush over to the other side of the bed. For a few magical seconds, I honestly believe I've acquired superhuman powers. Then I spot the girl crawling out from beneath Kat's bed. There's a smile on her lips and a syringe in her hand, and I know my days as a superhero are over.

"Busara? What are you doing here?" I whisper.

"Taking a risk," she tells me, sounding giddy with excitement. "I grabbed Marlow's projector from your locker at school, but when I got back to Elmer's, your body was gone. I figured the facility was the only place you could be, so I made an appointment to visit Kat." She points at the steel door that leads to the capsule maze. "I was planning to go through there and look for you, but then you spared me the trouble and came to me."

I glance down at Martin. "How did you just . . ."

"I found a syringe from the drawer and filled it with fluid from Kat's IV. Gave Martin a taste of his own medicine. Pretty clever, right?"

She called him Martin, I realize. "How do you know his name?" I ask, prodding the engineer's body with my toe. I must sound suspicious. Probably because I am. Busara's still got a way to go before she earns my trust.

"Geez, Simon. He used to work for my dad, remember? Stop thinking I've turned to the dark side. Give me a chance, will you?"

I'll give her a chance. But only because I don't have a choice.

"Are you sure you're strong enough for all this?" I ask. "I mean, your heart . . ."

"Is still beating as far as I can tell," Busara says. "And we've got to get out of here. Martin won't be unconscious for long. I'm parked outside."

"What about Kat?" I ask. "We have to take her, too. And Gorog—what about him?"

Busara's smile fades. "Simon . . ." She's going to tell me it's impossible.

"I am not leaving the facility without Kat," I insist. "I am not going to let them put her back in one of those capsules so she can die in a video game."

"Do you think Kat wants to be taken out of Otherworld?"

Busara asks. "She's obviously on a mission of her own. Do you think she wants it to end? Maybe you should ask her before you rip off her disk."

"I don't care what she wants; I will not let her die!"

"Calm down," Busara says. "As long as you're free, Kat's not going to die."

"What makes you so sure?" I demand.

"Because you know about the disks. And the Company will want to find you before you can cause problems. Kat's their bait," Busara tells me. "If she's here, the Company knows you'll eventually come back to the facility."

I hate to admit it, but she makes an excellent point. Right now, the best way to protect Kat may be to abandon her here. But there's no way in hell that's going to happen.

"I want to get you out of here so you can go back to Otherworld and get Kat through the exit," Busara is saying. "Then we'll figure out what to do with the projector."

"I can't go back to Otherworld. I don't have a disk and visor anymore," I tell her. "The Company took mine when they found my body at Elmer's."

Busara reaches into the pocket of her jacket and pulls out a well-worn set of gear. "Use these. They're all I have left. They might not be pretty, but they work. The disk isn't connected to mine, though. I won't know where you are in Otherworld, so I won't be able to help you. Now get out of here, and find a safe place to hide your body."

"I'm not going anywhere. Help me drag Martin to the bathroom," I tell Busara. "No one's going in there. It's been out of order for days. Tie him up and then head out to your car and wait for a signal. Don't leave the parking lot until you get one."

"What are you going to do?" Busara asks. "Where are *you* going to go?"

"Nowhere," I tell her. If Busara could fit under Kat's bed, I figure I can too. "I'm going to stay right here."

THE CHILDREN

"Simon." The whisper comes from above. I'd know the voice anywhere.

My eyes are still closed, but I'm where I need to be. I can feel lips pressing against mine. I reach out and find the girl they belong to. The body beneath my fingertips is soft and warm. An electric current courses over my skin. Every cell is tingling. Maybe none of this is real, but I've never felt so alive.

"Kat." My head is in her lap. Her hair has fallen across my face. Once more, her lips press against mine.

When she pulls back, I sit up and open my eyes so I can find her lips again. But the sight of her smile stops me short. It's been so long since I've seen it. I never want to look away.

"You came after me, just like you promised," she says.

"Of course I did. I'd go anywhere for you."

Kat takes my hand. "I'm sorry. I should have told you everything from the start," she says, her eyes on my fingers. "I was trying to protect you. I thought if I could just—"

"It's okay," I tell her. "We're in this together now."

"I know," she says. "If it makes any difference, it feels like you've been with me the entire time."

She sighs and her breath turns into a frozen cloud that hovers between us for a moment. We're no longer in Moloch's tower. Around us, I can see ragged rock walls and a cavern that's bathed in an ethereal blue light. What look like strands of stars are suspended from the ceiling. They blink in strange patterns that pass from one strand to the next as if they're creatures speaking in code. And they are, I realize.

"They're alive," I say.

"Yes," Kat confirms. "The Children cultivate them."

"Where are we?" I ask her.

"Beneath the ice fields," she tells me. "This is where the Children hide. They brought us here," Kat says.

"Why are they helping us?"

"Because they want us to help *them*. We know we don't belong here. The guests with headsets think this is a game—that the Children only exist for their amusement. You wouldn't believe the things I've seen while I've been here."

"I think I probably would," I say. "How did you figure out that the Children are different?"

"I was traveling through the wasteland outside the White City when I came across a caravan of trucks. Moloch's soldiers were rounding up all the Children they could find. I knew the minute I saw them that the Children weren't part of the original game.

So I snuck into one of the trucks and spoke with them. One told me they were being taken to a realm where guests hunt them for sport. I could see how terrified they were. That's when I figured out they were real."

"God, that's horrible."

"That's what I thought. So I killed all the NPC soldiers and set the Children free. I guess word got out after that. The Children have been helping me ever since."

"How did you end up getting caught?"

Kat laughs. "I didn't. I heard a rumor that Moloch was looking for a guest who wasn't supposed to be in the game. I thought that was probably you, so I let him find me. His tower wasn't as impregnable as he thought. I could have escaped at any time. The Children and I were just waiting for you to arrive. As soon as you're ready, the Children will escort us to the glacier to see their father. Do you remember the giant red avatar? It belongs to—"

"Milo Yolkin. How did you find out in here?"

She grins. "I'm a badass. How'd you find out?"

"I just sort of stumbled into it, really. But that's beside the point. We might need to kill him if he tries to keep us from going through the exit," I tell her. "Are you ready for that?"

"We can't kill him," Kat says. "Milo's the only one who can save us."

I'm about to question her sanity when three Children materialize at the entrance to the cavern, and I almost gasp. They are unlike anything I've seen before. Whatever digital DNA mixed together to make them, the results are truly spectacular. Two are females who look like they're twins. They're taller than most human women, with matte gray skin that reminds me of unbaked potter's clay. But something golden crackles within them, and bursts of light erupt on the surface of their skin as if fireworks were exploding beneath it. The male is enormous—at least as large as Magna—with the white hair and beard of a Nordic god. He looks more human than his companions, but there's something else in the mix as well. He's carrying several furry pelts over one arm. I assume they're what will keep us from freezing to death during our trek across the ice. It's hard to believe the guy has my safety in mind, though. He's glaring at me and his white eyes burn with hatred.

Kat rises to her feet. "Stay here. I'll go talk to them. They trust me."

I'm not convinced. "You sure you're going to be okay? I don't think that dude likes guests very much. *Any* guests."

"Can you blame him?" Kat asks. "Humans brought them to life, and then we set about killing them. I wouldn't be all that fond of us either."

I keep a careful eye on the negotiations, which seem cordial but tense. Kat returns quickly with the pelts in her arms and a stoic expression on her face.

"They say it will take a few hours to reach the glacier, and we have to move fast. Moloch's men are out in full force on the ice fields. They're searching for us, and the Children won't be able to hold them off forever." She offers me a hand and helps me to my feet. "Shall we get started?" she asks.

I would give anything for another hour alone with Kat. But that hour might cost us the rest of our lives. "Let's go," I tell her.

· · ·

The ice fields are a completely different experience with a disk. I can feel the frigid wind whipping around us. Beneath the heavy pelt the Children provided, my skin is numb to the touch. We move carefully across the treacherous ice. There are bottomless fissures wide enough to swallow us whole, and the blinding glare from the sunlight makes them difficult to detect. We pass over frozen seas where the ice beneath our feet is so thin that you can see the hungry beasts prowling the water beneath it. And we travel through storms that pelt us with hail and rip the sky apart with lightning. I wasn't afraid the last time I was here. I should be terrified now. But I'm not. There is nowhere I'd rather be than here with Kat.

When we set out, a troop of warrior Children surrounded us. Now, hours into our journey, I notice that our escorts have slipped away. I turn in circles, searching for some trace of them. Though I can see for what must be miles in every direction, they're nowhere to be found.

"We're alone," I tell Kat.

"Don't worry, the Children are watching," she says, taking my hand and leading me forward. "If Moloch attacks, they'll have the element of surprise."

"Do you think they can hear us speaking?" I ask.

She stops and turns back to me. "I have no idea what they can do," she responds. "You might as well say what you want to say."

"Kat, I really think we may need to kill the Creator—even if he lets us go through the exit. Milo Yolkin is the one responsible for all this. He's evil and he's addicted to the game he invented. He'll never make all the guests leave."

Kat shakes her head. "You're wrong about the evil part," she says. "Milo's not evil. He's *immature.* He thought he had a fun new toy to play with. He didn't know the technology was Pandora's box. He created Otherworld, but he couldn't control it. Now he's lost control of the Company, too. But he still has the power to shut both of them down, and that's what we have to convince him to do."

It's pretty clear that Milo's lost control of Otherworld. The evidence is everywhere you look. The rest of it is news to me. "Milo's lost control of the Company?" I ask Kat. "How do you know?"

"My beloved stepfather," says Kat. "Wayne works for the Company."

"Yeah, I heard," I say. "He told you about Milo?" It's hard to believe.

"Not exactly. Remember that little hut you added to our fort?"

I'm not sure where she's going with this, but I'll play along. "You really think I'd forget the fort?"

"Well, after you left for school, I'd go out there and sit and—"

"By yourself?"

Her head drops to her chest as if the memory is too much to bear. "I missed you," she said. "And Mom had just married Wayne and it was like the two people I loved had both deserted me."

Kat just said she loved me. Back in the real world, I think my heart just exploded.

"I'm sorry," I tell her. "You know I didn't have a choice."

"I know," Kat says. "And I knew that then, too. But whenever I started to forget, I'd go out to the fort to feel closer to you. Anyway, I was out there one day, and I heard Wayne talking on his phone. He always popped outside when he got work calls. He didn't want anyone else listening in. That day it was a call from someone named Swenson. I looked him up afterward—he's on the Company's board of directors. He and Wayne were talking about Milo. At first the things Wayne was saying made me think Milo might be sick. Then I realized what was really going on. Milo was obsessed with the new Otherworld. He'd even had some of his engineers build a weird capsule-thing for his body so he could stay in his virtual world as long as possible. For a while I thought Wayne and this Swenson guy wanted to help him, but then I realized they were planning to take control of the Company. They were pissed because Milo was using some amazing new technology they called the disk. But he'd forbidden the Company to make any more because the devices were dangerous. Wayne and Swenson wanted Milo out of the way so they could test the disk on more people. They'd keep Milo in his capsule and pull him out for a public appearance now and then, but . . ." She pauses and studies my face. "What is it?" she asks.

How do I tell her she's part of the test? I shake my head.

"I know I'm wearing one of the disks," she says softly. "I heard you talking about it in my hospital room right before I ended up here. Is my body in one of the capsules? I know Wayne was planning to build more."

"How?"

"I found blueprints for them in his office. When I figured out what they were, I was going to try to expose the Company. But then Marlow threw that party at the factory, and the rest is history."

I suddenly remember the blueprint photo I found in the Yoda sleeping bag at Elmer's. That's got to be what she's talking about. I'm an idiot for not putting the pieces together earlier. "Jesus, Kat. I still can't believe you didn't tell me any of this."

"I couldn't, don't you see? Not without putting your life at risk. Wayne was on to me. He had the whole house rigged with cameras and surveillance equipment. One of the cameras must have filmed me going into the fort that day, and Wayne realized I'd heard something I shouldn't have. He asked me a bunch of questions about it, and I played dumb. But after that, he tore down the fort and started monitoring everything I did. I tried to throw him off my tracks by wrecking his car and hanging around with those kids at school. I figured he wouldn't see me as a threat if I looked like some kind of druggie delinquent. I'm pretty sure I almost had him convinced. Some nights I didn't even go home. I slept at Elmer's instead. Then my best friend who'd been arrested for hacking shows back up in town and starts sending me thousands of dollars' worth of VR equipment. . . ."

"Which I would never have done if you'd told me what was going on," I argue passionately.

"True," she admits with a satisfied smirk. She was teasing me. Then her face turns serious once more. "But I was so scared when you came back to Brockenhurst, Simon. I knew I was in trouble, and I could handle that. But if something had happened to you— and it was all my fault—I don't think I could have survived."

There's nothing I can say in response. I step in front of her and put my arms around her. I kiss her and she kisses me back. We're standing all alone in a frozen wasteland, and Kat's lips are icy cold. And yet this is the best moment of my entire life.

"So do you see why we can't kill Milo?" she asks when we finally part. "We need to convince him to leave Otherworld so he can shut down the beta test and turn Wayne in to the authorities."

"You think he'll do it?"

"Maybe not for us," she says. "But he might do it for the Children. He knows how much they've suffered. Maybe . . ." She pauses. "What's that?" she asks.

There's a dark blotch on the horizon and it's growing bigger and bigger.

"I think someone's coming for us," she says, pulling an arrow out of her quiver. I take out my dagger. It's almost hilarious to think that it's my only weapon against whatever is thundering in our direction.

"Where are the Children?" I ask, scanning the landscape for any sign of our escorts. "Aren't they supposed to be protecting us?"

"They're not human. They have their own way of doing things," Kat says, managing to remain perfectly calm. "But in my experience, they always keep their word."

The dark mass in the distance is taking form. Giant white beasts race across the frozen expanse, human shapes atop their backs. On my first visit to Otherworld, I slew one such beast, a bear of prehistoric dimensions with long white hair like a yeti and teeth too large to fit in its mouth. It stalked me across the ice for miles, as if it wanted to study me before it tore me apart.

Now six of them are bounding toward us, and the men on their backs have their swords drawn. Riding the largest beast at the front of the pack is Moloch. As soon as he's within range, Kat pulls an arrow from her quiver and takes aim. The missile sails through the air and hits him square in the chest. But the arrow doesn't penetrate. I watch it bounce away and fall to the ground.

"What was the point of that?" I ask. "We both know the dude isn't going to die."

Kat doesn't bother with a second arrow. "I thought we might

be able to get rid of his avatar for a little bit, but he's wearing some kind of armor," she says. "Our weapons are totally useless."

"If he gets close enough, I'll just have to take him out with my own two hands," I tell her.

"Show-off," she jokes, and though we're probably facing imminent death, I feel the urge to kiss her again. So I do.

The bears are almost upon us when Moloch raises a hand and the animals slow to a trot. The six of them surround Kat and me. They tower over us, their black eyes fixed on our faces, their breath enveloping us in a rancid cloud. The beasts could destroy us in a matter of seconds, and yet I don't fear them. I've met plenty of creatures here that wanted to kill me. These just don't seem all that interested.

Moloch slides off his mount and joins us in the center of the circle. The NPC warriors he brought with him are in full battle gear, complete with helmets, but Moloch's handsome avatar is dressed like it's casual Friday at the investment bank. Then I detect a slight shimmer around him. It's some kind of protective shield.

"Hi, Todd," I say. It has to be Todd now. Martin's tied up in a bathroom. "Remember Kat? She's one of the people you've been trying to murder."

"Hey there." Kat gives him a cheerful wave.

Todd ignores her greeting and stands nose to nose with me. "Game over, you little shit. Do you have any idea what you've done?"

I share a look with Kat and shrug. "Do you know what he's talking about?"

"Nope," she responds.

"Martin is missing," he snarls.

"Oh, really?" I ask. "Maybe the serial killer lifestyle didn't suit him after all. Where do you suppose he went?"

"If he left, the Company will find him," Todd says, his voice cracking. "And then they'll kill him."

I'm finding it really hard to muster the appropriate level of sympathy. "What do you care?" I demand. "It's just another sacrifice for the advancement of mankind, right?"

"He was my friend!" Todd shouts. "We worked together for ten years. He might have been a sap, but he was a genius, too." Then, his teeth gritted and nostrils flared, he regains control. "Where is your body? We want the disk back."

I can't help but laugh. "Yeah, I bet you do. But you're not going to find it."

"Either you tell me where the disk is or bad things are going to start happening to everyone you care about. Starting with her." He shoves a finger at Kat.

It wasn't a smart move. I'm up in his face in an instant. "You do anything to Kat and I will punish you in ways you can't even begin to imagine."

I feel Kat tap me on the shoulder. "Can I help?" she asks.

"Oh, *absolutely*," I say.

"You think I'm joking?" Todd snarls. "I finally have permission from Gibson to get rid of her."

"Awww. How is dear old Stepdad?" Kat asks.

"Getting pretty sick of your shit," Todd snaps.

I really wish this asshole were wearing a disk. I've never wanted to make anyone suffer so much in my life. "You already came close to killing a thirteen-year-old today. You ready to murder another human being? You must have gotten used to slaughtering

Children by now. I'm guessing you've even learned to like it. Ever wondered what Otherworld is turning you into?"

"All I've done is take care of business," says Todd. "When I have a billion dollars and a Nobel Prize, no one's going to care what I did to get it. Least of all me."

"That's why we're going to do whatever it takes to make sure you end up in an orange jumpsuit instead," says Kat. Then she turns to me. "What do you think his Wikipedia entry will call him? Mass murderer? Mad scientist?"

"I'm gonna go with serial killer," I say. "Heck, you know what? Maybe I'll write the entry myself."

"Oh! Good idea," Kat says. "Be sure to add this part."

"Definitely," I reply. "It's such a dramatic moment, isn't it?"

"Shut up!" Todd shouts. He stomps back to his bear and climbs into the saddle. "Kill them both," he orders the beasts.

I pull Kat into my arms, but the attack never comes. The six bears stay where they are. The one nearest me leans over to its neighbor and licks the side of its face.

"Kill them!" Todd shrieks at the soldiers sitting atop the beasts. None of them moves a muscle. "Why are you sitting there? Do what I say!" Todd shouts in frustration. When it becomes clear that they aren't planning to follow orders, he goes for his own sword. But the scabbard is empty. "What the hell is going on here?"

The largest of the soldiers removes his helmet, revealing his white hair and beard. Back in the cavern, I didn't know what he was. Now that I see him atop the bear, it's clear that the two creatures share DNA.

"Filthy vermin!" Todd snarls. "Where did you come from? How did you steal my bears?"

"They are not your bears," the Child says placidly. "They are wild creatures. They don't belong to anyone."

"This is insane," Todd says. "Of course they do. I know the little asshole who designed them."

"The Creator gave life to this world, but it is constantly changing. Nothing here is what it was originally meant to be."

"No shit," Todd says. "But don't worry, we're going to clean things up. Starting with you."

"Your kind will not defeat us," the Child says. "With our father's help we will take control of Otherworld and drive your kind out."

"Your *father* is a pathetic addict," Todd sneers. "I'll get ten engineers working twenty-four seven to fix whatever he decides to screw up."

"And I will send thousands of Children to destroy every guest."

I glance at Kat. I totally agree that humans don't belong here, but setting out to destroy every guest seems a bit much. Some of them would really die.

Todd scoffs. "Thousands?" he asks. "There can't be more than a few hundred of you left."

The bears part and we can see a vast army of Children on the horizon. Looks like the Creator really got around.

"Oh my God," Todd gasps. Then there's a flicker in his avatar, and Moloch dims and goes still. Wherever Todd is, the coward's pulled off his headset.

"Take the avatar hostage," the Child orders the others.

Kat steps up to the Child's bear. "You never said you would kill all the guests."

"We will do whatever is necessary to take back our world," says the Child.

"But some of us never chose to be here," Kat argues. "We were forced into coming, and if you kill us in Otherworld, we'll die in the real world too."

Her pleas don't appear to make much of an impression. "The real world?" asks the Child. "Why is your world the real one? How can you be so certain you humans were not created by someone else? Does your history not speak of a Creator too?"

It's a good question—so good that even Kat can't find an answer.

"This is *our* reality," the Child continues. "Your kind comes here to use us for pleasure or murder us for sport. When we die here, there's no other place we can go."

"But killing hundreds of innocent humans can't be the answer," I argue.

"Then you must convince our father to banish the guests," the Child tells us. "That's why we've brought you here. Now do what you're meant to do."

When we reach the glacier, the Children leave us at the entrance. I look for the Clay Man as we enter the ice tunnel, but the spot where I first saw him is empty. I'm glad, because I'd rather there not be a witness to what I'm about to do.

"Hold on," I tell Kat. She stops and turns to face me. She's so goddamn beautiful I could die. "There's a really good chance we won't make it out of here, and I have something to say to you first."

I pause. The words were there just a second ago, but now I can't seem to find them.

"I love you, too," she tells me. "I always have."

I suppose I should be thrilled, but instead I'm crushed. "I can't believe I wasted so much time because I was too much of a wuss—"

"To risk destroying our friendship?" Kat finishes.

"Yeah," I admit.

"Simon," she says. "That's one of the reasons I love you."

I kiss her for the fifth—and maybe the last—time. When she pulls back, I don't want to let her go.

"It's going to be okay. This isn't over," she tells me.

"You're sure?" I ask.

"Yes. It's just beginning. I promise." She takes my hand. "Come on—let's get this part over with."

We walk side by side through the pale blue ice. Just before we reach the cave, she plants a kiss on my cheek. Then we step inside to find Magna sitting on his throne. His red body has cooled to gray metal. The avatar is just as colossal as I remember, but this time Magna's shoulders are slumped and his head is bowed. He seems exhausted, weak.

He looks up at us. His face takes form as it starts to glow. For the first time I can see the resemblance to Milo Yolkin. "Did Moloch send you?" he asks wearily.

"No," Kat says. "We came on our own. My name is Kat. This is Simon."

"I'm not in the mood for company," Magna tells us. "Get out." His body begins to burn bright red. He lifts one hand, and a glowing orb forms in his palm. As he does, the outstretched arm returns to stone, as if the effort has drained him. Yet there's little doubt that the orb remains a lethal weapon.

"Please, don't throw that, Milo. If you hit us, we could die in real life," Kat says calmly.

The avatar's stone limbs melt into swirling plasma. He's burning so brightly now that I can hardly bear to look at him. "What did you call me?"

I grab Kat and shove her into a crevice in the cave's wall just as Magna's orb sails through the air and hits the ground inches from where we were standing. The explosion leaves my ears ringing. I use my body to shield Kat, and I know my avatar's going to be black and blue from the chunks of ice that are pelting it.

"Guess he prefers to be called Magna," Kat says. "Good to know."

Kat can crack all the jokes she likes, but I can't see the humor in the situation. That evil little shit nearly killed us. I am going to make him pay for that. When I'm done, there won't be a bone in his body that hasn't been broken.

"Simon," Kat whispers. She sounds worried. "What's wrong with you? You look crazy. We both knew this wasn't going to be easy. You've got to calm down."

But I can't. The valve that once controlled my rage has been broken. The anger can no longer be contained. I can hear myself panting like a rabid beast.

"Stay here. Don't do anything," Kat warns. "You're not well. Let me take care of this."

She slips out of the crevice, and I follow her. The attack appears to have done more damage to Magna than it did to Kat or me. He's doubled over in his chair, his head in his hands.

"My apologies for offending you, Magna," Kat says to the avatar. "I was trying to tell you that Simon and I are both wearing disks."

He looks up. I assume he's surprised, but it's hard to tell. "Come forward," he orders weakly.

I hurry after Kat as she approaches the giant. I can feel the dagger tucked away in my boot. One wrong move and Magna's going to be tasting steel.

"Close your eyes," Magna orders Kat, and she does as he says. He leans forward and places his palms on either side of her face. One hand remains cold gray stone while the other glows red.

"Stop!" Kat exclaims, reaching up to grab the glowing hand. "You're burning me!" Magna immediately removes both hands from her face. The test is over.

"How did you get a disk?" he asks.

"The Company is beta testing them," Kat says. "They've kidnapped hundreds of people and stored their bodies in capsules. I'm part of the test."

Magna sits back in his chair. "They went ahead with it," he says to himself, seething. "Even after I forbade them to alter the business model."

Kat looks at me. "Business model?" she asks.

"The Otherworld headset app will make billions, but it's only a game. If the Company sells disks, the people who use them will have to turn to us for their most basic needs. They'll need a place to store their bodies and nourishment to keep them alive. Can you imagine how much we could charge for such services? Apparently my board of directors can. Those greedy bastards. I *told* them the disks weren't viable."

I can't keep my mouth shut. "Wait, we just told you that the

Company—*your* company—is kidnapping people and you're pissed off about the *business model*?"

Kat shoots me a dirty look, but Magna doesn't seem to give a damn about my outrage.

"You need to leave Otherworld," Kat tells him. "You have to return to the real world and stop the beta test. You're the only one who can do it."

"Why bother?" Magna asks. "Without me, the Company will never be able to fix the flaws in the disk. And no one will want to lease one of the Company's capsules when they find out there's a chance they might die in it."

"People are *already* dying in the capsules," I snarl.

Magna's eyes leave me, and his gaze focuses on a spot just behind us. "They aren't the first victims of this technology, and they certainly won't be the last. Humankind is taking a massive leap forward. There's bound to be collateral damage."

I glance over my shoulder and see a strange shadow on the wall of the ice cave. There appears to be a body entombed in the ice.

"Whose avatar is that?" Kat asks.

"It belongs to the disk's inventor," Magna says.

"James Ogubu?" Oh my God, it's Busara's dad. "You didn't kill him?"

"Kill him?" Magna scoffs. "Why would I do something so stupid? He knows the technology better than anyone. I might need his help someday."

"You need him *now*," Kat says. I can tell from her voice that she's stopped playing nice. "You've lost control. You've let Otherworld beat you. It found your weakness."

"Lost control?" Red veins spring up on the stone surface of Milo's avatar. "I created this world. I know every rock, every beast, every cloud in the sky. . . ."

"You may have created it, but it's not yours anymore," Kat tells him. "It belongs to the Children. They're alive and you *know* that. The guests are killing and slaughtering them one by one, but you haven't been able to stop it. You can't admit that your game needs to end. You're too addicted to playing God. Isn't that what you always wanted—what you couldn't get from the real world? The ultimate power? Otherworld gave you a taste and now you're hooked—just like all the people who came here to kill or steal or indulge their sick fantasies. . . ."

"I am not like them. Here, I *am* God!" Magna bellows. A new orb has appeared in his hand. I step forward, but Kat holds me back with one arm while she points at the exit on the far side of the cavern.

"Go through the exit, Milo. Close off Otherworld to visitors. Get rid of the disks. Keep the servers running and let Otherworld play on, but without any guests. Including *you*. If you want to save the Children—and save the real world from this technology—you can't spend your life in a capsule," Kat says. "Two worlds need you, Milo. You have to make the sacrifice. You have to go back. This is your chance."

She did it again. I watch Magna's arm rise at the sound of his real name. He's going to throw the orb. Maybe he'll miss. Maybe he won't. But I'm not going to stand here and let this crazy fucker and his overgrown avatar threaten the girl I love. If he won't go through the exit, I'm going to make him. He's already weak. The orb in his hand has drained the energy from the rest of his body. I pull out my dagger and charge forward.

"Simon, stop!" Kat grabs hold of my robe and won't let go. But I can't be stopped, and I drag her behind me as I make my way to Magna.

The orb is blindingly bright when he throws it. I'm dazzled, but I manage to duck. I hear the explosion behind me, but I keep going. Until I realize I'm no longer dragging Kat behind me.

I turn to see her on the ground, her copper curls fanned out around her face. Kat's eyes are fixed on the ceiling above and her mouth is open, but she doesn't seem to be breathing.

No. No. No.

I drop to my knees and take her in my arms. I can feel a feeble pulse, but it's already fading. Nothing else matters. *Let the world end,* I think.

"Please don't die," I beg her. "I love you."

I hear Magna making his way toward me. I don't even bother to brace for the blow.

"I'm sorry."

It's not Magna's booming voice. This one's boyish and quiet and I've heard it somewhere before. "Let me help. There's still time to save her."

"Milo?" I say.

He doesn't answer. The avatar gently lifts Kat off the ground. When I'm standing, he passes her body to me. "Take her through the exit," he says. "Do it quickly. I'll be right behind you."

THE BIG BOSS

Kat's body vanishes as I go through the exit. I'm not sure what to expect next. I'm used to having the disk ripped off the base of my neck, and I'm hoping this experience proves a little less painful. I step through the door and into a warm, bright room. It feels like a foyer between two worlds; all I need to do is walk forward. But I'm not in here alone. My grandfather is standing in my path. He's younger this time. Aside from his brash 1960s-style suit, he looks a lot like me.

"Off to rescue the damsel in distress?" he asks.

"Hopefully a few other people too," I tell him. "So I don't have time to chat."

He grins. "You got guts. I like it. Probably 'cause you got them from me."

"Did I?" I ask.

"Why not?" he replies. "I was like you once. Word of advice, though?"

"What?" I ask, annoyed that he's keeping me from Kat.

"Don't think you got it all figured out. Looks like you picked up a little problem back there in crazy world. And even when we've got our heads on straight, a lotta guys like us end up at the bottom of the canal."

I was expecting kudos, but I get a bullshit warning instead. I barge past him, through the light. When I can feel my hands, I remove the visor. The first thing I see is the ceiling of a capsule, which is all of four inches away from my face. They've found me. And getting out looks like it might be a bit of a challenge. I scoot down to the end and hook the tip of my shoe under the lever that opens the door. But when I pull, it doesn't budge.

Inside the capsule, it's at least a hundred degrees. Which might be great if I were naked. The sweat from my forehead is streaming into my eyes, and it's impossible to wipe it away. I try the door handle again. Again, it doesn't budge. My heart is racing now. It's probably my imagination, but the air in here seems to be growing thin. I'm on the verge of an all-out panic attack when I hear the capsule door open and feel a whoosh of cool air.

Someone pulls my shelf out. His face appears above me.

"Mr. Eaton."

"Hi, Wayne," I say, struggling to sit up. "Hope you don't mind if I call you Wayne."

He takes a few steps back until he's standing against the wall of capsules opposite mine. Only two of them are lit.

"Don't bother getting up," he says, gesturing at the metal shelf I've been lying on. "It will be time to go back soon. Right after you tell me where you've been getting the disks."

"You know what? I think I'll stay in the real world for a while,"

I tell him as I slide off the shelf and land on my feet. My legs feel wobbly, but I do my best to hide it. "I've been playing too many games lately. I need to spend more time outdoors. And as for the disks—go to hell."

"I'm afraid that's not the right response, son." He pulls out a gun and I almost laugh.

"Isn't that a little old-fashioned?" I ask him.

"I'm an old-fashioned man," he says. "A straight shooter, pun intended. I suppose I could go chasing after my enemies in some virtual world. But I'd rather just put bullets in their heads or make a few rotten floorboards collapse."

"That was you that night at the factory?"

"It was. And now you know just how far I'm willing to go if you don't do what I ask."

"Let me guess. You'll kill me?"

"Absolutely. And then I'm going to let your friends live."

I don't get it. Then he steps to one side, giving me a clear view of the capsules behind him. There's movement in one of them. A girl's hands are pressed against the interior of the capsule as if she's trying to force her way out. But there's no room to move, nowhere to go. I know her panic. It feels like being buried alive. And my own body almost collapses when I realize that the girl in the capsule is Kat. My eyes jump to the capsule beside hers. I see the toes twitch and I get a glimpse of male legs. It has to be Milo Yolkin.

"I'm guessing you didn't foresee this turn of events, did you?" Wayne Gibbons asks with a satisfied smirk. "The capsules don't open from the inside. I made sure of that. Katherine and Milo left Otherworld, but I think they're probably regretting that decision right about now. I switched off their meds. They're not paralyzed, but they're not going anywhere either. And this is exactly how they're going to stay unless you tell me where you've been getting the disks. I'm not sure I'd keep them waiting if I were you. How long do you suppose it will take for the two of them to lose their minds?"

I've seen people die in countless ways, but none compares to the horror Wayne Gibbons just described. "You're a goddamn monster," I growl.

"Not at all," he argues. "I'm giving the three of you a chance to return to Otherworld. Milo's private exit will need to go, though. We'll let him out from time to time. You'll have to stay in his nasty little world, of course. But heck, it's better than the alternatives, wouldn't you say?"

"What's all this for, Wayne?" I ask, trying to buy some time. "I'm just curious. What motivates a man like you? Is it money?"

"Nope. It's about progress, son. Well, and large amounts of money—but mainly progress. It's always required human sacrifice. You know how many men died building the Brooklyn Bridge? Or the Panama Canal? People like Mr. Yolkin here like to think that the world runs on their brainpower. People like me know that the world runs on blood. Now tell me what I need to know, Mr. Eaton. I'm finished with small talk."

"Me too," I tell him. "Go ahead and shoot."

I'm waiting for the sound of the gun. Instead my ears are assaulted by another noise. A siren has gone off overhead and a red light is flashing above Milo's capsule. Wayne Gibbons looks like he's just been punched in the face. He holsters his gun and peers through the capsule's window. Then he opens the latch and pulls the body out.

I'm frozen in place by the sight. Milo Yolkin barely looks human. His body is so emaciated that I can see every bone in his skeleton. Dark purple circles surround his eyes, and his shaved scalp is covered in strange brown patches. The heart monitor inside the capsule has flatlined.

"Help me, goddamn it!" Wayne shouts. "We need him alive!" He's started chest compressions and CPR. It's not going to make any difference. Even I can see that. But I let Wayne finish making the effort. Then I attack. I grab his gun from its holster with my left hand just before my right smashes into his face. Three more jabs and Wayne's down on the ground. I raise my foot, and I'm just getting ready to stomp him to death when I catch a glimpse of Kat inside her capsule. It takes all the self-control I can muster to pull myself back from the brink. I put my foot down and point the gun at Kat's stepfather instead.

"Get up and get on," I tell Wayne, pointing at the sliding metal shelf that I recently left.

He looks at the gun and then up at me. "You aren't going to shoot," he says, gasping for air.

"You sure about that?" I ask, giving him a quick kick in the gut. "Do you have any idea how many people I had to kill to make it through Otherworld? Do you really think one more would make a difference? Get on the goddamn shelf."

"Shoot," he says.

There's a deafening bang, and I have no idea what's happened until I see Wayne lying flat on the floor. I glance down at the gun in my hand and the finger that's just pulled the trigger. Wayne's groaning while a pool of blood spreads out around him.

What the hell did I just do?

I shove the gun into the waistband of my pants, open Kat's capsule and pull her out. "Simon!" she gasps as I peel off my T-shirt and help her into it. "What happened to Wayne? Oh my God, is that Milo?"

"I'll tell you everything when we're safe. But first we've got to get out of here," I say.

When Kat slides down to the floor, she shrieks with pain. "There's something wrong with my leg."

"Hold on to my neck," I tell her, and I gather her up in my arms. The time in the capsule has taken its toll on her as well. She's light as a feather.

"What about the others?" she asks.

"We can't save them if we're dead," I tell her. "We'll have to come back."

I carry Kat up the stairs and down the hall. We've gotten as far as the lobby when it becomes clear that we won't be going any farther. Black SUVs have pulled up in front of the building, and the men pouring out are already charging through the door. I have the gun in my waistband, but I'd have to put Kat down to reach it.

"Go!" she says. "Leave me here and get out another way."

"No," I tell her. I remember Carole saying the same thing. But Carole was sacrificing herself to save me. I'm saving myself. There would be no point in surviving if Kat were to die.

Then I spot movement in the parking lot. And I know what's about to happen, as if I've somehow managed to read Busara's mind. I drop to my knees behind one of the couches in the lobby a split second before the crash. Kat screams as glass flies in every direction. Large shards embed themselves in the walls. I'm up the second it's over, with Kat in my arms. Busara's car is in the middle of the large room. I open the back door and toss Kat inside, then throw my own body in after hers.

The door of the car is still open as we crash back out through the front of the building, skid across some grass and race down the driveway and onto Dandelion Drive. Busara runs every red light on the way out of Brockenhurst. I manage to get the door closed, but no one says a word until we're on I-95. I don't even know if we're heading north or south.

"So?" Busara finally asks.

I could spend the next three hours going through everything, but it would all boil down to two sentences. "Milo's dead," I tell her. "But your dad isn't."

Busara gasps and the car swerves across the highway. "What?"

"We saw him in Otherworld. He's trapped in the ice inside Magna's cave," Kat says.

"And his body?"

"It must be at the facility," I say.

"The one we just left?" Busara wails.

"I'm sorry," I tell her. "I promise we'll go back for him. And Gorog. And all the rest of them too."

"They won't be there when we do," Busara says. "The Company will have that place emptied out before sunrise."

"And they'll be looking for us everywhere," Kat adds.

"We don't have any money and we can't use credit cards," Busara points out. "And none of us can go home."

But I know what to do.

"I think it's time to pay a visit to my friend Elvis," I tell them.

EPILOGUE

There's only so far you can run before you have no choice but to stop.

We made it to Texas, but I don't even know the name of the town we're in—or if there's even a town around us. The wasteland we drove through could have been part of Otherworld. The sign that drew us here was the first we'd seen in a hundred miles. COLTON COURT, it said, and there was a picture of a gun next to the name.

Technically this is the first night I've ever shared a bed with Kat. There's little chance of anything happening with Busara asleep in the bed on the other side of the motel room. I'm sure we'll all wake up covered with bedbug bites, but we can't afford anything better, and I don't think any of us cares.

I'm so tired I'm delirious, but I still can't seem to sleep. I'm sitting on the edge of the bed, flipping through television channels. Most are just static, but every so often I come across one with a signal. Right now I'm watching the grainy image of a slick-looking salesman type who's speaking directly to the camera. The volume is down low enough so that I don't bother the others, but I wonder what he's selling. I have to lean forward and strain to make out his words.

"Then God said, 'Let Us make man in Our image, according to Our likeness; let him have dominion over the fish of the sea, over the birds of the air, and over the cattle, over all the earth and over every thing that creeps on the earth.'"

I flip to the next channel. Nothing. The next. Nothing. The next. Nothing. I just keep going like some kind of lab rat that's been trained to push a button. And then finally the reward—the nightly news presented by some Podunk Texas station. Right above the anchor's shoulder is a photo of Milo Yolkin. My heart picks up speed. The word is out. I bump up the volume. ". . . has announced he will be taking a sabbatical from the Company for health-related reasons. The Company issued a press release earlier this evening, and while it did not disclose the nature of Yolkin's medical problems, it did indicate that the twenty-nine-year-old CEO's leave of absence could stall the eagerly anticipated wide release of the Company's popular Otherworld game. In other news . . ."

"What the hell?" It's Kat.

"You're up?"

I come around to her side of the bed. She looks so beautiful that I have to lean over to kiss her. She kisses me back for a moment, but then her eyes seem focused behind me. She pulls back. "Look," she whispers.

We both glance over at Busara's bed. She has the covers pulled up over her head. The human-shaped lump beneath the blanket seems oddly still. I watch for signs of breathing but see none. I suddenly fear the worst—that her damaged heart may finally have failed her. I'm about to get up and check for a pulse when I see a faint flash from Busara's bed. It's almost imperceptible. I blink hard, trying to focus. There's the slightest movement of her covers. Busara is breathing.

WELCOME BACK TO
OUR REALITY.

OTHEREARTH

Autumn 2018

ABOUT THE AUTHORS

JASON SEGEL is an actor, a screenwriter, and an author. Segel wrote and starred in *Forgetting Sarah Marshall* and co-wrote Disney's *The Muppets*, which won an Academy Award for Best Original Song. Segel's other film credits include *The End of the Tour; I Love You, Man; Jeff, Who Lives at Home; Knocked Up;* and *The Five-Year Engagement.* On television, Segel starred in *How I Met Your Mother* as well as *Freaks and Geeks.* He is the co-author of the *New York Times* bestselling middle grade series *Nightmares! Otherworld* is his first novel for young adults.

KIRSTEN MILLER lives and writes in New York City. She is the author of the acclaimed Kiki Strike books, the *New York Times* bestseller *The Eternal Ones,* and *How to Lead a Life of Crime.* Kirsten is the co-author of the *Nightmares!* series with Jason Segel. *Otherworld* is the fifth novel she and Segel have written together. You can visit her at kirstenmillerbooks.com or follow @bankstirregular on Twitter.